Hush Hush

ALSO BY LAURA LIPPMAN

After I'm Gone
And When She Was Good
The Most Dangerous Thing
The Girl in the Green Raincoat
I'd Know You Anywhere
Life Sentences
Hardly Knew Her
Another Thing to Fall
What the Dead Know
No Good Deeds
To the Power of Three
By a Spider's Thread
Every Secret Thing
The Last Place
In a Strange City
The Sugar House
In Big Trouble
Butchers Hill
Charm City
Baltimore Blues

Hush Hush

LAURA LIPPMAN

WILLIAM MORROW
An Imprint of HarperCollins*Publishers*

HUSH HUSH. Copyright © 2015 by Laura Lippman. All rights reserved. Printed in the United States of America. No part of this book may be used or reproduced in any manner whatsoever without written permission except in the case of brief quotations embodied in critical articles and reviews. For information address HarperCollins Publishers, 195 Broadway, New York, NY 10007.

HarperCollins books may be purchased for educational, business, or sales promotional use. For information please e-mail the Special Markets Department at SPsales@harpercollins.com.

FIRST EDITION

Designed by Jamie Lynn Kerner

Library of Congress Cataloging-in-Publication Data has been applied for.

ISBN 978-0-06-208342-5

15 16 17 18 19 OV/RRD   10 9 8 7 6 5 4 3 2 1

For Sara Kiehne

Hush Hush

Transcript of interview with CAROLYN SANDERS, March 3. Filmed outside Friends School, Charles Street, Baltimore, MD. (Production notes: Interview was actually recorded on sidewalk near school, a public area, as school refused access. Permit was not obtained. Harmony Burns is off-camera. Transcript provided by our third-party transcription service, then edited by HB per her notes for clarity, transcription errors. Otherwise a full and unexpurgated transcript.)

> SPEAKER 1: Harmony Burns
> SPEAKER 2: Carolyn Sanders
> INPUT: HB

SPEAKER 1/HARMONY BURNS: I'll ask questions for clarity, details. But it's really just supposed to be you talking. When the film is edited, my voice will not be on it. You're telling a story, as if I'm not here.

SPEAKER 2/CAROLYN SANDERS: Why would I be telling the story if no one is here?

HB: I mean tell the story as if I'm not asking questions, as if it all just came out. As if the camera is your audience, which it is.

CS: Okay. Gosh, I'm glad it's not colder. Why didn't you want to do this inside?

HB: Production issues. Besides, it just looks like any school on the inside and it's dark, which is unflattering when you don't have the time to light professionally. People actually look better in bright light. Plus, this is a more interesting backdrop.

CS: You mean the tennis courts? Can you even see them from here? And it's not like they're just for the school. There's a club of sorts. People in the neighborhood pay to use them. Friends is a private school, but it's not super-fancy.

HB: Did you go here?

CS: No, I attended Roland Park Country. They had a summer program, too, but I wanted a change of scenery. I wish I had—I'd give anything not to have been here that day.

HB: Don't get ahead of yourself, okay? Just tell the story, beginning to end. Don't worry about pausing. Take all the time you want. And if you screw something up, stop, take a breath, and start over. There's no wrong way to do this.

CS: Okay. Now?

HB: One more check on everything—we good? Okay, go. Oh, and identify yourself. Name, age, your, um, role. What you were doing that summer.

CS: My name is Carolyn Sanders and I'm twenty-eight years old. I work at Sanders & Sanders, a local communications company that does advertising and PR. It was founded by my grandfather and his brother—my great-uncle—right after World War II. It is one of the oldest communications firms in Baltimore. My father is the current president and serves on several local boards.

HB: And twelve years ago? What were you doing then?

CS: Oh, yes. Right. On August eighth, 2002, I was working at the summer day camp here at Friends when a woman came in and asked to take her children home. The woman was Melisandre Dawes, the mother of two of our campers, Alanna and Ruby. She said she needed to get the kids and take them home. She said it was an emergency, but she wouldn't tell me the nature of the emergency. Only that she needed them, right now.

HB: Just keep going. You're telling a story.

CS: It was about ten A.M. and all the children had just left for a field trip to a local dairy farm. I was surprised that Mrs. Dawes didn't know because she had signed the slips two weeks earlier. Three kids had to stay behind because their parents forgot, and those kids had been dropped off by caregivers who couldn't give legal consent. Lots of our kids were dropped off by babysitters, nannies. The Dawes girls almost missed the trip because they were late that day, but their dad had dropped them off. Usually, it was the nanny, but she wasn't around that week. She was on vacation or something. Mr. Dawes had seemed a little absent-minded at drop-off, but he's that kind of guy, right? He didn't make all his money by focusing on details that others could take care of. That's what my dad always said. They knew each other a little, my dad and Mr. Dawes. They were on some board together. Anyway, Mrs. Dawes, whom I'd seen only once or twice that summer, came in, and asked to withdraw the girls. She said it was an emergency. Of course, I was very concerned when I heard that, but I had to ask—What is the nature of the emergency? And she just kept murmuring: "Can't you see? Can't you see? Isn't it obvious?" The only thing I could see was that she looked awful.

HB: Could you be more descriptive?

CS: Well, just awful. Her hair looked as if it hadn't been washed for days—and she had such pretty hair the other times I had seen her. Her skin looked bad, pale and waxy. She was breathing heavily, almost panting, and she wore way too much clothing for a hot day. She had on a turtleneck and this big baggy linen thing over it. It looked very Eileen Fisher and it was enormous on her. It was all very strange. Disturbing, like the homeless people you see wearing coats in hot weather. I didn't think she should be left alone. I told her to wait in the hall for me and that I would go get someone. I thought maybe she should see a nurse or a doctor, but I wanted to ask my boss. After all, I was only sixteen, I couldn't tell a grown-up to wait in one place, or make her have a glass of water. I wasn't gone more than five minutes, but when I got back with the head of camp, she—Mrs. Dawes—had left. When I heard later—I felt awful. If I had gotten her to stay, nothing would have happened. But I thought she was a risk only to herself. I mean, that's bad, but it's not as if I could see the baby.

HB: Are you sure the baby was with her?

CS: Not at the time. I mean, it was only after that I realized—there were straps, over the turtleneck, but under this poncho-like thing she was wearing, visible at the edges of the neckline. They had to be straps, right? So she had the baby in a carrier and she had put on the big poncho so we wouldn't see the baby. That's what I think.

HB: But are you sure the baby was under the poncho? Could you see the baby's shape, hear her? Was she moving?

CS: No.

HB: So the baby could have been in the car.

CS: Anything is possible, I guess. But I think the baby was with her.

HB: Go back and describe Melisandre again. In more detail if you could. Make people see her as she was that day.

CS: Her hair was almost flat with grease. I had seen her once or twice and she was a really striking woman, and her hair was what you noticed first. She had those big snaky curls, you know? And the color was amazing, gold and brown, almost like a topaz. She also had brown eyes and lovely skin. Normally. But on this day, her skin was grayish white and she was way overdressed, all these layers on a really hot day. She had on tights, too. And cowboy boots. Bright red cowboy boots. But, you know, some people overdress in the summer because they're in places that have really strong air-conditioning. I keep a cardigan in my desk drawer.

HB: And what did she say?

CS: She asked me to go get Alanna and Ruby. I said, "But they're on the field trip. They just left." She got so upset that I thought she might—do something to me. She was waving her arms, pacing, muttering, saying she had to take them right then. I went to get the head of camp, Mrs. Von. She's actually Mrs. Von Treffathen, but—well, little kids, you can imagine them trying to say that name. So she was known as Mrs. Von. I said that Melisandre Dawes was in the lobby and seemed to be in some kind of distress. I said—I said [next few words indistinct]. Mrs. Von came out with me, and Mrs. Dawes was gone. Everyone says it's not my fault. She probably ran out the second I left her, and what else could I have done? And I didn't know—I mean—if

I had known. I should have known. Where else would the baby have been? And we all knew that the family had a baby. Alanna and Ruby talked about her all the time. Isadora. But it didn't occur to me that she had brought the baby in with her, under her clothes.

HB: In court, you didn't mention the part about the baby carrier, did you?

CS: I wasn't allowed. They said it was conjecture. And they said even if I could swear to seeing the straps of the baby carrier, I couldn't know if a baby was under her dress. But she had to be. It became a big deal. That was the first time her lawyer moved for a mistrial, but it wasn't granted. People forget that sometimes, or get confused. They say, Oh, you're the girl whose testimony got Melisandre Dawes a second trial. The mistrial wasn't because of me, I didn't do anything wrong. I was only sixteen. Well, seventeen by the time it went to trial. [Indistinct words.]

HB: You know, Carolyn, Melisandre Dawes didn't go psychotic in a single morning. Think of all the other people who had a chance to intervene before that day. Her husband, her own mother, who had visited earlier that summer. Her mother-in-law, who lived right here in Baltimore and saw her grandchildren at least once a week. And you can't be sure that she had the baby with her. She might have left her in the car. After all—

CS: No, I'm sure the baby was there. I was the last one. I was the last person to see her that day. Isadora was there, inches away from me. Everyone says I can't know that, but I do.

HB: Did she say anything strange when you spoke? Melisandre. You've established that she acted oddly, but what about the conversation itself?

CS: No. I told you everything.

HB: She didn't say anything else? Something out of the ordinary? Anything about the nature of the emergency?

CS: No.

HB: Nothing?

CS: What do you mean?

HB: I don't want to lead you, Carolyn. My—our—standards for this—they're very high. I don't want to plant an idea in your head, lead you in any way. But are you sure you've recalled the conversation in its entirety?

CS: Pretty sure.

HB: She didn't say anything else? Something—I think this is okay—something to explain why she was dressed the way she was. Anything like that? About her arms, her legs, what was happening to them?

CS: No, nothing like that.

HB: Never mind. I just thought— Never mind.

CS: She thought something was wrong with her arms and legs? I don't remember reading about that.

HB: We asked you not to read, remember? Not to prepare in any way. We just want your memories, unfiltered.

CS: I read things at the time. Who wouldn't? And I was relieved that— The police came to talk to me, but my name was kept out of it until the trial and, by then, I was away at boarding school, which my parents thought best, although I came back for the trial. And to live, after college, but by then no one remembered anymore that I had a part in it. My dad always says Baltimoreans, the real ones, are like homing pigeons. Or boomerangs. We all come back. Anyway, everyone kept saying it wasn't my fault, but what else could they say?

HB: I thought you just said that people said the mistrial was your fault.

CS: Not the mistrial. The actual—thing. What happened. I could have saved her.

HB: You didn't know the baby was there, much less what Melisandre was going to do.

CS: But I knew Mrs. Dawes wasn't in her right mind. I saw her and I left her alone, to walk out and get in her car and—do what she did! I mean, even if she wasn't in her right mind, I might have been able to help.

HB: Even if? What do you mean?

CS: Nothing. I mean—my dad said not to go there. It's gossip. And the Dawes family has always been quick with a lawsuit. My dad says. When will this be on TV?

HB: No broadcast date yet. But it will be in theaters first, I hope. Theaters or on one of the premium cable networks, maybe one of the streaming outlets, which are doing original work now. We hope to finish shooting before summer, which means we'll take it to festivals the following year. So, if we're lucky—two years from now.

CS: Wow, I'll be thirty by then.

HB: Somebody has to be.

CS: What?

HB: I said that's a nice age to be. Camera off, end tape.

Part I

Monday

The first note appeared on Tess Monaghan's car on a March day that was cranky as a toddler—wet, tired, prone to squalls. But Tess did not know the note was the first of anything. There is no first until the second arrives. So this note was a mere curiosity, a plain piece of paper folded and placed under the windshield wiper on her car. From a distance, it had looked like a ticket and Tess cursed under her breath as she turned the corner and headed up Elm Street. She was sure she had fed the meter for more than enough time to stop and grab coffee and a bagel on the Avenue. Tess was sure because she had also fed meters for several other cars parked along this strip of Elm Street, a habit for which she had been scolded by parking enforcement types. One had even tried to claim it was illegal to feed another person's meter.

At which point, Tess Monaghan swore to use her spare change this way whenever possible. She saw herself as the Robin Hood of all endangered parkers, although she was stealing from the poor, the beleaguered city of Baltimore, and assisting the rich, at least this morning. Who was more disadvantaged in the end, a city that could no longer afford to pick up the trash twice a week, or a Proud Gilman Mom (according to the bumper sticker) who had parked her Porsche Cayenne outside the Wine Source without feeding the meter?

"Dammit, did I get a ticket?" Tess sprinted the last block to her car. It was a minivan, which she adored. Tess had never defined herself by the car that she drove. The only thing she disliked about her Honda Odyssey was that it didn't have a manual transmission. She had been proud of driving a stick. Tess was proud of a lot of odd things. She was proud, in general, although she sometimes lost sight of that fact about herself.

"If it is a ticket, why run now?" asked Sandy, her partner of a year, coming up the block at a more leisurely pace. A retired cop, he didn't waste words or motions. "Besides, there's no red stripe."

"Why are you are talking about beer at nine-thirty A.M.? The Wine Source isn't even open yet." The Wine Source was Tess's favorite liquor store. She knew its hours well.

"Why are *you* thinking about beer at nine-thirty A.M.? No red stripe *on the paper.* That's not a city parking ticket."

"Probably a flyer, then. But why am I the only one to get one?"

She opened it to find a handwritten note. Oh dear—had someone sideswiped her? She didn't see anything on this side of the Honda, which was named Gladys because everything in her life—everything—must be named and quantified, according to her three-year-old daughter. Carla Scout had recently asked Tess to name and count the moles on her body and Tess had chosen the names of first ladies. Martha, Abigail, Dolley, Lady Bird, Nancy, Mary, Jackie, Pat, Betty, Eleanor, Michelle, Hillary—it had been an interesting test of her memory.

But Gladys had been spared. The note said only: *I saw you feeding the meters. Hooray for you!*

"Well—that's nice," she said, showing Sandy the note.

"I guess so."

Her new partner held people in even lower esteem than Tess did. It was a valuable quality in a private investigator, occasionally enervating in one's only co-worker.

"Okay, what's the downside?"

"Could be sarcastic."

"Doesn't feel that way."

"Still kinda creepy. Like the person who wrote it—he or she, and I'm betting it's a he—thinks he's entitled to judge you. I bet he scoops up after dogs in the park and takes it to the owners' houses, leaves it on the doorstep."

"You told me you did that."

"I told you I *wanted* to. Big difference."

"The bottom line is, I'm not out thirty-two dollars. You squared away for the morning?"

"Yes. I have a meeting with the security company, and then the electronics guy is going to meet me at the condo, walk through, work up a proposal. Then you and I meet her tomorrow at Tyner's office, go over all of it. Look—I have to speak my mind—this is outside my comfort zone. I'm not a security consultant. And I don't want to be in some stupid TV show."

"Tell me about it. But Tyner is family, so I have to take this meeting. He probably thinks I need the money. And I do, but I am going to be candid with her: We're not going to be part of the film and this isn't our bailiwick."

"Bailiwick." Sandy repeated the word, rolled it in his mouth like a lozenge. English was his second language and, while well into his fifth decade in the United States, he collected words the way some people collected butterflies, impaling them on pins, considering them from all angles. A widower, born in Cuba, he didn't have a wisp of an accent. Blond and green-eyed, too. If it weren't for the fact of his surname, Sanchez, most people would have assumed he was just a typical Baltimore mutt. Like Tess, whose Irish name and freckles convinced some people that she wouldn't blink at an anti-Semitic slur. But her mother's maiden name had been Weinstein, and Tess did much more than blink when invited to share sentiments about cheapness and media conspiracies.

"I remember," Sandy said.

"You remember what *bailiwick* means?"

"No, when it happened. The thing with Tyner's client. It wasn't on my shift, thank God. But it's the kind of thing— Guys who could make jokes about anything, they didn't joke about *that*. Cases like that, they can really screw you up. And it's worse, in a way, when you don't even have the adrenaline of the investigation or the interrogation to work out the bad energy. You've got this person who's done a horrible thing and you're being told she's a delicate flower, that the usual rules are out the window."

"Do you have a problem with the insanity plea in general, or just the fact that it was accepted in this case?"

"No. It's fair. I guess. If you're really crazy, you can't be held responsible. And I'd like to think someone was crazy to do what she did. But—can you really get better if you're that crazy? In sex crimes, there are these guys—they never stop wanting to do what they do. Remember when Depo-Provera was the thing? It wasn't enough. You can take the starch out of the collar"—Tess was sure that *collar* was not Sandy's first choice, but he had a touching, old-school gallantry— "but you can't take the impulse away. It's always there. So this lady— is she medicated these days? Forget medicated. Has she been sterilized? What if—"

"I don't know, Sandy. I have trouble with the idea of forced sterilization under any circumstances. And that's one part of the female reproductive system the ultraconservatives haven't tried to stake out. They're all for freedom to conceive. In the missionary position, within a hetero-normative marriage."

"You know, I never know what you're going to say next," Sandy said. "Makes life interesting. See you tomorrow."

Tess felt flattered, then wondered if she had been insulted. Probably neither, just a simple statement of fact from a man who used words in the most utilitarian way possible, applying them to problems and needs. That was part of the reason she wanted him to take the lead in tomorrow's meeting. The woman, Melisandre Harris Dawes, was supposed to be a big talker. A former lawyer, which was how Tyner had known her. Maybe still one? As far as Tess knew, a finding of temporary insanity was not a reason to be disbarred. She'd say as much to Tyner, adding "insert your own joke here." For Tess was not only a talker, she was someone who sometimes planned to say funny things ahead. Forget *l'esprit de l'escalier*. Tess not only didn't think of the perfect retort too late, she often prepared it in advance. Yes, she would make just that joke in front of Tyner. "I guess being insane isn't a basis for being disbarred, or else there wouldn't be a single working lawyer in all of Maryland."

She would not, however, make a joke about whether a lawyer should be disbarred for driving to the shores of the Patapsco on a searing August day, parking in a patch of sun, and then sitting on the grass beneath a tree while her two-month-old child essentially cooked inside the car.

Tess looked again at the folded note, glanced around to find a trash can. None nearby. She imagined herself littering, something she would never do. She liked to imagine doing the unimaginable. *What if I grabbed a Goldenberg's Peanut Chew and ate it while shopping? What if I took money from that unsupervised tip jar? What if I sideswiped a car and just pretended to leave a note, for show, then drove away?*

Tess was reliably honest in her daily life, as opposed to her work one, which required some deceit. Still, she liked to think about being bad. She told herself it was part of her job to understand why other people broke rules that seemed inviolate to her. Insurance cheats, marriage cheats, embezzlers were part of her day-to-day life. But no one was truly pure. Tess had availed herself of office supplies and free long distance when she was a reporter. Long distance was no longer the perk it once was, but office supplies—oh, how she missed office supplies.

Could she ever imagine the disordered mind of a woman capable of what Melisandre Dawes had done? Can the sane understand the crazy? Was it un-PC to call someone crazy? Modern life was way too complicated. Tess hadn't even reached forty and she felt like a throwback. Then again, so did every true Baltimorean.

She tossed the note in Gladys's backseat, where it did not lack for company. Tess had not been a reporter for more than a decade, but she still tended toward the filth-strewn car, something of a journalistic trope. The note fell on the floor among the fast-food detritus that Tess blamed on her toddler daughter. Who had not, to date, eaten a single Chicken McNugget or Whopper, but that was at her father's insistence. Still, Carla Scout was a good fall guy for the messy car, although her vocabulary was such now that she could rat her mother out for certain transgressions. "Mommy bought me cheeseburger," she had told Crow the other day, and he had promptly quizzed Tess about its origins, whether it had been locally sourced, grass fed. Tess said it was from the Abbey Burger Bistro, Roseda Farm. It had actually been from Five Guys, and Tess had no idea where the beef had originated, but she did know that day's potato supply hailed from Wyoming. She did not consider this lying so much as a coping device, made essential by Crow's mild nutritional lunacy, which had come on without warning after Carla Scout's second birthday.

Carla Scout— She had to remember to pick up the right shampoo today, and the leave-in conditioner. Otherwise, combing the girl's hair after her bath was practically a violation of the Geneva Conventions. And they were out of milk, and it had to be the local, organic stuff in the glass bottles, which meant going to Eddie's on Roland Avenue, not one of the big chains, which stocked that kind of shampoo.

By the time Tess pulled away from the curb, the note was forgotten.

12:30 P.M.

Harmony Burns spent five minutes explaining the project to the restaurant manager, careful to play every professional card she had in her deck, paltry as her deck was. She mentioned her credits, all two of them, and noted they could be checked on IMDb, although she always hoped no one followed through. Oh, the credits were real enough, but IMDb had other information, too, links to articles and reviews she wished could be scrubbed from the Web.

She patiently reiterated that she really was in charge, not a production assistant, as if this project had production assistants. At thirty-three, Harmony looked at least a decade younger. ("I'm the director, but also the writer. No, it happens. I graduated from film school, but I have a solid background in journalism. And, yes, some of it has to be scripted.") She explained the film itself, how it had been commissioned and financed by the subject. This was the part that always made her queasy, yet the information had glided past everyone so far. *How could a documentary be scrupulously fair when it was being financed by the subject?* Harmony still had qualms about this, but Melisandre swore that nothing would be censored and Harmony believed her. She had no choice.

"It's about the criminal insanity plea, but we're using this one high-profile case to explore all the facets," she said, launching into her usual spiel, trying not to show her desperation to get the release signed, if only because the guy might shake her down. She began speaking faster and faster. She mentioned John Hinckley, still in St. Elizabeth's, probably forever in St. Elizabeth's, and Andrea Yates, the woman in Texas who had drowned all five of her children, although Melisandre disliked any comparison to Andrea Yates. She talked about the woman, also in Texas, who had been released from a psychiatric facility and taken a job at Walmart, only to lose it when a local television station outed her as the mother who had sawed her infant daughter's arms off in what was later determined to be postpartum psychosis.

The manager of the restaurant squinted at the form and said, "So, like a reality show?"

He wasn't the first one to ask this.

"No, it's a film. A documentary. Nothing like a reality show."

"But it's real, right?"

She wanted to sigh, but a sigh wouldn't get her what she wanted. Nor would a tortured explanation of the gulf between "reality" television and documentaries. So she said: "It's a film. Might go into theaters, might be on television."

"I thought you said it was real?"

Harmony, a native of a small town in southern Illinois, was not someone inclined to disdainful stereotypes about rubes and hicks and cultural backwaters. But Baltimore was really beginning to test her spirit.

"It is. Real. All real. We just want to film someone having lunch with her kids. We'll do it at the tail end of the serving hours, to be less obtrusive. We don't hang lights, or put down track or do anything to alter the space. I'm the entire crew and there's only one light."

"Why'd you choose Happy Casita? Did you find us on Yelp?"

"I'm told it's the girls' favorite lunch spot." What Harmony had been told was "No!" by every restaurant on the list provided by the girls' father. This place, a forlorn Mexican cantina that wasn't a chain but might as well have been, was the production's last hope. It was one of those doomed restaurants that was all location, with a nice view of the Baltimore waterfront but nothing else going for it. Harmony had paid off a good chunk of her college debts working in similar places in Austin, Texas.

"I guess so," the manager said. "But no one better flip a table or throw a drink in anyone's face. That's not the kind of trade I'm looking for."

Glancing around the almost empty restaurant, Harmony had to wonder that the manager wasn't salivating for any exposure, even a local feature on how bad the cleanliness standards were. But she had gotten what she wanted, what she required—a public place to film Melisandre's reunion with her teenage daughters.

Of course, she would have preferred it to be somewhere more private, but Melisandre's ex had been adamant. He had fought the idea that the girls should be on film at all, and he had the legal right to block it: they were underage and he was their sole guardian. But Melisandre had played him expertly, just as she had told Harmony she would. She readily agreed to defer to his wishes, saying he knew best, of course, then asked: "But shouldn't you consult them? They are seventeen and fifteen now and it seems only fair to ask what they think."

The girls said yes. *They said yes!* They would participate in the documentary and they would allow the reunion to be filmed. Harmony had been torn—getting the girls on film by themselves, in one-on-ones, was probably more important. But then Melisandre had dangled the bait of the reunion, allowing Harmony to film her first meeting with her daughters in almost ten years.

Now Harmony wondered if Melisandre had manipulated *her.* Since the day they met, in a suite at Claridge's four months ago, Harmony had felt as if she were in a circle with a snake charmer, swaying to her tune.

It had begun with flattery. Doesn't every seduction? Melisandre had contacted Harmony through Harmony's former agent, claiming to be a huge fan of the documentary of which no one was a huge fan, Harmony's second one, the one that had frittered away all the promise and potential of her first. It still hurt, the reaction to her second film. One thing to have her technique and storytelling critiqued; that was par for the course. Her small triumph with her first film had set her up to be savaged on the second. But to be called a racist, to be accused of pandering and manipulation, presenting a portrait that would allow better-off folks to laugh and jeer at the poor—that had been humiliating and unfair. No one understood that the studio had final cut, that the horrible mishmash was not Harmony's edit. In a world where every reality show participant blamed editing for her woes, Harmony's sincere protestations were meaningless.

And suddenly there was a woman on the phone, telling Harmony how much she loved her work, speaking in the most charming voice, full of tiny inflections and unusual cadences that came, Harmony assumed, from living abroad for almost a decade. She had to assume a lot during that phone call, because Melisandre Dawes was someone who expected people to know everything about her. Yet her name had meant nothing to Harmony.

"Oh, just Google me and then we'll talk," she told Harmony. "Face-to-face, I hope. I'm in London, closing down my mother's affairs here. Although she lived in Cape Town the last few years, she had an apartment she was renting, and a place in the Cotswolds that I'm going to sell."

"I'm in New York," Harmony said. She did *not* add: *in Inwood, broke and about to go back to waiting tables if I can't figure out what to do.* (She had turned down several reality shows, the only jobs offered.) She hung up, Googled Melisandre Dawes, and was on the verge of pawning her one nice necklace when a ticket was wired to her. Business class. Not to mention a comped room at the hotel, although not one as grand as Melisandre's suite. And Melisandre had set up reservations for most of their meals, relieving Harmony of the panic she felt about her maxed-out credit cards, her utter lack of liquidity. She could not believe how much things cost in London, even more than in New York.

Best of all, she *liked* the project. Loved it. She might have chosen it for herself. But Harmony hadn't chosen it. Melisandre Harris Dawes had chosen her. The project would always have that taint, even if Melisandre lived up to her promises, which included Harmony having a contractual final cut—*unless* the film did not find distribution within twenty-four months of completion. That was a cagey clause, a reminder that Melisandre had been a lawyer and knew her way around a contract. She also insisted on a confidentiality agreement, which Harmony found insulting. Having Melisandre tell her it was "pro forma" didn't make it any less insulting.

"We've both been treated unfairly," Melisandre said at their first meeting. "We have both been misunderstood."

It was hard, sitting at her table, eating the amazing tea that had been prepared for them, not to say: "I just made a film that was critically pilloried. I didn't leave my child to die in a car." Then again, Harmony had seduced every person she had put on film. Why shouldn't the subjects seduce back? In the months since her second film had tanked, when she had an unhealthy amount of time to think about her early promise and how she had wasted it, she would lie in bed and imagine the pitches that other doc directors had made to their subjects. What had the director said to the woman featured in *The Queen of Versailles,* for example? Flattery had always been part of the mix, always. Even here, in a third-rate Mexican restaurant in Baltimore, Harmony had to use flattery. And it had gotten the job done. They would return at 3:30, when the restaurant would almost surely be empty, and film the girls arriving.

She went back to the hotel—the Four Seasons, at Melisandre's insistence. "All for one, and one for all. If I stay here, you should, too. And there's only one of you, after all."

Harmony had decided to do this on her own, rationalizing that it was the chorus of enablers on her second film that had led her astray. If she hadn't had so many people around her telling her how brilliant she was, she might have seen how things were going wrong. She had to go back to the stripped-down ethos of her first doc—just her, not even a sound or lighting person, running and gunning. But with only one camera and her aversion to staging anything, Harmony had to make dozens of strategic choices every day. Take this lunch: Should she set up inside the restaurant, or try to film the girls' entrance, then set her one light? She thought it made the most sense to have the camera in the restaurant, trained on Melisandre, waiting for the girls. Melisandre would be miked beforehand, but that meant stopping and fixing up the girls, which would disrupt the flow of the meeting. Balance was always being struck between reality—she smiled to herself at the term, its meaning so perverted now—and technical considerations. If one more person quoted to Harmony that a thing observed was changed by observation, she might finally ask: *And how does anyone see what is not observed?*

She sat cross-legged on her bed, taking notes, eating takeout from Whole Foods. Melisandre had given her a free hand to create the budget, even oversight of Melisandre's bills. There was a per diem in the budget, but Harmony tried to pocket as much of it as possible. She had become a real schnorrer, a word she hadn't known in southern Illinois, where she had had the happiest of childhoods. Harmony probably should have moved back to her nonjudgmental hometown after the debacle of *The Western Slopes*. If family and friends there had never really grasped how successful she had been, briefly, then they also didn't understand how far she had fallen. She was just Harmony there, funny Harmony who wore black all the time and talked a little faster now, but still Harmony. Home would have treated her kindly.

But Harmony had no use for kindness. She wasn't going to learn from kindness.

Her phone tinkled, Melisandre's assigned ringtone, the sound of breaking glass. But when Harmony picked up, it was the bodyguard, not Melisandre.

"What's up, Brian?"

"No meeting today. With the girls."

"Did something happen?"

"Oldest says she has a migraine. Youngest won't come without her."

Shit. She should have set up the one-on-ones. They were backpedaling, she was sure of it. They were going to lose the girls. Melisandre had less control over her ex than she imagined.

"How's Melisandre? May I speak to her?"

"She's lying down." Brian was very protective of Melisandre. Too protective, in Harmony's view, and she had asked Melisandre, as the doc's executive producer, to remind him that he had to stay out of the way, that there would be moments in this that would be hard on Melisandre and he had to let them happen. Thank God Melisandre didn't want to see the dailies or read the files from the transcription service, although she was entitled to. That interview with the smug young woman from the summer camp would have devastated her. Harmony shouldn't have been sarcastic with her, at the end. But something about that self-possessed young woman had driven Harmony nuts. Carolyn Sanders would never end up in a studio apartment in Inwood, no matter how she screwed up.

"Did the girls reschedule?"

"I don't know. I just know it's not happening today. And if you don't mind my saying so, I would find another location. I looked at the Mexican place after you texted me. I didn't like the layout there at all. It's very exposed."

"Brian, there has been no significant threat to Melisandre since she returned to Baltimore. Those notes—"

"You make your movie," he said. "I'll take care of her."

"Yeah, well, the movie we're making is not *The Bodyguard*, Brian, okay?" But he was already off the line, as she knew he would be.

Fuck me, she thought. She should have pushed for the girls first, before the meeting. She didn't believe Alanna had a migraine, just a father who had ridden her for three days now, determined to keep the girls from seeing their mother despite saying it was their decision. What a creep. But he was a smart creep. Stephen Dawes was very smart to do whatever he could to interfere with this film.

4:00 P.M.

"Alanna?"

"Yes?"

The voice on the other side of the door was persuasively wan. Except Ruby wasn't persuaded. "Can I come in?"

"No. If you open the door the light will bother me."

"Then close your eyes," Ruby said.

A pause. Alanna was probably trying to come up with an argument for that. But one reason that Ruby had success with Alanna, where so many grown-ups failed, was that she took a no-nonsense approach, one she had learned from the various nanny programs on TV. Stay calm, stand your ground, don't criticize. Be consistent. Yes, it was weird for a fifteen-year-old girl to be using *Supernanny* techniques to deal with her seventeen-year-old sister, but the Dawes family was so beyond the country of weird that Ruby didn't worry about it. She was her sister's keeper. People expected it to be the other way, because Alanna was older. Maybe it had been that way, once, but Ruby had no memory of it.

"Okay," Alanna said, and Ruby opened the door and closed it quickly behind her, walking with the softest possible tread into her sister's room. She knew, from past experience, not to sit on the bed. Alanna would claim that aggravated the migraine. So Ruby sat cross-legged on the floor. The room was very dark. Blackout blinds had been installed when they moved into the new house, something Alanna had lobbied for since the migraines were diagnosed, three years ago. Alanna had felt vindicated, briefly, by that diagnosis. For years, her headaches had been dismissed as simple tension headaches, a convenient way to avoid doing anything she didn't want to do. But years of being called a fake had, in Ruby's opinion, persuaded Alanna that she was owed some fakeness.

"I could have gone without you," she said.

"That wouldn't be right." Alanna's words were muffled. She had her face pressed into her pillow.

"No." It wouldn't be. But if Alanna was faking today, then that wasn't right, either. Not that Ruby would ever say anything like that out loud to her sister. And if not to Alanna, to whom? Not her father. Not Felicia, never Felicia. Sometimes, when she was in a room alone with her new baby brother, Joey, she unburdened herself to him. Joey was six months now, so he just smiled and gurgled approvingly, no matter what Ruby told him.

She sat in the darkness, listening to her sister breathe. No point in asking any questions, such as *Why did you change your mind after you promised you'd do it? Did Dad get to you? I thought you were going to stand up to him, for both of us. That's what you promised.* She could not ask Alanna larger questions about their past. *Do you really think she meant to hurt us that day, too? Why did she give us up and move so far away?* No point in revisiting wistful arguments, either. *Maybe we could have saved her that day. Saved her and saved Isadora. She couldn't have left us in the car. We would have gotten out and run, gone for help.*

Ruby was four the last time she saw her mother.

"I have to go away for a while," her mother said. "To get better."

"Daddy said you are better."

"I am. But they want me to get treatment. Just in case."

"I thought you had a sickness that women get after having a baby."

"I did."

"Were you sick when you had me?"

"No."

"What made you sick?"

"They don't know. It's a sickness they don't understand."

"Are you still sick?"

"No, I don't think so. But we have to make sure."

"Do you miss Isadora?"

"Of course I do. Every day. Don't you?"

That had been a tough question. "She was just a baby and I was a big kid. I loved her—"

"Of course you did."

"But I don't miss her. Is that bad?"

"No. Ruby, you haven't done anything bad, okay? You and Alanna—you are very good girls."

"We weren't always good. When you were sick. We made noise sometimes."

"It wouldn't have mattered, sweetie. It wouldn't have mattered."

Ruby did not understand then that her mother was never coming back. That became clear only later, and even then Ruby wasn't sure why. Why couldn't her mother come back? She said she was going to South Africa because she had lived there as a child, but it felt as if she had picked the farthest location possible. For years, Ruby kept thinking she would come back, just walk through the door one day, the way the song promised. *Mommy always comes back.* Of course, she was thinking of the door of the old house, back in Bolton Hill.

In *this* house, you couldn't hear anyone coming through the door unless you were in the living room or dining room. This house was large, almost too large, with strange acoustics. If it weren't a new house, built to spec, Ruby might have thought it haunted. Right now, she could hear Joey crying—well, not exactly crying, but making the odd seagull noises he made when he was happy. That meant Felicia and Joey were nearby, probably in Joey's room, the smallest of the four bedrooms on this level, but also the only one with its own bathroom. Felicia wasn't awful. She was just—Felicia. Their father's second wife.

They still owned the old house. It sat empty. No one wanted to buy the house where the lady had gone crazy and murdered her kid, even if it hadn't actually happened in the house. Ruby knew enough about real estate to understand that if her father lowered the price enough, someone would buy it. But he kept the listing artificially high. So while it was true that no one wanted to buy it, it was also true that her father, for some reason, wasn't ready to sell it. He said he needed to find a special buyer, someone who appreciated what he had done to the interior. He said he might convert it to apartments. One day. It made Ruby sad that her childhood home sat empty. She couldn't have said why. She just knew it was terribly sad. Maybe it was because an empty house could hold only one memory, the big memory, the thing that no one wanted to remember. Whereas if a new family moved in, perhaps the house could start over. Her father had started over, with Felicia. New wife, new house, new baby.

How would Alanna and Ruby start over? When?

She decided to risk putting her hand on her sister's bed, as softly as possible, palm up. Seconds passed, but Alanna finally rested her palm, damp and sticky, on Ruby's. It was uncomfortable sitting that way, with her wrist bent back. But Ruby sat there for a very long time, listening to her sister breathe in and out.

SPEAKER 1: Harmony Burns
SPEAKER 2: Elyse Mackie
INPUT: HB

HB: Please introduce yourself and start by telling me when you were hired by the Dawes family.

EM: My name is Elyse Mackie. I was a nanny to the Dawes family. I started a month before Isadora was born. They poached me.

HB: Poached? And don't forget, try to keep talking without prompts, if you can. Just tell the story. Women are so polite. They always want it to be a conversation. Pretend you're a man and just talk and talk and talk. I'm kidding. A little.

EM: They hired me when I was working for another couple. It happens. And to be truthful, they were far from the first people to try. They were in Washington, D.C., at a park on Capitol Hill, with the older girls, Alanna and Ruby, and they saw me with the children I was caring for at the time. Mrs. Dawes slipped me a note, saying she liked the way I handled myself and suggesting she could do better by me, if I were interested in a change. Like I said, it wasn't the first time someone had tried that. I hate to say it, but I think it's because I'm white. All the other nannies in that park tended to be African-American or Latina.

HB: To clarify—you think that's why Melisandre Dawes tried to hire you, or you think that's why other families, in general, tried to hire you?

EM: All families. That and my age. I was in my mid-twenties, then. Old enough so people assumed I had chosen to be a nanny as a career. And I did have a good résumé. I spoke Spanish, although that's not as in demand as French. I'm very good at what I do. Mr. and Mrs. Dawes made it clear that they wanted me to help primarily with the older children, that Mrs. Dawes was keen to stay home with the new baby because she hadn't done that with Ruby and Alanna. So they were to be my charges, to free up Mrs. Dawes to care for the baby. Lots of driving, to activities, to school and back. And then, when they were in school, she needed help with errands, maybe an occasional break with the baby. I always wondered— Well, I really shouldn't speculate. That makes me nervous. I told you about the agreement, right? I have to be very careful.

HB: Don't censor yourself. I promise if you say something and you regret it, you can tell me and I can edit it out. We'll also have a lawyer review your interview, make sure you're not in violation of your confidentiality agreement. What was it that you wondered?

EM: I always thought that the arrangement must be a little odd for Alanna and Ruby. Their mother hiring help so she could be devoted to the new baby. I don't know if they thought of it that way. They never said anything. But they were very bright, those girls, and sensitive. Alanna's the one that everyone thinks of as sensitive, because she wears her heart on her sleeve, but Ruby is just as affected by things. I loved those girls. I was so glad when Mr. Dawes hired me back. After—you know, after. I had really missed them.

HB: We'll get there. Let's try to follow the chronology. Tell me about the Melisandre you met, in the park that day. What did she look like, what was she like?

EM: Well, it was like a movie star had walked up to me. I honestly thought she must be someone famous. She had that way about her. You know, the hair, the clothes. I have to admit, that's part of the reason I took her card and called her. Like I said, it wasn't the first time someone tried to poach me, and I am generally pretty loyal. But the family I was working for—they wanted me to do more and more housecleaning as their children got older. That's not why I worked as a nanny. I liked kids. And Mrs. Dawes—she asked me to call her Melisandre, but I never quite could—she seemed so nice. I mean she was nice. She was maybe six months along, but she was one of those women who looked beautiful pregnant. She carried high and round, and seemed unaffected by it. It really was like she was just walking around with a basketball up her dress. I liked her. And they made me such a good offer. I was almost suspicious. An apartment, rent-free, and not on their property, which is tricky. Living with a family. They say you'll have privacy, but you never do. I lived in one of Stephen's buildings, a mill redevelopment. They even gave me a car. They said they wanted to make sure that Alanna and Ruby were safe. They didn't like my little Datsun. They bought me a two-year-old Jeep Cherokee. Set hours, Monday through Friday. And, eventually, I was to travel with them, although that never happened. They had thought they might go to

Europe that summer, or rent a place on Nantucket, but Mr. Dawes couldn't afford the time off from work and Isadora was colicky. Bad colicky. It would have driven anyone crazy. Sorry. Oh, God, I'm so sorry—

HB: It's okay.

EM: I didn't mean to say it that way. I know it wasn't the colic. But I doubt the colic helped. We were all a bit on edge. Even the girls. But we got through the end of the school year, and they were in camp, and suddenly, Mr. Dawes told me they didn't need me anymore.

HB: Just out of the blue.

EM: It felt that way.

HB: Why?

EM: Why did it feel that way?

HB: Why did he say he had to let you go?

EM: He said it was at Mrs. Dawes's insistence. I don't know. Maybe that was when—her problems were starting. That would make sense, right?

HB: Are you asking me?

EM: No. I guess I'm still—still confused. About who asked me to leave. But Mr. Dawes was the one who asked me to come back. After. Only I had to sign a confidentiality agreement. Of course they were sensitive about people talking, given what was going on. I mean, factual stuff, that's not in dispute—the dates of my employment, my job description—that's okay. And when I talked to Mrs. Dawes—I guess she's not Mrs. Dawes anymore, but I don't know what to call her—she said I can say anything I want to about her, anything. But I wasn't there, when it got really bad. I was fired in June. Wait, I don't think I can say *fired*. I left in June and returned in September.

HB: Certainly that agreement doesn't apply retroactively. We checked. You signed that in September 2002.

EM: I don't have the, uh, luxury of finding that out. My first day back at work was September tenth. I remember because the next day—people were talking about the first anniversary of nine-eleven. I remember that Stephen—Mr. Dawes—told me that when nine-eleven happened, Alanna, she asked that everyone stop talking about it. Within, like, two weeks. She said, "Would everyone please stop talking about nine-eleven?" That was so like her.

HB: That's a good detail. I wonder if Alanna will remember that about herself.

EM: How's she doing? Alanna. And Ruby. She was adorable. I think about them a lot. I thought— Well, it doesn't matter. But I really loved them. Do they like their stepmother? I'm sorry, I guess that's none of my business. I always thought Stephen would marry—if he remarried at all—someone like, well, someone more like Melisandre. He cares about appearances, Mr. Dawes. I thought that might have been the reason he didn't get help for Mrs. Dawes.

HB: I don't want to press you, but about Mr. Dawes? He offered no reason at all when he asked you to leave the first time, in June, said only that it was what Mrs. Dawes wanted?

EM: It just came out of the blue. Also, it was summer. The girls had fewer activities, only the day camp. And it was around the time Mrs. Dawes began to get so strange. I guess, if she was psychotic, that was when it started.

HB: If? Do you doubt the diagnosis? Are you one of the people who believe she was faking?

EM: Oh, no, well, it's just that, it's like OJ, right? He was acquitted, but lots and lots of people think he was guilty.

HB: Do you, in particular, have a specific reason to believe that Melisandre Dawes was not clinically insane the day her daughter died?

EM: No, I didn't mean that. I was just talking in a general way. Don't put words in my mouth.

HB: Okay, in your own words, describe the woman for whom you worked that year.

EM: She was troubled. At first, she just seemed unhappy. I've worked as a nanny long enough to know that's not unusual. She was tired and Isadora cried all the time. It was as if the household had split in two, with her and the baby on one side, Stephen and the girls on the other. Like there were two families. And the more isolated she became, the stranger she seemed. But if she was hearing voices or having delusions—I missed it. She was unhappy and angry. I mean, that's what I thought. And she threw things when she got mad. I'd never seen anyone do that before, but I'm not sure it means you're crazy. Insane, whatever we're supposed to say. But she managed to hold it together around the girls, at least while I was there. I was let go in late June. I guess a lot can happen in six weeks. It must have. The woman I worked for—I can't imagine her doing what she did. It would make more sense if it were just a complete accident, if she forgot, like some parents do, you know? I can see her forgetting. I can't see her doing it on purpose. Or maybe I just don't want to. Are we done? I have an appointment at four.

HB: Sketch in your biography for me quickly. What you're doing now, if you're married or have kids?

EM: I manage a gourmet store in Belvedere Square, a place that imports food and olive oil from Spain. So my Spanish finally came in handy. I got married, but it didn't work out. I'm engaged to marry again, though, and I hope I can have kids of my own. I'd hate to think I'd missed out on that. I always thought I'd have kids. It was a real disappointment, you know, when things didn't work out. With my first husband, I mean. But I guess that was for the best, right? That wasn't the right situation for me, so it's better that I waited, that it didn't happen then. That's why I need to go. I have a meeting with my wedding planner and, I swear, it's like I work for her. I don't dare be late. She's really in demand and we're meeting with the caterers today for a tasting. I know it's silly, but my first marriage was such a rebound thing. I was young and I didn't really think it out. So this is my first wedding. I want it to be perfect. I know—people make fun of women, call us Bridezillas. But if you know anything about marriage, you know the wedding is the only thing that has a shot at being perfect, so why not?

HB: Camera off, end tape.

Tuesday

10:00 A.M.

"Danish?" Tess asked. "We're having a big platter of pastries and *Danish*? And bagels? With a carton of fresh-brewed coffee from the Daily Grind?"

"Nothing wrong with Danish," Sandy said, helping himself.

Tess continued to stare down Tyner Gray. Or try to. When it came to avoiding eye contact, Tyner's wheelchair was a distinct advantage. If she wanted to force him to meet her gaze, she'd have to crouch the way she did with Carla Scout, who also had a genius for avoiding eye contact when it suited her.

"I have been to, what, maybe three hundred meetings here over the years and you have never so much as offered someone a Luna bar and now you've put out a *spread*? What is so damn special about this woman?"

"She's an old friend," Tyner said.

"An old friend or an old *friend*?"

"I don't find those kinds of labels useful."

He was still avoiding her eyes, moving through the office and straightening up nonexistent messes. Even the converted Mount Vernon town house, remodeled years ago to be wheelchair friendly, looked a little shinier, a little spiffier than usual. And Tyner had a haircut so fresh that Tess could see the scissor marks.

"I forget sometimes what a dog you were before you got married," Tess said.

"I was a single man. I dated. Not a lot of hard feelings out there on either end, but if you want to call that being a dog, so be it. I knew Melisandre when she was in her twenties, before she married Stephen. I was there when they met. That's why she called me—and that's why you landed a pretty lucrative gig. So—*you're welcome*."

"Then I guess I'll enjoy myself, too." She started to reach for a chocolate croissant, only to catch the look on Tyner's face. "What? Are we not allowed to touch the food until Lady Bountiful arrives? You didn't give Sandy a dirty look when he had a cruller."

Tyner's pause gave her pause. "Are you in training?"

"It's been a little cold to be out on the water," Tess said, knowing she wasn't answering the question.

"But you've been erging over the winter, I assume?"

"I don't compete, so I don't need to erg in the off-season. I row for my own pleasure."

"There's a word for self-pleasure, and it isn't very nice."

"Who says?" Tess countered. "At least masturbation is always consensual."

Tyner let the subject drop, and that was more disturbing than anything he had said or implied. Tyner would normally have no problem telling Tess that she was going soft, literally and figuratively. And while Tess had never been one to worry about the numbers on the scale, which were more or less—okay, more—where they had always been, there was a slackness to her body these days. Still, if

Tyner wanted to tell her how to find time to get on the water when she had to be on kid duty five mornings a week, she'd love to hear it. She could find forty minutes to head out for a run, maybe put in an hour at the gym at lunchtime. But rowing was time-intensive, once you counted up the drive to the boathouse, getting her shell out and on the water, cleaning and storing it properly at the end of a work-out. And it could be done only in the daylight hours. Tess had never known how short a day was until she had a child. The old saying was that the days were long and the years short when raising a child. But the hours she had to herself certainly zipped by.

Maybe some fruit for breakfast was all she needed. Go figure; there was a selection of fruit, too, and even a box of tea set out. With sugar cubes. Sugar cubes! White *and* brown.

"So where is the guest of honor?"

"Running late," Tyner said. "There were photographers outside her hotel this morning."

"And she had to figure out a way to get out without being seen?"

"No, she waded right into them, as I understand it."

"With camera crew following. Well, that creates a scene for the documentary, right? Melisandre Dawes—does she still go by Dawes?—besieged by the paparazzi. Probably called them on herself."

"She's using Melisandre Harris Dawes. And she's not like that, Tess."

"No, she's just a very rich lady who has decided that her life's mission is to educate people about criminal insanity by thrusting herself back into public view after a decade abroad. Toward that end she has hired a film crew to make a documentary about her, even though her case couldn't be more anomalous. Why not focus on the women without money who didn't get the help they needed? By the way—you did tell her that I'm not going to allow her to film this meeting, right?"

"Technically, as her lawyer, that's my call—"

"No, it's not, Tyner. I'm not going to consent to be filmed for this, and if that's part of the package, she can take her big hourly fee and stuff it up—"

The announcement, over the intercom, that their client had arrived, kept Tess from completing her directions. Tyner had barely said, "Send her in," when Melisandre Harris Dawes strode through the door.

And *strode—strided?* Tess's inner grammarian queried—was really the only word. Melisandre walked with her head up, long tendrils of hair bouncing like some shampoo commercial. Tess initially had a sense of lights, but the "crew" that followed her was one small, thin young woman, pulling a wheeled suitcase and carrying a digital camcorder with one hand. A man in a dark suit was behind her.

"No filming," Tess said before anyone else could speak. "Sorry, but I don't want to have our interactions filmed. I don't even want to be in the same room as a camera. My work methods are confidential and proprietary, meant only for the paying customer."

"I'm not really up for being filmed, either," Sandy said. He managed to sound polite.

Tess had expected more of a fight, but Melisandre dispatched her entourage immediately, clapping her hands as if she were some magical nanny. "She has a point, Harmony," she said to the young woman. "Even if this won't be shown for months, it's probably not a good idea to provide insight into my security detail. You and Brian can take the plate of Danishes. I don't want them."

Did it even occur to Melisandre that others in the room might want them? Did she assume everything in the world was for her? Probably. Money could do that to a person. Money and beauty, and Melisandre Harris Dawes had plenty of both.

"What happened to your famed sweet tooth?" Tyner asked.

"I sometimes think it was overcome by one too many malva puddings in Cape Town. At any rate, I almost never eat sweet things anymore. Maybe it's the change of life."

"As if," Tyner said. "You're years away."

Sandy wiped his hands on a napkin and introduced himself with a brisk handshake. Sandy was big on manners, downright *lousy* with manners. Tess had hired him for his investigative skills and police experience, but it didn't hurt, having a male partner who could lay on the charm. Not in a smarmy way, but in a genuine, courtly way. Tess followed with the hearty, confident handshake that her father insisted was the key to success in all business ventures. Tyner kissed Melisandre's proffered cheek, only to have her offer the other one. She had lived overseas for a while and her mother was British. Maybe it wasn't *entirely* pretentious.

"So, cameras outside the hotel—and you decided to confront them," Tyner said. But his tone wasn't scolding, as it would have been with Tess.

"I decided to act like a human being, if that's what you mean. I'll never let anyone take my humanity away from me again. Let them take my photograph. It doesn't steal one's soul, quite the opposite."

It was an interesting assertion, the kind of idea that Tess wanted to dissect, debate. If the public gaze didn't affect one's soul, it did transform and might even corrupt. But Melisandre Harris Dawes was paying by the hour—and at twice Tess's usual rate. Tess had no desire to argue with the client that she and Sandy had privately dubbed the Windfall.

"I'm going to let my partner, Sandy, present the overview. I want to stipulate again that security is not our specialty, and your own bodyguard—I assume that was the man in black?—is probably better suited to some of the tasks you've assigned us. I appreciate your business, but there is a learning curve."

"My bodyguard is too well suited," Melisandre said. "To be in the security business is to be paranoid. I wanted a more pragmatic overview from someone who understands that I hope to live a somewhat normal life here in Baltimore. I have two daughters. I don't want them to feel as if they're shut up in a fortress."

"Will your daughters be staying with you?"

Melisandre, who had arrived with an enormous Starbucks coffee, took a second to adjust herself—putting her coffee and purse down, arranging her wrap, picking up her coffee, taking a sip. Tess tried to total up the cost of her outfit, including the jewelry. The wrap, almost certainly cashmere, had been layered over a turtleneck and leggings, which were tucked into suede boots with the telltale red soles and five-inch spike heels. Three gold chains of varying lengths and sizes, with complementary drop earrings. Probably $5,000, $10,000 with the jewelry. *On her back.* There were people driving around Baltimore in cars worth less than what Melisandre was wearing. Tess had been one before buying the minivan. Which carried a $450-a-month car payment—so, smile, suck it up. By the end of this meeting, she'd have covered most of this month's payment.

"That remains to be seen," Melisandre said. "I would like that, of course, but Alanna is a junior in high school, Ruby a freshman. They have lives of their own. Splitting their time between two houses may not suit them. Although my future home is probably more convenient than that strange house Stephen has built in the middle of nowhere."

"Your ex-husband has sole custody, correct? At least, it's my understanding that you surrendered your parental rights a decade ago."

Tess watched Melisandre for her reaction. She pulled on her gold chains, pushed up the sleeves of her sweater, exposing a Patek Philippe watch. Okay, make that another ten thousand. Melisandre said nothing, but now Tess had her tell—the tug at the necklaces, the sleeve. That was what Melisandre Harris Dawes did when she was being evasive. Good to know. It was always good to know when people were being evasive.

Tess nodded for Sandy to begin. He leaned forward, elbows

on knees, and fixed his soulful green eyes on Melisandre. Tess had known from the moment she made eye contact with Sandy fifteen months ago that she would hire him. Those eyes made people want to talk. Getting someone to talk was not as important to a private investigator as it was to a homicide detective, but it couldn't hurt to have a father confessor type on the payroll.

"I drove by and around your apartment building this morning," Sandy said. "The building is relatively secure—all visitors are required to sign in. The public areas, such as the gym, are on controlled locks. So even if someone got past the front desk, they couldn't, say, get into the gym. Okay, so worst-case scenario, someone is willing to, um, do harm to get past the front desk."

"Do harm?" Melisandre echoed.

"Hurt other people. The elevator is open, but your apartment is the penthouse. No entry without a key card. And given the location, on a point of land with only two routes out of the neighborhood, access is pretty limited. I like that. Anyone who wants to give you trouble will have to calculate that getting away will present certain challenges."

"Unless they come by boat," Melisandre said.

Tess understood that she was joking, but a sense of humor was not one of Sandy's strengths. "There's really no place to dock nearby, so I'm not too worried about that. The garage does bug me, though. While it has an underground entrance, the public is allowed to use the bottom floor for parking for certain public services —the wine bar, the salon. Someone could definitely get to you in the garage."

"I'll have my bodyguard." Said as carelessly as another person might have said: "I'll have my umbrella."

"I was allowed into the apartment after you closed, although there's still some work being done," Sandy said. "It is our recommendation that you put an alarm panel in every room. An alarm panel with a panic button."

"No," she said. "That would look hideous."

Tess's turn. She was the boss, after all. "For liability reasons, we're going to prepare a written report that outlines every suggestion we make and we'll ask that you sign a waiver, stating we're not responsible in the event of a breach."

Melisandre laughed. "A breach. I thought Tyner said you were a straight talker."

"I'd forgotten the sound of your laugh," Tyner said. "It's still delightful."

Am I too old to make a vomit noise? Tess wondered at her instant animosity toward this woman. Was it her money? Her relationship with Tyner? Or the fact of what she had done? The story had been legendary around the boathouse. But Tess hadn't thought about it for years. A child's death was different now, less abstract to her.

Melisandre kept her attention fixed on Tess. "Are you worried that I—or, more likely, my heirs—will sue you if someone hurts me?"

"It's not unprecedented," Tess said. "I cover the bases. For you, for myself. Besides, you seem to like legalities and penalties. I understand you wanted me to sign a nondisclosure clause, which is redundant given that you hired me via Tyner. He's your lawyer. I work for him."

"I like to have all the bases covered."

Their frosty antichemistry seemed to make Tyner nervous. He jumped in.

"As you can see, Missy"—Tess caught the nickname, shot Tyner a look—"Tess has done a thorough job assessing your new home. It is not without risks. I know you've closed already. But I'm not sure this is the best place for you. A gated community would have been better."

"I would never live in such a place. Besides, this is the best of the four-bedrooms I saw. And while my ex-husband may have abandoned the city, I'm still committed to it."

"Do you really need that much space?" Tess asked. "It's a gorgeous apartment, but it's huge for one person."

"I told you, it's my hope that the girls will be spending a lot of time with me there, although Stephen and I have no formal agreement. He's a little nervous about that kind of change."

Tess's restraint was hard-won, but she managed not to blurt out: "Hello? You killed one of his kids!" Yet Melisandre seemed to know what she was thinking. She had that way of looking deeply into someone's eyes, but it didn't promote the confiding feeling that Sandy's gaze did. Melisandre's look was probing, challenging. It put Tess in the mind of someone—or some*thing*—in a sci-fi movie, scanning her for weaknesses.

"I think Stephen knows I would never harm Alanna or Ruby. I left them in his care because I convinced myself it was in their best interests. And for ten years, I told myself that lie, every day. In Cape Town, my mother and I became close again, and when she died last year, I realized I had to try, if possible, to have a relationship with my daughters. That's a profound change. The woman I used to be, the woman to whom Stephen was married, didn't even like her mother that much. He doesn't understand why I've come back and it unsettles him."

"Do you think he finds it *unsettling* that you chose to buy an apartment in one of his buildings?"

"I told you—it's the only one that meets all my criteria."

Tess let an awkward silence build. She knew this wouldn't bother Sandy at all. Sandy was great at silences, expert at using them. Nor did Melisandre seem discomfited by the absence of conversation. It was Tyner who blundered in, like a host at a dinner party that was dying a slow, awkward death.

"Do we need to talk about the notes? The ones you've been getting at the hotel?"

"Threatening notes?" This was Sandy. Tess tried to look as if she knew what was going on, but this was the first she had heard of something concrete. Tyner had told her this security overview was primarily to assure Melisandre's ex that the girls would be safe. Did the ex know about the notes?

"Not exactly," Melisandre said. "More like taunting ones. The theme, if you could call it that, is that someone is onto me, knows all about me. I didn't even bother to bring them."

"Any idea who might be writing them?"

Melisandre shook her head. "Only that it's someone who knows me, at least a little. Or is very good at research. A few odd facts jump out—my boarding school nickname, Missy, which only a few truly close friends use."

Yes, Tess thought. Tyner being one of them.

"That was never in the press," Melisandre said. "But there are literally dozens of people who know it."

"Could the notes be written by your ex or his wife?" Sandy asked.

"Stephen and I have a decent relationship, all things considered. The new wife— Well, not to be rude, but I'd be surprised if she's clever enough. She was his physical trainer, I hear. I wasn't around, but it's my understanding that she landed her big fish quite expertly. But not, I think, via the power of the written word."

An old commercial jingle ran through Tess's head. *Meow, meow, meow, meow. Meow, meow, meow, meow.*

"Are you sure?" Tess asked.

"Sure of what?"

"Sure that you have a good relationship with your ex?"

Again, that intense, measuring stare. It was like being sized up by a velociraptor. A not very hungry one, because a hungry one would snap you in half, while Melisandre seemed to be deciding whether Tess was even a worthy snack.

"Do you know what I am, Tess?"

"A woman with enough money to make a documentary about herself?"

Tyner looked as if he wanted to bang his head on the table or throttle Tess, but Melisandre was unruffled by her directness.

"I'm every woman's worst nightmare. Because whenever a woman kills her child, every other mother—at least, every one who's honest with herself—has a flash of sympathy. Not empathy. They don't want to have done it, cannot imagine doing it. But they *know*."

"I didn't have a child when you"—Tess faltered, hated herself for showing that chink in her armor, and therefore had to double down on the active voice—"when you killed your child. But I can't imagine that would ever be my reaction."

"Wait and see, then," Melisandre said. "Wait and see. Because it will happen again. It's never going to stop happening. Filicide has been with us forever."

"Do you even consider yourself guilty of filicide? You were found not guilty by reason of criminal insanity. You were beyond choices, rational thinking, right?"

Tess thought she had scored a point off Melisandre at last, but the woman's smile appeared quite genuine. "Now, see? Wouldn't that have been a lovely exchange to have on film? You're a marvelous foil, Ms. Monaghan."

11:15 A.M.

Felicia collapsed at the kitchen table with a glass of green iced tea and her laptop, overwhelmed by how much she needed to do, how little energy she had to do any of it. The house was quiet. At last. Mornings were horrible. Joey was usually up by five, six if Felicia was lucky, and just as he began to calm down, there was the chaos of Stephen and the girls leaving, which seemed to set Joey off. He was still getting up in the middle of the night, too, despite no longer needing to nurse at 2:00 and 4:00 A.M. Nine months old, sixteen pounds, and he still wasn't sleeping through the night. Felicia had tried following the precepts of *The Happiest Baby on the Block,* she really had. Irony of ironies, this former personal trainer was a washout at sleep training. Felicia, who had literally made grown men cry for their own good, could not let her son cry it out for even five seconds.

"Well, if he's like everyone else in this family, he'll be out of tears before he's in kindergarten," Alanna had said at breakfast this morning, which for her was a cup of black coffee that she never finished. It killed Felicia that an athlete of Alanna's caliber ate so poorly, but she suspected her stepdaughter's black coffee was an attempt to provoke her, so she ignored it.

Alanna added: "If he makes it to kindergarten. Not all Dawes children do."

That was harder to ignore.

Welcome to the Unhappiest Family on the Block. Also the only family on the block, so they were the happiest, the unhappiest, the richest, the poorest. It was the Big House in the Big Woods, a lonely fortress that felt as if it were in the middle of nowhere, although the Beltway hummed with traffic not ten minutes away. It was everything Felicia had ever wanted—a house that she had helped design—and she was miserable.

Felicia had started agitating for a new house the moment she became pregnant. No woman wanted to live in a previous wife's house under any circumstances, and to live in *that* house with a baby—no thank you. But she never expected that Stephen Dawes, champion of urban living, would choose to move his family to a custom-built house on a private lane, surrounded on three sides by a wooded state park. Trust Stephen to find a parcel of land in the middle of state parkland, yet only twenty-five minutes from downtown. Felicia had imagined something with actual neighbors, shops within walking distance. She argued that she would be in the car all the time, living in a location this remote. Stephen pointed out that she never walked anywhere in Bolton Hill.

Fair enough. But if they had to move—and they did, for space;

the Bolton Hill house was huge but had only three bedrooms—why not another city neighborhood, or at least a more traditional suburb? Stephen glided past those questions when Felicia tried to ask them. The land had been purchased, the plan was under way. He said he would buy Felicia a new car, a hybrid that got better gas mileage. And give Alanna a car, too, so she could be responsible for getting herself and her sister to school. The girls might even change schools. They were in a decent school district here, and it would save a lot of money if the girls chose to attend public school.

The last piece of Stephen's argument scared Felicia a little. She had never known him to lobby for anything on the grounds of cost. Not that he was foolish with money. And he had always been careful not to spoil the girls. He bought Alanna a used Subaru Outback for her first car, for example. Of course, Alanna managed to get into an accident the first month—not her fault, yet not quite *not* her fault, Felicia suspected—and Stephen was so horrified at the body damage done by this small collision that he replaced the totaled Subaru with a cherry-red Mercedes. Used, but still.

The girls refused to change schools anyway, not that Felicia could blame them. Ruby had been about to start her freshman year when they moved last summer, while Alanna was a junior. It seemed hypocritical of Alanna, who had been complaining about Roland Park Country School for years, to embrace it the moment she was given a chance to transfer, but Alanna was nothing if not perverse. Ruby sided with Alanna. Ruby always did what Alanna wanted.

And even with Alanna driving herself and Ruby to school, mornings were still hell. Stephen always said, "I'll make sure the girls get off in time, don't worry, just hang out with Joey." But there were a thousand questions. Okay, a dozen. *Alanna's tracksuit?* In the laundry room, on the drying rack. *Ruby says she's going to someone else's house after school—did she tell Felicia? Can Felicia pick her up? Because Alanna has practice after school and the other girl's mother works.*

Stephen was evolved enough that he usually remembered to say:

The other girl's mother has a *job,* or *works outside the home.* Usually. But he spoke the words as if they were foreign-language phrases he didn't quite understand. What had he said when Joey was born? *Why not take some time off?* Felicia wondered now if it was because he wanted to save the money that child care would have cost, or if he feared what it would mean to his own day-to-day life if Felicia were working.

Still, it was hard to imagine how she could have kept her job after Joey was born. A personal trainer at Felicia's level worked long and odd hours. Her day often began as early as 5:00 A.M. and could run as late as 9:00 or 10:00 P.M. The kinds of people Felicia trained didn't go to the gym between nine and five, or even between eight and six, although one or two might try to squeeze a session in during lunch. Her clients worked out in the predawn hours or straggled into the gym at night, having done whatever they needed to do to make the kind of money that made it possible to hire Felicia. In just seven years, she had gone from being a fresh-out-of-college corporate gym trainer to owning her own company, the kind of trainer who ended up on various Best of Baltimore lists. It didn't hurt that she was sleek and blond and blue-eyed, the epitome of what people think a female trainer should be. Although when Stephen hired her, three years ago, he claimed he had not seen her photograph, simply instructed his assistant to find the city's best trainer.

Stephen was usually her last appointment of the night, paying for his sessions in advance on the theory that doing so would force him to come no matter how his workday had treated him. "I'm a wash-out," he said. "I used to row, but—" He didn't finish the sentence. Presumably, he assumed that Felicia knew how it had ended, why he avoided the boathouse. But in 2002, Felicia had been in college, and she didn't remember the story at all. It had sounded vaguely familiar when someone filled her in, and she had pretended she'd known all along; who wants to be the kind of twenty-something who doesn't pay attention to such a horrific story? Her ignorance spoke of self-involvement, an insularity beyond Alanna's. Felicia rationalized that it had been a Baltimore thing, and she was a Western Maryland girl. Her hometown of Cumberland was a world away, more likely to hear the news out of Pittsburgh. At any rate, the only things that Felicia knew about Stephen Dawes when he started working out with her were that he had a lot of money and he was in crappy shape. "I'm a single parent," he would say. "I need to be around for my kids." Then, with a truly charming, bashful grin: "I also might start dating again."

His body snapped back fast, former rower that he was. He supplemented his sessions with Felicia by running in the mornings, going to the occasional yoga class. The pale, saggy client who first came to see her was transformed within months into a trim man with healthy color. He was losing his hair, but in that charmingly wolfish way, in which a widow's peak remained while the hair on either side receded. The woman that Felicia trained before Stephen began asking her lots of questions about him, lingering to stretch. Felicia did not encourage her dawdling.

To be a personal trainer required one to be impersonal about people's bodies. One had to be like a doctor; not that there weren't bad doctors. (Felicia had been felt up by her ENT guy when she was just twenty-three.) Personal relationships were rare, at least among the elite trainers. They weren't good for business. She had a friend who had ended up in bed with a male client. "I went from getting eighty dollars an hour to boss him around and stretch him a little to getting zero dollars an hour to do everything he wanted," she quipped.

But as Stephen gradually unburdened himself to Felicia, she had found herself falling in love with him. And it was hard not to be proud of him as her creation, to look at the new and improved Stephen as *hers*. She had to hold her jealousy in check when he discussed his attempts to reenter the dating pool. Why should some other woman enjoy what Felicia had made? He talked about the ups and downs of dating under the judgmental gaze of his daughters. They disliked everyone automatically. He had tried to involve them in his social life, had asked if they wanted to go over his Match.com selections. They said they couldn't think of anything they wanted to do less.

This went on for three months or so. Stephen dating, telling Felicia about his dates, usually in a comic fashion. Felicia, who had moved out of her boyfriend's house a month or so before Stephen began training with her, returned to her ex after he made an earnest pitch. It didn't work the second time, either. She ended up back on her own, living in a crappy little studio, the best she could do in Baltimore's tight rental market.

On February 15 two years ago, she met Stephen for a training session in the gym of a new high-rise he had built in Locust Point. She didn't usually travel to him, but he said he wanted to use the gym there a couple of times, get a feel for it before the big sales push.

"Did you have a good Valentine's Day?" he asked as he warmed up on the treadmill.

She shrugged. Felicia didn't tell her clients anywhere near as much as they told her.

"It's a stupid day," he said. "So overloaded with expectations. Did you know that florists do a brisk business on the *fifteenth*? All these guys in the doghouse. But the good news is, the price of roses drops. Tells you everything you need to know about the Valentine's Day economy."

"I don't even like roses. I like peonies."

"You told me that once."

She had? She didn't remember that.

"You know what I want to do tonight? I mean, I know you're supposed to call the shots, but remember when you had me run up and down the stairs, how much I complained. What if we race? To the top?"

"To the top?" The building was thirteen stories. Stephen had told her once that Baltimore, unlike New York, called the thirteenth floor the thirteenth floor, and he loved his hometown for that. He had named this tower 13 Stories; its address was 1313 Locust Point. *When you've been as unlucky as I have,* Stephen told her once, *nothing really scares you anymore. Nothing silly, at any rate.*

"Scared?"

"Of course not."

Even for someone as fit as Felicia had been—and she had been in her prime that night—a race up twelve flights of stairs was taxing. Plus, she felt the pressure to win. It would be embarrassing to be bested by a client.

But she also wanted to win because Stephen was Stephen and this was the only advantage she had over him, being more fit. It was awful enough to have feelings for him. She couldn't lose the race, too.

He fell back by the third flight or so and, by the time Felicia reached the tenth flight, she couldn't even hear his footfalls over her own rasping breath, the blood pounding in her ears. It never occurred to her that he had slipped out of the stairwell on the third floor and taken the elevator.

When she burst through the door onto the roof, cold and startlingly bright, Stephen was waiting there. With a bouquet of peonies. In the solarium of the penthouse apartment behind him, a table was set with a white cloth, and a bottle of champagne could be seen in an ice bucket.

"February fourteenth is for suckers," he said. "Let everyone else have it. We can have February fifteenth. That is, if you'll consider going out with me."

They had married on that date a year later, and Joey had been born four months after that. Since then, Felicia's only client had been Felicia. She had managed, in the tiny pockets of time available to her, to rebuild her body to what it had once been. But she had sold her business. When, if, she went back to work, she would have to start all over, building a client list, regaining her reputation. Now Stephen worked out with the male trainer who had taken over Felicia's business. And she had gone from living in a studio apartment to a haunted house in Bolton Hill to this large and—*just say it*—scary, spooky house in the woods, where she spent entire days in which she spoke to no one but grocery clerks and the disembodied voice that took her order at the drive-through Starbucks on Nursery Lane, a big highlight of her day. When Joey was fussy, she put him in his car seat, got a chai tea at the drive-through, and drove around the industrial landscape near the airport, listening to what Stephen called girl music. "You have the musical taste of a teenager," he told her.

Not that the two teenagers in the house would have anything to do with her. Alanna and Ruby were cagey enough not to be outright rude to her. Stephen would have jumped on bad behavior. They were even loving to Joey, especially Ruby. But they acted as if Felicia didn't exist. No, as if she were—a *fart,* and they were ignoring her out of kindness, the way a trainer attempts to do in all but the most extreme cases of flatulence.

Stephen, in fact, had let go with the most amazing fart, in terms of sound, when Felicia was stretching him out one night. It couldn't be ignored. After a split second, he had laughed at himself, and she had joined in. She sometimes thought that was the moment she started falling in love with him. When he farted in her face.

Maybe that wasn't the best basis on which to begin a relationship.

But, no, be fair: The relationship had begun with a bouquet of peonies, underneath a cold February sky hard with stars. Later, she would hear the story—although not from Stephen—about how he had proposed to his first wife, the ring dangling from the tree, the friends and family hidden inside the boathouse. Stephen's mother, Glenda, had told Felicia that story, saying dryly: "Stephen always did like to make a production of things." What was her point? That Felicia wasn't so special? Or that a beautiful beginning was no protection against a bad ending? Felicia thought the real issue was that Stephen's mother, a widow since he was small, didn't want to share her son with anyone. Glenda Dawes had nothing good to say about Melisandre, and she had given Stephen an earful when she found out he was going to let the girls decide if they should be filmed with her.

A lusty cry on the monitor—the morning nap was over. Felicia hadn't accomplished a single thing. Joey was her accomplishment, she supposed. If she had once been proud of Stephen's body, she now felt that way about Joey a hundred times over. She had formed him, cell by cell. Her pregnancy had been an ecstatic time, so joyful that she considered being a surrogate. But now that Joey was on the outside of her—

A louder, more insistent cry rising to a wail. You couldn't say "Just a minute" to a baby, and even if you could, Joey would never hear Felicia in this vast, sprawling house. He didn't yet understand that she was a separate person, independent of him. She was his, he was hers. Maybe he would give her peonies one day. Lord knows, it had been a while since Stephen had. Last month, February 15 had come and gone without any acknowledgment from him. Felicia had ended up putting away the card and gift she had bought for him, not wanting to be caught out in her yearning. Turned out February 15 was for suckers, too.

12:30 P.M.

Alanna had cut school lots of times, but usually with friends and in the most benign and banal way possible. Going to Eddie's for sandwiches, sneaking out to someone's house for a smoke. *Benign and banal* was Alanna's phrase for what they did. *B-and-b,* she said, *how utterly b-and-b,* and her friends laughed. Alanna had a lot of friends, yet no idea why they wanted to be her friends. She assumed it was because they were scared of her. Why were they scared of her? Because she was brittle and smart and because boys liked her so much that it was worth putting up with all her shit. Why did boys like her? Because she was pretty and she scared them, too.

Alanna scared almost everyone in her life, except Ruby and Joey, who was too young to notice her sarcasm. Alanna was the first person for whom Joey had smiled. He patted her cheeks with his messy, gooey baby hands, drooled on her, even spit up on her. She liked that. Other people were always on eggshells around Alanna. When she competed in cross-country, Alanna ran the way she imagined people walked around her. She rose up on her toes as if the ground beneath her were fragile, a thin crust that could give way at any time. Running in this fashion, she won more often than not. Alanna needed to win because athletics were going to get her into a decent college. But Alanna also needed to run, get away. She hated leaving Ruby behind, but her sister should be okay without her. Perhaps even relieved, a little bit. Besides, if Alanna made a reasonable choice, a school in proximity to a school that would suit Ruby, then her sister could follow in two years. Alanna was looking at Division I schools in California, Michigan, and Minnesota. Unfortunately, Ruby kept dropping hints about St. John's in Annapolis, Georgetown in D.C. Not far enough, in Alanna's view. They needed to find a place where the name Dawes could sink, ordinary and thick as it sounded, where the sisters could start over. Where people would not be scared of Alanna. Where she would no longer need them to be scared of her.

Because, in the end, it wasn't about the sarcasm or her success with boys or her looks. The real reason that people were scared of Alanna was because they kept waiting for the switch to flip and for Alanna to go as crazy as her mother.

She looked exactly like her, except for the hair. Alanna had smooth, straight hair, while Ruby had the wild, snaky curls—only flat brown instead of their mother's caramel color—and no one could tame them. Perhaps their mother could have helped Ruby with her hair. When Ruby was small, someone had known how to do it, although that might have been Elyse. In early photographs, Ruby's hair was, if not as smooth as Alanna's, then at least presentable. But no one since then—no nanny, no caretaker, no relative, certainly not their father and not Felicia, never Felicia, because Ruby wouldn't allow Felicia to touch her hair—had been able to solve the problem of Ruby's curls. Sometimes Alanna thought that the curls fed Ruby's formidable brain or vice versa. It was as if there was electricity in there, almost making her hair stand on end. Some brats in Ruby's class, back in middle school, had tried to introduce Medusa as a nickname for her, but Alanna had put an end to that, *fast*.

She glided down the Jones Falls Expressway, conscious of the Mercedes's power. She actually missed the Outback. The Mercedes had just been another exercise in triumphing over her stepmother. Felicia was banal, if not benign. But she usually knew better than to try *mothering*. Alanna had put a stop to that early on, pointing out that Felicia was only fourteen years older than she was. "And although there is a fine tradition of teen motherhood in Baltimore, it's not generally practiced in our set." *Our set* was pure affectation, the kind of *Gossip Girl/Pretty Little Liars* dialogue that Alanna never heard in real life, much less used. But Felicia, ruthlessly normal Felicia, didn't get that, and she had been hurt.

"I'm from Cumberland," she had said.

"Is that like Middle Earth?" Alanna had asked.

Anyway, Felicia from Cumberland had decreed that if a seventeen-year-old girl was to be given a car, then it must be car with no style or cachet. If the point was transportation, then get something with four wheels that went forward and backward. Blah, blah, blah. Alanna had taken the Outback and waited for her first opportunity to wreck it. That had required time and planning, but Alanna never minded executing a plan. She studied the intersections near the new house, found a blind curve, observed that one could hear a car coming before one could see it, even estimate its speed. She sat behind the wheel of her shiny, innocent Outback, listened to a car wheezing up the hill, then pulled out just in time to take the hit on the passenger side. Her timing was slightly off; the car struck hers farther back than she had wanted. And, boy, did it hurt when the air bag deployed. There had been a moment of panic when she thought her lungs might be damaged. But the accident did the trick, and the Outback was replaced by a Mercedes, so—*she won, she won, she won.* Alanna cared nothing for status, and besides, few material objects could confer status at Roland Park Country School. She liked to win, though.

Being Stephen Dawes's daughter wasn't a big deal either at RPCS. But being Melisandre's daughter—that had its advantages. Alanna got away with a lot. Leaving school in her car, for example. She'd be in a lot of trouble when she got caught, but her father would make a call and say whatever he said—Alanna's so troubled, blah, blah, blah, let's just get her to graduation whatever it takes and how about a big donation for the latest capital project—and the trouble would go away.

Except the trouble never went away. And now her dad was double-dealing, pretending one thing to Ruby, telling Alanna something else. *You're old enough to handle the truth. Ruby isn't.* She could live to be ninety and she might not be old enough to handle the stuff her father had been laying on her.

Why had she never made this particular drive before? She wasn't a scaredy-cat suburban kid. She was a city kid, a real one, who had grown up in Bolton Hill. She could parallel-park, a skill she kept polished by visiting the old house, which she did all the time. Yet she had never before considered heading to the foot of the highway and making five simple turns toward her own past.

But when she turned on Waterview Avenue and saw the

boathouse—for the first time in her life, actually saw the place where everything had begun and everything had ended—she panicked. No, she couldn't go down there, look at the water, that fucking tree. Instead of pulling into the parking lot, she drove on, blindly. Before she knew it, she was lost in a worn-down neighborhood of check-cashing stores and "lake trout" restaurants and what even Alanna could tell were drug corners. She drove slowly, looking for someone—a middle-aged woman or even a really old man would be okay—to ask for directions. She could feel the weight of strangers' gazes. Not menacing, but definitely curious about the girl in the red Mercedes.

She was about to pull over and activate the GPS in her phone when she heard a woop-woop and saw a whirl of red-and-blue lights. She hadn't noticed the cop. If she had, she would have asked *him* for help. But surely she hadn't been going over the speed limit? Had she failed to signal, run a stop sign?

She offered her license and registration to the officer, giving him her best smile, but he was no Gilman boy.

"What are you doing in this neighborhood, Miss Dawes?"

"I got lost."

"Going where?"

What business was it of his? Could police officers ask such questions? It was a free country, right? He should write the ticket and get on with it. But a ticket—no, she couldn't afford a ticket. A ticket would tell her father *where* she had been today. She could get away with cutting school, leaving campus. But she didn't want her father to know she had gone to the boathouse, that she was searching for answers to questions she wasn't supposed to ask.

"I—I—" She was too slow, she could not come up with a lie that sounded plausible. "Officer, the truth is, I wanted to see the place where my mother intended to kill me."

"Funny."

In all seriousness, without thinking how it sounded: "Do you know who I am? It's right there on my license. Alanna Dawes. DAWES."

Perhaps the family name was not as well known as she thought.

They impounded her car and took her to the Southern District police headquarters. Hours later, when her father came to get her at the station house, no charges were filed, and Alanna was elated to find out the cop thought she was just a stupid suburban kid, trying to score drugs; that was pretty cool in a way, and a better cover story for her dad—the officer apologized to *her*.

"I just, you know, thought you were mouthing off," he said. "I didn't know—I'm sorry, I didn't know."

Felicia had driven Alanna's father into town and he drove Alanna's car back to their house, making threats all the way. He said she was going to be grounded, and she assumed she would—for three or four days, tops. Besides, she still needed to drive to school and then drive home after cross-country practice. In the end, it was too much of a *hassle* for Alanna to be grounded.

They were about a mile from home when he finally said: "But why, Alanna? Is this because—because of what we talked about the other night?"

Given how little time they had left in the car, he couldn't possibly want the truth. The truth would require miles.

"Oh, I just wanted to get it right for the college essays."

"You have until next fall to worry about your essays. We haven't even started visiting campuses yet. And I think you can find better topics."

"There was a girl—do you know this?—a girl who killed her mother and she got into Harvard. Of course, Harvard didn't know. And they rescinded the acceptance because she was lying. So it's lying that gets you in trouble."

He didn't get it. Or, if he did, was smooth enough to roll past it.

"That was a long time ago, before you were born. How do you know that story?"

"They told us at one of the sessions on how to apply. I think it was supposed to be an object lesson in not lying. But, hey, she came pretty close to committing a perfect crime at age fourteen. If that doesn't qualify you for Harvard, what does?"

"Don't be morbid, Alanna." He was turning in the driveway; their time alone together was almost over. They were seldom alone, Alanna and her father, and this made twice in one week. Whee!

"What did you think you were going to see, anyway?"

The tree. The parking lot. The pier. Her past, the destiny averted. But what she really wanted to see what was what in her mother's head that day.

And if it was coming for her.

"Maybe I really did go to Cherry Hill to buy drugs and the boat-house is the cover story. Did you ever think of that?"

She couldn't quite see her father's face in the dark car. But she was pretty sure that his expression was almost one of relief. Drugs? He could deal with drugs. Her mother's legacy was what made him nervous. Even her father expected her to lose it one day.

"I know you don't take drugs, Alanna."

"I think I want to see her, Dad."

"But yesterday—"

"All our troubles seemed so far away."

"What?"

"Forget it, Dad."

"If you really want to see her, it's up to you. I said as much. I took you into my confidence because you need to know the whole story. I just wanted you to be prepared, Alanna. For what it could be and what it will never be. *You're* my only concern. We'll talk, okay?"

But that was the one thing Alanna and her father never did. Oh, they used words, made sentences. Put them together like little rafts to sail across the surface of things, just like the boats her mother had taught Alanna and Ruby to sail down the gutters. But they never really talked. Because he knew and she knew it was Alanna's fault that her mother had gone crazy and killed Isadora.

6:00 P.M.

Tess arrived home to a tender scene: Crow and Carla Scout were entwined on the chaise longue in the sitting room, still napping. Father and daughter looked so much alike—dark hair, light eyes, fair skin. They were particularly beautiful asleep. Did Tess look pretty sleeping? Crow said she talked in her sleep. Argued, instructing various people to "cut it out" and "don't tell me that."

"Do I at least win the arguments?" Tess had asked. If she was going to fight in her sleep, she wanted to win.

But Crow and Carla Scout were serene in sleep, his face almost as lineless and smooth as the baby's, as Tess still thought of their daughter. The three dogs, also napping, had arranged themselves in a pile on the rug. They were twitchier sleepers. Esskay and Dempsey, both greyhounds, chased prey, hind legs rabbiting, while Miata, the world's sweetest Doberman, sniffed the air. If a stranger walked in, Miata would be the dog on her feet instantly.

It was, all in all, a lovely tableau, one that made Tess want to go in the kitchen, pick up a frying pan, then whack Crow on the head.

The problem with these naps, which Crow and Carla Scout took almost every weekday, was that they often lasted until Tess came home. Then Crow went to work, leaving behind a hyper child who, understandably, would not go to bed until ten o'clock. Tess had asked him repeatedly to put Carla Scout down earlier in the afternoon, in her own bed, or forgo the nap altogether, now that she was three. But Crow said he was simply following Carla Scout's natural rhythms and she was a night owl like her father.

Unlike her father, Carla Scout didn't run a bar with live music.

Tess stood in the doorway, aware that she was polishing a little grudge—and aware that her temperament required such grudges, that she needed to stockpile any evidence of Crow's flaws. Because—surprise, surprise—Crow was an exemplary father, a natural parent. The perfect postmodern boyfriend, as her friend Whitney Talbot had once dubbed him, had segued seamlessly into the perfect postmodern father. He had standing to make pronouncements about Carla Scout's needs because he was with her for a good part of the day, supervising her diet, arranging her playdates, channeling her energy in all sorts of creative and nurturing ways.

Crow's only real failing as a hands-on daddy was that the house was never as neat as Tess would like. He said he had read something somewhere about how clean houses were never happy houses. To Tess, this sounded like the kind of aphorism offered by an actress or a model, someone pretending to lead a normal life while employing a phalanx of factotums. Their house wasn't *dirty,* not quite. Given its population of three humans and three dogs, it was relatively clean. But there was always something somewhere that needed to be put away. Toys, laundry, another load of dishes in the dishwasher. Tess should have taken advantage of this quiet moment to have a glass of wine or start dinner or—in the great tradition of mommies everywhere—have a glass of wine *while* starting dinner. Instead, she busied herself with the Brio trains and tracks that had been left in the middle of the sitting room.

She dropped a wooden train on her foot and said a very bad word. She knew it was a bad word because Carla Scout opened her eyes and told her so.

"Don't say that, Mama."

"I won't." She held out her sock foot. "I have a boo-boo. Do you want to kiss it?"

"No."

Carla Scout yawned, grabbed the hideous stuffed clown that was her constant companion—a kangaroo in a clown suit, known only as Clownie, for Tess had not wasted any effort on naming him, figuring the ugly thing for a short-timer when it was presented to Carla Scout on her first birthday. Naturally, Clownie became *the* toy, the boon companion, the One That Must Never Be Lost. If Tess had charged her hourly rate for finding and retrieving Clownie, Carla Scout's college tuition fund would be much more robust than it was.

"How 'bout a show?" she asked, sliding from the chaise without disturbing her father.

"How many did you have today?"

Her daughter was not really capable of lying—yet. But when she wanted something that she suspected she was going to be denied, she could and did launch into rambling arguments. "Daddy said, Daddy said, Daddy said—we watch MY show. A daddy show. We watched the show with the horsies. But that was a daddy show. I didn't get to watch *my* show."

"Horsies?"

"Horsies. ON DADDY'S SHOW."

"Black and white horsies?"

Carla Scout thought about this. "Yes. And the men came and they said go and the horsies and they run. They run!"

Go? Let's go? But Crow would never have shown her *The Wild Bunch*. Tess had a brief pang, remembering how much her friend Carl, who had inspired Carla Scout's first name, had loved that movie.

She also remembered how his death had been almost too much like a scene from it. If her hands hadn't been full of trains, she would have stroked the scar on her knee, the reminder that she had survived that ghastly night while Carl hadn't.

"Crow?"

He didn't open his eyes, but he replied. "We watched *She Wore a Yellow Ribbon*. It was fine."

"Would it kill you to watch something kid-appropriate with her?"

He opened his eyes and smiled at her. Tess used to think Crow had no idea how charming he was. "No, but it won't kill her to be subjected to good things. You don't advocate letting her choose what she eats every day. Why do you want her to consume the cinematic equivalent of Fruity Pebbles and Chicken McNuggets? All those bright colors and *lessons*. What a racket. What did you grow up watching?"

"At three? Probably reruns of Yogi Bear and the Flintstones. Whatever they showed on *Captain Chesapeake*."

"See. You were entertained by the antics of a petty thief stalking pic-i-nic baskets and an animated version of a series that celebrated domestic violence."

"Fred never threatened to send Wilma to the moon."

"No, but his size, his manner—I don't think all was well in that household. And Fred clearly had a crush on Betty."

Tess laughed, and the tension of the moment—her frustration over the late nap, an afternoon spent watching a Western, the long evening ahead of her—dissipated.

Carla Scout Monaghan—Crow was so evolved that he had insisted their daughter have Tess's surname—had not been planned. In hindsight, it was almost fortunate that preeclampsia had kept Tess here, on this very chaise longue, for the last trimester of her pregnancy. The forced rest had given her a little time to prepare herself mentally for something she had never assumed she would do. It was not that she had decided *not* to be a mother, just—not now. She and Crow weren't even married when she got pregnant.

They still weren't. They had said they would marry after their child's birth, in the new modern style, but Carla Scout's arrival in the world had been tumultuous, life-threatening to mother and child. By the time the baby left the neonatal care unit and came home with them, a wedding seemed like too much to plan.

Now three years had gone by and it was just too embarrassing to have a wedding. It would seem as if they were trolling for presents.

When, Tess thought grimly, starting on dinner while Crow went off to the shower, the last thing they needed was more stuff. The house, so perfect for two, felt cramped with three. Six, if one counted the dogs, who jumped on the chaise the moment Crow vacated it. Carla Scout climbed up with them and giggled as they licked her. Well, Miata, the Doberman, whose maternal feelings toward Carla Scout rivaled Tess's, was licking her. Esskay, the greyhound, was gently kicking her with her hind legs, forcing the child to yield territory to her, while Dempsey sniffed her delicately. Dempsey, an Italian greyhound, was definitely working an Evil Queen vibe with Carla Scout: Every day, he seemed to weigh the evidence before him as to which one was the fairest of all. So far, Dempsey seemed confident he was winning.

Tess shooed the dogs off the chaise, set Carla Scout up at the kitchen table with a semihealthy snack. Crow recently had informed her that yogurt was now being vilified for its sugar content and that dairy products in general were suspect. He had even started sneaking almond milk into Carla Scout's cup, which she left untouched. Throughout her life, Tess had always had her share of feeling overmatched and incompetent, but nothing made her feel like more of a failure than being a mother. Especially when she compared herself to Crow, who made perfect meals and never left the house without a well-stocked diaper bag. Whereas Tess often found herself with a diaper bag that had everything *but* diapers.

Those days were behind them. Almost. Carla Scout was down to one overnight diaper. Of course, diaper changing was one thing at which Tess excelled. She could even do it in a moving car, as they had found out on one memorable trip to the Delaware shore last summer.

Crow headed out to work. No music at the Point tonight, but he had to be there Tuesday through Saturday. The restaurant had become as important to the Point's bottom line as its lineup of bands and PBR on draft. They were doing the whole locavore thing, a challenge in March. But while the Point's location in West Baltimore enhanced its reputation with the hipsters who loved out-of-the-way discoveries, it made it hard to get as much traffic as they needed. Crow's partner, who happened to be Tess's father, couldn't imagine finding a place of similar size in a more desirable location. Crow, for his part, worried that some essential gestalt would be lost if they relocated. Tess had heard about this when her father called her to ask what the hell *gestalt* was.

The evening flew and crawled by. Tess made Crow-approved fish tacos. Carla Scout picked out the pieces of canned corn, leaving behind the halibut, shredded chard, and avocado. They had two shows, a *Dora the Explorer* and *Wonder Pets!*, which was Tess's favorite. She liked to sing along when the duck cried: "THIS IS SEWIOUS. THIS IS SEWIOUS." Carla Scout allowed—there was no other word for it—Tess to rub her back as they watched. These days, Carla Scout was prone to demand "Daddy do" even when Daddy wasn't there. Tess didn't have the heart to ask Crow if the tables were turned when she was gone, if Carla Scout ever insisted that "Mama do."

At 8:30 Tess crawled into the bath with her daughter, held her tight against her body. *Damn, Melisandre was in good shape,* she thought, remembering the taut body in those sleek leggings. But then—Melisandre had given birth to her last child eleven years ago, not three. Melisandre, according to the overview of her life she'd provided for the security assessment, had a personal trainer, worked out every day. Tess was lucky to work out three times a week these days, and she was eating more without realizing it—Carla Scout's rejected fish tacos tonight, for example.

But the bath was the one place where Carla Scout was completely Tess's. They rocked together, talked about their day to the extent that they could. ("Mommy and Mr. Sandy saw Uncle Tyner and met a lady." "A friend?" "No, not a friend. Just a lady.") Because of Carla Scout's early weeks in the NICU, Tess had never really known her daughter as a newborn, had not experienced the exhilarating terror of holding a child so fresh and fragile. The girl was sturdy now, strong and thin, a lanky string bean. Her father's genes.

The bedtime book was *Bear at Home,* which had been the running choice for seven nights now. How Tess yearned for the day when they could read chapter books—the Shoes stories by Streatfeild, Betsy-Tacy, *Charlie and the Chocolate Factory,* perhaps her all-time favorite, although she had been less enchanted by his subsequent adventures in the Great Glass Elevator. Tonight, she found herself envying Bear's orderly, well-kept house. Carla Scout insisted on turning the pages, holding the book at an angle that made it difficult to read. Book finally finished, there was a brief disaster when Clownie could not be found. Someone—Tess suspected Dempsey—had hidden the doll under a chair in the living room. "I can't close my eyes," Carla Scout announced dramatically, as she did almost every night. "Then don't," Tess told her. "I'll be back to check on you every fifteen minutes." She showed her daughter on the bedside clock when she would return. Carla Scout seldom made it past the second bed check.

Still, true to her worst-case scenario, it was ten o'clock and Tess needed an hour to set the kitchen to rights—so it could be destroyed again tomorrow. She fell asleep on the sofa, too tired to finish her second glass of wine, and that was where Crow found her when he returned at two. She would be up at six with Carla Scout, seven if she was lucky, out the door at eight and en route to the babysitter they used for a few hours every morning, so Crow could get a decent amount of sleep.

And now Crow was lobbying for another child and he had enlisted Carla Scout in the campaign, although she wavered when Crow admitted he couldn't guarantee a sister. A second child would mean finding a new house, as Tess's beautiful little cottage simply couldn't hold yet another person, and it had already been expanded as much as possible. Maybe, she thought, as she drifted back to sleep in her bed, she should tell Crow it would ruin the gestalt if they had to move because of a second child.

Transcript of Interview with Poppy Widdicombe, Treemont Hotel, March 11

SPEAKER 1: Pauline "Poppy" Widdicombe
SPEAKER 2: Harmony Burns
    INPUT: HB

PW: Hi! Thank you so much for the hotel room. This was almost like a vacation for me. And the breakfast was great. So what do you want me to say? They said it was a coincidence, although I don't think either one of us ever believed it. And then they said, You know what? Maybe you'll be friends. Those two ladies down in Texas, they became friends. And that's when Melisandre said to me—

HB: Okay, okay, that's great. I know I told you just to start right in and tell the story your way. But let's get the context first, okay? The things that happened before you met Melisandre? Introduce yourself, as if you were giving a talk to a group of people interested in what you have to say. Because this will be seen by a group of people very interested in what you have to say.

PW: I hate telling that part.

HB: I know, but it's important. I wouldn't ask you otherwise.

PW: But— Okay. For Melisandre. My name is Poppy Widdicombe and, in 2002, I, I, killed my eight-month-old daughter. I was found not guilty by reason of criminal insanity. I had postpartum psychosis. I was sent to a psychiatric hospital in western Maryland, near Frostburg. My roommate was Melisandre Dawes. She killed her daughter, too. She was famous, all over the news, though, because she had a trial and a mistrial before she was found not guilty. By reason of criminal insanity, but—that's still NOT guilty. A lot of people don't get that. That's part of the reason I've had so many problems. By the way, Melisandre told me I'll be paid for this?

HB: We'll talk about that later. Off-camera. Also, Poppy? A little slower. If you talk too fast, the transcription app makes errors.

PW: The thing about Melisandre is that people thought she made it up. The whole being-crazy thing. Whereas with me, people knew I had to be. What I did—it was so awful. Only I didn't do it, as my doctors always tell me. I have to understand that wasn't me, that when you are as sick as I was, you can't blame yourself for the things you do any more than you would blame yourself for throwing up when you have the flu, or having bad diarrhea with food poisoning. I was sick and the thing that I did was a symptom. My husband took me to church, where they were all Hell this and Hell that, and you must strike at the Devil when he speaks to you. I needed a doctor, not church. But my husband wouldn't take me to a doctor when I got sicker and sicker. He just yelled at me, said I was a bad wife and mother. And then, you know, Satan started talking to me. That is, I thought it was Satan because whenever I tried to talk to people about my problems, they said God didn't give you more than you could handle and I was being tested by Satan and if I would just listen to God, I would know what to do. So one day, I realized Satan was in my baby and I had to get him out. So I did it.

HB: Did what, Poppy?

PW: Do I have to tell this part?

HB: I'm afraid so. Part of doing what we're doing, what Melisandre is trying to do, involves speaking hard truths. Because if we don't, others will speak them for us and we will look as if we're trying to be duplicitous. False.

PW: Sometimes you sound just like that preacher. Not the same words, you understand. But the way you say things.

HB: Well, I'm not saying you have to do anything. I'm just explaining why things need to be done a certain way.

PW: Is there a difference between those two things?

HB: I think so, yes. I'm just telling you what Melisandre wants. Your friend, Melisandre.

PW: My friend. Yeah. Okay. I took a kitchen knife and I stabbed my baby. More than once. She bled to death. [Walks o/c] I'm going to need a minute, okay? You might think it gets easier to say that. But it gets harder. Every time. It gets fucking harder, okay?

HB: Camera going off here.

HB: Camera back on. I'm sorry, Poppy. I know that was hard. You're very brave.

PW: Well, I guess I have to say it. To get paid.

HB: I need to tell you again, for the record, Poppy, that you are not being paid to say anything. You are being paid for your time away from work, and your travel here.

PW: I wish I got a thousand dollars a day at Sheetz. It was nice, sending a car for me. I'd never been in a Town

Car before. And this hotel last night. It was really nice. I had room service for dinner, too. I hope that's okay. I know you told me I could go out, but it was like a vacation for me, to sit in a room and have someone bring me dinner on a tray.

HB: We wanted you to be rested. And, as agreed, we're not going to tell people where you live now, or even where you work. We'll edit out that part about Sheetz.

PW: But if people see this, someone who knows me, but doesn't, you know, know, might figure it out.

HB: Probably. But it's been in the newspaper, how you became friends in the hospital. People know the story.

PW: People forget stories. Faces not so much. Can I change my mind?

HB: Withdraw your release? Sure. You might have to pay the production back for certain costs, though.

PW: Really? I hadn't thought about that. Okay, so—surprise surprise—the two women who killed their daughters end up as roommates. They didn't expect us to be friends, or comfort one another. They expected us to rat each other out. They wanted me to find out if Melisandre was really crazy.

HB: Did someone tell you that?

PW: Melisandre told me. She said: They put you in here to find out if I was crazy. They're after me. And I'm not paranoid! That's the kind of joke you make, when you're in one of those places. I liked her right away for making a joke because it had been so long since anyone had made a joke to me. That's one of the weird things about being me. Being us. There's this whole piece of life that people think you don't want to have anymore, when you need it more than ever. Jokes, silliness.

HB: But didn't someone on staff corroborate what Melisandre said? That you were there to spy on her?

PW: You know, I've been thinking about that. I mean, I thought someone did, but the more I think about it—and, you know, my memory isn't great because there's a lot of stuff I want to forget—the more I'm not so sure. Would it make a difference?

HB: We just want you to tell us what you remember. There are no right answers.

PW: But do I get more? If I say someone on staff told me that?

HB: Poppy, you are not being paid to say anything. You are being paid for your time. It's important only that you tell the truth. That's the only thing that matters. You are not being paid for your appearance in the film, but for your out-of-pocket costs.

PW: My pocket's never had a thousand dollars in it. There was this one TV producer who got in touch with me, but no one wanted my story. Everyone wanted Melisandre's, but she could afford to say no. She was the hot ticket. Although if they had made a movie, I would have been in it. I mean, an actress would have played me. Not like this.

HB: Let's talk about the technical stuff off-camera. What did the staff say to you, if anything?

PW: I don't remember anyone saying anything to me, word for word. But everyone knew, you know? A lot of people doubted Melisandre was ever sick like I was. For one thing—and this is kind of interesting—there was no religious angle. Turns out that's really common. And she didn't have an official diagnosis. Before, I mean. That was kind of a big deal. How did a guy like her husband not see that she needed real help, why had he taken her to see his old friend, that doctor who ended up being a liar face? But the main thing was, you know, how she did it. It was kind of all over the place. She tried to get the older girls. Did she know there was a field trip or not? She signed the slip, but did she remember? I mean, when you're in a bad way like I was and like she was, there is stuff you plain don't remember. Leaving the baby in the car—that's a weird way to kill a kid if you're hearing those voices telling you to save her. She said she was going to drive right down that pier into the river. Only she didn't.

HB: Did you ever doubt that Melisandre had a psychotic episode?

PW: Me? No. But a lot of people did. And they wanted me to tell them if she wasn't—if she was faking. When she explained that to me, I said, "I have your back." I have ever since. I've had hers, she has mine. When I got fired from my first job because a local TV station told people I was working at the Discount Warehouse— Melisandre sent me a check. She even said she was going to fly me over to Cape Town or London, although that never happened. But that was because I could never get enough time off work. I've never had more than a week off. By the time you fly all the way to South Africa, a week is practically gone, that's what Melisandre always said.

HB: Why are you so sure that Melisandre, like you, was psychotic?

PW: Well, you have to be, right? If you're not sick, you're evil. You know those women, the ones who make up stories because they just want their kids dead? Because there's money in it for them or because they have a new boyfriend or because they want to get back at their husbands. They're evil, they have a reason.

HB: I don't actually know of a case like that. One where a woman killed her child to get back at her husband. Are you thinking of something in particular?

PW: Well, Melisandre, of course. That's what some people said about her. But I never believed it. Hey, is it okay if I ask the car, when it takes me back, to stop for lunch? Can a Town Car use the drive-through? There's a Roy Rogers in, I think, Hagerstown, and we don't have any of those where I live. You hardly see them anymore. It's such a treat. They have the best fries. I'll buy the driver some fries, out of my—what did you call it? Per diem. Out of my pocket!

HB: I'm sure that's fine.

PW: And do you think I'm going to see Melisandre before I leave? We haven't talked in forever.

HB: I'm not sure. I'll text her.

Wednesday

"One more," Silas said

"Last one?" Melisandre said.

"Last one."

The final combination was two crosses, two uppercuts, two jabs. It would be easy to get sloppy. Who cared about the last minute in a ninety-minute workout? Melisandre cared. She believed it was the final set that showed one's mettle. She focused on form, making sure to put her full weight behind each punch, pivoting so her midsection was engaged, especially on the uppercuts, trying to land the punches so that each one made a sweet, perfect thud when she connected with the flat pads that Silas used.

Melisandre wore her own gloves, ordered after her first session with Silas because she didn't like having her hands in gloves that others had used. But the real offense had been the color of the gym's boxing gloves, a bright, girlie pink. It took Melisandre a while to find what she wanted—gray gloves, with black trim. The good thing about owning her gloves was that Silas had to tell her, in advance, if they were going to do a boxing workout. He couldn't spring it on her.

Melisandre liked to know, as much as possible, what was going to happen each day. She made a schedule every night, writing down not only the appointments but everything she expected to happen—the hour she would awaken, the times at which she would take her meals, what she planned to eat, television shows she might like to watch, time for reading. Her calendar could be mistaken for that of a very busy person.

She had begun keeping this detailed daybook after her release from the hospital and the move to Cape Town. She had wanted to be as far away as possible. To be in a place where it was hot when Baltimore was cold, where there was almost no shared popular culture—that helped, as much as anything could have helped. She regretted giving up the girls, but it was too late. She had tried to talk about it with the psychiatrist assigned to her at Frostburg, but she couldn't explain the entire situation, so it made no sense. "Legal custody, whatever you signed—it may curtail certain rights, but nothing can stop you from being a part of their lives," he would say, well-meaning man. She couldn't confide in Poppy, either.

Poppy. Although Melisandre generally didn't watch dailies, she had gone into Dropbox and opened that file last night. It was a shame Poppy kept talking about money. And that she didn't remember anyone on staff affirming that there were suspicions about Melisandre. Harmony had taken Poppy through the interview four times, but just as Harmony had warned Melisandre, such retellings flattened the stories out, made them seem more rehearsed. In the hospital, Poppy had been able to talk for what felt like twenty minutes straight without a pause. She had driven Melisandre crazy sometimes with her incessant chatter. But she had been a friend, in her way. Melisandre really had believed the friendship might continue once they were both released. But it was hard to know who you were going to be, once outside again. It wasn't that she had been insane before she was admitted. Melisandre was stabilized long before she was sent to Frostburg. The hospital had been a sop to the judge, a way of letting him acquit her without causing a political uproar. It was sometimes reported that it was part of a plea bargain, but that was inaccurate. The judge had found her not guilty by reason of insanity, after receiving assurances that she would seek treatment.

"Good work," Silas said. He was at least fifteen years younger than Melisandre, maybe twenty, with the long, lean look of a yoga teacher. She didn't want a muscle-bound trainer. She didn't really want a trainer at all, but she couldn't achieve the stamina and strength she wanted without someone else pushing her. That hadn't been an issue until she hit her forties. She had followed her mother's example—walking, gardening—and that had been enough to stay thin. Then her metabolism had taken the hit of age and other things, and she'd had to find help. She hated the fact that Stephen was married to a trainer. An ex-trainer now, from what Melisandre could discern, not that she had ever met the woman. If she had, she would have probably said something like "Oh, honey, Stephen makes all his wives quit their jobs. You think it's your choice, but it wasn't."

"Tea?" she asked Silas. To pacify Brian, who disapproved of this off-site workout, Silas picked Melisandre up at the hotel and then walked her back, staying for tea if he didn't have another appointment. She suspected that he had begun to plan his mornings around having tea with her, not out of some cougar fascination but because he liked this glimpse into a privileged life—the view from her suite, the porcelain cups that Melisandre had unearthed from her storage locker when she returned to Baltimore, the matching sugar bowl.

The sun had barely straggled into the sky. How Melisandre hated daylight saving time's early start, which was new to her. Back home in London—she stopped, corrected herself, *London is not home, you didn't even have an apartment there, you just ended up there after Mother died because you had to close up her apartment, take care of things*—the clocks wouldn't be reset until the end of the month. Melisandre had awakened at first light all her life, and she felt deprived of an essential birthright when she had to rely on an alarm clock, as she had this morning. The eight-block walk to the gym in darkness was a misery. But the walks to and from the gym were also highlights of her day, among the few times she was allowed out without Brian, who took his job much too seriously. She was determined to live without him once she was in the new apartment. Not that she had told him that.

Silas chattered amiably on the walk back to the hotel, and Melisandre listened with the top of her mind, making the correct comments at intervals. It was not unlike talking to Poppy, back in the day. Silas was a nice young man. If Melisandre were inclined toward cultural cliché, she would seduce him. But it was unthinkable to her, and not just because Stephen had married a trainer. Melisandre preferred protectors. She was aware that was her downfall, but she wanted a man who could take care of her. That had been Stephen's charm, even if he was a bit of a rebound, not that anyone had suspected as much. Stephen seemed like Prince Charming to everyone else—rich, decent-looking, not in a wheelchair.

They reached the Four Seasons and went up to her rental apartment. Lord, she was sick of hotels and corporate apartments. She realized this was an entitled, bratty thing even to think, but Melisandre's family had always had money, although they had been rich in the old Baltimore way, not making a show of things. Money was like skin. She had been born with it, she was used to it. Money offered her some protection, some comfort, and she couldn't live without it. But it didn't make her invulnerable. It had not saved her in her darkest days and it could not get her what she wanted now, except indirectly. She should have come back sooner, but she hadn't been strong enough to face Alanna and Ruby. She was so ashamed of what she had done. But with her mother's death, and then the news of Stephen's new child, a son, she knew she had to return. Not that she believed Stephen would neglect the girls in favor of his new child, but one never knew.

In the kitchen, she made a cappuccino for herself, a tea for Silas. A vegan and very pure, almost sanctimonious, about what he put in his body, Silas had one interesting dietary tic: He adored sugar. She used to adore it, too, she told him. Had been famous for it among her boarding school friends. That was one of the things that her anonymous taunter knew. But her note writer didn't know that she no longer loved sugar. Sweet things tasted like ash in her mouth now. She watched Silas heap sugar into his green tea until it was practically a soda. She liked him better for this one weakness. Melisandre always liked to know what others' weaknesses were. Silas had been a fat kid, and this sugared tea was one of the highlights of his day. She left him to it, heading to the shower. Soaping herself, she wondered idly why she didn't want to have sex with Silas. She hadn't been with anyone for a while. Perhaps it would take the edge off? Maybe it was because he brought out something maternal. She saw the fat kid, not the buff young man. She had figured out his history before he shared it, asked him point-blank: *You were fat as a kid, weren't you?* Stephen had once accused Melisandre of not caring about other people's feelings. If anything, she cared too much. She could feel other people's feelings sometimes—and it was terrifying. When Isadora had cried, it was as if Melisandre had colic, too.

Showered, she changed into clothes that were really just a more luxurious version of her gym gear—velvet leggings, an Armani T-shirt, a loose cashmere sweater, soft ankle boots—and fluffed her hair, an entity with which she had made peace long ago, although she still sometimes resented it for all the attention it received. She did not wish to be loved for her curly hair alone. Checked her phone:

Brian had texted that he would be three minutes late and, knowing Brian, that meant he would be two minutes, fifty-nine seconds late. She hoped—

Just then, she heard a thump from the living room, then the sound of something breaking. Clumsy boy. That sugar bowl was an antique.

But it was not just a bowl that had fallen. Silas was on the floor, body in spasms, surrounded by fragments of his morning treat, the rug soaked with tea.

Melisandre was still standing there when Brian arrived. He dropped to his knees and felt for the young man's pulse, then called 911.

"I froze," Melisandre murmured. "I just—froze. I'm sorry. I'm so sorry. I just froze."

She had no idea how much time had passed. And that frightened her even more than the young man convulsing on the floor.

11:00 A.M.

Tess Monaghan believed no one should speak on a phone while driving a car, no matter what device was used. Hands-free, headsets, earpieces, Bluetooth—all of it took one out of driving. It was unsafe at any speed.

Still, she did it all the time.

She supposed that made her a hypocrite. And a really crappy mother, too, as she did it even when Carla Scout was with her. But Tyner had called her three times this morning and she had ignored the first two. When his number flashed in the dashboard caller ID a third time, she decided it must be urgent, possibly even personal.

"What's up?"

"There was an incident with Melisandre this morning. It appears that someone tried to drug her or poison her—we're unsure. At any rate, her trainer drank something while in her apartment and he went into a seizure. He's going to be okay, but it was clearly meant for Missy."

That nickname again.

"Why 'clearly'?"

"Remember, Melisandre told us the notes she's been receiving are from someone who knows things about her past, things that not everyone knows. Well, she was a sugar fiend once. Used to pour tablespoons of sugar into her coffee, over her morning Rice Krispies. Remember, I was surprised that she didn't want the sweets at breakfast?"

Tess remembered. She almost drove through a red light, thinking about how well Tyner knew Melisandre's breakfast habits.

"So?"

"We think someone doctored her sugar. Her trainer used it, she didn't. Could have been the tea, which was loose, but the sugar seems more likely, as it was in a bowl. The doctor thinks it could have been a large helping of one of the date rape drugs—they don't normally see seizures from those, but it can happen."

"What do the police think?"

Did paraplegics squirm? There was a squirm in Tyner's long pause, Tess was sure of it.

"She didn't call the police. The boy stabilized quickly, was breathing and alert within minutes. Melisandre chose to take him by private ambulance to her doctor. She goes to one of those boutique practices, one that's available to its clients around the clock."

Of course she does.

"The doctor attended to the boy as quickly as any ER would have," Tyner added. "Faster. Melisandre made the right choice."

"So why are you calling me? Sandy and I are not responsible for the security in her current location."

"She wants to move as soon as possible. She doesn't want to spend another night in the Four Seasons."

"Then tell her to call a moving company. Anyone but Mayflower, though. Then people in this town really won't be able to forgive her." Mayflower had been the company that had moved the Colts out of town in the dead of a snowy night. Thirty years and two Super Bowl victories later for the Ravens, Baltimoreans still carried a grudge against the moving company that had taken their beloved Colts away.

"I'm on top of those details, thank you very much. But I want you to go over to the Four Seasons, make some discreet inquiries. We need to figure out who had access to Melisandre's suite."

"Isn't that Brian's job?"

"It was. She fired Brian. Perhaps a little impetuous and unfair, but that's Missy. She will not tolerate failure."

Missy.

"This could have happened in the plant where the sugar was packaged. It could have happened anywhere. Did the hotel provide the sugar? Did Melisandre shop for her own groceries? The opportunities for contamination are endless, from the store to the delivery, to whoever put it in a bowl to begin with. And who still puts sugar in a bowl, anyway? Why so fancy?"

"Melisandre was raised in a household where things were done in a certain way. Her father was from here, but her mother was British and Melisandre was born in London. Certain rituals were observed."

Again, Tess was irked by this intimate knowledge. Sure, it was something any friend could know. And it wasn't as though Tyner was a virgin when he married her aunt a few years ago. Her fabulous, gorgeous aunt, who was much too good for him. But Tess's preferred narrative about her aunt and Tyner was that both were sexual adventurers who had discovered true love with each other. Okay, Tyner and Melisandre had dated back in the day. Tyner had dated *everyone*, back in the day. But family facts, breakfast knowledge—you couldn't say it was TMI, but it was more "I" than Tess needed.

"She's terrified, Tess. I've never seen anything like it." He disconnected without saying good-bye. Presumably to go tend to poor little Melisandre. *Missy.*

Tess turned to Sandy, riding shotgun. Oh, yes, that was the other thing she hated about taking phone calls in the car: Sandy had heard every word of the conversation, through the dash. She always forgot to tell callers when someone was listening, although she knew that was the proper etiquette.

"What do you think?" she asked him.

"Weird. She's a puzzler."

"Like all women?"

"No. On an individual basis. I understand a lot of women. You, for example."

"The other day you said you never knew what I was going to say next."

"I never know what you're going to *say*, but your feelings are all but written on your big mick forehead. I just don't get her agenda, which means I don't get *our* agenda. When I was a murder police, I always knew the objective. Find out who did what. Get it cold. Pass it on to the state's attorney, and if some defense attorney wanted to say, Well, Pinky killed Peaches because his mother didn't love him, fine with me. Not part of my job."

"So what's going on here?"

"Got me." Sandy's shrug implied something else.

"You have an opinion, though."

"No. I specialize in not having opinions. But—"

"But what?"

"Don't lose sight of the fact that no one had more chances to doctor her guy's drink than she did. Doesn't mean she did it. But the obvious answer . . ."

Is the obvious answer. Tess knew that was an article of faith in Sandy's old job.

"Okay, then why?"

"Not my favorite question, as you know."

"Possibly mine. As you know."

"Well, they're making a movie about her, right? Maybe she just needed something to happen."

"Tyner said she's terrified. That's hard to fake."

Another shrug. It wasn't a who-knows shrug. If anything, it seemed to indicate a world of knowledge that Sandy didn't want to share.

"Guy had a seizure. If she's responsible, then she's worried that she's gone too far."

Tess chewed on that. Chewed on it almost literally, absentmindedly grabbing a pen from the pocket between the seats, putting it in her mouth, and gnawing on the top.

"I see you doing that and I think two things," Sandy said. "One is that, one day, I'm going to have to give you the Heimlich."

"And the second thing?"

"I never want to borrow a pen from you."

"I feel like there's a third thing you want to tell me."

Sandy grabbed the handle above his seat. He claimed Tess's driving made him nervous. "Unfinished business here. She didn't hire you because you're the best of the best of the best. Sorry—but you said it first, security isn't our *bailiwick*." He was clearly proud of himself for remembering that word. "So what do you want to do?"

She wanted to finish the work as contracted and be free from Melisandre Harris Dawes. But visions of sugarplums—food, clothing, braces, college tuition—danced in her head. A visit to the Four Seasons meant more billable hours.

"Is it okay if I drop you at the hotel and let you approach management alone? This is going to be delicate and you still have your cop gravitas. You'll probably get further than I ever would."

"Sure. What are you going to do?"

"I thought I'd go to the boathouse. I need to think, and I think best on the water."

"Fine with me. But I thought you said you couldn't go back on the water until April, that it was too cold to row yet."

"All the serious rowers get back on the water by March. I'm just not serious anymore."

Tess retrieved her shell from the rack at the boathouse. Rowing technology had come a ways since her time as a mediocre college rower, and she now had a shell that was extremely light, yet hadn't killed her bank account. Workout clothes were different, too, concocted of magic fibers that wicked moisture away and kept warmth in or, depending on the weather, wicked moisture away and let the warmth out. The magic of Under Armour. Like a lot of native Baltimoreans, Tess was amazed when anything from her hometown became a national phenomenon. Yet there was Under Armour's headquarters on her rowing route, a thriving hive of activity where Procter & Gamble had turned out Ivory, Tide, Dawn, and Cascade. Locust Point, a working-class neighborhood once, was making a move on hip and trendy. It was even the site of a couple of swank condo developments, including 13 Stories, Melisandre's new home.

But for everything that had changed about Tess's rowing routine, one thing remained constant. Tess went to the water to think. Or, more precisely, *not* to think, which was when solutions came to her. Today, her body was a little stiff from winter; she never worked out as much as she intended to over the cold-weather months, not since Carla Scout's arrival. Ah, well, she wasn't even forty. She could return to her peak shape with a little effort, not that her peak was that formidable. More like a Maryland mountain, certainly nothing you'd find out west. Not that Tess had ever been out west. She had barely left her home state. She had never traveled abroad. She could probably count on her fingers the number of times she had been on an airplane.

How had this happened? No one *planned* to be a boring stick-in-the-mud. But in her twenties, working as a reporter, Tess had had almost no money and very little vacation time. And then she had had all the time in the world—and zero money, because she had been laid off. Circumstances had thrown her into her PI gig, and she was good at it, even if the local newspaper, the *Beacon-Light,* had hung that stupid moniker, the Accidental Detective, on her. Crow had said that article was practically a blueprint for stalking.

Then she became an accidental mom. Soon, Tess supposed, she would be an accidental spouse, assuming she and Crow ever found time to get the license, go to the courthouse. But there was never time.

Money. Time. The first was theoretically infinite. Tess had always embraced the wisdom of Mr. Bernstein in *Citizen Kane*: It's not hard to make a lot of money, if all you want to do is make a lot of money. But the pursuit of money blinded one to the finite nature of time. There was no truer democracy than time. Everyone got twenty-four hours in a day. But, like that game show with the briefcases full of cash, the one that Tess never got the hang of despite having watched it compulsively while being on bed rest during her pregnancy, no one knew how many of those days they were going to bank. So how did you value your hours? Tess wanted Melisandre's money—and felt dirty for wanting it. Because Sandy was right. Melisandre hadn't hired Tess because she was Baltimore's Gavin de Becker, the best of the best of the best. Melisandre wanted Tess because she provided a connection to Tyner. Why? What was the unfinished business between them? Why couldn't Melisandre just stalk Tyner on Facebook and leave Tess out of it?

The day was cold, typical of this wretched winter, and Tess's stiffening fingers forced her to turn back early. Walking her shell into the boathouse, she remembered how shocked everyone here had been when Melisandre's madness had brushed up against this close-knit world. Stephen Dawes had rowed with a private club, competed in all the local races, some regional ones. He never came back to the boathouse after that day, and who could blame him? Melisandre wasn't really part of the community, except as Stephen's wife. Tess didn't even recall seeing her around, back in the day—and Melisandre wasn't a person who would escape notice easily.

Feeling nostalgic for the person she was ten years ago, even though that person had been lonely, broke, and miserable, Tess went to Jimmy's, her post-workout haunt when she had lived in Fells Point above her aunt's bookstore. She loved Jimmy's, but she had stopped going there after that newspaper profile—that Accidental Detective nonsense—had mentioned how she always ordered the same thing for breakfast, a toasted plain bagel. Tess's monomania was a private quirk, thank you very much. Besides, it was now almost two o'clock, so she had a grilled cheese and bacon sandwich and read the *New York Times* that she grabbed off the front steps every morning and almost never opened. She probably couldn't pass a grade school current events quiz these days.

She hit the restroom, and her check was waiting on the table for her when she returned. *Okay, okay, I get the hint, you want me out of here,* she thought. *It's not like people are waiting for tables at this time of day.*

Upon closer examination, however, she saw that it wasn't her check, just a piece of paper, in the same handwriting as the note on her car, two days earlier.

All it said was "No bagel, Tess? So people are capable of change. Good to know."

2:45 P.M.

It was a truism in Baltimore that one was forever running into people one knew. Good old Smalltimore. Kitty Monaghan, a native, was used to it.

However, she was not used to seeing her niece walk by her bookshop, head down. Why wouldn't Tess drop in if she were in the neighborhood? How busy could she be? But then, Tess was a mother now, much less carefree with her time. Not that she complained to her aunt, but Kitty had noticed over the holidays that Tess, never exactly a relaxed person, was more tightly wound than usual.

Kitty went back to the calendar for the store's upcoming events, more important than ever to her business. Even with an online store that did a booming business with Baltimore expats, Kitty needed to get people into her physical space if she was going to sell books, and that took more than just throwing a writer behind a card table. Kitty had a weekly music series, four different book clubs, and a story-telling hour for children every Saturday. She had created something called the RUI club—Reading Under the Influence—a kind of anti–book club in which women from book clubs came to get title sugges-tions and free wine, provided by Bin 604, who sent a store employee to conduct themed tastings. It was all working, but it required that *she* work pretty much every day.

When Kitty had opened her bookstore twenty years ago, buoyed by a settlement over her wrongful termination from the city school system, she had thought she was opting for an easy life. Sit in a pretty space surrounded by books, make friends, ring up sales. Even in the beginning, it had been much harder than she had anticipated and there had been a moment—six months in reality, six very long months—when the world economy imploded and she thought she was going to have to surrender. The use of a war term was apt. She was besieged on every flank—by online stores, by the popularity of digital readers. Kitty felt that even the so-called binge watching of television had begun to eat into people's reading lives. If you could sit down and watch four hours of *Break-ing Bad* or *Downton Abbey* in a single night, when did you read? Even there, she took on a can't-beat-them-join-them mentality. She did events for the novels of Julian Fellowes, leaning hard on the

Downton connection. Perhaps inevitably, she started a small event called WireCon. It had been a local show, and there were more than two dozen books to date that could be linked to *The Wire's* writers and stars. The "convention" had started three years ago with seventeen people sitting on folding chairs, pretending they were being called to order by Stringer Bell. Last month, the fourth annual WireCon had sold out the Senator Theatre, and Idris Elba, the actor who played Stringer Bell, had appeared. Along with, in Kitty's estimation, every African-American woman in Baltimore, and maybe the surrounding counties. Anticipating this audience, she had cannily thrown Zane's backlist into the mix, figuring the Maryland erotica writer, a trailblazer, was due for a rediscovery in the wake of *Fifty Shades of Grey*. Yes, Kitty was nimble, Kitty was entrepreneurial. To quote the Sondheim song, she had gotten through all of last year and she was still here.

Next year? Yes. The year after that? Harder to say.

Running a business had brought out a competitive part of her nature heretofore unknown to her. The youngest of seven and the only girl, Kitty had never had to compete for anything. She had been born lucky. Her beauty was part of the luck, but far from the whole story. Kitty had led a charmed life. Most of the time. She lived to please herself, which sounded selfish. Yet she believed it made her more generous—with her friends, her family, her husband. Her happiness secure, she could make others happy.

She had always felt that birth order had much to do with her lack of interest in motherhood. Kitty had never wanted children. Correction: Kitty had always *told* people that she never wanted children, which wasn't exactly the same thing. But if the birth order in her family had been switched, she would have been expected to be a second mother to her brothers. Instead, she was spoiled, although those who loved her insisted she wasn't spoiled in the least. And everyone loved her. This was a fact about herself that Kitty understood only externally. She heard it over and over again, accepted it as true according to others, but never felt the reality of it. It was like being told about an interesting mole on the small of her back. "Everyone loves you!" "There's a mole the shape of the Liberty Bell back there." Oh, okay. Sure. That's nice. But she couldn't *see* it.

Her innate happiness drew people to her, just as it drew people to pick up all those self-help books promising happiness. When she was younger—not young, just younger, in her thirties—this quality had attracted men. Lots of men. Young men, usually, perhaps too young, but she'd had no interest in marriage, so that was good. She really didn't see the point of marriage if one didn't want children. Lately, science had been catching up with what Kitty had long suspected: Women had no innate talent for monogamy. They, too, became bored with partners at midlife. But Kitty had married at midlife. She loved Tyner, considered him a soul mate. Like oil and vinegar in the right proportions, they balanced each other. Tyner being the vinegar, of course, but only in the world at large. With Kitty, he was sweet and loving.

She had always assumed he had fallen in love with her because she was not as self-congratulatory as some of his exes. Tyner had cut a great swath through Baltimore. ("Well, rolled," he liked to say.) But he had been dubious of the women who were drawn to him. He called them *Coming Home* groupies. "I didn't go to Vietnam. I got hit by a car outside Memorial Stadium. And I'm not Jon Voight. I'm better-looking."

He was, and aging with far more grace. Kitty glanced at the rack of magazines she felt obligated to carry—there was no real newsstand left in Fells Point—and shuddered at the surgically altered, cosmetically heightened, orthodontically enhanced faces that grinned back. She had read somewhere that one could see the effects of long-term bulimia in a woman's face, that the chin and cheekbones formed a striking triangle. This month's cover models—three actresses and three reality-TV stars—were five for six on the triangle scale.

Kitty wasn't immune to the desire to look good. She believed in maintenance. She liked facials. She touched up the gray in her auburn hair and availed herself of a professional colorist four times a year in order to restore the subtle balance of shades that had once been her birthright. She shaved her legs, moisturized, watched her weight. Kitty had always felt very good in her own skin.

Then she had met Melisandre Dawes at dinner last week.

The woman was a little younger than she was, but it wasn't Melisandre's youth that intimidated Kitty. For one thing, she didn't look young for her age, not particularly. Melisandre looked every inch the forty-something she was, but in the best possible way. And then there was that hair, which could only be described as an aureole. Her tawny skin. Brown eyes with the light hair, once the Elizabethan ideal of beauty, and the eyes had flecks of gold that complemented the hair. Sure, the hair was highlighted, the skin cultivated, the body buffed, but why not? These ministrations were in service to a world-class beauty.

"So wonderful to meet the woman who tamed our Tyner," Melisandre had said, and it felt as if she were leaning down from a great height, although she was no taller than Tess and certainly less broad, and Tess never made Kitty feel this small. Maybe it was that familiar possessive, *our* Tyner. Kitty had not thought of Tyner as belonging to anyone but her. To whom did *our* refer? Kitty and Melisandre? Or the community of women in Tyner's past?

They had met at Cinghiale, in a private room, for Melisandre's "security." Kitty had thought such caution over the top at the time, although this morning's events had proven her wrong, she guessed. She had said as much to Tyner, after Melisandre called this morning. They had been having a lovely lie-in, a perk of self-employment. Kitty may have had to work every day, but she could arrange the schedule so someone else opened.

"I guess I was wrong," Kitty said. "About her security issues being overblown."

"You *guess*?" Tyner was almost never sarcastic with her. With others, yes, but not with her. He hurried through his morning routines, keen to go take care of the shaken Melisandre. Kitty worried this was a harbinger of things to come. Melisandre, for all her seeming confidence, had no problem leaning on others.

Whereas Kitty was self-sufficient. She had never lived with a man before Tyner, never wanted to. Technically, she had been engaged, for all of a red-hot minute, but that was kid stuff. They hadn't been serious.

Well, *she* had never been serious. Who could be serious about getting married at seventeen?

But he had been. Paul. She wondered what had happened to him. The modern thing would be to look him up on Facebook, but Kitty wasn't on Facebook. The store had a Twitter account and a Facebook page, maintained by one of her employees, although Kitty wasn't quite sure she approved. It seemed strange, reaching out to people through computers and phones to lure them into a bookstore. In the battle for people's eyes, computers and phones were more competition.

Then again, her single most successful signing of the year to date was for a blogger turned memoirist with a huge Twitter following, so maybe there was something to it.

She glanced at the clock in the upper right hand corner of her computer screen. Almost three. Tyner hadn't checked in since he left this morning. He didn't, usually. It didn't bother her. Usually. She thought again about Melisandre, the dinner. People *jumped* to do things for her. Men and women. They couldn't have known, Kitty thought. If they had known what she had done, they wouldn't find her charismatic. No one was charming and beautiful enough to transcend that story. Yet Tyner knew and he didn't care. Ah, but Tyner had known her before all this happened. *We dated,* he'd told Kitty. *No big deal.* Kitty had laughed. "One of the cast of thousands, eh?"

But Melisandre had let it slip, during dinner, that she had broken up with Tyner only because he made it clear he had no interest in marriage or fatherhood.

Or was it a slip?

Another advantage of being the boss was that Kitty didn't have to close most days, although she had always worked the last shift on Saturdays so she could go over the week's receipts. She went upstairs to change and take down her hair. In her younger days, Kitty had favored a vintage look verging on costume, but now she wore simple, timeless clothing. Still vintage, but the more expensive kind, found in consignment shops instead of church rummage sales. She overdressed, perhaps, for the role of a bookstore owner, but she liked her tailored black dresses, which she paired with old jewelry— Bakelite bracelets, Chanel pins. Dressing for work, she often thought of dowdy Mildred Pierce, her attempt to create a fancy uniform for herself at her restaurant, only to look a little odd and wrong. Kitty never looked odd or wrong. There were some who said she was more beautiful than ever. Tess's Crow, for example, who had once worked in Kitty's store, and had nursed a little crush on her before falling for Tess. Did her employees still get crushes on her? She hadn't stopped to think about that for a long time. She paused, facing the mirror, hands holding the ends of a distinctive choker, a chalky white number that contrasted beautifully with the black dress's neckline, but also looked like a ghastly fake smile.

She put on an apron—no role playing here, it was just good sense to protect a dry-clean-only dress from grease and splatter—and made sure that dinner was one that Tyner would like. Pork tenderloin, roasted vegetables. They usually ate at eight, then spent the evenings in companionable silence, reading for work. They also had a secret habit—not a guilty one, but a secret one, key distinction—of watching *Mary Tyler Moore* reruns on Netflix. Tyner laughed so hard during these shows. Although Tyner was more of a barker than a laugher, coughing up a single harsh syllable of approval when he found something funny. Kitty had worked out recently that *The Mary Tyler Moore Show* had gone off the air not long before Tyner's accident. Did he laugh because it was funny or because it reminded him of a time when he'd laughed more freely?

At 7:45, Tyner called.

"I lost so much time today, dealing with Melisandre, the hotel, the expedited move. She forgets that she's not my only client. And I'm in a good rhythm, here in the office. If I leave now, I'll just disrupt the flow of what I'm doing. Would you mind terribly if I work for a few more hours?"

"Of course not," she said quickly. She would not nag. She would not remonstrate. Plus, he sounded genuinely put-upon, harried. He did not enjoy the demands Melisandre put on him. He couldn't say no to her. *Why couldn't he say no to her?* Kitty ate her share of the supper she had prepared and put the rest away on the lower shelves of the refrigerator, so Tyner could reach and reheat them. She changed out of the dress that no one had seen her in and put on a nightgown and a kimono she had owned forever. She curled up in her usual spot on the sofa, but she enjoyed television only when she could watch with someone else. There was nothing to do but read a book. Which, in the life of a bookseller, meant reading galleys for the next season. She settled in with a sigh, plucked one from the pile, and started in. She fell asleep on page 79—at least, that was where she found the book, spine spread, lying on the floor when she awakened. It was 11:30.

And she was still alone.

11:30 P.M.

Ruby had learned as a child that attempting to muffle or conceal a sound only drew attention to it. If you whispered, people leaned in to catch what you were saying. If you tried to tiptoe, or close a door without being heard, people wondered why you didn't want to be heard. So when Ruby went to her listening post late at night, she simply got up and walked downstairs. If someone ever challenged her, she would say: "I'm going to get a glass of water."

But no one ever challenged her, possibly because no one else, not even Alanna, had discovered that one could hear everything being discussed in their father's bedroom while standing in the hall closet.

Ruby wasn't sure why this acoustical anomaly existed. Every-where else, the house seemed to smother or distort sound. She as-sumed it was some shortcut in construction, a missing layer in the wall that the closet and bedroom shared. Atypical of her father, a perfectionist known for overseeing every detail, but then the house was atypical for him. Brand-new, built from scratch, not rehabbed. Suburban. Beyond suburban. Rural in feel, surrounded by trees, yet almost close enough to hear the humming cloverleafs of the Belt-way and various interstate exchanges. Now, late winter, was the most light-filled time in the house. And when the trees were bare, one could see the house's glowing windows from a great distance, and that was cozy—from a distance, looking in. As spring turned to summer, the house would grow darker and darker.

The house was also unusual in that it had a master bedroom suite on the first floor, with the other bedrooms on the second and third floors. It made Felicia crazy, going up and down the stairs so much. She had taken to wearing a pedometer to show Ruby's dad how much she walked. Silly, but then Felicia thought it mattered, how many steps a person took in a day. Ruby specialized in getting out of gym class whenever possible, no small thing at a physically rah-rah place like Roland Park Country, especially when one's sister was a track star. Her latest condition, supported by a forged doctor's note, was an enlarged spleen. That should be good for a week or two.

She slipped her coat from a hanger, careful not to make a sound, then made a nest, leaned her back against the rear wall.

"I don't see why this concerns us," Felicia was saying.

Her father's voice was indistinct; he must be in the bathroom. Luckily, Felicia had trouble hearing him, too, and he had to come out and repeat himself.

"It concerns us, Felicia, because we gave the girls permission to see Melisandre if that's what they want."

"You gave permission. I wasn't consulted."

"Jesus, Felicia. Can we not have that conversation again?"

"It was really hurtful. When they said they didn't want me to adopt them."

"Understood. But there's nothing I can do about it."

"I waited until I was pregnant to ask because I wanted to emphasize that we would be one family."

This old thing. It wasn't the first time that Ruby had heard Felicia complain about their refusal to be adopted. She had felt bad at the time, but she was glad now. Alanna had been right to say they shouldn't go along with it. Alanna used to have Ruby's best interests at heart, but now it wasn't so clear that she did, not after what Ruby had heard in this same spot a few days ago, Alanna agreeing with her father that it might be better if they avoided seeing their mother as long as possible. Ruby hadn't heard enough of the conversation to know why Alanna was suddenly on their father's side, and you couldn't go to someone and say: "Last night when I was eavesdropping, I didn't quite catch everything, could you fill me in?"

"Is that why Melisandre came back?" Felicia asked. "Because she knows I asked the girls to let me adopt them?"

"She came back to make this stupid film, best I can tell. But she has been getting threatening notes, apparently, which I just found out about. And now this."

"I know Silas, a little. He was just getting started when I sold my business. What a crazy thing. Do they know what happened?"

"It's just a clusterfuck as I understand it. He knocked the sugar bowl to the ground when he fell and it smashed, and some maid with a Dustbuster cleaned it up while they were out getting him medical attention. Tyner Gray is trying to spin it as a good thing—he says the Four Seasons will probably be more cooperative with his private investigator if there's not a police investigation, that the promise of discretion is a powerful carrot. I don't know. I don't really care. Look, I'm worried for Missy, even if the seizure, whatever caused it, probably wasn't the intended outcome. Her doctor thinks someone used a drug, maybe GHB."

"What would be the point of drugging her?"

"To scare her. To put her on guard. Same with the notes. And in both cases, there's a sense that the person knew her back—back then. She used to be a sugar junkie. Before. She had gestational diabetes with Isadora, and her sweet tooth never came back."

A memory swam into Ruby's mind, almost overwhelming her with its power. *Don't tell Daddy.* A wink and a smile, as they settled in for gelato at Vaccaro's. Did Ruby really remember that? Or was it something that Alanna had told her? She was not quite four when their mother left forever. Alanna was only six. It seemed unfair that Alanna should have so many memories, Ruby so few.

Then again, Ruby didn't have migraines. Maybe that was the trade-off.

"At any rate, she's out of the hotel. As of tonight. I think she had a mattress delivered to 13 Stories and she's sleeping there until her things are delivered from storage."

"I still think it's weird that she wants to live in one of your buildings. Maybe she wants you back."

Her father laughed as if this were the most ridiculous thing in the world, and Ruby felt as if a hand had grabbed her heart and choked it. "Not a chance, Felicia. And you should be glad she bought that apartment—it's a big chunk of money for us. I've never been able to sell that penthouse. It's out of line, price-wise, with that part of town."

"Still—she wants to see the girls. Ten years, no communication, and now she wants to see them."

"Or wants to be seen as wanting to see the girls. Her film can milk it either way, right? Heartfelt reunion or isolated by the evil ex. At any rate, it doesn't matter what she wants. And it no longer matters what the girls want. Not after this. No visits anywhere, anytime, until we understand what's going on. On top of everything else, she fired her bodyguard without a replacement. That's insane."

"Insane," Felicia said, and the word seemed to echo for a very long time.

What do I want? Ruby thought, sitting on the floor of the closet in the long T-shirt she wore for sleeping. Before her mother arrived in Baltimore a month ago, Ruby had had a long-range plan, one she hadn't shared with anyone. She was going to go to a college with a good foreign exchange program, then do a year abroad in London. Her mother had family in London, or had had. Even if she had sold the apartment there, she probably still visited. Ruby figured she could go see her mother on her own terms, by herself. In London, no one would care if Melisandre Dawes walked down the street with a young woman, met her for lunch. In London, Ruby could have had her mother all to herself, something she had never known.

Don't tell Daddy. I'm not supposed to be eating sweets during my pregnancy, but this one won't hurt. A wink, a smile. Did Ruby remember it? Or did she remember Alanna telling her about it? She pressed her face into her hands, leaned into the memory with all of her senses. Stracciatella, flakes of chocolate in vanilla. Yes, the memory was hers, she could taste what she had eaten that day, see her mother struggling with the tiny café table, her enormous belly pushing and prodding, making it awkward for her to eat. Ruby had put her hands on her mother's belly, felt the kick.

What should we name the new baby? It's a girl, of course. One more for our team. One for all, all for one, the four musketeers.

"Isadora," Alanna had said, *offering no explanation.* Isadora it was.

Transcript of Interview with Ethan Hinerman, his office, March 12

SPEAKER 1: Harmony Burns
SPEAKER 2: Ethan Hinerman
INPUT: HB

HB: We are in the office of Dr. Ethan Hinerman, in the five hundred block of Cathedral Street, Baltimore, Maryland. We really appreciate you agreeing to speak to us, Dr. Hinerman.

EH: I'm not a doctor. I have a doctorate, but I'm not a medical doctor.

HB: My mistake. I thought you used to identify yourself as a doctor.

EH: I use my title as appropriate. That was never meant to confuse anyone. It only became an issue when— Well, there was a piling on. I suppose that's natural. I made a mistake. An honest mistake, but it was costly to some.

HB: Right. The one thing I have to caution you about is speaking from what I'll call deep context. Not everyone knows everything, the ins and outs. So we have to be very linear. It helps to tell the story in chronological order. So let's start with how you knew Stephen.

EH: Stephen and I met at Gilman when we were eleven years old. He was a scholarship student who enrolled in sixth grade. I mention that only because it's often forgotten, in the wake of Stephen's success, that he's self-made. His family wasn't poor, but his mother was a widow, a schoolteacher, and they lived pretty simply.

They lived in Hampden, actually, when it was one hundred percent working class, no yuppies. I think part of Stephen's philosophy, if you will, is a desire to create more organic spaces, buildings that don't fight the neighborhoods so hard, don't make the old-timers feel as if they no longer belong. That's why he used existing structures, like schools and churches, whenever possible, and tried to add ground-floor tenants that were open to the community, local businesses. Anyway, he had good timing, for the most part, and he ended up richer than most of the kids he went to school with. But he still had a fascination with people who were born with money. That was a big part of Melisandre's appeal.

HB: Her money.

EH: Not money, per se. Class, status. Stephen's probably worth more, at this point. And Melisandre comes from one of those WASPy Baltimore families that don't spoil kids. She was comfortable, but she didn't have control over the family fortune. I assume she does now. I heard her mother died.

HB: From whom?

EH: I don't know. Someone.

HB: Stephen?

EH: Maybe.

HB: How did they meet? Stephen and Melisandre.

EH: At a regatta. The Charm City Sprints. Stephen had just taken up rowing, but he was already quite good, which was typical of him. I'm not sure why Melisandre was there. I think she knew one of the coaches or rowers with another club. He introduced them, I think.

HB: Were you present? Or did you just hear about it?

EH: I was, actually. I mean, I was there that day. I can't tell you that I remember their first meeting or saw it. But at one point that afternoon, Stephen pointed her out to me. "I got her number," he said. Boy, that marks us as old, doesn't it? If you can remember a time when all you aspired to was a phone number? And then you used it to call someone, not text. This was long enough ago that you didn't even Google your dates. I got divorced a few years ago. It's a different landscape out there. Most of the people I know are meeting online. What does it say that I, as a therapist, don't trust online dating? Why am I holding out for chemistry when I spend my days counseling people who had nothing but chemistry and are now making each other miserable?

HB: Not to get too far ahead, but you did not see Stephen and Melisandre professionally, right? You were not their therapist.

EH: No, that would have been unethical.

HB: And you were Stephen's best man? At his wedding?

EH: I was. Almost a year to the day after they met. He proposed to her three months after that regatta, at the boathouse. It was like a surprise party. He brought her there, to a big tree where he had tied a jewelry box to a ribbon hanging from a low branch. I actually had to stand guard over that jewelry box until I saw his car pulling into the parking lot, then I sprinted inside. It's not the greatest neighborhood, you know? He proposed beneath the tree, she accepted, then he brought her inside for the party, where all their friends were waiting. It was great. Better than the wedding in some ways.

HB: Why?

EH: Oh, weddings are so stuffy, you know. This was looser, more fun. Plus, I think Melisandre was—well, not a Bridezilla, but she did sweat every detail on that wedding. She was one of those women who had to be as skinny as possible, so she basically didn't eat for a while there and it made her pretty darn tense. She was always high-strung, in her way. I think that's why it was hard for Stephen to notice at first. When things went wrong. Moodiness, depression, a tendency toward drama. Big highs, bigger lows. That had been part of the package from the start. It just became more pronounced after Isadora's birth.

HB: But, as far as you know, she was okay during the first five years of the marriage. Happy?

EH: If you're asking me what I know, as a trained professional, then—yes, I saw a normal woman with the usual highs and lows. In hindsight, there seems to have been mild postpartum depression with Alanna and Ruby. At least, that medical opinion was presented in court, by one of the experts she hired. I don't really have the credentials to make that judgment. But she never received an official diagnosis before the, uh, incident, nor was she treated. I do know that it wasn't Stephen who pushed for a third kid. That was what Melisandre wanted. And she was the one who said she should stop working, for good. She had taken two leaves by then. She wasn't a partner and she probably wasn't going to be one. It also was her choice to hire a nanny to be with the two older girls. Look, Stephen is a wealthy man, but given his background, he chafes at some expenses. He couldn't justify two nannies if

Melisandre was going to stay home full-time. I mean, why was she staying home? It was her choice to care for the baby and let the nanny take over the two older kids, do all the driving and after-school stuff. I heard the way her lawyer was trying to spin it in court, that Stephen was this heavy-handed sexist who wanted a traditional wife. But that wasn't true and it wasn't fair. If she was not guilty by reason of insanity, then she was not guilty by reason of insanity. But the defense attorney was trying to suggest that Stephen's behavior caused her psychosis. That makes no sense. Okay, I understand it intellectually—they throw everything at the wall to see what sticks, they don't have to be consistent. They just have to create a reasonable doubt. But a man's reputation was being dragged through the mud. Stephen's daughter was dead. His wife appeared to have lost her mind. He had two small children to protect.

HB: That's twice now that you've hedged Melisandre's mental illness. "Appeared" to have lost her mind. Do you doubt it?

EH: I didn't treat her. I have no standing to pass judgment.

HB: You harbored doubts at the time, certainly. That was evident in your testimony.

EH: I made a mistake. A mistake born of memory, nothing more. That has no bearing on what I've said here.

HB: I know it's probably painful, but will you tell the story about what happened when you were called to testify?

EH: The prosecution, as you may know, has the option to present additional evidence after the defense has put on its case. That's how it worked in Melisandre's trial. I contacted the prosecution after the trial was under way because I remembered something disturbing: I had seen a folder of clippings on infant deaths in the Dawes house.

HB: Tell me about these clippings.

EH: Some of them centered on children dying when they were left, usually by accident, in a car on a hot day. That was right around the time Isadora died. Look, I've tried very hard not to have an opinion on this. But it was the prosecution's contention that Melisandre's defense, not guilty by reason of insanity, would be more convincing if she had done something, well, more violent to her child. What she did—it's still a horrible way to kill a kid, but it wasn't hands-on. It was passive. She didn't even have to be there. All she had to do was park the car and wait. I know she later said that she believed it was her plan to drive into the Patapsco with all of her children, to kill herself and all three daughters. And maybe it screwed her up, even in that psychotic state, to find out that Alanna and Ruby couldn't come with her. There are parts of her story that make sense—going to the summer camp, having no memory of the field trip.

HB: To get you back on track—you testified, right? For the prosecution. But you didn't come forward until the trial was under way.

EH: I remembered that I had seen this folder of clippings at the house, on a little table that Melisandre used as a desk. I didn't think much about it at the time—that is, I assumed that Melisandre, like a lot of mothers, was overly concerned with her children's safety, that she had a morbid habit of reading that kind of stuff because it was what she feared most. I picked up the folder and read it. I remember one article was absolutely brutal because it was about an assistant principal who simply became overwhelmed, forgot that she was supposed to take her kid to day care, and drove to work, parked in the lot outside her school, came out at the end of the day to find her child dead in the backseat.

HB: Were you in the habit of picking up things in other people's houses and reading them?

EH: No. No. But—Stephen was like family. I was over there all the time. It was like, it was like picking up a magazine.

HB: Right. At any rate, you testified about seeing those clippings. You mentioned that one article in great detail, right?

EH: Yes. I mean, if Melisandre had read that article before Isadora died, it would have been relevant.

HB: But she didn't, right? You were wrong. Those clips had been gathered after Isadora died. How did you make that mistake?

EH: I don't know how I got the time line confused—perhaps because I was trying so hard to understand what had happened, and my mind changed the sequence of things. You can see why I thought I had to testify. It was embarrassing for me, but I'm glad they caught the mistake when they did.

HB: Why?

EH: Because, well—she would have served time, right? If the mistrial hadn't been declared then and there. She might have been found guilty and gone to prison. And that wouldn't have been fair.

HB: Have you ever thought about why you got confused? As a therapist, do you wonder if there was something, well, Freudian about the way you flipped the events?

EH: I'm a clinical social worker. I don't tend toward Freudian interpretations. But, no, I didn't have any subconscious desire to present false evidence against Melisandre. It wasn't a lie, what I said. I found a folder of articles on Melisandre's bedside table. It would have been normal to take that information and try to create a narrative that made sense. Why would she have those clippings after the incident? It didn't occur to me that it was Stephen's file, that he was working through his grief by reading about other people who had lost their kids in horrible ways. That certainly wouldn't have been my professional advice. And that's why I didn't speak to him about what I saw before I went to the state's attorney.

HB: But it turned out the chronology was wrong, that you had switched the dates in your head. How did that come out?

EH: The one incident, involving the assistant principal who had left her child outside her office? I had remembered that one in the most vivid detail and talked about it at great length. But it happened a month after Isadora died. I remembered it was hot that day, so I associated it with summer. I got it wrong. The brain does that, you know. It gets stuff wrong, all the time. It wasn't malicious. My brain was trying to find a narrative for something that didn't make sense.

HB: Yes, I noticed you contradicted yourself in the course of this interview. You said you saw the clippings on Melisandre's desk, then said it was her bedside table.

EH: Did I? How strange.

HB: I know. I mean, given how many times you must have gone over it.

EH: Gone over it?

HB: For the trial, of course. I assume you were deposed, that this information was made available to the defense.

HB: I'm sorry, if there's too long an interlude, if no one speaks, the transcription app will turn itself off. Anyway, so a mistrial was declared. And Melisandre's not guilty by reason of insanity plea was accepted when she opted for a trial by judge the second time.

EH: Yes.

HB: Could you say those words? For the film?

EH: I'm not sure I see the point in my saying them. It's not something I orchestrated.

HB: It isn't?

EH: Excuse me?

HB: I'm sorry, I meant only that a mistrial meant that Alanna didn't have to testify, right? She was on the witness list, too.

EH: What does Alanna have to do with anything?

HB: She was on the witness list. She didn't testify because of the mistrial.

EH: I don't really remember that.

HB: So you don't know what she was going to testify to?

EH: I wouldn't have any insight into the ins and outs of the trial. I wasn't a lawyer.

HB: Didn't you ever ask Stephen why his daughter was scheduled to testify?

EH: No, I didn't consider that my business.

HB: But you must have thought about it. What could a

five-year-old girl have to say that would have been relevant to her mother's trial?

EH: No idea. None.

HB: Are you still close to Stephen?

EH: We don't see each other as much as we once did. But
that's just how life evolves.

HB: What do you mean?

EH: Same old story. He remarried, had a kid, moved to the
suburbs. I got divorced, stayed in the city, never had
kids. Our lives are in different places, literally and figuratively.

HB: And that's the whole story? You just drifted apart?

EH: Pretty much.

Thursday

11:00 A.M.

The staff at the Four Seasons almost fell over itself providing information once the manager heard the magic words *We are trying to bypass the police in this investigation.* A conference room was put aside for interviews, and the hotel even offered Tess and Sandy coffee and snacks.

Perverse Tess wanted to call the hotel union reps and make an anonymous complaint about the privacy violations of the employees. When she found out the employees had no union representation, she was even angrier and thought about calling the newspaper. But she wasn't sure she knew anyone at the *Beacon-Light* these days.

"Maybe after we finish the interviews," Sandy cautioned her when she vented. "I have a decent relationship with the cop reporter, Herman Peters."

Now this was something else Tess liked about her new partner. Sandy found a way to make his opinions known while still letting

Tess be the boss. He was very satisfactory that way. His predecessor, Mrs. Blossom, had been too deferential. Then again, Mrs. Blossom had always been up for emergency babysitting, whereas Sandy was not. Alas, Mrs. Blossom had moved to Arizona after the winter with almost seventy-five inches of snow. That winter had broken Mrs. Blossom.

Sandy was also more meticulous than Tess. After just a little more than a year together, she had come to see that Sandy always gave 100 percent to anything he did, whereas she could be satisfied with 90 percent. Hey, it was still an A-minus. Today, for example, she wanted to avoid using their favorite hacker for full financial sweeps on the employees they were interviewing.

"Always good to know who's in debt or has financial problems," Sandy said.

"It's 2014," Tess grumbled. "Everyone has financial problems. And Dorie is expensive when we have a rush job. You know that."

"Yeah, but Melisandre Dawes is paying three times your normal rate right now," Sandy reminded her. *This* was a cheering thought. They were on the clock, being paid by a woman who actually said things like "Money is no object." Tess was pretty sure that money was *always* an object, even when you had a lot of it. Especially if you had a lot of it. She imagined the minutes as coins falling into a bank. It helped a little, but it didn't make her stop feeling like an enormous bully as she quizzed housecleaners and room service waiters and parking valets and bellmen. A few struggled with English, and Sandy stepped in, speaking a slow, careful Spanish that was the aural equivalent of a car whose engine hadn't been started for years.

By lunchtime, the only thing that Sandy and Tess had been able to establish was that far too many people had had access to Melisandre's suite and it was for the best that she had moved to her penthouse, even if they hadn't persuaded her to take all their suggestions on security.

"I have to say, I'm not that impressed with her bodyguard," Tess said. "He deserved to be fired. She's really been pretty vulnerable all this time."

"He's just that. A bodyguard for hire. Not a security expert, just another retired cop. Stands next to her twelve hours a day with a gun. She got what she paid for."

"That's what I mean. Money isn't a problem for her. So why didn't she want twenty-four/seven protection? I really think he was more of a prop, for this documentary. A nice visual, you know—the misunderstood woman needs a bodyguard by her side because some deluded person might want to cause her harm. Who, though? The kinds of nuts who get upset enough to contemplate violence don't care about women killing their children. They only come out when women want to terminate pregnancies."

Sandy coughed. It could have been a cough, nothing more. But Tess heard a world of argument in that cough.

"What?"

"There are reasonable people who believe that abortion is wrong. As wrong as murder."

"But the second they cross the line and try to harm someone, they are no longer reasonable, right?"

"I'm not speaking for myself. I don't believe in God, not really. But my wife did and she believed abortion was wrong. Even if she had known—"

"Known what?" But this was a part of Sandy's life where he always shut down. His wife had died from cancer several years ago, Tess knew that much. There was a son, too, grown now, and Sandy never spoke of him. She had inferred something was wrong, although she had assumed it was drugs or drink. Could it be something that might have led another couple to choose abortion?

"It's not important," Sandy said. "And in all other things, Mary and you probably would have agreed. Especially on everything that was wrong with me."

That was Sandy's way of changing the subject, Tess understood.

She could never decide what a truly good friend would do when people didn't volunteer personal information. Should she push for the confidence or let it go? She let it go.

"You want to go over the threatening notes that Melisandre has received? See if there's anything in them that can be linked to what happened in the suite? Or just anything at all that could help us?"

An hour later, they had the notes spread across the Parsons table in Tess's office, along with the remains of their lunch from Iggies—a salad for Sandy and a sausage-fennel pizza for Tess, who had decided not to think about losing weight until the weather was reliable and she could work out every day.

The notes, five in all, had been written on a computer, printed on plain white paper, sent in basic envelopes. They had not been preserved in any sensible way, another sign of Brian's incompetence. Melisandre had shoved them into a manila folder, not even bothering to log where and when she had received them. Some had come by mail, one had been dropped off at the Four Seasons front desk.

And one had been slipped under her door.

"I thought you said Brian was ex-police."

"He is. After my time, left the department about a year ago. He was a vice detective. Left two years short of his twenty, which is weird, but it happens. They've got some pretty big jerks over there these days."

Sandy's tone made it clear that "vice detective" was many rungs below murder police, his preferred term for what he had done.

"So why would he just gather up these notes as they appeared and not treat them like evidence?"

"Probably following orders. Based on what happened this week, Melisandre Dawes wants to avoid the police whenever possible. She put that kid's life at risk by not calling 911."

"She told Tyner she panicked, that it was almost like post-traumatic stress disorder. She froze."

"Yeah, she froze, he broke the sugar bowl when he passed out, she had a private physician take care of him, the maid happened to clean up the mess while they were at the doctor's office, so there's nothing to examine."

Normally, Tess liked working with someone even more cynical than she was. But this seemed a bridge too far.

"You do think *she* did it. But why? She didn't get any footage out of it. And according to Tyner, her ex now wants to renege on letting her see the kids in anything but public settings. No visits to her new apartment. So there was no benefit. Quite the opposite."

Sandy looked through the notes again. The ones that had arrived by mail were postmarked Baltimore. *Well, there's someone who still needs the postal service*, Tess thought. Stalkers. E-mail was too easy to trace. When it came to threats, you wanted good old-fashioned stamps, maybe some magazines to cut up. *Or maybe just a notepad to leave missives on someone's car as the opportunity arrived*, Tess thought, remembering her own notes. Melisandre's correspondent had typed these not-quite-threats on a computer, then printed them out. A first-rate computer expert might be able to find these keystrokes on a computer, but you'd have to know which computer to search.

"They're not exactly threatening," he said. "If she were writing them, I think they'd be more dramatic."

"Melisandre says the writer uses tiny details that only she knows. Her nickname, references to personal habits. Including her sugar habit."

"I still think she would do something more overt. These are a little creepy, although I can't put my finger on why. But I bet she knows and she's not telling us everything."

"Why wouldn't she tell us?"

"Because everybody lies."

Tess knew that was a murder police's axiom and Sandy was old-school murder police, a term that was dying out in Baltimore. And she didn't disagree. She had the sense of being an unwitting player in someone else's drama, just another Rosencrantz or Guildenstern, being sent off to England while things were happening at a far higher level.

The first one said:

> Dear Missy—Just wait and see what fun we'll have. (That's what Bear said. Remember?)

"Missy? Is that the boarding school nickname?"

"Yes," Tess said. "But Tyner doesn't know from Bear and Melisandre says she doesn't, either."

"Here's number 2. Sent a week later."

> We bake cake! And nothing's the matter! Nothing's the matter! Still have that sweet tooth, Missy?

Then there was

> But he will not know about that. He will never find out. Isn't that what you promised, Missy?

"Wait, which is the next one? Do we have the chronology right?" Tess asked.

"This came next."

> We will have to shut you up where you can't do any more harm. And yet you can, Missy. Wherever you are, you can still do harm.

The final note was the cruelest, to Tess's way of thinking. And also annoyingly familiar, yet just out of reach.

This kid is driving me CRAZY! Literally true in your case, right, Missy?

"I hate to nitpick, but her child didn't literally drive her crazy unless it had a driver's license," Tess said. "So—not an English major. And don't tell me about the OED. The OED is wrong to change its stance on this."

Sandy was uninterested in the Oxford English Dictionary and its position on *literally*. He also had probably abandoned the fight for *hopefully*. "Five notes. Harassment, but not illegal."

"Yeah, I've gotten only two and the second did bug me, even though there was nothing overt in it."

"Wait, another one? Like the one the other day? What did it say?"

That's right. She hadn't told anyone about the second note. Crow didn't even know about the first. It had gotten lost in all the details of day-to-day family life.

"Just wanted to know if I had enjoyed my breakfast," Tess said. It felt wrong to talk about the notes with Sandy when she hadn't had a chance to tell Crow. But she and Crow were so exhausted that when they had time together, she didn't want to speak of upsetting or distracting things. "I figure real life is starting to imitate Facebook now. 'Friends' you've never met comment on every aspect of your personal life. Everyone's always looking for a Like button."

Sandy looked baffled. He had no use for social media. Antisocial media, maybe.

"I did check to see if the daughters had Facebook accounts," Tess said.

"Why?"

"Melisandre has one and it's wide open. You should see the things some people write. I thought the girls might be lurking there, or be part of her network. I felt kind of sleazy, doing it. I mean, I wasn't going to send a friendship request to either of them, although I have an account I use for that sometimes. It's come in handy for some of the insurance stuff I've worked on. People who are suing over slip-and-falls will post photos of themselves finishing marathons."

"Why would they let a stranger see that?"

"You'd be amazed how many people will 'friend' an average-looking woman named Marge Gunderson, who lists her address as North Dakota. Sometimes they even say, 'Hey, did you know you were a character in a movie called *Fargo*?' I always feign amazement. Anyway, I looked to see if the daughters had public accounts, but I didn't find anything. Either they're not there, or their privacy settings are really high."

"Good for them."

"But frustrating for a mother intent on reconnecting. Because you just know that Melisandre has probably tried to reach out to them that way. How could she sign away her rights to them, Sandy? How does someone walk away from her kids? If anything, she should have been keen to show the world—show them—that she was capable of being a good mother."

Sandy kept his eyes on the papers in front of them. "Guilt? I mean, she was going to kill them, too, right? That's a hard one to patch up. And sometimes, when things get bad—when you haven't done the right thing by someone—it's hard to make your way back."

Tess suspected he was speaking from experience.

"Everyone has bad days—I still can't imagine walking away. Carla Scout drives me crazy sometimes. Figuratively."

"I'd like to tell you it gets better," Sandy said. "But my kid—well, he's kind of like a forever three-year-old, so I don't know what happens next. But I hear it gets better."

Tess went back to studying the notes, aware that Sandy had finally offered up a clue about himself, while she had been lying. No, she couldn't imagine abandoning her daughter, but she sometimes thought about the life she used to have, almost as if it were an alternate reality. Some evenings, marching through the routines like a zombie, she asked herself: *What would I have been doing five years ago on a night like this? Eating dinner out, without being interrupted seventy thousand times. Reading a book. Going for a run.* Something for her, and her alone. She had been so self-centered. Why not? She'd had only herself to tend to.

But once you were a parent, how did you walk away? Especially given what Melisandre had done. And it wasn't like Melisandre had sought a do-over. She didn't remarry or try to have more children, although it might have been possible at her age. Not easy, but not impossible for a woman of means, although perhaps risky given her history of postpartum depression.

Maybe Melisandre was making her play for a do-over right now.

So who tainted the sugar? Who sent the notes? Nothing seemed to connect.

"Want to break early and go for a drink?" Tess asked Sandy hopefully.

"We got three more interviews back at the hotel," he said. "Some people just coming off their shifts."

He was more conscientious than she was, too. She should probably consider that a point in his favor. And they would be in Harbor East when they finished today. They could go to the cool sushi place there or drop by Cinghiale or— No, she couldn't go anywhere. She had to be home by six so Crow could go to work. Drinks and dinners out were enjoyed by Alterna-Tess.

1:30 P.M.

The thing about being grounded was that it just made it more logical to cut school, especially on a day practice was canceled. If Alanna didn't have cross country to look forward to, she certainly wasn't going to hang around for chemistry and English. As long as she was there to drive Ruby home—the reason her car had not been taken away—no one would know. Besides, there was someone she needed to see downtown.

But first, she wanted to see the old house.

Alanna still had a set of keys. Why wouldn't she? Why shouldn't she? They hadn't sold it, merely moved. Most of their furniture was still there, although her father had let Alanna and Ruby take a few favorite things to the new place. She parked on the street, then circled around to the back, unlocking the garden gate.

"Hello, you," she said.

It was a distinctive-looking house from the front, a freestanding yellow-brick Victorian with turrets and a lone gargoyle, a standout even in a neighborhood full of idiosyncratic houses. That was the problem. The house became the stand-in for the family when the family was not made available. Newspapers and television stations used two images over and over—the house and her mother being led away from her bail hearing, her wild hair flying.

Even then, *after*, they never considered moving. The house was their father's dream, old on the outside but reconfigured within, his vision of what a family home should be. The living room and dining room were formal, retaining the grand proportions of a nineteenth-century town house. Her father was ahead of the curve there, renouncing child-centric lifestyles while others were building houses with tiny living rooms and so-called great rooms abutting kitchens. Stephen Dawes didn't believe that children should be seen and not heard, but he did think that adults had ceded too much territory to their offspring.

Not that their kitchen, which she entered through the deck-to-ceiling glass doors, was small. It was large and open, the heart of their family's life. A builder's daughter, Alanna realized that the appliances and fixtures there were now slightly out-of-date, but she still loved the island, whose base was covered in a mosaic of blue tiles. It should have clashed with the coral-verging-on-orange Aga, yet it worked. The family had spent a lot of time here, but it was not a great room, and it was not meant for play. Instead, the entire fourth floor had been given over to the children's playroom.

Alanna climbed three flights of stairs to this space. While the rest of the house was her father's design, this had been her mother's creation, inspired by a book she had read as a child, a book she had planned to share with Alanna and Ruby when they were older. But by the time they were older, their mother was gone, so Alanna never did find out in what children's book the kids played in something called the Office. She knew only that her mother had attempted to re-create it from memory. There was a big rag rug over a floor that her father had soundproofed, a trapeze bar hanging from the ceiling, a piano, although no one in the family had ever learned to play. A box full of dress-up clothes, two easels. One wall was slate, so it could serve as an enormous chalkboard. The television had never been hooked up to cable, but it had a DVD player, so Alanna and Ruby could watch films here. An entire wall of bookshelves, only half full now. After the divorce, her mother had demanded some of their books and toys, putting them in storage. "See?" Ruby had said last week, when she nagged Alanna into agreeing to see their mother. "She always planned to come back."

Yes, she planned a lot, their mother. She planned more than anyone knew.

A circle of three beanbag chairs faced the bookshelves—bright blue, bright yellow, bright green. And although the blue one was Alanna's, she felt like Goldilocks as she tried out each one, not that any of them gave way. Each was just right. One for Alanna, one for Ruby.

And one for Isadora.

They had chosen these chairs while their mother was still pregnant. *One for all, all for one,* their mother said. *You will be my three musketeers. We will be the four musketeers, always looking out for each other.* No one told Isadora about this arrangement, apparently. She was a difficult baby. Crying all the time, not any fun. Boring. Alanna might have even pronounced her banal, if she had known that word at age five. Before Isadora was born, Alanna and Ruby had quarreled a lot. Or so she was told. She didn't remember that part. What she remembered was that the real musketeers were her, Ruby, and their nanny, Elyse. They did everything together, while her mother was stuck with boring Isadora. Her mother wandered through the house at night, her face pale and Isadora wailing on her shoulder. She would pass her and Ruby's open bedroom doors, not even thinking to check on them as she once had. The Night Mother, Alanna called her. Soon it was as if the Night Mother was with them night and day. She didn't notice anyone but Isadora. It was embarrassing, the way her mother was always unbuttoning her shirt to feed the baby. It was gross. Had Alanna felt that way at age five? Yes, yes, at age five she had begun to find everything about people's bodies to be silly at best, vile at worst. When they said she would have to share her room with Ruby so that the baby could have a room of her own, she had been furious. How would she change her clothes with Ruby in there? Even at five, Alanna required a lot of privacy.

That was the flaw in their father's dream house—it had been built for a family of four, not five. With the fourth floor taken over by the Office, there was room for only three bedrooms—two on the third floor, a master suite on the second. More than a master suite, a room with a hidden room, her father's study, reached by a secret door through the walk-in closet. There was no reason for her father to hide the study that way. It was just for fun, he said. "I always wanted a secret room," he said. He didn't need one.

Or so Alanna thought until the day she got hungry and wandered down from the Office to find Elyse and ask for a snack. She didn't call her name—her mother had gotten very harsh on people being "shouty," especially as the new baby's sleep patterns were so unpredictable—so she went from room to room on tiptoe. She had to be somewhere. Elyse had put Ruby down for a nap, then told Alanna she could watch anything she wanted on the television in the Office, for as long as she wanted, an unheard-of privilege. Her mother was at the pediatrician's with Isadora, *again*. Alanna soon grew tired of her video feast. So she went looking for Elyse. She had been up and down the stairs three times before she thought to slide open the secret door.

And there was Elyse, her head buried in Alanna's father's lap. *His* head was thrown back, but he had his fingers in Elyse's hair, his eyes closed.

To this day, she could not remember what happened next. Did she speak? What would she have said? She couldn't get back to the girl who stood there, a five-year-old who knew nothing about sex, much less this strange game her father and Elyse were playing. She probably thought her father was rubbing Elyse's head, the way he did with Alanna and Ruby at bedtime. So why was he the one falling asleep?

But they saw her. And overreacted. How could they not? Whatever they did, whatever they said, Alanna understood that much: They had been doing something wrong and they wanted her to keep the secret. Her father said Elyse had bad news and she was crying and he was trying to make her feel better. *Ooooo-kay.* He asked what Alanna wanted most of all, said he would buy it for her, but she had to keep the secret. Why? Because Elyse was very private about the things that made her sad. And if Mommy knew Elyse was sad and talked about her sadness, she wouldn't let Elyse come over anymore.

Okay, that made no sense. But Alanna got an American Girl doll out of it. One for her and one for Ruby. Isadora was too young. Alanna waited for her mother to say something about the dolls. Her mother had said they couldn't have American Girl dolls, that they offended her on some principle. But she didn't even seem to notice the dolls. She didn't notice anything anymore. She was like a ghost, wandering through the house at odd hours, holding Isadora, who was forever crying, crying, crying.

Then Elyse went away anyway. "Did Mommy find out Elyse was sad?" *Shhh. We don't talk about that. Respect Elyse's privacy, okay?* Then Elyse came back, after, and stayed for another year. Then she got mad and quit. She had said Alanna's daddy wasn't fair. Well, Alanna knew that to be true, sometimes. He wasn't always fair. He had a hard time keeping promises, although he had kept the one about the American Girl dolls.

And for a long time, she was never sure if he knew that she had broken her promise, too. Not on purpose. But Mommy was having a bad day. That's what she would say. *I'm having a bad day, Alanna. Mommy's having a bad day.* Ruby would cry and say, *No, it's a good day, Mommy, don't say that, it's a good day.* But Alanna was older. She knew that some days were bad, especially for her mother. Alanna, without thinking, had said, *A bad day like Elyse when she was crying in Daddy's lap.* And Mommy, vague and checked-out as she was, had asked Alanna what she meant. It was too late to keep the promise, but she had begged Mommy not to tell Daddy that she'd told.

She thought her mother had kept that promise. But then one day, grown-ups came over and said they had to ask her about that, and Daddy said it was okay, she could talk about it. They gave her dolls, asked her to act out what Daddy and Elyse did. They asked if she could tell the story to a roomful of people. She said yes, but she didn't mean it. She had stomachaches every night. It might have been when the migraines started, too, although she didn't have words for her headaches then.

Then, two days before she was to go and tell the story, Daddy came to her and said she didn't have to. That she would never have to tell the story and she probably shouldn't.

Five, six, maybe seven years passed before she realized, while reading a terrific dirty book that was making the rounds of Roland

Park Country middle school, that she had seen a blow job and that she was supposed to describe that in her mother's trial.

The why of it had taken a little longer to piece together. But it was part of the before time, when Isadora was alive. Alanna told her mother, by accident, what she saw. Elyse was fired. A month later, Isadora was dead.

Good-bye to the musketeers, who never were.

Last year, in an avant-garde film class, the teacher had screened a film called *1900*. You had to have a permission slip to watch it. The parents had to sign off on a Wikipedia entry that described the plot and emphasized there was nudity and graphic violence. Alanna had high hopes, but the film didn't live up to most of the dirty books she had read. There was one scene where two lovers, interrupted by a child who spies on them, rape the child. The man then swings the boy around by his feet until he ends up bashing his brains out on a rock. Was it on purpose or by accident? She couldn't figure that part out. But whatever he had seen, the memory was gone.

"I protected you," her father had said the other night, when they fought. "I was thinking only of you." But was that true? Who could tell her what was true?

She had time to kill before her appointment. She climbed the trapeze in the Office, swung her legs and sang a song, the one about the mockingbird and the diamond ring and the looking glass. Who had sung that song to her? Mommy? Elyse? Daddy? No, it had been a woman's voice, she was sure of that. Sweet and high. *And if that diamond ring turns brass*—was that even possible? Don't say a word. Don't say a word. Daddy will buy you whatever you want. Don't say a word.

5:00 P.M.

"This isn't how I imagined the interview with Ethan going, Harmony. I have to tell you, I am not happy with this one."

Harmony, seated in the living room of Melisandre's new apartment, took a deep breath. This was the moment she had feared since taking the project. Until last week, however, Melisandre had been almost *too* hands-off. Then, out of nowhere, she'd asked for the camera and a quick overview of Harmony's protocols, saying she had a "mystery guest" to interview, someone who wouldn't speak to anyone but her. She also had said she wanted to review dailies, although Harmony had assumed the events of this week had pushed those plans out of her mind.

No such luck. Despite her last-minute move, Melisandre had managed to review all the video shot to date and summoned Harmony to her new apartment, which already looked polished and perfect. Rich people. It helped that Melisandre's furniture and household items had been chosen weeks ago and warehoused, so she had only to summon her decorator, who supervised the movers. Still, Harmony could not get over the fact that last night this apartment had been empty and now it was furnished. Even art had been hung, although it felt impersonal, the kinds of things a decorator would choose.

"This is raw footage," Harmony said carefully. "Unedited."

"I know what *raw* means, Harmony."

This was not the woman that Harmony had met in London four months ago. This woman had no desire to charm or seduce. She was jumpy, agitated. And she still wouldn't tell Harmony whom she had interviewed yesterday. Nor had she uploaded the video for Harmony to transcribe. But the transcription app would kick it to her soon enough. Assuming Melisandre had remembered to use it.

"I think the interview with Ethan isn't as bad as the interview with Poppy, in some ways. That's going to be very difficult to edit, with her bringing up money all the time. There's a big difference between paying someone a per diem and travel expenses and paying for an interview, but it confuses the issue, having Poppy reference it over and over again."

Harmony did not add that she had been blindsided by Poppy's talk of money. Melisandre had made that arrangement through Tyner. Harmony wasn't sure what she found more disturbing, Melisandre's failure to tell her about that deal or the fact that Melisandre wouldn't even get on the phone with her former roommate once she was in Baltimore. Melisandre had addressed the latter at least, explaining to Harmony that Poppy's preoccupation with Melisandre's wealth had driven a wedge between them after they left the hospital. They had been the same there. They weren't in the outside world, and Poppy could never stop dropping hints about things she wanted. Poppy was the one, Melisandre said, who kept asking about visiting her, but made it clear that Melisandre would have to buy the tickets, and could she have a companion fare and would it be okay, as long as she was making such a long flight, to go to Paris, too?

But it wasn't the Poppy interview that bothered Melisandre. It was Ethan on whom she had fixated. Careful, clipped Ethan. To Harmony's amazement, Melisandre was angry that Harmony had pushed him on the issue of his testimony. But how could the documentary ignore it?

"The whole point of the documentary—our smoking gun—is what Stephen and Ethan did to guarantee the mistrial, then how Stephen used that opportunity to manipulate you," Harmony told her.

"That is *not* the whole point. I confided in you about Stephen and Ethan so you would have the big picture. I never expected that to become your central inquiry. The mistrial, Ethan's mistakes—I don't want this to get bogged down in a discussion of legal technicalities."

"He made a slip, though. He said at one point that the articles were on your desk, then another time that they were on your nightstand."

"So what? Anyone could make that kind of mistake. You let it go pretty easily."

"I'm not—this isn't *60 Minutes,* Melisandre. I'm trying to be unobtrusive, stay out of it. I can't be adversarial during the interviews. That's not right for the tone of the piece I'm creating. We're creating."

"Ethan perjured himself. He's never going to admit that oncamera."

"I know that's what you think happened, Melisandre."

"It's what happened, Harmony. No 'think' about it." Lord, her voice was icy when she was mad. Harmony had a moment of wondering what Melisandre had been like as a mother. The woman had a mercurial streak that was hard enough on Harmony. How had two small girls felt when her moods jumped like this? Harmony thought of her own mother, a working-class woman of great charm and wit. She was loud but direct, shouting instructions at her children and husband. But Harmony never had to wonder where she stood with her mother.

"Melisandre, this is supposed to be a documentary about the insanity defense and our society's inability to grant people the verdict that the court bestows. You won in court. You were judged not guilty. As you know, the same circumstances happened in the Andrea Yates trial. The original guilty verdict was vacated, based on inaccurate testimony, and she went on to be judged not guilty by reason of insanity."

"No one has ever doubted that Andrea Yates was insane. And Andrea Yates is still hospitalized. Like Hinckley, she'll probably never get out. I'm the one that people think rigged the system because I had money. I'm the one who has to prove that this is real, that it can happen to anyone, not just some silly Bible thumper with a substandard IQ. Not that I think of Yates that way."

The last sentence was said hastily, in a tacked-on way. Harmony tried to keep her face neutral. Yet she was sure that was exactly how Melisandre thought of Yates.

"But that's what *others* think," Melisandre continued, up and pacing now, raking her hands through her hair. "There's always a reason to look away when mental illness is involved. When someone even opens the door to the question, as Ethan does here, that I might not have been ill—I can't tell you how hurtful that is to me. The others hint at the same thing. It was bad enough to do what I did, to live through it and have to go on. You know there were suicide attempts, Harmony. You know because I told you, and I'm willing, in our film, to share that with the world for the first time. I lost my mind. You have no idea how apt that phrase is until it happens to you. I lost my mind. I got it back. But I lost everything else. My daughters, all of them."

Not your money, Harmony thought. But she realized that was *her* obsession. Melisandre had suffered. She missed her daughters terribly. Her money was no cushion against those harsh realities.

"I signed those custodial papers under stress. Ethan doesn't tell that part, does he? And believe me, Ethan knows all about what happened when I left the hospital. Ethan *conspired* against me. But it's Stephen who has to admit what he did. Not the affair, so much, but his desperation to keep it from coming out."

And here was the Melisandre of Claridge's in London again. Warm, empathetic, seductive.

Harmony, eager to please, said, "I can't really afford the time to edit this right now, but I could edit the transcript, show you how it might appear."

"Is that the best use of your time?"

"I told you: Transcribing the audio really seals the information in my head, gives me perspective. The forest and the trees, you know? I doubt this interview with Ethan will even be a big part of the final project. You're right—it covers ground that's been covered. But with Stephen reneging on his agreement to let the girls participate in the film, this is all we have right now."

"*For* now," Melisandre said. "He'll change his mind."

"Let me edit the transcript, show you what I think we might use, and how. Then we'll take it from there. I'm not opposed to sitting down again with someone. I just want to avoid meeting over and over. People get too smooth after a while. We want this to feel, you know, real. Unrehearsed. I wish we didn't have to do so much with talking heads and voice-over. And you know I won't do re-creations, I just won't. No fuzzy scenes with actors portraying the past. But— the things we had hoped to be filming this week. Well, it may be a while."

She was trying to be as tactful as possible about the impasse over the girls. The incident with Melisandre's trainer had given Stephen more juice. Perhaps Melisandre thought owning an apartment in Stephen's building would force him to concede her surroundings were safe, but it wasn't working out that way.

"That's another thing—I don't want it mentioned in the film, ever, that Alanna was called to testify. I don't want to go down that road. Not because of me. Because of her. I wouldn't do that to her. Believe me, I have no problem revealing that Stephen wasn't quite the saintly husband and father people think he was during my illness. But it would hurt Alanna, and that's all that matters. That was my concern at the time and that's my concern now."

Harmony took a deep breath. "I'm not sure we can leave it out. It's a salient fact. The prosecution was attempting to build a case that you were not criminally insane, that you had cause, that you knew about the affair."

"The prosecution thought I was Medea, is that what you're saying? Perhaps Medea was mad, too. Again, this isn't about me, Harmony. It's about Alanna. Maybe if Stephen understood we weren't going to go there— Well, I will reassure him about that, and watch his objections to the film disappear."

"Even after the incident with your trainer?"

"Stephen's not the least bit concerned about Silas. He's terrified his secret is going to come out, after all these years, and he's using this as an excuse. Poor brave Stephen Dawes, bewildered by his wife's behavior, sought solace with the nanny. *The nanny.* How did I ever marry such a cliché?"

The question had occurred to Harmony, although not in the context of a cliché. Why had Melisandre married Stephen? She had filmed Melisandre's version of the proposal story, beneath the now winter-bare tree where it had happened. She couldn't put her finger on it, but there was something off about the story, an emphasis on the romantic gesture but little reference to any genuine romantic feeling. Maybe that was because Melisandre had to tell the story from the vantage of hindsight, knowing how it had ended.

"The other dailies are fine, Harmony," Melisandre said. "Even Poppy. And I assure you, I am not going to censor your film, or try to structure it. You do have final cut."

Final cut contingent on the film being accepted into a major festival within one year of completion or finding distribution within two, Harmony thought. *No pressure there.*

"Thank you," Harmony said, hating herself for being submissive, subservient. How had she become this person? "And I look forward to seeing what you did this morning. The 'mystery' interview."

"All in good time. Maybe I'll use your method, transcribe it in order to better understand it. Now how about something to eat? There's a restaurant on the first floor that will send food up. Very good, doing that hyperlocal thing. And I have wine. Or tea if you prefer. I promise you won't have a seizure."

Harmony managed a weak smile. That should have been funnier than it was. "Wine would be great, as would dinner. May I use one of your bathrooms?"

"Sure," Melisandre said. "There are four of them. Although I'm not even sure where they all are."

Harmony headed down a corridor of closed doors. Framed film posters lined the hall. They were all one-sheets by Saul Bass, but lesser-known works, not the iconic *Anatomy of a Murder* poster. She wondered if Melisandre even knew who Saul Bass was, or if he was just a new affectation, something else to acquire as she reinvented herself as a film producer. Harmony was only a human version of these posters, a bit of cred that Melisandre had purchased.

She opened a door at random, but it was not a bathroom she had found. It was a girl's room, a sophisticated teenager's room, straight from the pages of an upscale catalog, except for one small detail: an American Girl doll, an incongruous note on the pillows of the double bed with its silken linens of teal and rose. Harmony walked over, picked it up. The doll had glossy brown hair and an old-fashioned dress, nineteenth century. She had never been much for dolls. She found their eyes unsettling, and this one wasn't any different.

"That was Alanna's," Melisandre said from the doorway. "I had some of the girls' possessions put in storage. I never knew why, but now I'm glad I did. I can't wait for them to see their rooms here."

Harmony smiled weakly, embarrassed. There was no way to disguise the fact that she had been snooping. "I'm sorry—I came in here by accident. I was just looking for the bathroom."

"My life is an open book," Melisandre said. "To you especially."

A bathroom connected this bedroom to another one. Ruby's room, Harmony guessed, but she didn't so much as crack the door, although she was curious to see if the decor was different, if Melisandre had distinctive ideas about the two teenagers her daughters now were. And if so, what had formed those ideas? She washed her hands and splashed cold water on her face. Melisandre believed that she was getting her girls back. She was so confident that she had created bedrooms for them. Of course, this could be the delusion of a woman who was used to getting what she wanted. Yet Melisandre's confidence, as reflected in the completeness of the decor, struck Harmony as specific, rooted in something that Melisandre knew and others did not.

And why wouldn't she tell Harmony whom she had interviewed today? If Melisandre was an open book, then that book was hollowed out, like a volume used to hide secrets now concealed elsewhere.

March 13, 2014, Tyner Gray's office

SPEAKER 1: Melisandre Harris Dawes
SPEAKER 2: Tyner Gray
    INPUT: MHD

MHD: Okay, I think I've done it all correctly—I didn't bring the light, but the light here in your office is fine unless you're vain. I have the app I'm supposed to use, and the camera is set on the tripod so I don't have to hold it. Checked voice level. So—go.

TG: I don't really understand why I'm doing this, Missy. As your lawyer, I'll probably forbid you to use anything—

MHD: Just tell the story. That's what Harmony does. Says. She gets people to tell the story, tries to stay out of the way. It's like I'm not here. Ignore me.

TG: No one has ever been able to ignore you, Missy.

MHD: You did, the first time we met. Do you remember?

TG: Impossible. If I was ignoring you, then I hadn't seen you for whatever reason. So, no, I don't remember it that way.

MHD: It was in a restaurant downtown. That cute old-fashioned diner on Redwood with the wooden booths and tiled floors. You stopped to talk to my boss on your way out. You both ignored me. I had to introduce myself. I was a baby lawyer, with nothing to contribute to the conversation, but still. I wasn't used to men ignoring me.

TG: Werner's. I was probably distracted. Lunch there was always a big networking thing. And that place was hell to navigate in my chair. Very narrow aisles, so many people. But I will apologize for ignoring you. What has it been, twenty years?

MHD: Twenty. Exactly twenty. Almost to the day. It was February 1994. I saw you in the courthouse a week later. That's probably what you remember. I was stalking you.

TG: Very funny, Missy.

MHD: I was. The moment I saw you I realized you were someone I had to get to know. You were kind of legendary. You had worked so hard to achieve something, to make that Olympic team, and then it was taken from you, through no fault of your own, and you had gone on, without bitterness or rancor. You are the strongest man I've ever known, Tyner.

TG: There was bitterness at the time it happened. Some would say I'm bitter still, but I always had a prickly temperament. It just got pricklier. Missy, why are you doing this particular interview? Especially after everything that's happened this week. Isn't it enough to produce and star in the film? Do you have to be your own crew, too?

MHD: Today's the only day that Harmony can meet with another one of the subjects and we're behind schedule. I didn't know it was possible for a documentary to get behind schedule. I thought you just lived it. But Harmony is concerned about the budget. She was accused of exceeding her budget on her second film. It matters to her. And I guess it should matter to me, as it's my money. But I've never cared about money.

TG: Who is Harmony interviewing?

MHD: I think it's Poppy. My roommate at the psychiatric facility. Anyway, let's establish how we know each other and then we'll talk about what happened to me. At the end.

TG: I have known you—

MHD: Not me. I mean, you can't say *you*. You—Tyner— are talking to the camera, to the audience beyond the camera. I'm not here. Talk about me as if I'm not here, as if you're telling other people about me. I always wanted to know what you said to other people about me.

TG: Missy— Okay, fine, here goes. I've known Melisandre Dawes since 1994. She was Melisandre Harris then. I first became aware of her in the courthouse—she was working as a young lawyer with one of the bigger firms in Baltimore, Howard, Howard & Barr, but she said she was interested in coming to work for me. She was not well suited to my one-man practice. I took on associates for two to three years, but tried to avoid anyone who hoped to have a partnership. My office is a good place for a lawyer to apprentice while studying for the bar, then move on. Melisandre was past that. Besides—

MHD: Tyner?

TG: Yes?

MHD: That's almost thirty seconds of silence. If this were film instead of digital, you'd be costing me money. And it screws up the transcription, if the silences go on too long. I think that's what Harmony told me.

TG: Sorry.

MHD: Now finish the sentence. Why didn't you want me to come work for you? I lobbied pretty hard for the job.

TG: I didn't hire you—

MHD: Say, "I didn't hire Melisandre."

TG: Sorry.

MHD: Why do you keep saying sorry?

TG: Because I'm screwing up, aren't I? Okay. Deep breath. Focus. I didn't hire Melisandre Dawes—Melisandre Harris—because I was interested in her. In dating her. It was the Anita Hill era, or not long after. I had dated some of my other young hires. Before. And it was consensual. I really hadn't thought too much about it. If one works long hours, where does one meet people? But I saw that I had, in fact, abused my position. To be clear, no one ever complained. I like to think that was because I was always very—up-front. I was up-front with all the women I dated. I had no intention of marrying, no intention of having a family. Do men still say that, *up-front*? Does anyone believe them if they do? A lot of women didn't believe me when I told them what I wanted. They really thought it was just a matter of me meeting the right woman. But not even Melisandre Harris could change my mind, and she was one of the most alluring and charming young women I had ever known. We dated for six months, a long time for me. She ended the relationship on December thirty-first, 1994.

MHD: You remember the exact date?

TG: It's not hard to remember being stood up on New Year's Eve.

MHD: I didn't stand you up. I called you that morning and said it was time to move on. That I needed a commitment or there was no reason to go forward.

TG: Yes, you did.

MHD: No *yous*, Tyner.

TG: We broke up on December thirty-first, 1994, at her initiative. It seemed like the next thing I knew, she was dating Stephen Dawes, a friend of mine. Well, acquaintance. We knew each other through the boathouse. He rowed, I coached. Our paths crossed a lot. I might have even introduced you—Stephen and Melisandre. All I know is it happened very fast. He proposed to you three months after the Charm City Sprints.

MHD: He proposed to Melisandre.

TG: He proposed to Melisandre three months after the Charm City Sprints. He did it up in a big way, planned a surprise party at the boathouse. He even arranged for people to arrive on a shuttle, so there would be no cars in the lot, which would have been unusual at that time of day. The ring was in a jewelry box dangling from a tree by a ribbon. He proposed to her there, near the site where they had met, then took her into the boathouse to celebrate, where friends and family waited with champagne. He was very sure that she would say yes, I guess.

MHD: How do you know the details of the proposal? Were you there?

TG: I was invited to the party. No hard feelings. Everyone was an adult. Melisandre had broken up with me because she very much wanted a husband and children. Stephen wanted a family, too. It was a whirlwind courtship.

MHD: You consider getting engaged in three months to be a whirlwind courtship?

TG: I do.

MHD: Could you repeat that back in full?

TG: I do consider three months to be a very swift courtship, yes.

MHD: How long did you and your wife date before you married?

TG: I don't think that's important, Melisandre.

MHD: Don't address me by my name. That's like saying *you*.

TG: I don't want this to be part of the documentary, Missy.

MHD: I just—I mean, I'm entitled to ask. How did you end up marrying? After all those years of saying it wasn't what you wanted?

TG: I changed, Melisandre. People do change over a twenty-year span. I'm not the man you knew. And I didn't change my mind about children. I didn't have the temperament for fatherhood. When Tess comes over with her little girl, I find it charming. For about twenty minutes. Kitty, as a doting aunt, is good for the whole visit, but even she sighs with relief when Carla Scout leaves. I had thought the only reason to marry was to have children. Kitty— Look, I don't want to talk about this.

MHD: On film, or at all?

TG: At all. I've told you several times now, I'm very happy. I have no regrets.

MHD: I think you also told me once that anything modified by the word *very* is suspect.

TG: Move on, Melisandre.

MHD: Did you see much of Melisandre Dawes after she married?

TG: Baltimore is small in its way and you're apt to run into people, so, yes, probably here and there. I remember sending gifts to each child after their births.

MHD: What did you send them?

TG: Okay, I had my secretary select and send the gifts, but I wrote the notes. I was very happy for you—for Melisandre. She had what she'd always wanted.

MHD: Did you ever see her alone?

  TG: Once.

MHD: When was that?

  TG: Missy.

MHD: It matters. You have to talk about this.

  TG: On August eighth, 2002. The day she killed her daughter.

MHD: And what happened?

  TG: She came to my office.

MHD: And what did she say?

  TG: I cannot tell you. Because two weeks before that visit, Melisandre Dawes had retained me as her attorney and all conversations subsequent to that time are privileged, in my view.

MHD: Did you, in fact, serve as her attorney when she was charged with murder?

  TG: No, I referred her to a criminal attorney who had more experience with the insanity plea. But as of that morning, I was technically her attorney. She had never told me why she wanted an attorney of record, only that she did. I didn't think it meant anything. She told me she was scared and in trouble, but she wouldn't tell me anything more.

MHD: Can you tell us what happened that day?

  TG: No, ethically I cannot.

MHD: But the visit, in fact, represents the missing time? The gap that has never been explained between Melisandre leaving the camp at Friends School and arriving at the boathouse?

  TG: I'm not going to comment. Nothing relevant to the case happened, and she was here for no more than fifteen minutes. If I had been asked to testify, I would have been happy to say that she appeared upset and I tried to persuade her not to leave, but I failed. I thought she was drunk, or had mixed up a prescription. She kept saying that her legs and arms felt strange, as if she were growing scales. But it's hard seeing someone you have known, as crazy. It doesn't compute. Also— Well, life with Melisandre was not without melodrama. She was capable of throwing scenes, then reverting to her usual nature, as if nothing had happened. But she did not have her child with her. Apparently, the child was in the car, which I didn't know. Couldn't know. I'm still shocked that her car sat behind my office for as long as it did without anyone seeing the child in there. And I did not think she was on the verge of harming anyone, including herself. I have to live with that. I do live with that.

MHD: Is it possible that Isadora died here?

TG: Here?

MHD: In the garage behind your office?

TG: I don't remember how precisely the time of death was determined, but I think not. It's very cool and shady. The temperature inside the car would not have risen quickly enough for that to happen.

MHD: What did she do? Melisandre, when she visited you. What did she say?

TG: I can't say.

MHD: She told you that she still loved you, that she wanted to be with you.

TG: You always said you don't remember anything that happened that day.

MHD: I don't. But you told me about it.

TG: At your insistence. Yes, I did. You told me you needed to know in order to prepare for your trial.

MHD: I told you that I still loved you, that I would always love you.

TG: Well, as you know, you weren't in your right mind at the time.

MHD: You told me that you didn't want children. That we could be together, if it weren't for the children.

TG: I never said that. Never.

MHD: Not that day. But you said it before. And suddenly I had three children and the littlest one had colic and would never stop crying and I was so unhappy and I just wanted to be with you again.

TG: You can't possibly remember what happened that day. You know these things because you badgered me to tell you.

MHD: But I did say I would give up the children for you, didn't I? I said I could free myself if you would let me, that I would let Stephen take the children.

TG: The ultimate proof you were sick. You would never have voluntarily given up your girls.

MHD: That's one way to look at it. I wouldn't be the first woman to decide her children were standing between her and her romantic future. But you never told anyone what I said. You protected me, Tyner. You stood by me, never doubted me. Oh, sure, you were my lawyer at the time, but if you had a second's doubt about whether I was mad, you could have used what I said against me. So which is it, Tyner? Did you think that I was mad? Or did you still love me enough to try to protect me from myself? Both?

TG: Turn the camera off, Missy. Now.

MHD: Tell me you love me. Still. I know you do.

TG: Turn the camera off.

Friday

2:00 P.M.

Joey down for his afternoon nap, Felicia risked a bath, the monitor perched near the tub. Her tub was a beautiful thing, a freestanding soaking tub that Felicia had selected, Stephen grousing about the cost every step of the way. But a good tub was more important to Felicia than a good bed. She considered it vital to her well-being to steep herself in warm, vibrating water on a regular basis. Yet this was her first bath in weeks. Joey had a genius for sensing Felicia's rare moments of relaxation. If she even started filling the tub for herself, he cut his naps short. But even Joey was cooperating with date night.

Date night! Felicia was so wiggly with excitement that she barely needed the jets to move the water around. She had arranged for Alanna to babysit—a nice deal for someone who was grounded, making fifteen dollars an hour when she couldn't go out anyway—and gotten reservations at Pazo, an old favorite from their courtship days. She had tried to persuade Stephen to book a car so both of them could drink, but he had said pointedly that she was still breast-feeding, so how much did she plan to drink, anyway? Only maybe—maybe Stephen wanted to make sure she was wide-eyed when they returned, so she could devote her full attention to him? Okay, fine, she would limit herself to a glass of wine or two, be the designated driver. Ruby had a sleepover, so they didn't need to worry about picking her up.

Felicia heard her cell, ringing in the dressing room, but couldn't imagine what might be urgent enough to lure her from this tub. As long as she could hear Joey's snuffly breaths on the monitor, nothing could be wrong. Felicia had been one of those parents who stood by the crib in the early months, checking that her son's chest was rising and falling, that he was alive. She still did it sometimes. Being a mother was like being trapped in the first fifteen minutes of a horror film. Everything was fine, lovely. But there was this persistent sense of dread. Joey wasn't even a year old, and already there had been a series of averted crises. His first crib had been recalled, and it turned out the little seat he used was considered dangerous, too.

Then there was the house itself, a never-ending source of potential dangers. You would think a man who had had two daughters—*three,* her mind amended—might remember what children got into. Oh, and don't even talk to her about lithium batteries. Joey wasn't even crawling yet, but Felicia had identified all the devices in the house with such batteries and hidden them. Stephen grumbled that getting the remote for the AppleTV device was akin to signing out documents in a government agency. Felicia didn't care.

Joey slept on, considerate for once. She had time to do all the things she never had time to do anymore—shave her legs, wash and dry her hair, slather herself with lotion. Felicia's looks had never depended on makeup, but she needed a little help these days, especially with her sleep so disrupted. She studied her face in the mirror, wondering how Melisandre Dawes had aged, then wondering why Melisandre still used the surname Dawes after all these years.

Her phone again. The cell. Stephen. She almost didn't take it. The quiet was delicious. She was as close to being alone as she ever was these days.

"Listen," he said. "About tonight."

No, she thought. *No, no, no.* "Yes?"

"Something has come up."

"At work? On a Friday?"

"Melisandre wants to meet with me. She says it's for the documentary. And you know what? I might as well get it out of the way. Tell her face-to-face that I won't do it and the girls have changed their minds. That the girls aren't going to see her at all, with or without a camera. Then she'll be out of our lives forever."

"But tonight is date night."

"What? Oh, I'm sorry, I forgot. Well, we can still go out. I'll just be home a little later. I mean, maybe not some big fancy meal, but we can have some time to ourselves."

"We'll see," she said with a tight-lipped fury that didn't seem to register with him at all.

"I'll be home by nine, I'm sure. See you then, okay?"

No, she decided, after hanging up the phone, *it's not okay. I'll treat myself to a night out. Alanna's already agreed to babysit. I'm going to go out on my own, see a movie, stop somewhere for a drink. Let Stephen arrive home and wonder where I am. That would show him.*

She went to her closet, selected a knit halter dress. Although it left her shoulders bare, it would be warm enough paired with a jacket. Felicia's shoulders had always been among her best features. She might not be in peak condition, but she still looked pretty good. Lots of men would look at her tonight, offer to buy her drinks, maybe even flirt with her. Nothing wrong with flirting, especially if one's husband was going to spend date night with his ex-wife.

3:15 P.M.

Sandy looked skeptically at the machine on his desk. He was no Luddite. The department had not relied much on computers at the time of his retirement—Google was barely used, as Sandy recalled—but he had always used databases, especially when he came back to work cold cases.

But this thing, this *tablet*. How had he allowed himself to be sold this? He didn't even understand why it was called a tablet. The young woman had been so enthusiastic, though, and the demo at the Apple Store had been seductive. All you have to do is take it home and plug it in, she kept saying, after setting up basic programs for him—his e-mail, the text message function, an iTunes account, and his first-ever Facebook account, which was the whole point of this exercise.

Had she looked at him strangely when he expressed interest in that particular application? It was probably in his head. But she had seemed almost a little pitying when he offered the lie "I need it to keep in touch with my grandkids." She said: "Kids don't use it as much as older people, actually. I hope you won't be disappointed if they're not in touch with you as often as you hoped."

How much would she have pitied him if she knew the real story?

Sandy opened the Facebook app. His profile had no photo attached, and he currently had zero friends. Strangely, there were already requests, but he ignored those. Facebook urged him to share his "status." He ignored that, too. He was a faceless man, using his proper name—Roberto—trolling these strange waters. The things that people shared here! And so many had clearly ignored the privacy settings.

But that was to his advantage. It took a while, but he found what he was looking for. Some people would call what Sandy did playing hunches. Or, perhaps, making an educated guess. He had given up on trying to explain that what he did was a kind of science, informed by a lifetime of experience. True, he hadn't really known what Facebook was a few days ago. But once he understood, he was sure he would have better luck with it than Tess would, and here was a solid lead, justifying his confidence. He would have to do more research before he shared the information, make sure he was right. He felt a little cocky, having bested her in a milieu where she should have been able to outthink him.

Before he signed off, he did an odd thing, knowing it was odd, yet incapable of stopping. He searched for women with the name Mary Bailey. His late wife's maiden name had been Bailey. She'd made a joke about it on their first date, but it had gone over his head. As a boy in Cuba, Sandy had never seen *It's a Wonderful Life*. As a teenager in the United States—essentially a refugee, orphaned within months of arriving—he'd had no desire to see a film with such an incomprehensible title. Eventually, Mary had gotten him to watch it one Christmas Eve, and he had tried not to let her see how much he hated it. Really, people thought this was a warm, celebratory movie? It was the saddest thing he had ever seen. Nice guy spends his whole life never getting what he wants. Sandy had lived it. He didn't need to see that in a movie.

And yet George Bailey, holding Zuzu aloft in his arms, ended up being one up on Sandy. They both had their Mary Baileys—lovely women, much too good for them—but Sandy's son was not the kind of child to be held placidly. Bobby would have torn Zuzu's petals to bits, knocked down the tree in a rage, chucked his toys at his parents' heads.

The boy had been institutionalized since age six. The best thing about Mary's death was that Sandy could stop pretending to care about him. Once Bobby's problems emerged—and once his rage nearly cost Mary her life—Sandy could not regard Bobby as his son. It was more as if they were in some horrible fairy tale and had given birth to an animal, one prone to attack and hurt those who loved him best.

So when Tess talked about how hard it was to be a mom, or how she could not imagine someone not having a relationship with her children, Sandy didn't *share*. What could he say? She was a nice young woman, but she didn't know from hard. One of the advantages to not being a big talker was that no one noticed when you shut down.

There were a lot of Mary Baileys on Facebook, but none was as lovely as his own, in Sandy's opinion. He started to power down the tablet, then saw that the lady at the Apple store had added gin rummy and hearts to the games folder, probably because he had admitted he liked to play both of those on his laptop. And you could name your opponents. That was pretty nifty. He set up the gin game so his opponent was named Mary. She beat him soundly, just like the real Mary. Sandy was never sure what he thought about the afterlife, but for a half hour or so, he allowed himself to believe that his beloved wife was playing gin with him. Game after game, he took wild chances, played stupidly against the odds—and lost happily.

4:30 P.M.

The Tasmanian Devil, Looney Tunes edition, was spinning in the narrow, sloped aisle that connected Eddie's of Roland Park's liquor department to the grocery store at large. Spinning and screaming and demanding something in garbled, guttural oaths that could not be understood. It was a fascinating display, something that Tess could have watched in awe—if the Tasmanian Devil were not Carla Scout Monaghan, who had just been told that she could not have a can of Pringles potato chips. Not now, not ever, per her father's instructions. The only chips on Crow's approved list were Kettle, which were certified GMO-free. And those were for emergencies. He preferred for Carla Scout to eat homemade chips.

"Oh, is wittle you having a bad day?" A well-intentioned Roland Park matron lowered herself on creaky knees to Carla's eyeline.

The child responded with a scream that should have shattered the nearby bottles of Scotch and gin and tequila. *Lovely, lovely tequila,* Tess thought. Could she have a shot now if she bought the bottle? Would that be so wrong? She couldn't really blame Carla Scout for responding that way to baby talk. It set Tess's teeth on edge, too.

The books said to ignore tantrums or remove the child promptly. They said other things, too, but Tess tended to forget what they were when she was in this situation. She was frozen, watching her toddler thrash it out in a high-traffic area, blocking anyone who wanted liquor, beer, wine, and snacks. And it was Friday at Eddie's. Everyone wanted liquor, beer, wine, and snacks. Including Tess. TGIF? In her life, it was more like FMIF—fuck me, it's Friday. Friday and Saturday were big work nights for Crow, requiring him to go in by 4:00, then stay until almost 3:00 A.M. Which, of course, meant sleeping until noon on Saturday and Sunday mornings. Tess dreaded Friday nights. All she wanted to do was pick up some prepared dishes at Eddie's—curried chicken salad for her, mac 'n' cheese for Carla Scout, a bottle of sauvignon blanc—get home, and survive the next five hours.

Carla Scout had a slightly different agenda.

"What you should do—" the matron began.

"Is get my husband a vasectomy. We're saving up!" *Why did I call Crow my husband, why am I putting on a front for some stranger?* Because enough of her life was hanging out in public. Much of Carla Scout's rear end was hanging out in public, as her dress had bunched up, exposing the fact that she was wearing no underpants. On a rather cool day in March. How had that happened? Tess had a vague memory of picking up Carla Scout from the Friday babysitter who helped cover the gap between Tess's and Crow's work schedules, a hurried visit to the potty, where Carla Scout had asked Tess "to give me some pri'acy." Silly Tess had assumed she had come out with her Dora the Explorer underpants on beneath her long, smocked dress, not Carla Scout's usual style at all, but it had been clean this morning. Matched with miniature suede boots bestowed on Carla Scout by her fashion-conscious grandmother, it had made for a plausible outfit eight hours ago. But, no, Dora the Explorer was apparently exploring the floor back at the babysitter's house. Was having a bare-butt child in Eddie's grounds for being reported to social services?

Tess crouched down and said, in what she hoped was a persuasively no-nonsense voice: "Carla Scout, I am going to count you down and if you can't calm down, you'll be going into Quiet Time. Right here, in the store. One . . . two . . . three."

The girl's wails rose and Tess felt as if everyone in North Baltimore was staring at her.

"Four . . . five . . . six."

Carla Scout, although several aisles from Emeril's signature spices, kicked it up a notch.

"Seven, eight, nine"—oh, Tess so did not want to say it—"ten."

At that, Tess picked up her writhing daughter and deposited her in a corner. "Quiet Time. Right here, in the store." It was this or leave, and she'd be damned if she was going to leave when she had everything she needed but the wine. And she was really damned if she was going to leave without the wine. She could feel herself flushing from embarrassment. She tried to tell herself she didn't care. Tess had always maintained she didn't worry about what people thought of her. Maybe she was lying to herself, or maybe motherhood was just the ultimate test. Every day she was judged a dozen times—and almost always found wanting. But she weathered the stares and smug glances, and Carla Scout finally calmed down, and they returned to their shopping with just the occasional dramatic sniffle. Carla Scout's, not Tess's, although she was tempted, too.

It had been such a crappy day. Tyner had asked Tess to meet him, then raked her over the coals for having made so little progress in developing leads about Melisandre's harasser. He didn't particularly appreciate Sandy's theory about the sugar bowl. "That's overwhelmingly cynical," Tyner said. "This is clearly someone from her past. Someone close to her."

"Like you, Tyner?" Tess had said, and then Tyner had just freaked the hell out. Told her she was indolent and insolent, that he had referred her as a favor because he knew she could use the work and would it hurt for her to be grateful for once. Tyner was always cranky and prone to tongue-lashings, but this was unlike anything Tess had known. She had been grateful that Sandy didn't witness it, given how close to tears Tyner pushed her.

She had left Tyner's office just in time to get caught in the rain without an umbrella, forgotten it was Friday and gone home without picking up Carla Scout, then driven over to Medfield, where the Friday babysitter lived. And now this. The thing was, she would happily buy her daughter Pringles. But she had agreed to try to do things Crow's way. No soda, ever. No store-bought cookies, crackers, cakes. Carla Scout could have junk food—junk food made with straight-up white sugar, white flour, butter, et cetera—but it had to be pedigreed or homemade. Oven-baked potato chips, sliced with a mandoline that was probably going to take a hunk of someone's finger someday, deep-fried sweet potatoes, even tortilla chips. Crow had started baking bread, too, old-fashioned Irish brown bread, which was delightful. And he baked like a madman on his days off. Whoopie pies, perhaps the most aptly named food ever, because Tess really did want to say whoopie when she bit into one. Homemade Twinkies. Something called compost cookies and chocolate sandwich cookies with buttercream icing that were the closest thing to a Hydrox that Tess could imagine. All in all, a good deal.

But Carla Scout still yearned for the occasional can of Pringles or a package of Gummi Bears, and it grieved Tess to deny her. She thought a little crap, in moderation, wasn't that bad. Crow said if she wanted to take over the cooking, she was welcome to it.

Okay, no Pringles.

Carla Scout was calming down, slowly but surely. It felt as if the tantrum had gone on for hours, but it was less than five minutes by Tess's watch. Tyner's tantrum had probably lasted longer. They procured a bottle of wine—"Mommy juice!" Carla Scout announced to everyone in earshot—and checked out without further incident. Roland Avenue was a madhouse, as usual, so Tess had to leave her cart and go get the car, two blocks away, carrying Carla Scout, who complained about the wind and rain. It was nice, Tess thought, to live somewhere a person could leave a cart of groceries on the sidewalk for five or ten minutes. When they got home, the dogs needed a quick walk, so she put away the perishables, left the other groceries to sit. Tess being Tess, she had forgotten to bring the recyclable bags for shopping, but that was okay: a woman with three dogs could always use some more plastic ones. Carla Scout took Miata's leash, as the Doberman was actually the gentlest and most patient of the three dogs, while Tess wrangled the two greyhounds, large and small. It was still light at 6:30, a nice change, and the walk restored some equilibrium between mother and daughter. Carla Scout, as was her wont, was fascinated by her own bad behavior in the grocery store, quizzing Tess about it. "I lie on the floor. I kicked. Why I do that, Mommy? Why I do that?"

"I'd love to know," Tess said. But she could feel her jangled nerves settling. The key to these grueling weekends was to adapt herself to Carla Scout's rhythms, to let her take the lead the same way she let the greyhounds pretend to be in charge. They would go home and have a "picnic" tonight—dinner on a blanket on the floor of Tess's bedroom, the dogs shut out, while they watched a movie on Tess's computer. Carla Scout loved these picnics, as did Tess, because they involved paper plates and plastic cutlery. Nothing to wash but

Mama's wineglass—and that was always the last thing to go into the dishwasher each night.

The rest of the evening was as sweet and easy as Tess could dare to hope. It was only at 10:00 P.M., when Tess was lying in Carla Scout's bed, the girl curled into the nook of her arm, that she remembered the groceries that had never been put away. She extricated herself carefully—Carla Scout had a habit of throwing an arm and leg across Tess, like some sci-fi parasite securing its food source—and went into the kitchen, feeling loose and warm and happy.

At the bottom of the last bag, she found a can of Pringles. How had her daughter smuggled them into the cart without her noticing? Then again, part of Eddie's cachet was that employees still unloaded the contents of one's cart onto the belt, with another person bagging at the end. Tess dug out the receipt to make sure she had paid for it. Carla Scout had serious klepto instincts, although she usually took what she called tiny things—keys, coins, earrings. No, there wasn't a can of Pringles on the receipt. But when could Carla Scout have grabbed it?

There was a note, however, written on the back of the receipt, in now-familiar block printing:

> YOU MAY HAVE GOTTEN A LICENSE TO BE A PI, BUT
> YOU'D NEVER GET ONE TO BE A MOTHER. YOU'RE
> A CRAPPY MOTHER.

Midnight

Melisandre poured herself another glass of wine, checked her e-mail, noticed a quiver to her hands. Why hadn't Harmony answered her? What else could she have to do on a Friday night in Baltimore? The young woman worked all the time. She had no life outside the project. Melisandre almost felt guilty about that. Almost.

Harmony was right: It had been a risk, forcing Stephen to meet with her. But she couldn't wait. That was her lifelong problem. When she wanted something, she couldn't wait. This was not a consequence of being spoiled or indulged as a child. Melisandre had been raised by fond but detached parents who delegated as much child care as possible, then sent her to boarding school at age fourteen. Her father, so much older than her mother, had died when she was seventeen, and she had felt grief, but also sadness for not having a father she could miss more sincerely. Yet losing her mother last year had sent her reeling. They had grown closer during Melisandre's time in Cape Town. It was her mother, facing stage 4 breast cancer, who had urged Melisandre to find a way to reenter Alanna's and Ruby's lives by any means necessary. But her mother didn't know the whole story. Only two people did, Melisandre and Stephen.

Stephen had been so angry with her. She had insisted on setting up the camera to record their talk, as insurance, but he had given a curt "statement," then told her to turn it off. She hadn't expected that. Resistance, yes, but not anger. "We had an arrangement," he said when she turned the camera off. "An agreement. I could have asked for child support, other financial concessions during the divorce. You agreed to leave—with half of my savings. We said we would put the past behind us, forever. Those things cannot be undone on a whim."

She argued that she had been desperate, unwell, but that made him only angrier. Which must be why he said such hurtful things.

They had been in the kitchen of their old Bolton Hill house. It had been her idea—inspiration, she thought—to meet and tape her ex-husband there. She honestly thought that she and Stephen, back in their old house, could recover a fragment or two of their good times. She had loved him in a fashion. Not as profoundly as she should have, which may have been why he had devolved into the utter cliché, the husband who fucks the nanny. Really, how lazy could men be? Elyse wasn't even that pretty or interesting. She was just *there*. Melisandre had certainly never seen her as competition. She never considered other women competition. They usually weren't.

It's never going to happen, Melisandre. Never. Get over it. You look like a fool. You are a fool.

The rage she felt at that moment—it was like nothing she had ever known. It wasn't madness, which was the term Melisandre had always preferred for her illness. Unfashionable and imprecise as it was, *madness* seemed right to her. There had been something vicious inside her, something apart from her, all those years ago.

Stephen had said: *It's never going to happen. Get over it.* How dare he tell her what could happen? He still knew her well, and he used that knowledge to wound her. His words had the force of a physical blow.

She checked her e-mail again. Harmony had finally answered her question about the protocols, explained the transcription app again, then advised Melisandre not to worry about doing her own transcription because Harmony would want to do it. She wrote that it helped her stay on top of the material. Melisandre ignored the latter. She began the laborious task of stopping and starting the tape, typing Stephen's words. When her cell rang at one, she was tempted to ignore it, but then she saw DAWES in the display.

"Melisandre? This is Felicia Dawes. Stephen's wife." It was a high voice, to Melisandre's ear. Maybe even a little whiny. And overly enunciated, the way people talk when they're trying to appear sober but aren't.

I am Stephen's wife, she thought. *You are just another nanny. Trainer. Whatever. I am Anne Boleyn. You're Jane Seymour.* She didn't want Stephen, nor had she expected him to pine for her forever. But he could have done better than *this.*

"Could you tell me what time you left Stephen? He hasn't come home and he's not answering his phone."

"I think it was no later than nine. I know I was home by nine-thirty or so, doing e-mail and transcription."

"Did he stay behind? Were you at a restaurant or his office?"

"No, neither. We met at our old house."

"Oh." A pause. "Oh."

"He was still there when I left. Do you need the address?"

"No, thank you. I did live there for a time. Before our son was born."

"Stephen loved that house. I'm surprised you got him out of it."

The rude girl didn't even bother to say good-bye.

Poor thing, Melisandre thought. *Poor thing.* She had gotten in over her head. The nanny, the trainer. Stephen really was the laziest man alive. Why not the clerk at the dry cleaner's? A barista? Cruel—but he had been cruel to her. Heedlessly cruel. Sticks and stones.

Melisandre went to bed, although it was almost dawn before she found sleep. She had one of her old anger dreams, which she had had at frequent intervals during her marriage, although they had subsided over the past ten years. She yelled at people, she grabbed them and struck them, but she was harmless as a kitten. Her rage grew and grew. She pounded her fists on a table. The table was in a courtroom, but she was not working. Nor was she on trial. She knew these things in the way people know things in dreams. She was yelling at everyone and they laughed at her. She pounded and pounded and pounded and pounded—

But, no, the pounding was outside her dream, in the real world. At her door. How could anyone be at her door? No one was supposed to be able to get to the penthouse without calling first or having a special key for the elevator. She would have to speak sternly to that girl, the one Tyner doted on. His stupid wife's stupid niece, whom Melisandre had hired as a favor to Tyner.

She pulled on a robe and instinctively fluffed her hair, which she could tame no matter how wild or bedheaded.

The man at the door introduced himself as a policeman, Lieutenant Martin Tull, showed her a badge. Stephen, Stephen, something about

Stephen. What was he trying to tell her? She really shouldn't have taken an Ambien after drinking wine. Maybe this was a dream, too?

"I told his wife that I left him at the Bolton Hill house at nine," she said. Was it 9:00, 9:30, 9:45?

"Yes, ma'am," Tull said. "A police cruiser went by there a few hours ago at Mrs. Dawes's request."

"I didn't request it. Oh—of course."

"Ma'am I'm sorry to tell you, but Mr. Dawes is dead. He went through the glass doors at the back of the house and bled to death."

Bled to death. Death. She saw Isadora's lifeless body, pulled from the car by a crabber who had broken the window in his desperation to save her. She saw her trainer, Silas, convulsing. She saw herself. Why did death stalk her? What did it want from her?

I should sit down, she thought. Then: *I am going to sit down. Where do I sit down? How do I sit down? It's like Isadora all over again except I'm here for this, I know what's going on.*

"He fell through the doors? I always worried about that glass," she said after groping her way to one of the dining room chairs. "It's because of the way the flooring was done—it's the same inside and out, which is a lovely effect—we could open the doors in such a way that it was like one big room. But dangerous. I worried about the girls so."

"We'd like to talk to you about your evening with him. Downtown, if you don't mind."

"Am I under arrest?"

"No, ma'am."

"But you want me to come downtown?"

"Yes, ma'am."

"I need to dress, call my lawyer and ask him to meet us."

"You're not under arrest, ma'am. It's no big deal, really. Just want to talk."

"I'm a lawyer," she said. "I wouldn't dream of speaking to you without one present."

She knew that insisting on a lawyer would escalate things, but she didn't care. Only a fool would speak to police without a lawyer present.

She made him wait for forty-five minutes while she showered and dressed, changing her outfit three times. She realized this could be the only power she would have for a while, making this detective wait. She began to put on her usual uniform of leggings and cashmere, then decided to wear a dress instead. A blue knit dress, paired with boots that added three inches to her height. She kept her jewelry to a minimum, wearing only diamond studs and her watch, which had belonged to her mother. Poor Mum. She had done the best she could. Almost every mother did, in Melisandre's view. *She* had done the best she could, no matter what people thought.

While in the bathroom, she managed to send Harmony a text:

> Take all materials related to film to Tess Monaghan
> and tell her they are now privileged. I'll arrange for her
> to pick up what I have here.

Of course, Tyner really needed to be the one to hold the videos and transcripts, Harmony's shooting schedule, whatever ephemera the film had generated. But Tyner was going to be with Melisandre all day. Tyner was going to be with her for hours and hours.

She fluffed her hair, put on eyeliner, and smiled at her reflection. She looked very good, all things considered.

Part II

Saturday

10:30 A.M.

Tess had no choice—today was going to be her own impromptu take-your-daughter-to-work-day. It would have been unfair to Crow, who had arrived home at 4:00 A.M., to shake him awake five hours later and ask him to watch Carla Scout while Tess ran around town at Tyner's bidding. For one brief, ungenerous moment, she had tried to rationalize that it was in Carla Scout's best interest to be left in her father's care. It was going to be a boring Saturday morning for her, strapped in her car seat. But Tess recognized she was being selfish even as she tried to be selfless.

"I want Dada," Carla Scout announced from the backseat, for the fifth or sixth time, not the least bit placated by the treats Tess had plied her with—a cruller (from a Crow-approved bakery) and chocolate milk (organic, but Starbucks, iffy in Crow's world).

"Sorry, kiddo, you're stuck with me."

"I want a Dada day, I want a Dada day," she chanted, thrumming her feet.

"That makes two of us," Tess said.

"Huh?" It never occurred to Carla Scout that anyone yearned to have a day without her.

Their first stop was Melisandre's apartment, where she said she had left her iPhone, iPad, digital camera, and laptop, all of which were to be collected. Once that was done, Tess had to drive to the Four Seasons on the other side of the harbor and meet Harmony Burns, who would add her gadgets and papers to the pile.

But the apartment first. Tess had to admit, Melisandre was a pretty cool customer, remembering to leave these items behind. Tess entered the apartment with the keys given to her during their security checks, trying to keep Carla Scout from running amok. But it was hard, locating things when Melisandre hadn't provided precise locations. While Tess was searching, Carla Scout ended up seizing a doll she found in one of the bedrooms. An American Girl doll, Tess realized. She had been trying to keep Carla Scout from knowing of their financially ruinous existence.

"Mine," she said.

"No, it's not, Carla Scout."

"MINE." Carla Scout believed that "No" was the result of not having been heard, so she simply amped up the volume at the first denial. And on the second, then the third.

"Not yours," Tess said firmly, removed it from her daughter's grasp, and walked it into the bathroom, thinking to stow it in a cabinet there. Oh, thank goodness, there was Melisandre's phone on the sink, and the tablet was on the back of the toilet. She threw those into her battered leather knapsack with the laptop and camera, which she preferred to a purse, as it kept both hands free when she was walking. She instructed Carla Scout to follow her to the car, only to discover, upon fastening her into her car seat, that she was clutching a book, *In the Night Kitchen*. Fuck. She should take it back, but she couldn't bear the idea of unbuckling, then rebuckling, Carla Scout.

Wait—why did Melisandre have a copy of *In the Night Kitchen*? That was appropriate for little kids. Why did she have an American Girl doll, come to think of it?

Harmony was waiting for Tess on the circular drive at the Four Seasons, all her materials loaded onto a bellman's cart.

"How long will I have to go without my iPad?" she asked. "And my phone? How am I supposed to cope without my phone?"

"Tyner said go over to the AT&T store on Fleet, say you lost yours, and buy a new phone and tablet. He'll reimburse you. I assume everything is backed up somewhere?"

"I use—"

Tess held up a hand. "Don't tell me. I'm not sure how it works in this brave new world. And when it comes to your laptop, well—la, la, la, I can't hear you, you don't even have one, okay? We have a grace period, maybe a long one, in which no one is going to ask for this stuff. The detectives assigned to this case are old school. They believe in interrogation above all. And they're good at it. Tyner is more worried about the state's attorney's office requesting these items down the line, but—better safe than sorry."

"He's right to be concerned," Harmony said. "Federal prosecutors sought all footage from a reality show last year after they indicted two of the people on it. I'm talking about stuff that had never aired. The network fought the request, but I'm not sure how it ended up."

Harmony looked thin and frail in her black clothes and her cherry-red Doc Martens. She could pass for a teenager. Maybe that's why Tess felt an almost maternal desire to cheer her up.

"But this is good for your project, in the long run? I mean, something has happened. You have a story to tell now."

"No, it's horrible. Other media is going to swamp us. And I don't understand why Melisandre was meeting with Stephen. That was terribly premature."

"I assumed that was because of the kids. She was desperate to see them."

"Yes, but why—" Harmony stopped herself.

"Why what?"

"Never mind. Melisandre usually knows what she's doing, even if she doesn't always tell me. I'll leave it at that."

Tess lingered for a minute in the driveway. There was something likable about Harmony Burns. She had seen her only once before, at Tyner's office, and then the young woman had been not so much a person as a person associated with the film that Tess wanted no part of. But Tess, forever inquisitive, had Googled Harmony after their encounter and read her slender backstory—the accolades that had greeted her first documentary, the criticisms that had buried the second and tarnished her reputation. She had been accused of exploiting her young subject, affirming racist stereotypes, not stepping in when the girl's cousin huffed spray paint on-camera.

"I used to be a reporter. Too." The tacked-on word was a bit of conscious flattery. "The story goes where the story goes, no?"

"It's not what I signed on for. I don't do crowd scenes, headline drama, CNN crazy-lady-of-the-week. I wanted to make a film about a woman who was trying to rebuild her relationship with her daughters."

"I thought it was a broad look at the criminal insanity plea."

"Yes, it's that, too. But I also wanted to document the return to something that others would call normalcy. Insanity by any name—there's still such a taint. Young actresses can go to rehab seven times. And be forgiven, seven times. But no one's allowed a comeback from crazy."

What do I believe about Melisandre Harris Dawes? Crazy? Crazy then, but not now? Never crazy? Tess decided she preferred not to think about Melisandre at all. The story was just too awful—the mother sitting mere yards away, shielded from the sun by a shade tree, while her daughter essentially baked to death in a luxury SUV. Of course it was crazy, but what did crazy *mean*?

Tess got back into her car and headed to police headquarters to see if Tyner needed anything else from her. There wasn't much news on the radio on a Saturday morning. The death of Stephen Dawes was still unknown to the city at large. She wondered how long that would hold true. Even if an enterprising reporter had been listening to the police radio overnight, the report would have been for an ambulance dispatched to a Bolton Hill address, then a call for homicide detectives. A reporter would have to look up the address to learn that it was the home of someone well known, then go to the scene to understand the circumstances of the death. After all, it would initially be investigated as an accident.

And it might have been an accident. It was possible that Stephen Dawes had walked or fallen through the large plate-glass doors along the rear of his Bolton Hill home. There was evidence that he had been drinking, although it was unclear how much, just that an empty wine bottle had been found at the scene. It also appeared that he had died very quickly, blood gushing from his femoral artery. Even if someone had been there, he couldn't have been saved.

But if someone had been there, why hadn't that person called 911?

Tyner had no more work for Tess after she dropped everything off. No praise, either, but that was comfortingly in character. Carla Scout, bored with the book she had stolen from Melisandre's apartment, was breaking bad after a long morning in the car. But Tess had a solution for that—Saturday story hour at her aunt Kitty's bookstore. Carla Scout was a regular there. Kitty didn't tell the stories. For all her personal warmth and magnetism, Kitty didn't really have a lot of rapport with kids unless, like Carla Scout, they were related to her. She hired a smiley, happy lady to tell the stories on the children side of Women and Children First, then busied herself in the Dead White Men annex.

And that suited Tess, who needed to talk to someone, anyone, today. There had been no opportunity to tell Crow about the third note last night, especially given that he didn't know about the first and second notes. Besides, she was afraid that Crow, kind as he was, might share the sentiment of the note writer. She *was* a crappy mother. She lost her temper. She yelled. She couldn't plant herself in the moment the way Crow could. She tried to blame it on being six years older, but did the reason matter? Crow was an innately great parent. Tess? Not so much. The accidental detective had become the accidental mother, and the learning curve was even steeper in this line of work. Tess remembered a PI friend, one who hadn't started out so friendly, telling Tess that she held her gun like a blow dryer. That was even funnier if one had seen Tess with a blow dryer. But she had learned to hold a gun, even to use one with lethal force when it came down to it. Her hand reached for her knee, for the slightly raised scar that reminded her that she was alive, and lucky to be so, that a gun had saved her life. She touched this talisman of flesh much less frequently since Carla Scout was born. Tess no longer needed to be reminded of her own mortality. Carla Scout did that job very nicely.

"Three notes so far, but this was the first overtly cruel one?" Kitty asked with her instant, easy empathy. She had always been more like a big sister than an aunt.

"Sandy nailed it from the first. He said that if someone had the power to approve of my behavior, they also had the power to disapprove. The second one creeped me out, but my eating habits are, thanks to the *Beacon-Light,* public record. As Crow said, that article was a blueprint for stalkers. That, and the coverage of the Epstein affair, when I went into premature labor after throwing an antique bedpan at someone's head."

"Ah, yes. My gift to you. More fortuitous than I would have dreamed."

"You've always had a way of anticipating my needs better than I can."

Kitty nodded, but she was distracted today. Abstracted, to use that rare word that sounded like Baltimore malapropism but was actually proper English.

"You okay, Kitty?" Tess asked and realized she seldom had cause to ask this question. Kitty was always okay, better than okay. Happy, stable, a rock. It had never occurred to Tess until this moment that no one, not even Kitty, could be happy all the time.

"Stephen Dawes's death—I don't even know the man, but it's clearly going to be at the center of our lives for a while. Melisandre called Tyner at seven or so. We weren't even awake. Even before this horrible accident, the last few days have been exhausting. *She's* exhausting. I hate the habit of calling women high-maintenance—as if they were cars or appliances. As if women, in general, require care in a way that men do not. But Melisandre Dawes is high-maintenance. Besides—she makes me feel short."

Tess recognized that her aunt was trying to divert the conversation with that little joke at the end.

"You *are* short."

"But I never feel that way, ever. In my mind, I'm taller than you. So—what are you going to do about the notes?"

"Well, I guess I'll do my own security assessment on myself. We have a good alarm system, although I never have installed outdoor cameras. I also think it would be hard for someone to follow me now that I'm on guard. What I find unnerving are the places I can't control. Day care, the part-time babysitters. I don't want to tell them about the notes, though. It's bad enough . . ."

Her voice drifted off. She was unwilling to say the rest, but Kitty knew. Kitty understood.

"You're a good mom, Tess. Don't let some crazy person convince you otherwise."

"I'm not as patient as I could be. The other day, Carla Scout took my phone out of my purse and pretended to make a call. She said, 'Hello, hello, hello. What's happening. Not AGAIN!' And then she told her mysterious caller—'I don't like it.'" She dropped her voice almost to a whisper, although Carla Scout hadn't been whispering. "'I don't like it when Mommy yells.'"

"Well, that just shows how extraordinary a circumstance it is, Mommy yelling."

"Maybe," Tess said, keen to believe this. "Maybe."

"You know, Tess, your own parents were a little overwhelmed when you were small. The house in Ten Hills—when they bought it, they knew they would need two incomes to keep it."

"I thought they bought a big house because they were going to have lots of kids."

"They were, but they hadn't thought it through. Judith had to go back to work as quickly as possible after you were born. And your dad— I love my brother, he's such a good man, Tess, but he didn't lift a finger to help with you. That's how it was. It's part of the reason I never wanted kids. I remember reading Nora Ephron, writing about the women's consciousness movement in the seventies, how it basically involved men agreeing to clear the dishes after dinner."

"Is the point that I have it so good?"

"No, the point is that your mother yelled, too. Probably more than you even remember. And yet, you love her and you don't dwell on those things."

"She hated messes so much," Tess mused. "You know how she is about her own clothes. Everything perfect and matchy-matched. She wanted me to be the same, but I was a slob. Made her crazy."

"Have you ever thought about what your mother might have achieved if she had started at NSA even a decade later than she did? Or considered how her wardrobe was one of the few things she controlled back then?"

Tess, to her chagrin, had not. She had never contemplated her mother's side of anything.

"Okay, okay, I am the poster girl for first world problems," she said. "And the one thing I don't have to worry about is billable hours. Assuming Melisandre gets charged and indicted, which sounded likely when I talked to Tyner. There's a lot of legwork when he has a big criminal trial."

"Tyner's not going to represent Melisandre. After all, he didn't represent her last time. He just happened to be the only person she could reach on a Saturday morning."

Tess started to contradict, tell Kitty that Melisandre was insisting Tyner represent her, given that the insanity plea wasn't part of the mix this time. But she didn't want to give her aunt another reason to feel short.

1:00 P.M.

Felicia felt as if she were running up a flight of stairs in a skyscraper in which someone added another floor for every flight she ran. She could never make it to the top. Even if she made it to the top, Stephen would not be there. Stephen would never be there again. But if she stopped running, she would have to think about what her life was now, so she kept going. Move forward, do something, anything. Feed Joey. Make breakfast, even though Alanna was still asleep and Ruby had not yet returned from her sleepover. Every minute that

Alanna slept, that Ruby lingered at her friend's house, was one more minute of happiness for them. Felicia was glad, inside her own shock, that she wanted this for the girls. She was going to be their only parent now.

She called her mother and stepfather, who said they would come as soon as possible. Felicia's mother had lost her father as a teenager. She might be helpful to Alanna and Ruby, if they would allow her to be.

Who would help Felicia?

When the police had come to the door before sunrise, she knew. She *knew*. She willed herself not to break down, if only because she needed Joey to sleep a little longer. She could feel the officers judging her, noting her composure, and realized that she was probably a suspect. They led her through the events of the evening—where had she been, why did she wait so late to call? She told them about her night out, how she had fallen into bed at midnight, clothes still on, foggy even on two glasses of wine. She had checked on Joey, who was sleeping, but had not even bothered to knock on Alanna's door. She remembered calling Melisandre at one or so, when she realized that Stephen was still not home. But she couldn't leave. She just kept calling and texting him.

They asked her if she needed help, if she had someone to call. She didn't have anyone local to call, but she didn't want to admit that. Her parents would be here later this afternoon. All she had to do was hold it together until then. And get through telling the girls.

Keep moving. Keep moving. With Joey down for his nap, she made their bed—no, never theirs again, just hers—picked up the clothes she had dropped on the floor the night before. She had expected to find Stephen waiting up for her, perhaps a little pissed that she had gone out. Hoping he would be a little pissed. She was puzzled that he wasn't home, but also buzzed, so she went to sleep. The wine rebounded on her, and she woke up at 1:00 A.M. with a dry mouth and a vague sense of things not being right. Stephen's side of the bed was empty.

Wide awake, if cotton-mouthed and cotton-headed, she called Stephen's cell. It rang, but went to voice mail. Finally she broke down and called Melisandre, who was no help at all, seemed downright amused by Felicia's predicament. Hours later, even as Felicia dialed 911, worst-case scenarios filling her head, she did not believe that the worst had happened. The whole point of imagining horrible things was that it prevented them from happening. Think of the worst thing you could ever imagine and it wouldn't be.

Yet it had. It had happened. Her husband was dead. She was a widow, with a young son, and two stepdaughters who couldn't even be bothered to hate her. Except, of course, she would be their mother now. Stephen had said, back when the girls declined to be adopted, that he would go ahead and appoint Felicia as their guardian. He didn't need the girls' permission for that. The executor—had he ever replaced Ethan?—would oversee the girls' inheritance, while Felicia would supervise Joey's trust. The key thing, Stephen had said, was fairness. Everyone must be treated the same. Toward that end, Stephen had come up with a complicated bit of math, in which Felicia's share, instead of being half the estate, was one-half minus one-third, because technically Joey's share would be her share until he was eighteen. It had all been so speculative, almost laughable. Felicia had gotten dressed up and gone downtown with Stephen to discuss it with his lawyer, happily playing the game in which she was the scheming stepmother who would try to undercut the girls' inheritance. She herself made no will—what did she have to leave anyone?—and Stephen had agreed that Joey's guardians would be Felicia's parents, still relatively fit in their sixties. After the meeting with the lawyer, they had enjoyed a long, flirty lunch at Petit Louis.

She went to the safe in the closet to retrieve a copy of that will. It wasn't there. Strange. She started going through his other files.

Could it be at his office? She found Stephen's old-fashioned Rolo-dex—he held on to a lot of old-fashioned things—plucked the law-yer's card from it, and called him at his home.

"Mr. Jacoby? This is Felicia Dawes. Do you remember me? You drew up my husband's will."

"I remember our visit. But you know, Mrs. Dawes, I can't speak to you about Stephen's will without his permission."

"Of course." This was her life for the foreseeable future. She was going to have this conversation over and over. On the phone to her mother, she had been too dazed to register it, but now she saw how it was going to be: She would have to tell people, all sorts of people, that her husband was dead. For how long? How many times would she have to say the words? Would it become easier or harder?

She also was aware of an ugly sense of self-importance. It was such grave news, the biggest she would ever deliver. And she still needed to tell two teenage girls.

"My husband died this morning. An accident." To say he was killed, to speak of the police's suspicions—that seemed tacky, sala-cious. Stephen wouldn't want her to spread gossip. He was a proud man.

"I'm so sorry, Mrs. Dawes. That's horrible news. How are you doing? An accident—"

"An accident," she repeated with an emphasis that she hoped would shut down any inquiries. "So, of course, I need to know where the will is. Possibly a safe-deposit box, but I thought it would be here, in the house."

"Mrs. Dawes, I'm sorry, but—"

"I know. I'm not your client. But how does this work? I don't really know anything about our finances. We have a joint checking account, but Stephen paid the bills, and he had corporate accounts, which is where he kept a lot of his money, transferring sums every month. It's awful, but I have to be able to pay our mortgage and buy groceries. I don't want to be talking about this, but I have to."

"No, Mrs. Dawes. That's not what I was going to say. Stephen never executed his will. There is no will. We had the discussions, yes, but there were some key issues he couldn't decide."

"Key issues?"

"He didn't name a guardian for the girls."

"He intended for me—"

"I'm sure he did. But with nothing set, a judge has to decide. I'm sure it will end up the same way, but custody, the distribution of the money—that's now in a judge's hands."

"Are our accounts frozen?"

"The corporate ones will not be accessible. But I'm sure your lawyer will be able to get the estate to pay out living expenses, even while it's in probate. And there will be Social Security, although not much, and I'm not sure when it starts."

"But—" She didn't want to ask, but how could she not? This was about Joey, his life, his future. Focusing on the practical, the day-to-day, gave her purpose, blunted the grief. "Will I get any money at all beyond that?"

"Typically under Maryland law, the estate is divided evenly between a surviving spouse and the children."

"So we each get a fourth?"

"No, the spouse gets half, then the children split up the remaining half. Typically. I can't swear to you how it will turn out."

Alanna came into the kitchen just then. Her incuriosity about her stepmother was ingrained at this point. Felicia could start singing "The Star-Spangled Banner" while sobbing and the girl wouldn't look up. But she seemed particularly inside herself today, even for Alanna. She stared into the refrigerator.

"Why is there never anything good to eat in this house?"

Felicia was shocked at the thought that flitted across her mind just then, swift as a bug darting when the lights went on. *You're get-*

ting only a sixth. I'll get a half and I'll control Joey's sixth. That's two-thirds. She excused herself from her phone call, not caring that she was abrupt to the point of rudeness. Insensitivity was her right, at least for a little while.

"Alanna? There's something I have to tell you."

She faltered. There could be no pleasure in saying what she had to say, no matter how cruel the girl had been to her. At age five, Alanna had been told that her sister was dead, killed by her mother. Now she was seventeen and her father was dead. Killed by her mother. Not that the police had told Felicia that, but what else could have happened? Stephen never would have walked or fallen through those doors.

"Alanna?"

"Jesus, *what?*"

1:30 P.M.

Daisy's dad made a big deal about listening to some show about the Beatles. It was funny about the dads—they always wanted you to listen to their music, educate you, while the moms wanted to hear what the girls thought was cool. Daisy's dad lectured the girls on the Beatles between songs. Daisy and Ruby, the last girl in the car as she lived the farthest out, might have giggled over his earnestness if they hadn't been exhausted from the usual sleepover antics.

It had been a good party. Ruby, although not pretty or outgoing, was well liked by the other girls. They didn't mind that she disapproved of certain things—texting boys, calling people out on Facebook. If anything, they seemed to respect her for her principles. The other girls longed for her approval, just as she had always longed for Alanna's.

Ruby wished she could throw a sleepover, too, but their new house was too far out. Not that the other parents would have objected. Other parents were always happy to do extra things for the Dawes girls. Too happy. Thank God she was only a year away from getting her license, and then she would get a car, just as Alanna had, or maybe take over Alanna's car when she went to college. And given how few rules Alanna had to follow, Ruby would probably be allowed to do whatever she wanted, whenever. Even without a chronic migraine problem. Her dad was too lazy to discipline them and Felicia didn't care. She *pretended* to care, but since Joey was born, the difference was obvious to Ruby. Joey was Felicia's son. Alanna and Ruby were her husband's children. Felicia was nice enough, especially to Ruby. She had no idea that Ruby was the one who had refused to allow Felicia to adopt them, that Alanna had gone along with her for once, not asking her reasons. Alanna probably figured that Ruby was entitled to her secrets, given how many secrets Alanna had.

Only Ruby knew almost all of her sister's secrets. She knew that Alanna had gone to Cherry Hill to find the boathouse—and gotten grounded for it. She knew that Alanna had a twenty-three-year-old boyfriend. She knew that Alanna was worried about getting pregnant, but was safe so far, based on the blank pregnancy tests in their shared bathroom. Not that Alanna was careless enough to throw them out in plain view. Ruby went through trash cans, too.

It had been a relief to have a night off from thinking about Alanna's secrets, knowing she was at home, grounded and watching baby Joey. So many times Ruby had lain awake, worrying, because she knew Alanna had gone out to see her boyfriend. What kind of twenty-three-year-old man wanted to hang out with a teenager? *Creepy.* No, it was a nice break to giggle with Daisy in the backseat of her dad's car, laughing at his detailed explanations about why the Beatles *mattered.* They laughed so hard that the back of his neck flushed and he started punching the radio buttons, saying, "Fine, we'll listen to WBAL, then." They rode in silence, letting the words roll over them, playing punch buggy.

"Punch buggy," Ruby said, jabbing Daisy's upper arm. "Green."

"That wasn't a Bug."

"It was a VW."

"It has to be a VW BUG," Daisy said. Ruby knew this was true, but she was laughing too hard to say anything else.

A familiar name jumped out of the radio: ". . . Stephen Dawes was found dead today in the Bolton Hill home he once shared with his wife . . ."

What? No. It didn't work that way. This is not the way the world ends. Wait, that was a line from a poem, or close to. But Ruby was fumbling toward something similar. This was wrong. You did not, while playing punch buggy on the Baltimore Beltway, hear that your father was dead. *No, no, no, no. How had it happened the first time?* But Ruby had been spared that memory. She remembered crying after the fact. Sadness throughout the house, a feeling so physically present that it was as if it were raining inside all the time. But she could not remember the actual moment she was told that her sister had died.

How had this happened? It wasn't supposed to happen. People were supposed to come to your house and tell you these things in soft, gentle voices, arms around your shoulders. Did Alanna know? Joey? But Joey was a baby. He would never know, never understand. He would just go through life as Ruby had, with a hole inside him, a hole through which everything leaked oh so slowly.

Daisy's father was pulling the car over. "Ruby? Ruby?" Daisy was saying: "Ruby? Ruby?" They were nice people. Daisy was her best friend. Daisy had her father. Daisy had her mother. Ruby hated her more than she had ever hated anyone.

She heard her own voice coming from far away: "We have to get home. I need to see Alanna. Not call her. I need— She has to hear this from me, not anyone else."

Monday

Tess Monaghan woke up with the blasphemous, horrible thought: *Monday! OH, THANK GOD IT'S MONDAY.* It was her morning "off"— Crow had Carla Scout for the day. Monday, Monday, love this day. Everyone in the house liked Monday, the least manic day of the week in their household.

The second thought was more in keeping with Monday: *And I get to go play mind games with a freshly minted widow with a baby. Hooray for me.*

Sunday, the one carefree day the family shared together each week, had been lovely. They had gone to the zoo, where the cool but spring-scented day seemed to energize the animals. Carla Scout had fed a giraffe, giggling with delight, and brushed a goat. They had eaten lunch at Suburban House, an old deli of which Tess was fond, drawn more by nostalgia than by the actual food. They had finished the day with a movie at home, *Despicable Me,* which Tess and

Crow loved. "Did you like it?" they asked Carla Scout. "No," she said thoughtfully. "That was not my favorite movie." Tess never loved her daughter more than when she was being her own person, exhausting as that person could be. She didn't want to raise a mini-me, or even a minion, who parroted back her parents' preferences and opinions.

Well, so far, so good, Tess thought, stretching out in bed next to Crow. He and Carla Scout, night owls by nature, would sleep in, have a late breakfast at one of "their" places. *Now all I have to do is help Tyner prepare for a criminal case he shouldn't be trying.*

Melisandre had been charged with homicide and would go before a judge this morning. Tyner was confident that she would be given bail, although it would be a high one, possibly requiring a surety bond on her new home. A flight risk because of her time overseas, she would be required to surrender her passport, although Tess was pretty sure that Melisandre had at least two passports, a consequence of her dual citizenship. Not Tess's problem if a judge missed that fact at the hearing. The apartment that Tess and Sandy had vetted for security would also be good for avoiding media scrums. Once released, Melisandre would be able to come and go without being observed. She had been photographed when she was transferred to the city jail Saturday night, but that was probably unavoidable. Tess had watched the footage on the news. Harmony had been there, too, looking miserable. Tess had spotted her in the background, but she didn't even appear to be filming. Was the project dead—or better than ever? At least something was finally happening.

Not Tess's problem. Her first order of business was to speak to Felicia Dawes. As Tyner had explained it, they had a seven-hour window to play with. Stephen Dawes had met with his ex-wife in his home on Friday evening. His body was discovered at least seven hours later. What Tyner hoped to establish was that there had been plenty of time for someone, anyone, to enter the house and push Stephen through the glass doors after Melisandre had left. An intruder would be an easy case to make in that part of town—say, a burglar who had assumed the long-vacant house was ripe for picking. And if nothing could be shown to have been taken, then Tyner would argue that the intruder had surprised Stephen Dawes, pushed him in a panic, and fled.

Time was the one thing that they could manipulate. Time, Tess's inflexible enemy in day-to-day life, was on their side.

Time was on their side. Monday, Monday. Just another manic Monday. Jesus, it was as if her fillings were pulling in an oldies station this morning.

She grabbed a notebook from the nightstand. Once she left her bedroom, the dogs would clamor for their morning walk. Working from memory, she jotted down the established points on the clock. Melisandre arrived at her apartment sometime between 9:00 and 10:00. Her garage and elevator entry would establish the precise time. Felicia called her at 1:47 A.M. That was on the confiscated cell phone; Tess had checked it. However, Felicia had not called the police until almost 4:00 A.M., apparently feeling sheepish for her worry.

Tess's job was to go over what Felicia Dawes knew—and determine how confident she was in what she knew. By the time Tess left, she would be a lot less confident. Tess was okay with that.

Tess wasn't okay with the secret directive Tyner had given her last night—to try to develop alternative suspects. That wasn't what defense attorneys did, much less private investigators, and she had argued that point. She might have actually said, "Who are you, Perry Fucking Mason? O.J.?" But Tyner was clinging to the idea that they could find the real killer and spare Melisandre a trial. "I don't think she'll survive it. Emotionally, I mean. She can win an acquittal, but at what cost?"

"Wouldn't it be better to focus on getting the charge knocked down, go for a plea? I mean, there's no intent, right? Maybe there was an argument, she shoved him—maybe she was defending herself—maybe—"

"Tess, Melisandre said she didn't do it. Can you understand how important it is to her not to be accused of a crime where the mitigating factor would be rage? She wants to be exonerated. If we could do that outside a courtroom, it would be a bonus."

It was work. It was groceries, the utility bill, maybe the start of a private school tuition nest egg. Hers was not to question why. Hers was to question Felicia Dawes.

"I told you," Felicia Dawes said. "I'm not sure why Melisandre was so adamant about meeting him Friday night, only that Stephen wanted to get it over with."

Her voice scaled up. She was young enough that many of her sentences ended as questions. And young enough to be too timid to ask Tess to leave, although she was clearly growing impatient with her presence. The second Mrs. Dawes was younger than Tess by several years, although she didn't look it, not today. Grief and a young child did not do much for a person's appearance. The young woman who met with her in this oddly secluded house had a ravaged look.

"But it was for the film? Are you sure he said that?"

"He said— We were supposed to be going out and he called. No, I'm sure he said it was about the film."

"He *told* you he was meeting Melisandre about the film. Is there any chance he might not have been forthcoming with you?"

"No—no. I mean, why? Is there something I don't know?"

The monitor at Felicia's side crackled with a baby's cries, and she sat up a little straighter, listening. Then a woman's voice was heard, laughing and cooing, and Felicia relaxed.

"Do you have a nanny?" Tess asked. She couldn't help herself. She always wanted to know everyone's child-care arrangements.

"I'm a stay-at-home mother," Felicia said. "My mother and stepfather came to help me, when they heard. But I'm not sure how long they can stay. They both have jobs, the kind from which you can't take long leaves. They live in Cumberland."

The last bit—the mention of the jobs, Cumberland—seemed weirdly defensive, but Tess understood. Felicia was telling her that she wasn't rich, or to the manner born. As for the proud way she declared herself a stay-at-home mom—well, Tess knew better than to engage in *that* discussion.

"Anyway, did Stephen tell you why he felt he had to see Melisandre when she insisted on it?"

"Why do I even have to talk to you?"

Not so timid, after all.

"You don't. Not now. But you will, eventually, at great length. You'll be deposed by Melisandre's lawyer, and you'll be grateful that you spoke to me when your memory was sharpest. It's in your best interest."

"You work for her lawyer."

"I do. But all I care about are the facts, as you remember them."

"Facts that you'll shape to your agenda."

"Facts can't be shaped," Tess lied. "Facts are inert. Facts are neutral. I just need to know them. My personal opinion? Things look very bad for Melisandre."

"Because she had a motive." Felicia had no problem making *that* into a declarative sentence.

"Homicide investigators care little for motive. She was there, she had the opportunity. But why do you think she had a motive?"

Ah, good. Felicia looked perplexed by Tess's dismissal of motive. Perplexed and troubled.

"Stephen had changed his mind about the girls seeing Melisandre."

"About them being in the film?"

"About *everything*. The girls didn't know that, but he had never been comfortable with the idea, and after that thing happened with Silas—he made up his mind. No film, no visits at all."

"When did he tell Melisandre this?"

"He hadn't, as far as I know. But maybe he told her Friday night. Maybe that's why—"

Oh, no, that was unfortunate. But better to know now than later.

"If that's the case, why would *he* participate in the film? Melisandre shot film of him, although no one has reviewed it yet. Why not just tell her on the phone that the deal was off? He was supposed to go out to dinner with you? Why put that off to meet with Melisandre?"

"He forgot our date." Felicia stared at the floor, looking as if she was going to cry. Then, to Tess's horror, she did.

"I'm sorry," she said. "I'm sorry, I'm sorry, I'm sorry."

"It's okay," said Tess. "When my daughter was your son's age, I pretty much cried every day, and I wasn't in your circumstances."

She hadn't meant to mention Carla Scout, but it was hard, watching a stranger cry.

"How old is she now?"

"Three. Don't believe what you hear about the terrible twos. It's all about three. It's like living with Maria Callas."

"What do you do for child care?"

"Pretty much reinvent the wheel every day. Or at least every week." That got a semismile from Felicia. "We have a patchwork of day care, babysitters, and parental care. My husband"—there she went again, calling Crow her husband—"works nights, Tuesdays through Saturdays. My hours are unpredictable at best. We have day care three days a week, a babysitter on Fridays, and my parents in emergencies. Don't you have any help at all?"

"No. Thank you for asking. Most people assume that it's a life of leisure, staying home with a child. It's the hardest job I've ever had. Only I'm not supposed to call it a job, am I? And now—" She began crying even harder. Oh dear, Tess had done too well at creating empathy with the widow Dawes. It now seemed awkward to try to steer the conversation back to her memory of Friday night, to ask for precise times and words.

A young woman who bore an uncanny resemblance to Melisandre, although absent the curls, appeared in the doorway. Tess assumed she had been drawn by the sound of Felicia's tears, but the girl stood where she was, stone-faced.

"Who are you?" she asked.

"A private detective. I work for your mother."

"How do you know who my mother is? I haven't told you my name."

"Well, I—" Tess was floundering. The girl was enjoying it, too. "You look exactly like her."

"So some people say. I've never seen her."

"Never?"

"Well, not since I was five and she killed our baby sister."

"You're the oldest? Alanna?"

"Oh, so you're a math whiz. Yes, twelve plus five equals seventeen equals me, Alanna."

"Where's Ruby?" Felicia asked, trying to gain control of herself.

A shrug, perfected. Alanna Dawes should patent her shrug, make YouTube instructional videos on shrugging. Watching her, Tess felt as if she had never before seen a human being lift and lower her shoulders in order to communicate her complete lack of interest in something.

"So if you work for my mother, does that mean you think she's innocent?"

"Actually, I work for Tyner Gray, your mother's attorney," Tess said, knowing that Alanna would see through that linguistic sidestep. "But when I help him, I need to focus on facts, whether they help or hurt her case. There's no point in ignoring inconvenient facts, given that the prosecution will find them and use them."

"Such as?"

"Your mother met with your father Friday night. And the meeting might not have been friendly, based on what Felicia tells me."

"Really?" Alanna trained her eyes on her stepmother. Tess would not have wanted to be on the receiving end of such a gaze. She probably would be, though, when Carla Scout was an adolescent. "Felicia, you gossip. What family secrets have you been sharing?"

"I don't think this is the time to be—a time to be proper," Felicia said.

"Proper." Alanna's echo managed to convey with admirably controlled mockery that she didn't think her stepmother had standing to decide what was proper.

"I'll probably need to speak to you as well," Tess said. "And your sister. Not today. I didn't expect to find you home today."

"Why do you want to talk to me?"

Because you were grounded and can verify what time your stepmother arrived home—and if she went out again at any point. But saying that would be impolitic in Felicia's presence. Still, Felicia would have to account for her hours, too, from Friday 9:30 P.M. until—well, 1:47 A.M., when she called Melisandre. According to what Felicia had told Tess, Alanna had been asleep when she got home.

"I'm just trying to rebuild the day, understand where everyone was and what everyone knew. You might have to testify, if it goes to trial."

"Yeah," Alanna said. "They said that last time." Then, at Tess's puzzled look, "I think you might have more facts to gather. If you really want to know where everyone was and what everyone did, you might have to go back a ways. Twelve years, to be specific. More math: 2014 minus 12 equals 2002. But if you want it broken down into geometry or calculus, you'll have to find Ruby. She's the family brain."

The girl walked away. She even moved like her mother, with that cool glide. Tess glanced at Felicia, but she seemed just as confused.

"Okay," Tess said. "May I go over the sequence of the evening one last time?"

2:00 P.M.

No one would have expected the Dawes girls to attend school that day, but Ruby had lied and told Felicia there was a test she couldn't miss. She didn't dare ask Alanna to drive her, because Alanna might actually figure out that Ruby had lied about the test. Ruby had a hard time lying to her sister. No worries, Alanna was in her room, not even bothering to claim a headache. Alanna would never go to school if she could get a day off. It wasn't that Alanna hated school. But it bored her. She was like a princess in a tiny country where she had long ago exhausted all the perks of her power. She needed to move on.

So Ruby got a ride from Felicia's stepfather, essentially a stranger. She couldn't imagine a better companion for the thirty-five-minute drive. Frank Davidson was a quiet man who kept his opinions to himself. This was in marked contrast to his wife, Roberta, who had a lot of opinions on everything in the Dawes household, which she criticized with feverish admiration. "So big, you must get tired trotting around here all day," she had said to Felicia. "What a strange layout—the master bedroom on the first floor, the laundry off the kitchen. Don't you get tired of hearing the dryer rumble? And even if you have a monitor, can you really get to Joey fast enough? I know this pediatric nurse and she always said, bad things don't happen often, but when they do happen, they happen *fast*."

But Roberta's critical chatter was preferable to the constant keening of their real grandmother, Glenda Dawes. Grandma Dee's grief was so large and vocal that it took over the house when she visited. She roamed from room to room, clutching Joey, who was terrified by this sobbing, incoherent woman who had replaced the grandmother he knew. He cried with her until it seemed like some sort of contest. Ruby felt sorry for Felicia. Or did, until she overheard Felicia discussing the guardianship issue with Ruby's grandmother.

"Stephen didn't leave a plan in place for the girls," Ruby heard Felicia telling her mother-in-law over the monitor in Joey's room. The monitor was great for eavesdropping, although it was tricky for Ruby to linger near the central unit in the master bedroom, as she had no business being there. Those were Felicia's words: "You have no business here." Ruby always wanted to reply: "It's not business. It's family. This is my father's room and he would never ban me from it." But Ruby was not good at fighting people face-to-face. Secrets were her specialty. She had discovered so many secrets, but she didn't know what to do with them. She still didn't.

"So are you going to petition the court to raise them?" Grandma Dee asked.

"Of course," Felicia said. "Although I assume Alanna will seek independence at age eighteen. But it makes sense. They are Joey's sisters, this is their home, I'll control most of the money. Without a will, that's the way the law usually works. The spouse receives half, the other half is divided among the children."

"I'm sure that Stephen meant to provide for me." Grandma Dee wasn't crying then. She sounded hard, angry.

"I'm sure he did, too, Glenda. And when everything is sorted out, I promise I will, too. To the best of my ability."

"Sorted out? What needs to be sorted out?"

"Stephen kept much of his money in corporate accounts, then transferred cash to cover our expenses on a monthly basis. I have no access to the corporate accounts. I am the beneficiary on his retirement plans, but I need legal advice on what happens if I tap into them now. It's all really complicated."

"Maybe I should be the girls' guardian. I'm their blood."

"Joey is their blood, too, Glenda. Would you really split them up?"

"What's splitting? Alanna's off to college in eighteen months. It might be better for Ruby to live with me."

"How so?"

"Are you telling me that you can love Ruby as you love your own child?"

There was a long pause on the monitor, then footsteps. Ruby worried that Felicia might have left the room in anger and she would be caught snooping. She should leave to be on the safe side. But she couldn't. She had to hear Felicia's answer.

"I could," Felicia said. "If she'd let me."

That had been yesterday. Now, hiding out in the school library on the pretext of working on a term paper, Ruby thought about Felicia's words again. They sounded nice. But were they true? Grandma Dee wasn't the only one who was dubious on this score.

Ruby checked her watch. School was out in an hour. Getting to her appointment was easy, but then there would be the problem of getting home without anyone knowing where she had been. She had told Felicia that she had to go to the Central Library to research something and Daisy's mother would drive her home. But wouldn't Felicia find it odd if "Daisy's mother" didn't come in and offer her condolences?

Secrets used to make Ruby feel powerful. Now she felt loaded down, as if she had eaten all her Halloween candy the first night. She wanted to make everything okay. But could anything ever be okay again? Had it ever been? She didn't even remember Isadora, not really. She remembered being told about her and about a time when things in the family had been good, actually good. It was like being told that the stories in her childhood books were true—that there was a monkey who lived with a man in a yellow hat, that a boy fell through the sky, that a lonely doll made friends and your mother would love you forever. She yearned to believe it all, but it only made her sadder.

Was it so wrong to wish that she could have been born into a happy family?

8:30 P.M.

"Ready for a eureka moment?"

Tess, cradling the phone between shoulder and ear, was ready for many things. A glass of wine, bedtime, her daughter's or her own. An easy compromise over what to watch on Netflix tonight. She wanted peace on Earth, a Democratic majority in the House and the Senate, and a national health care system that didn't make people insane. She wanted a pair of really comfortable boots that looked dressy enough to wear with skirts. She wanted good Chinese food within a ten-mile radius and home delivery from her favorite pizza places. She wanted someone to figure out who had the secret recipe for the Asiago cheese dip known as Federal Hill crack, a commodity that was currently MIA since the woman who held the recipe had changed jobs again.

But she would settle for a eureka moment.

"What do you have, Sandy?"

"So you've heard of Facebook—"

"Yes, I remember mentioning it to you. And have you heard about this thing called the horseless carriage?"

"I had no reason to know this stuff. But now that I do— interesting."

"I looked for both girls last week and couldn't find them."

"You looked under Dawes, right?"

"Yes."

"Alanna's there under her mother's maiden name, Harris. And

that led me to her sister, who goes by Ruby Dee. Even has a photo of the real Ruby Dee for her picture."

"How did you figure out to check Alanna under the mother's maiden name?"

"I got to thinking—Alanna Dawes, Ruby Dawes—those names come up, on a Google search. Harris falls between the cracks. Anyway, her friendship circle is relatively small. Alanna's."

"Define relatively."

"Fewer than three hundred."

"Have to put the phone down for a sec and put you on speaker, okay?" Tess soaped Carla Scout's back. "Good work finding Alanna, but I don't see how that's going to be helpful. What are we going to do with three hundred random names on Facebook?"

"'Scuse me, Mama. 'Scuse me, Mama. 'Scuse me, Mama."

"Don't need to look at all three hundred—"

"MAMA STOP TALKING UNCLE SANDY STOP TALKING."

"Well, yes, I guess there are ways to filter—maybe by location or certain circles, but even—"

"MAMA MY SHARK IS GOING TO BITE YOU ON YOUR BOOTY IF YOU DON'T STOP TALKING."

Carla Scout rose from the bath, ribbons of soap running down her ridiculously perfect body, a toy shark in her hand. Whenever Tess looked at her daughter, she had to wonder how a flat stomach had become the aesthetic ideal for women. All women should be convex. Carla Scout's belly was a taut little drum and it was glorious.

"Carla Scout! Sometimes Mama has to talk. Uncle Sandy has something important to tell me."

"Uncle Sandy is BORING." Carla Scout was not being rude. She had been told frequently, when Tess had to head out the door for work, that she was going to talk about "boring stuff with Uncle Sandy." Carla Scout had no idea what boring was, only that she was against it.

"Yeah," Sandy said. "It's a big old haystack all right. But when you see that little heart thingie next to one name—that's something, right? Especially when the guy looks to be in his twenties."

"Alanna has a boyfriend?"

"Uh-huh, and he's twenty-three. Tony Lopez. Sealed juvie record, some burglaries, although he hasn't been picked up for three years and hasn't done time. Yet. Unemployed since December, when he got fired—from his job as a bellhop at the Wyndham. If you go to his Facebook page, you discover he has lots and lots of friends in what they call the hospitality industry. Including three at the Four Seasons. And one is a room service waiter."

Tess was glad the phone was balanced on the back of the toilet, as Carla Scout seized this moment to throw a virtual tsunami in her face. She couldn't even get mad. She shouldn't be trying to multitask this way. Carla Scout had been with Daddy all day. This was supposed to be Mama time.

"You there?" Sandy asked.

"Yes, just mopping up a spill. So—do you think—I mean, it could all be a coincidence, right?"

"Could be. But I think the first order of business is visiting Tony Lopez at his residence. What do you bet he sleeps in most mornings? Let's get there early. I'll bring the coffee."

10:00 P.M.

When the phone rang, Kitty knew it would be Melisandre. She also guessed the call would be urgent, as that had always been the tenor of Melisandre's calls, even before she had any real right to urgency. *There has been a development. It can't be discussed on the phone. It can't wait until morning. It has to be discussed now face-to-face.*

Tyner wasn't happy about being at her beck and call. But that only made it worse, watching him go grumbling into the night. He had confided in Kitty that he was worried about Melisandre's mental state, that he didn't dare ignore her for fear she would harm herself.

What was it like, Kitty wondered, to always get your way, or to expect to? She wanted to point out that the one thing Melisandre had never done was harm herself. Instead, she kissed Tyner, said she understood. The problem was—she did understand. Kitty almost always understood why people did what they did. Guilt worked on Tyner. Guilt and getting to be a hero.

The temptation was to play armchair analyst, break it down, connect his desire to be a hero to the accident that had taken a physically vital man, an Olympic-caliber athlete, and made him someone—not dependent so much as a person who had to fight for his independence every day. Thirty years ago, Tyner had been forced to remake his entire world. Not just the physical spaces but his interior ones as well.

Once—only once—Tyner had asked Kitty how many wheelchair-bound men she could name, from life and pop culture. Her list had read:

Ironside
FDR
Bobby Udeki (neighbor)
The lawyer in *The Player*
Everybody in *Murderball*
Lincoln What's-his-name in Jeffery Deaver's novels

"No *Coming Home*?" he asked. "You don't harbor fantasies of being awakened to life by sensitive, sensual Jon Voight?"

"Never seen it," she lied. Tyner later said that was when he realized he was in love with her. Kitty was happy. Kitty was complete. She saw Tyner as being—well, not happy but also complete. She had never understood the point, to continue with pop culture clichés, of one person saying to another, "You complete me." She didn't want someone with a hole inside that she had to fill. She was not a half. She was not, Yeats be damned, part of the platonic ideal described in "Among School Children." She was yolk *and* white. She was complete.

She was also alone on a Monday night, an intact egg, while her husband was figuratively, perhaps literally, holding the hand of a woman who had no problem saying, "I need you. Now."

Kitty's first love had snuffed out the neediness in her. She had fallen, hard, for the biggest lunkhead in the neighborhood. Handsome, an athlete. He had attended Mount St. Joe. Her parents had approved of him. Her brothers had not. She had thought them overprotective and silly, but they knew Paul, or his type, much better than her parents did. Later, much later, Patrick, Tess's father, would tell her that he had predicted it all. He told her this with real sorrow. Patrick became a father the summer that Kitty was sixteen. That same summer, Kitty went to a stone house on a bluff in Hampden, a hidden place because the girls there were to be kept hidden until they gave birth.

Oh, Paul had wanted to marry her and Kitty had even announced to her parents that they were engaged. They would have let her go through with it, too. It was her band of brothers, six strong, who told her she did not have to do this. Brendan, the oldest, even dared to speak of abortion. But she saw how that would rend her family—her parents would disown her and take hard against the brothers who supported her. So Kitty went to the stone house on the bluff in Hampden, gave birth in August, and returned to school in September. No one was fooled. A Catholic girl's high school uniform could not hide a pregnancy into the sixth month. But her family had held fast to the lie that Kitty had a glandular problem and that "surgery" had cured it over the summer.

Paul was angry. He should have been relieved. His young life had been spared, too, by Kitty's decision. But knocking up Kitty Monaghan was the only real achievement of his life outside of basketball and baseball. He told his friends that she was a slut, that no one knew who the father of her child was. He did not tell them how he bought a cheap ring and got down on one knee. Or how he cried when Kitty gave the ring back to him three days later, saying: "I cannot be married to you. I don't think I want to be married to anyone. I don't want to be a mother or a wife."

And for decades, this had held true. She had lived life on her own terms. She still did. Those terms had expanded to include marriage to Tyner, but never motherhood. She was not meant to be a mother. Marriage was tough enough. Were there moments when she yearned for the solitude she had taken for granted? Did Tyner have habits that grated? Of course. The phone rang late at night and he rushed out. Always to help someone. There had been a client out in the suburbs, a striking redhead who was almost certainly involved in prostitution, not that Tyner would ever say. Other times, it was Tess who needed him, although she had been less likely to get into trouble over the past few years. And now there was Melisandre. No different from anyone else. Just another client.

A client who happened to be his gorgeous ex-girlfriend.

Kitty trusted Tyner. He was a professional. He wouldn't attempt to represent a woman toward whom he had unresolved feelings.

Now there's a sad little rationalization if there ever was one, Kitty thought, turning off her bedside lamp. *I know my husband isn't cheating on me because it would be* unprofessional.

He didn't come home until almost two. She pretended to be asleep even when it was clear that he saw through the pretense. It was lonely, inside her shell, but no one had ever promised that being complete could save you from loneliness. Quite the opposite.

Tuesday

8:30 A.M.

Sandy brought steaming travel mugs of his homemade Cuban coffee for their morning field trip, but the caffeine was superfluous. Both Sandy and Tess were amped on the adrenaline of this mission. It was an ugly feeling, she conceded to herself, but when their target was a twenty-something man in a relationship with a seventeen-year-old girl—well, why the hell not? This was legitimate bullying. Even Crow, who disliked this side of Tess, approved of the plan to make Tony Lopez sweat. Crow had a daughter now.

Lopez's last known address was an East Baltimore rowhouse, one that had been cut up into more apartments than would seem possible in a fourteen-foot-wide building. Sometimes as many as thirty men, usually Central American immigrants, crowded into these rowhouses, which allowed them to send more money back home. There had been a horrific fire a few years back, flames feeding on the plywood partitions the men had used to create tiny sleeping lofts.

But Tess had a hunch that Lopez, despite his surname, was at least one generation removed from the hardworking immigrant class. His rowhouse had been carved up into *only* six apartments, two per floor. She leaned on the buzzer to 3B with great glee, assuming that Lopez, who was still drawing unemployment checks, was not someone who usually rose at 8:30 A.M.

"WHAT THE FUCK?" he shouted down the stairwell after releasing the door. "Haven't I told you a million times not to ring my fucking bell when that bitch in 2A doesn't answer?"

"But we're not looking for the *lady* in 2A," Tess said, bounding up the stairs. "We're looking for you, Tony Lopez."

The face that stared down from the top floor was handsome enough. At least, a teenage girl would consider it so. Dark eyes, olive skin, a full mouth. Points to Alanna for not picking the pallid vampire type. It was a shrewd face, too, the brown eyes quickly taking in the situation. What did Tony Lopez see? Two strangers, on official business, a man and a woman. She could almost hear the calculations clicking off in his head: *Should I run? I'm in bare feet and sweatpants, no shirt. And I have to knock down two people, not one. I could take the woman. I could take the old guy. But I can't take them in combo. Cops? Maybe. Okay, they've got me. For now.*

He stood in his door, wary, his arm up.

"May we come in?" Tess asked, after providing their names but not pulling out ID.

He didn't drop the arm.

"Who are you?"

"Investigators."

"Not cops."

"Former cop," Sandy said.

"I know my rights," Lopez said. "I'm not just off the bus, you know? I was born here, I'm legal as they come. You can't fuck with me."

"Is Alanna Dawes? As legal as they come, I mean."

He had been resting more on one leg than on the other, cocking his hip, thrusting his crotch forward. Now he planted himself on both feet, crossed his arms over his chest.

"She told me she was eighteen, a freshman at UB."

"The law doesn't care what she tells you," Tess said. Sure, Alanna, at seventeen, was legal. But Tess was willing to bet that Lopez wasn't up on Maryland's statutory rape laws, much less Alanna's official birth date. "She's fifteen."

"No way, man. She drives."

"Did you ask to see her license? 'Cause you sure didn't ask to see her birth certificate." This was Tess again. Sandy's job was to glower over her shoulder, eye-fuck this kid into jelly. So far, so good.

"No, I mean—"

"Let us in, Tony. We'll sit down on your futon—I just know you have a futon—have a nice talk. It's not really about Alanna so much as it is about her mother."

"Who's her mother?" he asked. But he let them in.

Tony Lopez did have a futon. A futon and a very sad chair that looked as if it were made from two squares of foam rubber. The two pieces of furniture filled what had probably been a child's bedroom on this top floor. Small to begin with, it was even tinier now that a galley kitchen and bathroom had been carved out of it. Tess walked around, checking to see if there was a fire escape outside the bathroom. No, it was the complete firetrap.

"So you worked at the Four Seasons," Tess began. She took a seat on the futon and almost fell into the cavernous crack in the frame. Sandy remained standing. Standing and eye-fucking.

"Before the Wyndham, yeah. I worked a lot of places."

"Where you working now?"

"I'm between gigs."

"How do you pay the bills?"

"Unemployment."

"You got unemployment after being fired from the Wyndham?"

"That's how you get unemployment. You get fired."

"Even if you get fired for stealing stuff?" A guess, but a reasonable one for a guy with a rap sheet of burglaries. He'd either defend himself or rationalize.

"That was bullshit. They were just looking to trim the staff at the end of the summer."

"You've got priors."

"Juvie, mostly. And not from hotels."

"Still—is that why you got fired?"

"I was the fall guy. Some stuff went missing. It wasn't me and they couldn't prove anything, which is why I got unemployment."

"Who was it, then?"

"I didn't tell them and I won't tell you. I'm not a snitch."

On this point, Tess believed him. He wasn't a snitch. Just a guy who liked teenage girls. And to be fair to him—as much as it killed her to be fair to him—Alanna probably had lied about her age. The girl could pass for a college freshman. A little creepy, but not illegal.

"Alanna's mom lived at the Four Seasons for a while."

"So?"

"Yeah. But she had to leave, just last week. Bad things happened to her there."

"Like what?"

"You tell me."

"I don't know."

"Really? You don't know? Your friends didn't help you gain access to her suite?"

"What would I want to get in her suite for? I told you, I don't do that anymore."

I don't do that anymore. He was stuck on burglary. Strangely, that made him more credible. He didn't seem to have any idea what Tess was alluding to. She decided to switch up. "How did you meet Alanna?"

She thought it an innocent question, but the way Tony's eyes cut from left to right to left indicated that the answer was not.

"Around."

Sandy walked over to him, bent slightly at the waist, and forced eye contact. "That's not an answer."

"All the one you're going to get, old man."

Given the construction of the chair on which Tony sat, it was almost too easy for Sandy to push him over. Still, it was impressive when Sandy did just that, applying little more than the palm of his hand. Tess watched with great glee as Tony flipped over the back of his own cheap chair. He came up sputtering, ready for a fight, but the look on Sandy's face seemed to convince him he was at a disadvantage.

"You're not cops. I don't have to tell you shit."

"No," Tess said cheerily. "You're right on that score. The cops don't know about you. Yet. And the cops are investigating the murder of Alanna's dad. Should we tell them to pay you a visit?"

"Alanna's dad?" His voice squeaked on that one.

"Stephen Dawes. Don't you watch the news? Read the papers?"

The confused look on Tony Lopez's face indicated that Tess might as well have asked him if he spent his evenings contemplating the mysteries of quantum physics.

"Did Alanna ask you to gain access to her mother's suite at the Four Seasons? Or was that your idea, Tony? It's no big deal. Yet."

"No—no. I don't know what the fuck you're talking about."

"Alanna didn't ask you to do anything?"

"With her mom? No. Was this Friday night? Look, I didn't even want her to come see me Friday night. That was her idea."

Friday night. Sandy was poker-faced. Tess hoped she was, too. Alanna had been home Friday night. According to Felicia, Alanna had been babysitting her baby brother. But Joey wasn't in a position to contradict his sister, and Felicia couldn't know where the girl had been during the hours she was out.

"You better tell us everything about Friday night, Tony. We're not cops, and that's in your favor. We're interested in gathering facts. They're interested in closing a case, fast." If he didn't know about the murder, Tess reasoned, he wouldn't know about the arrest, either. "If they find out that Stephen Dawes's daughter was dating an older guy, a guy with priors, and that she came into town the night Dawes was killed—"

"Alanna told me she had to babysit, so I didn't expect to see her. Then she showed up with her little brother, and what could we do with him around?"

Yeah, what else was there to do with a girl but have sex with her? Tess felt a pang for Alanna Dawes, another girl giving herself away too freely to someone who didn't begin to deserve her. But she had to focus on Friday night.

"What time did you meet up?"

"About seven-thirty, eight. We like Two Boots pizza, over by UB. She texted me, said she was free. I get there and she's with the kid. What the fuck? So we had some pizza, but the kid was fussy, a real pain."

"So where did you go?"

"I was with my guys by nine-thirty." Tony produced his phone, proudly displayed an Instagram of five young men grabbing their crotches with one hand while holding bottles of Coors Light with the other. Of course, the time stamp was proof only of when it had been posted. But Tony had to be relatively sure that the four other men in the photo would vouch for where he was, when.

"Where did she go? When you left?"

"Home, I guess. What do I know? It's not like there was anywhere we could go. Although—"

He stopped. He was trying to be chivalrous, in his way. But he was scared, and the fear won out. He didn't want cops coming to his door.

"She has a key, you know."

"A key?"

"To the old house. She goes there. We've been there. To—you know. We don't go all the way. She's a virgin. I'm kinda in love with her."

"You go to the house in Bolton Hill. To fool around."

"Yeah. After pizza."

"Look at you, Romeo," Sandy said. "Do you even pay for the pizza?"

"I love her, man. I really do. I met her down at the harbor last fall. She's so pretty. I don't know what she wants with me."

Tess did. It had started as a safe little rebellion, an older but not so smart guy, something sure to annoy one's father. But perhaps it had progressed. Perhaps Tony Lopez was not only the reason that Alanna had sneaked out but the reason she had been grounded as well. Two Boots pizza was perhaps a two-minute drive from Bolton Hill—and the house where Stephen Dawes died. The house to which Alanna had a key. Yet Tony, based on what he was saying, hadn't known until minutes ago that Stephen Dawes was dead.

Pry open the window, Tyner had said of the evening's time line. Introduce as many possibilities as you can. Find an alternative suspect.

The problem with prying open a window is that you can't control who crawls through.

10:30 A.M.

"Probably going to say she was crazy. After all, it worked before."

Melisandre couldn't help overhearing what the woman was saying. And it wasn't because her ear had, as one's ear will do, separated out the sound of her own name in the jangling acoustics of this suburban Starbucks. This woman intended to be heard. The hand cupped by the mouth, the lowered head—it was all a pantomime of whispering.

Melisandre knew what she needed to know. She should expect to be recognized, anywhere. She hadn't been paranoid after all.

She had driven out to the suburbs thinking to enjoy a moment of anonymity. Now it was official: She had no anonymity. Had it been like this after Isadora died? She couldn't remember much about the immediate aftermath, which she had always considered a blessing. But she was sure that things had been less circus-like even when her trial was under way. Yesterday, back in her apartment after the bail hearing, she had seen her face over and over and over again on the various news channels. *Melisandre Harris Dawes, acquitted of killing her child, now suspected in her ex-husband's death.* It was interesting to see how different points were emphasized depending on the channel's slant. On the local news shows, they were almost giddy with the geography of it all—a big story! Happening here! The more conservative outlets leaned on the idea that justice had not been done the first time and now see what had happened, neener, neener, neener. But even the liberal ones, the programs that should have been allied with a woman who had been acquitted, indicated subtly that they were not giving her the benefit of the doubt this time.

The one thing that everyone seemed to agree on was that she was a big fat juicy bite for all of them to chew. She was a commodity, something capable of filling the infinite space on the Internet and cable television. "CRAZY" MOM MURDERS AGAIN. That headline, on one particularly scurrilous site, was wrong on so many levels that she couldn't help deconstructing it. *"Crazy."* Did they doubt she was crazy then, or were they anticipating that she would claim to be crazy now? *Mom.* She was not Stephen's mother. *Murders Again.* But that was a legal term. She had never murdered anyone. That verb implied intent. Melisandre may not have practiced law for more than a decade, but she still understood the concept of intent.

But now she knew the truth, all for the cost of a drive to Turners Grove. Her privacy was gone, and not only in Baltimore. Thanks to the *Daily Mail*, she was receiving attention in London. Probably Cape

Town as well. A notorious figure on three continents. Should she buy a wig, wear dark glasses? Never leave her apartment?

Over *her* dead body.

She stood up and walked over to the whisperers, forced eye contact.

"Thank you for your interest in my legal standing," she said. "Although the details of my defense are not something I can discuss publicly, I thought you'd like to know that we do not currently plan to enter a plea of not guilty by reason of insanity. The plea will be not guilty. Because I am. Not guilty."

The whisperer pressed her spine back against the soft chair, creating the maximum space possible between her and Melisandre. But she was not completely cowed.

"Baby killer," she said.

"How original," Melisandre said. "Do you think I haven't heard that before?"

She raked her eyes over her accuser's outfit, her nails, her hair. The woman reached out and put a hand on the stroller next to her, as if Melisandre were the bad fairy at the christening. What was the bad fairy's name? Melisandre never thought she would forget a single word of the stories she had read to Alanna and Ruby. But she had deconstructed those stories for her children, too, and rephrased things as she saw fit.

"Stay-at-home mom," she said in the manner of a doctor making a nonserious diagnosis. "The little boy in the stroller isn't your only child. The other is school age, or at least in preschool. Montessori, I bet. Well fixed. You have time to get your nails done, although your roots are due for attention. You've opted out, as they say. I did, too. Had a career, decided not to work anymore. I'm sorry—decided not to work *outside the home*. Opting out is a badge of status, as surely as your car is, probably a high-end SUV, with DVD player in the backseat and seat warmers. You spend your days taking care of two children, rushing here, rushing there, hunkering down in this coffee shop for a bit of gossip. And you are bored out of your mind."

"I'm not bored," the woman said, but not convincingly.

"Really? If you weren't gossiping with your friend, I bet you'd be staring at your phone, checking e-mail and posting to Facebook."

The woman winced. Target located, hit.

"One thing about having been crazy," Melisandre said. "I get to tell the truth now. All the time. Twelve years ago, I wasn't that different from you. Then something happened. This weekend my ex-husband was killed, tragically. My children, who lost their sister when they were small, have lost their father. Perhaps, instead of whispering about me, you might want to visit, show your concern. They live not twenty minutes from here. Do you know how to make a casserole?"

She walked away, proud of her ability to remain composed. Melisandre had once had the makings of a good trial lawyer. Tyner had been the first to tell her that. "Whatever you do, you should be a litigator," he said. "You're a cool customer, hard to shake. Nothing rattles you." But inside, she was jelly. It took a toll on her, saying such things. Sticks and stones—what a silly saying. Words were incredibly potent. Words wounded terribly. She would tell her daughters as much when they came back to live with her. Because they would. She had to hold on to that belief, her vision of her future. They were all she had now.

She bided her time, waited until the two gossipers left, then trailed after them just to be provocative. Ah, a Porsche SUV. So she had been on the nose there. Melisandre drove a Lexus hybrid, for the sake of the environment, but she also liked the car's quiet motor, how it crept through parking lots. Under the right conditions, you could sneak up on someone in this car. Minutes later, she glided past the woman, who was still struggling with collapsing the stroller, her toddler crying lustily in the car seat. Melisandre waved cheerfully.

Maleficent, she remembered. The name of the bad fairy was Maleficent. How ham-handed, that use of *Mal.* Was that Disney or the source material? But the fact that it was close to *magnificent—that* was clever. There was a kind of magnificence in being bad. She felt better than she had in days.

6:30 P.M.

"A pizza party!" Tess told Carla Scout. "We're having a pizza party!"

The party was, in fact, an evening meeting at Tyner's law office. He had asked to meet face-to-face after Tess told him about Lopez. All her emergency babysitters and backups were unavailable tonight, so Carla Scout sat at the conference table, drawing contentedly. Novelty went a long way with Carla Scout. An unusual place and the promise of pizza might keep her under control for however long it took Tyner to praise Tess and outline their strategy.

"You did good work," he said. Simple words, but not ones Tyner used easily, and Tess preened a little. Maybe he had demanded that she come downtown because he wanted to tell her face-to-face that she was getting a bonus. "Too bad we can't use a bit of it."

"What? You asked me to develop alternative scenarios and I've given you *three*—her alone, him alone, or, my favorite, the two acting in concert. He's got a B and E past, she's as sullen and angry a teen as I've ever met. And she's six blocks away the night it happens, a fact that she has kept to herself."

"Do you really think Alanna took her baby brother with her to murder her father?"

"You're not paying me to think. You're paying me to develop new information. This is a gold mine. What did the police say when you told them?"

"I didn't. We work for Melisandre, not the city of Baltimore. And she's furious. She asked me if I thought there was any circumstance under which she would implicate one of her daughters. Her only goal now is to clear her name so she can have custody of those girls."

"Aren't you obligated to tell the cops what Sandy and I found out?"

"All you found out is that Alanna left the house Friday night and went out for pizza."

Tess wanted to throw a Carla Scout–style tantrum. It was infuriating to have this information discarded. And possibly unethical. Wasn't it Tyner's responsibility to overrule his client when she wasn't making decisions in her best interest?

"This is crazy." Tyner glared, and Tess realized her gaffe. "I mean, not *crazy*, but— No, sorry, *crazy* is the best word. I did exactly what you asked and now it's not right? This is like some damn fairy tale where a mercurial princess keeps changing the rules."

"Tess—even if you had something more substantial, think about it from Melisandre's point of view. She's not going to save herself at her daughter's expense. If anything, she might lie to protect her daughter. She could even be withholding key information."

"You can't allow that."

"No. And as things progress, if we end up going to trial—then I'll do my best to persuade her that there is no gain in her trying to paper over these facts. But we have to drop this for now. Forget Alanna."

"I should at least talk to her about that night. After all, she's also the person who can ascertain where Felicia was, and when."

"Stay away from Alanna and Ruby. Those are Melisandre's orders, and you work for her."

"Fine. She still owes me for the time that I put in, right?"

"Of course she does. She's not contesting your billable hours, just asking that we leave her children alone. How much time have you put in this week?"

Tess pretended to do a swift calculation on her iPhone. "Ninety hours and about three thousand miles."

"Very funny, Tess."

"It's hell finding parking in East Baltimore. I don't know how many times we circled the block."

"I understand you're upset. But, for now, concentrate on other things. Melisandre has suggested you talk to Ethan, Stephen's best friend. When he was interviewed for the documentary, he indicated he's not as close to Stephen as he was. Who knows what he might say?"

"Okay. Maybe I should go through all the documentary interviews and notes then—"

"*No.*" Tyner's tone was sharp, even by his standards. "I mean, I just don't want to open that can of worms yet. The state's attorney's office hasn't requested them."

"But they will," Tess said. "And we'll need to know what's on them."

"Harmony can brief me on that. Just go to talk to this guy Hinerman."

"What about the interview with Stephen?"

"Harmony transcribed it. He gives a two-minute statement, saying he will not be participating in the documentary, but wishing Missy well."

"Okay, but—"

"Jesus, Tess, stop second-guessing me. I know what I'm doing."

Tess didn't doubt that Tyner knew what he was doing. She was less sure of Melisandre. But she was being paid, so she went home and did as instructed. Made an appointment with Ethan Hinerman, read his interview, then watched it using an encrypted Internet link that Melisandre had provided. The interview seemed flat on paper, but *seeing* it— She watched it again. There was something pulling at her memory, but it wasn't about Melisandre. No, there was another case, another mistrial. And Hinerman contradicted himself on a small but telling detail. Of course, people got stuff wrong all the time. But they got it wrong in the same way. He got it wrong twice within seconds. Where had he found the file of papers?

After Carla Scout went to sleep, Tess sat in her own bed, laptop on her stomach, and Googled various search strings, each more horrific than the last. Strange to fall asleep in the middle of such a task, but it had been a long day. Hours later, she awakened to Crow's concerned face—he clearly had seen the article on her screen, was possibly contemplating a call to social services. But Tess was instantly awake, jumping up so suddenly that she had to catch her laptop to keep it from sliding to the floor.

"Nailed, him!" she crowed to Crow. "NAILED HIM."

Wednesday

Ethan Hinerman's office was in a mildly run-down block of Cathedral Street. The trash-strewn street depressed Tess. Baltimore had always had a scruffy side, but it had felt vibrant, a lovable mutt of a city ready to play or brawl. Now swaths of downtown were being replaced by apartments and condos, but there seemed to be fewer and fewer *people* downtown. Definitely fewer jobs. Hinerman was a holdout, someone who hadn't decamped for a suburban office with convenient parking, and property records showed this elegant brownstone as his residence as well. She should like him for that.

Inside, the first-floor office was gracious and well kept. An anxious or depressed person might start to feel better just sitting in this waiting room, with its working fireplace, lush rug, deep, soft armchairs. Oh, and new magazines! Tess, who was fifteen minutes early for the appointment she had arranged this morning, grabbed a *People* with someone on the cover whom she didn't even recognize. This was happening more and more, and not because Tess lived in some rarefied cultural bubble. Now if a Wonder Pet had been on the cover— she opened the magazine, enjoying the fire's warmth, reviewing her day in her head. Carla Scout went to day care on Wednesdays, then was picked up by Tess's mother, then was taken to the house. Or was it the babysitter? Tess had to get to the dry cleaner's before it closed today—*never mind, read about the pretty people even if you don't know them.*

The next thing she knew, someone was shaking her shoulder. Jesus, she had fallen asleep. This chair was really comfortable.

Ethan Hinerman, bigger and shaggier than he had appeared on Tess's laptop, was at the stage of life where his beard was outpacing his hair. The beard was thick and almost entirely red, while the hair on his head was thinning and running to more of a mousy brown with gray at the temples. He wore what Tess thought of as hyper-stylized preppy garb—a bright green-and-white-checked shirt, a bow tie, a brown tweed jacket with elbow patches. Old Baltimore. As opposed to the Full Towson, which was white belts and white shoes.

"Tess Monaghan?" he asked. "Don't worry, you're not the first person to fall asleep here."

"Are therapists' waiting rooms supposed to be so comfortable?"

"I don't know about other therapists. I want people who come to see me to associate our time together with good things, pleasant things. Because, in the end, it should be positive."

"Yeah, well—" Tess wasn't about to confide that her only time in a therapist's office had been court-ordered. "Given the parking situation in this neighborhood, that's a good idea. I had to park over on Hamilton. I don't understand why there are so many cars when there seem to be fewer and fewer people."

"I've wondered that myself," he said, leading her into his office. This room was even more beautiful, with another fireplace, although no fire. "I've been here for twenty-five years. When I first started working here, I could walk to Louie's Bookstore for lunch or get takeout from Sascha's. I'm such a Baltimorean that I still think of Donna's as being the new place—and the Mount Vernon location closed years ago. I think I used to see you in the bar at the Brass Elephant. Ah, well, I can still walk to the library. And Iggies pizza."

"I love Iggies," Tess said, still trying to find her equilibrium. It was humiliating, being awakened by someone she was interviewing. But maybe it would lower his guard. "So—Melisandre Dawes."

"She still uses that name?"

"She prefers the full handle, Melisandre Harris Dawes, but yes. She still uses her ex-husband's name. I understand you were his friend, go all the way back to Gilman with him."

"Yes, but I didn't really have a relationship with Melisandre."

"And why did you assume I was going to ask that?"

"Because—well—you work for her, right? Work for her lawyer. And this is clearly about her trial—"

His fumbled words helped her recover, find her footing in the conversation.

"I'm here because Melisandre suggested I speak to you."

"Why?"

"I haven't a clue. She told me to watch the interview you taped for the documentary. I did. Seemed pretty ordinary to me."

"Oh, that. Yes, I agreed to speak for the record. As a favor to Stephen."

"A favor to him?"

"Yes."

"Yet you say in the interview that you're not close anymore?"

"Did I?"

"Your exact words were, I believe, 'literally and figuratively.' Full props for using those terms correctly. Go, Gilman."

"Well, thank you. I guess." She had thrown him off his stride. Gilman boys were allowed a certain mock humility, but others were supposed to be awed by their alma mater. "Yes, Stephen remarried and moved to the suburbs. He's in a different phase of his life. Was. I still can't quite believe he's gone."

"What did you think of him marrying someone younger?"

"I thought it was his business. And that he should get a prenup. Not that he asked me."

"Because you no longer spoke?"

"You make it sound as if there were a feud. It was nothing like that."

"No, Melisandre made it sound as if there were a feud. She's the one who suggested I speak to you, after all. Based on the video. Man, she must have been furious with you back then. When you testified against her."

"No, not really."

"No?"

"Melisandre understood why I felt I had to testify. That it wasn't malicious or perjury. Just an error."

"Are you familiar with the Andrea Yates case? She went to trial several months before Melisandre did. The woman who killed all five of her children?"

"Vaguely."

"You know what's really interesting? She got a mistrial, too, the first time around."

"Really?"

"The state's expert witness, a psychiatrist, testified that there had been a *Law & Order* episode in which a woman used postpartum psychosis to disguise a homicide. But there was no such episode. In Yates's case, the evidence didn't come out until after the trial and she won a new trial three years later, in 2005. In Melisandre's case you testify Thursday, and, boom, her attorney has the goods to contradict you on Friday. Mistrial on Monday."

"Was that the timing? I think I testified on a Wednesday?"

"Oh, so you think that's what matters? The calendar?"

"Well, speaking of the calendar—if you're trying to link the two things, that makes no sense. Melisandre's trial was in 2003. You said the Yates conviction was thrown out on appeal in 2005."

"But it came to light before the sentencing phase in Yates's trial in 2002. The mistrial was requested then."

"Then I guess Melisandre's lawyer had followed the Yates trial closely."

"Okay, let me see if I understand what you're saying: Melisandre's lawyer follows the Yates case closely. Sure, that makes sense. So when a psychiatrist—"

"I'm a family therapist. And I testified as a friend of the family, not an expert witness."

"So when a therapist—excuse me, a family friend, although you said you weren't really Melisandre's friend—when the *husband*'s friend testifies that he saw this folder of newspaper clippings, Melisandre's lawyer immediately finds it suspect, does the research, and contradicts the witness in cross the next day."

"It was a famous incident, the one I described. Melisandre's lawyer was the mother of two small children, a harried professional not unlike the woman in the article. She remembered it well."

"Huh. Wow. Well, lucky for Melisandre, right, that you went into all that detail about the one case? Or was she the one who got lucky? I mean, you were Stephen's friend, not hers. But she was the one who benefited from your testimony. Or was she?"

"I'm not sure, I can't— Look, it was a mistake. An honest mistake. I didn't commit perjury."

"Yeah, I'd say that, too, because there's no statute of limitations on perjury in a criminal trial in Maryland." Tess was only 75 percent sure of this information. It didn't matter. What mattered was what Hinerman said next.

"Yes, I know."

Bingo. "Why?"

"Well, because, because it came up in some other context. With a client."

She nodded and smiled at him in the fakest way possible. "I'm sure it did. Anyway, false statement, mistrial requested, mistrial granted. I guess Baltimore judges are a little more liberal than Texas ones, and a folder of newspaper clippings is worse than just saying a TV show aired. Shows more intent, planning. If such a folder ever existed."

"It did. I mean—I was told—" He was smart enough to correct himself in midsentence. "I saw it."

"You were told that it existed." Tess tried to assume the comforting, confiding pose that came so naturally to Hinerman. "Hey, I know you can't undo what was done. But being truthful now counts for a lot. I'll protect you to the extent that we can. Just tell the truth."

Hinerman sighed and tented his hands, speaking more to his fingers than to Tess. "Stephen told me about the folder, said he couldn't bear to be the one who testified about it. He told me he had been so upset that he had thrown it away, but he briefed me on what was in it. Article after article about women harming their children, under all sorts of circumstances. He said I could call the prosecutor, say I had just remembered it. It was for his daughters, you see? He couldn't bear to be the one who offered the testimony against their mother. That's what he said and I believed him. I gave the testimony. And the next day, I was sandbagged. I had no idea that the dates were wrong. I had trusted Stephen's memory."

"Is that why your friendship with Stephen fell apart?"

"No, not then. I assumed it was an honest mistake on his part. It was only later—really, only a few years ago—that I realized why Stephen needed me to testify, why he set me up. Alanna was on the witness list. Alanna was going to testify."

They said that last time. Tess saw Alanna, standing in the doorway. Now she understood.

"And he wanted to spare her that?"

"He wanted to spare himself. Alanna had seen him having sex with the nanny. Then told her mother. Stephen didn't want that to come out. Not his image, you know? He'd rather suppress relevant information about his wife's intent than let the world know that he cheated on her. But I didn't figure that out until a few years ago."

"How?"

"In my experience, a lie can be like a tiny seed lodged in a tooth. You can't see it, you barely feel it, but there's always this sense that something's off, that the pieces don't fit. And then one day, it falls out and you think, *Oh, that was it.* Around the time when Stephen decided to remarry, I counseled him to get a prenup with Felicia. He was offended, but I was just trying to look after Alanna's and Ruby's interests. He said something about how this was real love, not like the other times, and I thought, *What other times?* He could have been referring to his dating life, but he hadn't been serious about anyone since his marriage ended. Then I realized there must have been someone during the marriage, maybe several someones. I asked him point-blank, and he admitted it. He denied that he had set me up at the trial, but I knew. I knew. It was so obvious all of a sudden. How could Stephen have confused that sequence of events?"

"So you're pretty angry with your old friend."

"*Disappointed,* I think, is the better word. I don't blame him for having an affair. But his cowardice, his willingness to manipulate a trial for his benefit, with no interest in what the truth of the matter was—I found that sad. He pulled every string he had for Melisandre's retrial—wrote a letter on her behalf to the judge, paid for the experts who supported the diagnosis of postpartum psychosis."

"You know I have to ask where you were Friday night."

"At a very boring professional dinner at the Sheraton in Towson, one where I was in full view for the evening. I gave the keynote."

"Sorry." Tess gave him a lopsided smile. "Just doing my job. It's interesting, what you've told me, but I can't decide if it's helpful. I mean, if Stephen set you up as you suspect, that was good for Melisandre, right? As you said, Alanna's testimony would have created the case for intent, a revenge killing of a sort. Could he have been so coldhearted that he would have let his wife slide on homicide just to keep his reputation intact?"

"I don't know. At one time, I would have told you that Stephen was incapable of that kind of deviousness. But, at one time, I would have told you that Stephen would never expose his oldest friend to a perjury charge. Maybe he rationalized that it was okay, as long as he was going to have full custody of the children. Maybe he told himself it was in their best interest. Miss Monaghan—"

"Um, Ms. But Tess is fine."

"There's one more thing I should probably tell you."

In Tess's experience, one more thing was usually the most boring, irrelevant thing in the world. But she brightened with what she hoped was plausible enthusiasm.

"Yes?"

"I'm not the only person who figured this out. Alanna did, too."

"When?" *Not last week, not last week, not last week.*

"She came to see me Thursday—"

Tess lost a few words then to the part of her brain screaming, *Oh, Jesus fucking Christ.*

"She came here, to the office. She asked me point-blank about the mistrial."

"But who told her? Or did she figure it out like you did?"

"Stephen had told her that Melisandre had 'sold' the girls to him after she was acquitted, taken a lump sum and agreed to leave, never see them again. But Alanna saw how he benefited. She believes the real story is that he paid her mother never to speak of the affair."

"Was she angry?"

"More sad, I would say. She kept asking me, 'How could they do it?'"

"Do what?"

"Put her in that position, at such a young age. I told her that her father was thinking of her, too, that it was better that she never testified. What if her mother had been found guilty? How would a five-year-old make sense of it? Whatever her father's motives, it was for the best."

"Did she believe you?"

A sad smile. "No."

Tess went back outside. She'd have to tell Tyner eventually, sooner than eventually, but she didn't have the heart for such a conversation today. She rounded the corner onto the tiny, secret lane of Hamilton where she had parked. There was a piece of paper on her windshield. *Fuck. Again?* She was almost relieved to find a ticket, even though she knew she had put enough money in the meter. The meter had shortchanged her. She could contest the ticket, ask for a trial, but that would mean trading a half day of her time to fight a thirty-two-dollar fine. Hard not to think the city had figured that out.

God, she hated the new meters. But a thirty-two-dollar fine was better than being called a crap mother by a stranger. Assuming the person was a stranger. In her darkest moments, Tess feared it was someone who knew her all too well.

4:00 P.M.

Harmony's phone issued a single bell-like tone, the sound she used for signal alerts and push functions. She glanced at the display while continuing to pack. A file had landed from the transcription company. So what? The project was dead, as dead as— But that was in bad taste. She couldn't be angry at Stephen Dawes for being dead. And having watched Melisandre's interview with him, Harmony was pretty sure that Melisandre hadn't killed him. The "interview" had been useless, way too short. It was also about as dispassionate as anything Harmony had ever seen. For exes, those two had zero chemistry. Harmony should have taken a firmer stand on Melisandre's participation. It was one thing for her to conduct that interview with her lawyer. Strange and uncomfortable as that footage was, it wasn't central to the film. Sure, it established that she had gone to see him before driving to the boathouse, but it also had established a pattern—Melisandre had left baby Isadora in the car at every stop that morning. At the school, outside Tyner's office, in the boathouse parking lot. Who cared what Carolyn Sanders thought she saw? That was all hindsight, a self-involved young woman's attempt to heighten her connection to something big, and thereby make herself more important. Melisandre had been disturbed enough to leave a sleeping child in the car everywhere she went that day. It hadn't mattered at the school, where she was parked briefly, or at Tyner's office, where she evidently used a garage. But there was a consistency in her strange behavior. And, in this case, the consistency established her insanity. A woman intent on homicide via neglect, then faking insanity—that woman probably would have had the child with her on those two previous visits. She wouldn't have risked a concerned citizen busting her before she could execute her plan.

But it didn't matter what Harmony thought. It never had, really. Since Melisandre had been charged with homicide, the cable vultures were circling. They both agreed there was no room for the kind of project they had planned over tea in a London hotel suite. Harmony had tendered her resignation yesterday, over the phone.

Melisandre had made a perfunctory attempt to dissuade her, even pretended that they might resume the film. "Once this is over," she said, although it sounded like false bravado to Harmony's ear. "Meanwhile, what do I do, with the files, everything that Tyner's little friend gathered up?"

"Whatever you want, Melisandre. The material is yours. You paid for it. You paid for me, too, but I was just a loaner."

If anything was over, it was Harmony's comeback. Back to Inwood, back to waitressing until she could find a gig. Maybe she would start looking for a job in reality television.

And yet—the notification from the transcription app lured her back to her new laptop. She perched on the bed, clicked on the Dropbox icon, began watching the unedited footage again. *This could have been something special.*

Harmony had been surprised by Tess Monaghan's naïveté. She didn't expect Tyner Gray to be particularly tech savvy. An unfair stereotype of an older man, perhaps, but a true one in her experience. Even Melisandre had interesting gaps in her skill set, a consequence, Harmony had assumed, of having too many people doing things for her over the years. Melisandre could be flummoxed by a digital thermostat. She had actually called Tyner and asked him to explain how to work the one in her apartment.

But Tess wasn't that much older than Harmony. Besides, Harmony had essentially told Tess that everything that had been recorded on various devices was also in the so-called cloud. Tess had to know that Dropbox would be accessible to Harmony on any computer, that it would be there when she got a new phone and accessed her account. Physical possession meant nothing in the digital age.

Only—when she tried to go back to the new footage, still in the cloud, it turned out the password to the Dropbox account had already been changed. *Wow, Melisandre, that's a little cold.* But Harmony had told her to do this when they met over lunch today. At least Melisandre had sent her out in style, over a bottle of champagne at the Wit & Wisdom.

She went into Netflix and watched her second documentary, but not before reading the comments. "Condescending." "Patronizing, racist, classist." "Lorita's quinceañero deserved to be captured by someone who wasn't sniggering at this dim-but-sweet Hispanic family as if she had discovered the Telemundo version of *Here Comes Honey Boo Boo.*"

"It's in the editing" is, of course, the first line of defense for the wronged reality television star—but it was also true in this case. Harmony had been given a big budget to make her second doc. But the studio had essentially taken it away from her in editing, making this mishmash. She had no recourse. She could have taken her name off it, gone the Alan Smithee route, but her agent persuaded her that would be career suicide. She still ended up dead, career-wise.

She pulled up the e-mail Melisandre had sent Friday night, which had included the clip with Stephen. Melisandre also couldn't figure out how to upload a video on her own, so she had sent them as attachments. Two minutes. Two dull, unnecessary minutes. Why had she even wanted to film Stephen? Melisandre had been back and forth on the issue of the affair. She wanted it in, she wanted it out. She wanted it in but didn't want to involve Alanna. Harmony understood it was a spiky topic, but they could have gotten more out of Stephen than this say-nothing two-minute *statement.*

Two minutes—she glanced at the clock. She had lost too much time to her little mournful memory walk. She would have to rush to make the 5:30 train.

11:15 P.M.

Tess was still amazed by how motherhood had changed her hearing. She could hear Carla Scout sigh in her sleep yet was capable of sleeping through a car accident in front of her house. Literally. A car had driven into a tree directly across the street and she had not heard a thing.

The ringing telephone fell somewhere in between, rousing her by the third or fourth ring. She had fallen asleep in a chair, reading.

Tess glanced at the clock—11:15 P.M. Not necessarily a scary, world-ending phone call, but an urgent one.

"You didn't answer your cell," Tyner said.

"Hello to you, too." The iPhone was on the table next to her, its face blank. "It's out of juice. I forgot to charge it. What's up?"

"There's no easy way to say this, so—you're fired."

"What the—?"

"I'm sorry, but Melisandre is adamant. She believes you went behind her back and—well, no one can convince her otherwise. Knowing you, I doubt you did it, but it doesn't matter. She wants you off her case and I can't overrule her."

"Tyner, I still don't know what I allegedly did."

"Leaked to the *Beacon-Light*. Melisandre has a Google alert, and the story went live about a half hour ago."

"I didn't tell them about Alanna."

"No, and Alanna's not mentioned in the story, which is the only reason *I'm* not fired. But everything else is there—the anonymous notes, including the content, the incident with the trainer. Maybe she'll cool down, Tess, but—I doubt it."

"I didn't do it. I didn't do anything." Tess remembered Sandy mentioning his friendship with a reporter at the *Blight*. No, he would never take such action without consulting her.

"I believe you, Tess. But Melisandre doesn't, and that's all that matters for now."

She heard a woman's voice in the background.

"Wait, are you there right now? Is that Melisandre or Kitty? Put Melisandre on the phone and let me talk to her."

"I don't think that's the best idea right now. She's terribly upset."

That makes two of us, Tess thought, hanging up. She should be glad to be off the job. Melisandre was self-destructive, determined to ignore the growing evidence against her own daughter. And she was quick to fire people—look at Brian, the bodyguard, who had been fired after the incident with the trainer.

Look at Brian—yes, look at him. *He* knew about the notes. He knew about Silas. He could be the source. What had been his full name? Hell, Silas could be the source. Or Harmony.

They had all signed that nondisclosure pact, Tess remembered. The one Melisandre had wanted her to sign, and Tess had refused. And Tess was the one who kept finding links to Alanna. That had to be her real crime. Not talking to the press, but getting too close to the truth.

11:30 P.M.

Ruby was not supposed to be on her computer after ten. But that had been her father's rule. Felicia didn't care. Felicia didn't care about her at all. Felicia wanted to be her guardian just because of the money. Alanna said it didn't matter who their guardian was. She was out of here in a year. Well, it mattered to Ruby. She had three more years until she was eighteen.

She read the story again. How could her mother not have recognized the source of those notes? True, taken out of context, read one at a time, they might not jar one's memories. But Ruby recognized them instantly. The familiar sentences washed over her as a series of colors—green, blue, yellow. The light slanting through the window, a soft rug underfoot. She always thought she had no memories of those times, yet here one was, at last. For so long, she had yearned to remember something, anything, from the before time.

Now she had, and it was the worst thing that had ever happened to her.

What should she do? What was right? What was best for everyone? Who deserved her loyalty? She wished she could unknow things. People joked about bleaching their brains all the time now. If only that were possible. She had been warned, eavesdroppers hear no good of themselves. But it wasn't what she knew about herself that was the problem.

Ruby wished she were a baby again. She would be the sweetest baby in the world, a child so sweet and lovable that her parents wouldn't dare to have another one because the new baby could never be as wonderful as she was. They would still live in the yellow-brick house, just the four of them. No Isadora, no Felicia. No Joey, either, but so it goes. She would trade her little brother to have her family back, intact. But all she kept doing was splintering it. She had lost a sister, a father. Now she was going to lose someone else, but who would it be? There was no end to it, no end.

Part III

Thursday

10:30 A.M.

Tess sat at Golden West, looking at the *Beacon-Light,* rereading the story she had read online the night before. On this, her seventh or eighth read, it was, to her eyes, relatively innocuous. Yes, it included the incident with Silas, which wasn't good for Melisandre's defense. Not calling 911, seeking private treatment for him. That did look weird. What if the same thing had happened with Stephen? Say he slipped and went through the doors and Melisandre had this bizarre PTSD reaction, then panicked because she realized no one would believe her, so she slipped away. Given the nature of his injury, he would have died very quickly.

But the article also mentioned the notes, and that seemed like a plus to Tess. The notes established that someone had been harassing *Melisandre.* That would be another foothold in Tyner's defense. Someone was stalking her. And it was fair to think the sugar was meant for her. Was it not reasonable to assume that person had gone to her old house and found Stephen there? Okay, it was a coincidence that almost groaned under its own weight, but defense attorneys were allowed coincidences, given that life was full of them.

Besides, Tess felt a reluctant sisterhood with anyone on the receiving end of cryptic, vaguely sinister notes.

Tyner knew there was no way Tess was the "source close to Melisandre Harris Dawes," as the article had it. But the lady was on a tear. And Tyner had to placate Melisandre—*Missy*—for now. And while Tess should have been relieved to be relieved of the job, instead she was incensed. She had already raged to Tyner, then Crow. Now it was her best friend's turn to hear her lament.

"No spawn?" Whitney asked when she arrived.

"Daddy took over at ten," Tess said. Then, in that kind of confessional gush that one's best friends can inspire: "He's better with her than I am. He never loses his patience."

"You're too hard on yourself," Whitney said. Surprising. Whitney Talbot, who had probably been voted least likely to spawn by her graduating class at Roland Park Country School, was not celebrated for her empathy. But in the past few years she had been softening. No, not softening, but smoothing out a little. Supervising her family's foundation had introduced a vein of kindness into this superhuman creature, who found failure incomprehensible. Certainly, being rich and intelligent was no guarantee of success, but Whitney honestly did not understand how anyone who tried could end up failing. It had been bizarrely comforting, when Tess Monaghan was waist-deep in failure, that Whitney refused to believe Tess couldn't turn things around. Comforting and frustrating. The concept of "too hard" on oneself was not something Whitney would have expressed even two or three years ago. She was the friend who told you to stop whining, slap on a helmet, and get into the game. And yes, she said "helmet," not big-girl panties.

Still, Tess felt tentative talking about her struggles with motherhood to her happily childless friend. "No one tells you that it's, well, kind of boring. Being a mom."

"Did you expect to be in thrall all the time?"

"I didn't know what to expect. Maybe I should have read *What to Expect When You're Expecting*." Tess, ordered on bed rest, had read novels while pregnant. She had tried to read a couple of baby manuals but decided she would rather read classic horror novels or watch horror films in which aliens burst out of orifices that bore an uncanny resemblance to Georgia O'Keeffe paintings. At least Shirley Jackson was honest about her desire to scare the piss out of people. The baby books claimed to be about joy and anticipation but specialized in fear and anxiety.

"My parents are going to his funeral," Whitney said. "Dawes, I mean." Now that was the old Whitney, changing the subject when she became bored.

"When is it?" Tess asked.

"Not until Sunday."

"WASPs," Tess said.

"I know."

Their food came, and Whitney picked at her Elvis, pancakes served with peanut butter and bananas. Food did not really interest her. Tess, who had chosen an abstemious egg-white omelet, eyed Whitney's plate with undisguised yearning, then summoned the waitress and asked for a side of *sopapillas*.

"Back to Melisandre. *We* know you're not the source," Whitney said. "It's got to be the bodyguard, don't you think? She fired him. She's quick to do that, isn't she? She likes to fire people. Why not make an anonymous call to the newspaper if you're that guy?"

"Or Harmony. Yet Harmony is the one who's given us the best leg up in defending Melisandre, by providing that videotape that shows her having a perfectly civilized exchange with Stephen. Well, not *us*, not anymore. But as long as Melisandre refuses to use the information about Alanna—no, I can't see Harmony doing it. The classy thumb sucker of a film she envisioned is now just one big Nancy Grace three-ring circus. That's why she quit. Doesn't matter if the charges against Melisandre are dropped and Alanna is charged. It won't save the film. Besides, the source didn't mention Alanna, or her boyfriend. The source had the contents of the notes and the incident with Silas. Who else knows about that?"

"The person who wrote the notes, and the person who put the date rape drug in the sugar bowl. That person knows. Will the reporter at least confirm that you didn't tip him off? He could do that, ethically. Tell Melisandre you're not the source, but not reveal who the source is."

"Sandy called him for me," Tess said. "He said he couldn't help me even if he wanted to, because he doesn't know his source. He received a letter at the paper, then played that game where you call someone and say, 'So, will I be wrong if . . .' Melisandre, for all her sophistication, got took. She thought she bluffed him, but she was wrong. She ended up confirming everything in the letter. On the record, yet. Oh, well, there wasn't that much for me to do, anyway. I'm not allowed to talk to Alanna or Ruby."

"Allowed? If you're fired, I guess you can do whatever you like, right? Meanwhile, if the source was anonymous, that makes it more likely it's someone who signed a nondisclosure statement, no?"

Tess smiled. "I knew there was a reason I have you in my life, Talbot."

"Yeah, now remind me why I have you in mine."

"To eat your leftovers," Tess said, spearing a triangle of Whitney's barely touched pancakes.

Noon

When Tess suggested that Sandy chat up the fired security guard, she said it would go better "mano a mano." She probably meant one to one, or man to man, not hand to hand, but Sandy would never point that out. Besides, in his mind, the real significance was that it was cop to cop. Even if Brian had been a crappy cop—and that was Sandy's hunch—the two spoke yet another language. Tess got that. So he would do the cop, she would do the trainer.

Brian was also someone who had witnessed Melisandre in a moment of crisis, when her trainer was doped. The obvious answer is the obvious answer. If Romeo and Juliet hadn't decided to take the dad out, still Sandy's preferred scenario, then Melisandre was the only possibility. He understood that Tyner didn't want to build a defense on post-traumatic stress or anything psychological. But it might be all they had.

Brian Griffin was easy enough to find. He lived in the kind of suburban apartment complex that screamed Divorced Dad. White brick, a series of three-story buildings, divided into two stairwells with six units per stairwell. Brian lived in a "garden" unit, which meant going down a half flight.

"What do you want?" he asked at the door. Not surprised, but not expecting Sandy, either. Kind of beyond caring who came to his door. No dark suit today, but jeans with a crease and a Ban-Lon knit top, well-shined loafers. A cop at heart, Sandy thought, looking at the glow on those slip-ons. Cared about appearances.

"Wanted to ask you a few questions about our gal."

"Not my gal. Not even my boss now. As you probably know, she fired my ass."

"Unfairly, seems to me," Sandy said. He had followed Brian into the living room. It should have been a good thing, having one wall of sliding glass doors overlooking the pool, but it limited where the furniture could go, so the room was kind of awkward. Still, Brian had a view of the pool. He probably told himself that a lot. "I have a view of the pool." Brian took the Papa Bear seat, the wide, comfortable-looking easy chair, let Sandy perch on the small sofa.

"She blamed me. For the breach. The thing with the sugar bowl.

I just think she figured she didn't need me anymore, once she moved into the apartment."

"So why not give you your notice, let it be all peaceful?"

He shrugged. "Nobody knows what goes on in that head of hers. But if I had to guess? She's one of those people who likes there to be someone to blame. She can't stand for stuff to just happen. I tell you, sometimes I felt sorry for those kids of hers. Had to be hell to have her as a mom."

"Yeah?" Very casual. But if Sandy were a superhero—which he was very clear he was not—he would have said his Spidey senses were tingling.

"I broke a cup. A *cup*. And she was, like, gray. She really had to fight that temper of hers."

Okay, the defense probably would not be calling Brian Griffin to the stand.

"So was she angry at the kid who broke her sugar bowl?"

"I wasn't there. But I guess if you have a seizure, you're exempt from the wrath of Queen Melisandre. Maybe I should have tried that. Hey, maybe he faked it, knowing what a nut job she was. High maintenance doesn't begin to describe it."

There was a familiar tone to the guy's talk, but it took Sandy a moment to process it. He knew this. He had heard this kind of talk before. Where? A Spanish word popped into his head, as it did from time to time, leapfrogging over that divide in his mind, the separation between his time in Cuba and his time here. The Cuba portion of his life was all but forgotten, in part because it had been painful, those memories of his parents, whom he left behind, thinking he would see them soon. They died in a car accident a few months after he arrived in the United States. But every now and then, a memory broke through. It was like a slant of light, bright and golden. *Escuela,* his mind whispered to him. *Escuela.* This guy was like a boy in school, saying a girl was too thin or too fat, when all he wanted was to walk home with her, hold her hand.

"You liked her," Sandy said.

Brian looked out the sliding glass doors. "I didn't mind her. Too much. Until she fired me for something that wasn't even my fault. She just wanted to exercise the clause in which she didn't have to pay me two weeks' wages. She was cheap in some ways."

"You *liked* her liked her."

"I did not." But the tone was still there.

"You the one who went to the newspaper?"

Brian waved an arm at his surroundings. "Do I look like someone who can afford to get pissy and risk a hundred-K fine? Because that was the penalty for violating her confidentiality agreement. Maybe if I hit Coinstar." He patted a large jar of change at his side, which doubled as his end table. More copper than silver in it.

"You were a cop. Vice, right? You know how to play the game. All you had to do was feed Herman Peters the info that he printed, tell him not to disclose your identity."

"I wouldn't pick up a phone to yell at a reporter about my newspaper delivery, much less help one out. You're way off base."

"Has anyone been to see you to talk to you about the murder, your boss's temperament?"

"Only you, Sanchez. So far. And if your employer—once our employer—needs me to go on a long vacation, that could be arranged."

Another tingle. "You were dirty, weren't you? That's why you didn't make your twenty. That's why you live in this shithole and work private security, even though you're not much good at it. Something went down and they just turned you loose, quietly."

"Weren't we all a little dirty? If you get down to brass tacks?"

"I wasn't."

"Good for you. I'm supporting two households. And I'm not like you."

"What do you mean?"

"Gossip cuts two ways. You know I didn't make my twenty. Well, I also didn't make the state support my kid when it turned out he was a retard."

Sandy counted to ten, in both his languages. So there it was, the judgment he was always afraid to face. This is why he didn't talk about family stuff with Tess. Yet now that he had heard the dreaded words from Brian, they hurt less than he had thought they would. He remembered his wife, going to her parents and begging them to help pay for the institutional placement that Bobby Junior needed after he all but killed Mary. He thought about his son, whom he had stopped going to see because, since Mary died, they simply had no connection. She had held them together. She was what had made them a family and, once she was gone, it was as if there had never been a family at all. Sandy stood, smoothed his tie, shot his cuffs. He still dressed like a murder police. He still had his pride.

"You liked her," he repeated. "You were jealous of anyone who was close to her. Maybe you did the trainer. Maybe you did the husband."

"Don't be stupid."

"You want to tell me where you were Friday night?"

"I don't want to tell you shit, beaner."

Beaner. Guy couldn't even get his ethnic slurs right.

"Well, I have things to do. You know how it is, when you have a *job*. Oh, wait—you don't." Sandy took out his business card, placed it on top of the jar of coins. "I hear the Harem down on the Block is looking for a bouncer. Feel free to use me as a reference, I'd be happy to say you're not the biggest asshole I've ever met."

3:30 P.M.

Alanna sat in front of her car outside the Roland Park library. She wouldn't be able to stay there for long, even though she was out of uniform. Anyone who looked remotely school age got hassled by the librarians. Same at Eddie's across the street, which had a policy about how many kids could enter at one time. But she figured she wouldn't have to wait for long, and she looked old enough that someone would think twice before trying to play ad hoc truant officer. She might even be mistaken for a mother or babysitter, waiting to get in line for pickup. Because Ruby being Ruby, she wouldn't cut school to do whatever secret thing she was going to do.

Sure enough, here came Ruby, looking as furtive as all get-out. Kid had no game. She was trying so hard to look nonchalant as she walked down the street toward the bus stop. She must have checked the schedule, too, being Ruby, for the bus arrived only a minute or two after she took her post. Hell, Alanna could follow a bus. Anyone could follow a bus. The trick was not overtaking it. She meandered along, keeping back, not that Ruby would be looking for Alanna's car. Ruby thought her sister was at home, defiant in her ongoing school boycott, although Felicia still made Alanna take Ruby to school now that her parents had returned to Cumberland.

What Felicia had actually said was "I don't give a shit what you do, but you're going to take your sister to school because there's no way I can."

Back at you, Felicia. Love you, too.

It was during the drive this morning that Alanna had figured out something was up. During the drive and before, when she had gone through Ruby's backpack. Ruby was chattery, not at all her style. Just one inane comment after another, about music, her classmates, Alanna's college plans. *Did Alanna know that there were schools that recruited girls to row even if they had never rowed?* It was all about Title IX. On and on, and blah, blah, blah. Well, lying wasn't easy and Ruby was new at it.

Then she had said: "I won't need a ride today. I'm going over to Daisy's house, like the other day, and her mom will bring me home."

That's when Alanna knew Ruby had something on her mind that was neither benign nor banal. She went home, in part because it was too hard to kill a day on her own, but also because it was fun, walking out the door that afternoon with Felicia yelling that she was still grounded.

When she saw Ruby get on a bus headed for downtown, she thought her sister might be going to the old house. But why would she do that? Probably couldn't even get in it now. Felicia said they would sell the house, although not for a while, and it might not get as much as it should, given— Here Felicia had paused, struggled and, to Alanna's surprise, opted against the euphemism. "Given your father's murder," she'd said.

"It could have been an accident," Alanna told her. "We don't know what happened, right? Innocent until proven guilty?"

Felicia had just looked at her. "I'm pretty sure what happened."

It had been tempting, then, to tell Felicia what she didn't know about that night, how Alanna had sneaked out with baby Joey. She knew she wouldn't have any fun with her brother along for the ride, and she had been planning on getting caught eventually. What was the point of flouting her father's rules if her father didn't know? The idea had been to show him that he couldn't make her do anything— stay home, stop seeing Tony. She didn't even like Tony that much, but once her father had gotten wind of it and told her to stop seeing him, there was no way she could stop. Especially once she knew what she knew about her father.

Fine, Dad, she had thought that Friday night before heading out. *But if you want to keep someone in prison, you need to hire a few guards.* She left the house not even thirty minutes after Felicia did and beat her back by only an hour or so. Sure, Joey knew everything, but it wasn't like he could tell anyone.

But, no, Ruby wasn't going to Bolton Hill. The number 61 meandered on, into the city proper, and Ruby got out on Fayette Street, began walking east. Unfortunately, Fayette was a one-way street heading west. Alanna tried to figure out how to make a series of ever-smaller loops, so she would stay even with Ruby as she continued east, but the lights were against her. Where would Ruby go in this part of Baltimore? Alanna passed the courthouse, City Hall, that string of sad-silly strip clubs on Baltimore Street. Bail bondsmen.

Police headquarters.

No, Alanna reasoned. What could Ruby know? She didn't know anything. Did she? Her backpack. So that was that. She was going to show the police what she had in her backpack.

Alanna idled outside the building, trying to persuade herself that her sister had gone somewhere, anywhere else. What did Ruby know? What could Ruby know? What did Ruby think she knew? They were three different questions, in their way.

The Mercedes shot forward on Fayette, almost as if it had a mind of its own. Alanna wasn't sure where she was going. She only knew that she couldn't go home. She didn't have a home. If Ruby had turned against her, she truly was alone in this world.

4:00 P.M.

They made her wait awhile. Because she was fifteen, they said. They needed permission to talk to her. Who could give it?

"My mother," Ruby told them.

"Your stepmother?"

"My real mother. Although she doesn't have custody. Technically, no one has custody. I don't have a guardian. My father died without a will. But my mother is here in town. Somewhere."

"Do you know how to get in touch with her?"

"Not really. My dad—my dad knew."

More back-and-forth. They asked her again if she was sure she

wanted to make a statement, and that's when the confusion was finally resolved. It turned out that they thought she was here to *confess*.
No, no, she said. She just had information that she thought she should
share. Well, they could talk to her as long as she wasn't confessing.
No permission needed for that. Was she sure she wasn't trying to
confess?

"Very sure," she said. A confession would be so much easier than
what she had to do.

So finally, the two detectives sat opposite her. She knew all about
good cop, bad cop, but this was pretty much good cop, good cop.
They asked her if she wanted a soda, and she discovered that she did.
Orange. Why did she say orange? She never drank soda at all. That
was one battle Felicia had won. No soda in the house, ever. Ruby's
mouth was dry. She had been psyching herself up to do this for hours,
but now that the moment was here, it was like one of those dreams
where you open your mouth to scream and nothing comes out.

"What do you want to tell us, Ruby?" asked the handsome one,
Tull. He had a few acne scars, but they only made him more attractive, the way a flaw can, sometimes.

"You saw the paper? About the notes my mother has been getting? I told you—I know who's been sending them."

"Right. But it's not you. We need to be clear on this. You haven't
been a party to these notes."

"Is it against the law, sending notes like that?"

"Not exactly. But that's why we made you wait. If you are here to
admit to any criminal act, you need a legal representative. Because
you're under eighteen. But you are allowed to share material information with us."

"No, I had nothing to do with it. But I know who did."

"How?"

"Because I recognize the source. There's a pattern."

"A source? A pattern?"

"Yeah, I realized when I read the paper online last night."

"You read the paper? You're a very unusual fifteen-year-old kid."

Shit. That did sound weird. She thought fast. "Yeah. I am. I'm the daughter of a woman who killed her youngest child and now my dad has been murdered. You'd read the paper, too, I think."

"I probably would." He was agreeable, kind. The other cop was trying to arrange his features into a nice, agreeable face as well, but he wasn't as good at it. "So what did you see in the paper?"

"The notes. I know what they mean. Well, not mean, exactly. But I know who wrote them. Alanna. It has to be my sister, Alanna."

Nothing really changed at that moment. Perhaps the handsome detective slouched a little less, but there was nothing to indicate that what she had said was significant. Yet. Ruby knew it was.

"You know that how?"

"Because I know where the lines are from. They're from books, particular favorites of my mom's. Alanna read them to me after our mom was gone. I have four of them with me. I couldn't find the fifth."

And with that, Ruby took the books from her backpack. *The Lonely Doll. Curious George. Love You Forever. The Cat in the Hat Comes Back.* There were Post-its affixed to the key pages. The lines, reclaimed by the books, were at once more and less sinister. Curious George was in trouble for setting off a false alarm. The angry father in *Cat* would resent nothing more than the damage done to his suit. She didn't know why Alanna had sent those threatening notes to their mother. She wasn't sure what they were meant to achieve. After all, if Alanna wanted only for their mother to stay away, she had a powerful ally in their father. But Alanna was angry at Dad, too. They had fought furiously after he grounded her, although Ruby had caught only part of that quarrel.

"Alanna has a key. To our old house. She goes there. She doesn't think anyone knows. But I do."

"Was she there Friday night?"

"She could have been. I don't know. I think so, yes."

You have to follow your conscience. I can't tell you what to do. I know only what I must do.

Ruby looked at the old books. *Curious George* had been her favorite. *The Lonely Doll*—she understood that others found it creepy, but she never had. If you thought about it, *Curious George* was far creepier in the way it had glossed over the fact that the monkey was kidnapped, taken from his real parents, whoever they were, and raised by a man. What did the man in the yellow hat have to offer except for the yellow hat? How could George be happier with him? And how could someone not love the Cat in the Hat? He always cleaned up after his messes.

The truly creepy book, in Ruby's opinion, was *Love You Forever*. She knew it had been written by a man whose two children were stillborn. Alanna had told her that. And their mother had told Alanna. Still—creepy. The idea of your mother crawling through your window and holding you when you were an adult. Then growing up, doing the same thing to your mother.

"Where did you find the books?"

"They're mine." She showed them where she had printed her name in the books in big block letters, using a purple crayon. Ruby and the purple crayon. Alanna had used blue.

"Okay, so maybe your sister wrote the notes. That's interesting. But why do you think she was involved with this thing with your dad?"

This thing. Yeah, murder was a thing, all right. Ruby had not thought the police would make her say more, put it in words. She had hoped that all she had to do was put the books in front of them and they would do the rest.

"There were fights. Two. One Sunday, then another one Thursday night. I—I eavesdrop. I don't know why they were fighting, only that Alanna was mad at him. She said he was a liar, that he was always trying to control everything, but he couldn't control her."

"What was she talking about?"

"I don't know. She has a boyfriend. But I didn't think our dad knew that."

"Was Alanna in the city Friday night?"

Ruby swallowed hard. "I don't know. I had a sleepover. But she was home, alone, with baby Joey. And she did go out."

"How do you know that if you weren't there?"

"When I got back the next day and everything was so crazy? Joey's car seat was in Alanna's car. So she definitely went out with him at some point. Nobody else noticed. I mean—so much else was going on. But I saw it in her car and then, later, it was back in Felicia's car. When we had to go to the funeral home." She began to cry. "Can she go to the funeral? It's not until Sunday. Will you let her go to our dad's funeral even if she's under arrest for killing him?"

7:00 P.M.

The house phone rang, followed by the cell a few minutes later. Tess, who was sitting down to dinner with Carla Scout—a proper dinner, roast chicken and two vegetables, a dessert of fruit, and who cared if the chicken had been roasted by the grocery store?—tried to obey house protocol and ignore the phones. No screens at the table! She had been expecting a call from Sandy; they had been swapping voice mails about their equally futile interviews today. Brian was vile, but Sandy didn't think he was the leak. Silas the trainer was clearly starry-eyed about his former employer. What was it about Melisandre? She really was like a sorceress when it came to men. Like Circe, Tess thought, seeing Tyner's number on her screen.

Or Medea. Medea was a sorceress first.

"No phones at dinner, Mama," Carla Scout reminded her. Crow had empowered Carla Scout to say such things. Encouraged her, in fact.

"It's work, Carla Scout." Tess walked away with her phone.

"In this house," Carla Scout said, "we sit down when we eat." More of Crow's dogma.

"We try, Carla Scout. We try. But this is Mama's work."

Tyner had told her an hour ago about Ruby's visit to police headquarters. Tess had joked to Crow that maybe Ruby was going to be fired, too. But Ruby wasn't the source for the newspaper article, she was only reacting to it, offering up a piece of the puzzle. No, Ruby couldn't prove that Alanna had written the notes, but if she had— Well, the notes had started before the time that Alanna, according to Ethan Hinerman, had found out how her father and mother had used her as a pawn. It wasn't exactly logical to be angry at a long-missing parent for returning, but teenagers weren't known for being logical.

Alanna for her father's murder—that was logical. The working scenario now was that Alanna had gone downtown to see her boyfriend, become incensed when he blew her off, and then taken it into her head that it was her father's fault. She knew her father was at the old house because Felicia had told her. She drove over there, waited for her mother to leave, then went inside and confronted him. Maybe she planned it, maybe she didn't. Maybe he put his hands on her first. The cops were in no hurry to drop the charges against Melisandre, but they did want to talk to Alanna as soon as possible.

Problem was, Alanna hadn't come home today. She had sent a text to her stepmother, saying she was at a friend's house, failing to specify the friend.

"Have they found her?"

"Not yet. They've thrown the boyfriend in a room. He's adamant he wasn't there Friday night. Not budging off his story no matter what they offer him. But he admitted to getting a friend to deliver one of the notes."

"Do you think she assumed her mother would be blamed? And I still can't figure out how she does this with a kid in a car seat. I have trouble ordering a coffee, much less having a conversation with someone when Carla Scout is around."

"Maybe she left him in the car."

"No one would do that, Tyner."

"Someone might," he said with an odd laugh. "Of course, the fact that she's missing heightens police interest in her. Although we're playing it as not missing, just inconsiderate."

"How's Melisandre handling it?"

"Pretty well, all things considered. She's being her best self. She's upset, but her primary focus is to get Alanna whatever help she needs. I could tell she was appalled when she realized how juvenile law has changed in her time away. There's virtually no chance of anonymity for Alanna, not at age seventeen, not in a red ball like this. If she's charged, she'll be arraigned as an adult, then have to petition for juvenile standing."

"Tyner, I know this sounds flaky, but is there any chance they, well, collaborated on this? Mother and daughter?"

"Yes," Tyner said, his voice cold, "that *does* sound 'flaky.' Alanna hasn't spoken to her mother for more than a decade. And she was sending her threatening notes."

"Ruby *said*. It could be Ruby, you know. Ruby could have sent the notes, then blamed her sister."

"Except Ruby's whereabouts for Friday night are quite definite and she adores her sister."

Adores her so much she voluntarily went to the police and put her in for her father's murder. What would Tess have done in the same situation? Not having a sibling, she couldn't be sure. She couldn't even be sure what she would do if Carla Scout were in serious trouble. She wanted to believe that she would stand for principle. She feared she would Thelma and Louise it, only making sure that Carla Scout jumped out of the car before it headed into the Grand Canyon.

"Is there anything I can do?"

"Yes," Tyner said. "I'll need you tomorrow, no matter what. And Missy may still come around."

"Keep me posted," Tess said. She walked her plate back to the table and focused on having the best evening possible with Carla Scout. Sometimes that was all it took, mere focus, abandonment to the moment. She fitted herself to her daughter's schedule, let the evening flow. Tonight it worked. The girl was asleep, the house clean by 9:30. Tess actually had time to read the newspaper. Which, come to think of it, was still on the front walk.

She grabbed the plastic bag and unfurled the paper. Oh, hell, the carrier had screwed up again, as sometimes happened. It was the *Beacon-Light*, not the *New York Times*. (The *Beacon-Light* had refused to hire Tess more than a decade ago and Tess excelled at grudges.) Adding insult to injury, it wasn't even today's *Beacon-Light* but yesterday's.

She looked more closely. No, no, the *carrier* hadn't screwed up. Because there, affixed to the story about Melisandre Harris Dawes, the one that had cost Tess her job, was a Post-it covered with a now recognizable handwriting. The first part was an address, vaguely familiar to Tess, although she couldn't pin it down immediately.

Then, in block letters:

HYPOCRITE. YOU WORK FOR A CHILD KILLER. HAVE YOU NO SHAME.

The article hadn't named her, though. Her stalker was pretty stalkerish if he knew this. What the— And then the address clicked. It was in Medfield. Tess hadn't recognized it because the address wasn't what she thought of when she drove to the little white house on Fridays. She just thought of it as the little white house, home to Carla Scout's Friday babysitter.

Home to Carla Scout's Friday babysitter. The place where she was due to go in less than twelve hours.

As the little duck on *Wonder Pets!* liked to say: This was sewious.

Friday

2:00 A.M.

"When did we stop talking to each other?" Crow asked.

They were in bed and Tess was reminded of the saddest poem she knew. She should have been cheered that her seeping, sieve-like Mombrain could conjure up a single line of poetry, but she would have preferred not to think about Philip Larkin's "Talking in Bed," with its searingly intimate knowledge of what it's like to be estranged from your spouse. Not that she and Crow were in any trouble. They were just parents. Overworked, underpaid, and now in a full-fledged crisis.

"There was never a right time to say, Oh, I'm getting these weird notes."

"*Weird* isn't the word I'd use."

"But at first, that's all they were. A compliment—I thought—on feeding meters. A creepy observation on my breakfast habits. And then when I got the one on being a crappy mother . . ." Her voice trailed off. She could not bear to tell Crow that she worried he would agree.

"You told Sandy."

"Not about the last one. He was with me when I got the first one. And the second one came up by accident. Really, Crow, I wasn't trying to shut you out. But there's never time to sit and *talk*. Our life is like an air traffic control tower with one very busy plane coming and going all day."

She thought of the early days of their courtship, when talking in bed *was* easiest. Everyone knew the famous adage about newlyweds, about how if you put a penny in a jar every time you had sex the first year, you wouldn't hit that figure again for the rest of your lives. But that was also true of those aimless, intense conversations that happened *after* sex, when you had hours and hours to lie around and just talk. Crow had found her fascinating then. He had pursued her ardently, made it clear that he found everything about her intriguing. But he had also run away twice, always because he doubted her affection for him. No, that wasn't quite right. The first time, Crow had doubted her love for him. The second time, he had felt that he couldn't protect her and it turned out that Crow, for all his evolved qualities, still wanted to be a protector.

How many times was she going to have to learn this lesson? She had been threatened. She hadn't turned to him for help. It made him crazy.

"We're talking *now*," Tess said. "Let's figure out what to do about child care tomorrow. I still don't think this is a real threat, just someone who wants to fuck with my head for some reason. But, okay, he or she has won. What should we do?"

"Can you take the day off?" Crow asked.

"I wish. Tyner says he needs me."

"Okay, so it's the nuclear option. Your mom."

"Yep. Carla Scout will come home with her hair curled and shoes that match her purse."

Will Carla Scout be safe even here? Tess wondered as she drove to her mother's house later that morning. Did Tess's stalker know where her parents lived? She kept a careful eye on the rearview mirror and drove the most random route she could devise. She was reasonably sure she hadn't been followed, but then—she had been followed at least three times. That first morning on Elm Street, the day outside Jimmy's, the afternoon at Eddie's. Perhaps one of those encounters had been random, but no more than one. And the note leaver knew about Melisandre, too. Then someone had managed to drive down her street, a tiny lane that saw almost no traffic, and switch out her newspaper, although that could have been done at any time yesterday. Still, that was the creepiest part, imagining this person walking up her walk, taking her *New York Times*, leaving the older copy of the *Beacon-Light*.

"Okay, I've dropped Carla Scout off over on the west side of town," she told Tyner on her cell, sitting in her mother's driveway. Carla Scout had been so delighted to have a day with her grandmother that she barely registered Tess's departure. "I figured I'd call in to find out where I'm going, just in case it's closer to where I am."

Tyner paused for so long she thought the call had been dropped.

"I don't know exactly."

"You don't know where I'm going. I thought you said you had something urgent for me to do today."

"I do. The good news is—Melisandre has, as I told you she would, cooled off. She wants you working on her case again."

"You know, Tyner, whenever anyone says 'the good news is,' that means there's bad news."

"I wouldn't say it's bad. Only—challenging."

Okay, then it was really bad.

"Melisandre wants you to find Alanna. She knows it looks awful, her disappearing like this. We have a great attorney for her, once she comes in. Gloria Bustamante has agreed to represent her."

"That old lush?"

"She's better drunk than most attorneys in this town are after a week in Bible camp. Besides, she's stopped drinking. Secretly. Last time I had lunch with her, I caught her sneaking water into her water glass. She had the staff trained at the Center Club to make it look as if she were drinking vodka all day."

"That's just bizarre."

"I know. Besides, she was always a Scotch drinker. I should have been onto her from the start."

"No, I mean it's bizarre for Melisandre to think I can find Alanna. I don't know anything about her."

"You found the boyfriend."

"So did the cops."

"Tess, it's work. It pays by the hour. I can't make you do it, but can you really afford to turn it down?"

"Probably not. I'm going to have to buy Kevlar vests for everyone in the family."

"What?"

"Never mind. Did Melisandre have any suggestions where to start?"

"Only one. The former nanny."

"The woman who had an affair with her father? That seems unlikely."

"Melisandre believes she was in touch with Alanna, around the time filming started."

"Why?"

"Mother's intuition. Plus, someone had to wind Alanna up, right? Why did she show up at Hinerman's office out of the blue, asking about his testimony?"

"Do you have her details?"

Tyner did. Elyse Mackie managed a fancy food store at Belvedere Square, on the city's north side. But she wasn't in when Tess called. She was, a colleague offered when pressed—Tess might have intimated that she worked for a lawyer who did probate work and there was money at stake—at a bridal shop, making an event of selecting her dress. "It's a new thing, I think," the co-worker said. "They make it a hen party of sorts, champagne and hors d'oeuvres. It's up in Timonium."

Or, in other words, about as far as someone could be from where Tess was right now and still be in the Baltimore metro area. That was okay. She got paid by the hour *and* the mile. And she hadn't been joking about the Kevlar vests. For all she knew, she'd be hiring her own security detail soon. Hey, Brian needed a job.

The bridal boutique was in a strip mall, but a high-end one. Tess, who seldom ventured into Baltimore's far suburbs, thought of her city as down-and-out, a little dowdy. Yet there were places such as this, a bridal shop offering couture in a town where most of the citizens couldn't pronounce the word. Seemed pretty pricey for a young woman who managed a store that imported olive oil, even if some of the balsamic vinegar there did go for as much as a hundred dollars a bottle. Elyse Mackie must be one of those women who threw around the phrase *my day*. Tess vowed never to use those words. Should she and Crow actually get their act together and pick a date.

The party was well under way, with two champagne bottles upended in the buckets and a third being passed among the five women. The dress-shopping-as-brunch concept seemed risky to Tess. Didn't they worry about getting champagne or grease stains on the gowns? The bride to be was easy to spot, as she stood on a raised platform, modeling a mermaid-like concoction. The dress was so narrow around the ankles that Tess had to think it would take hours for her to walk down the aisle. She'd make better time in a sack race.

"We're open by appointment only," the boutique's owner said to Tess with one of those bright, fake smiles that conveys nothing a smile is supposed to convey. She was taking the measure of Tess's net worth, as evidenced by her clothing. How had Elyse Mackie ever passed muster here?

She was a pretty woman, although not in Melisandre's league. Not even in Felicia Dawes's league, come to think of it. She had the kind of prettiness that comes from long mornings at the mirror until hair and makeup are just so. Felicia Dawes, ravaged by grief, lack of sleep, and the plain old rigors of motherhood, was a natural beauty. And Melisandre was a force of nature, Tess had to admit. If Melisandre had walked in here in an Old Navy peacoat, jeans, and Frye boots, she would have been treated as if she wore couture. Some women make clothes look better simply by putting them on.

Not Elyse Mackie, though. She was out of her depth, trying on dresses and a lifestyle clearly beyond her means. Maybe Elyse Mackie was marrying well. But Tess had a hunch she either had saved diligently or was prepared to go into debt for her special day.

"Miss Mackie? I hate to bother you under these circumstances, but it's urgent. I'm a private investigator trying to find someone, and there's a possibility—remote, to be sure—that you may be able to help me."

Elyse looked confused, which was understandable. Strange enough to have a private detective call on you. Stranger still to have one invade your—what was the event called? Not a shower. Not really a hen party. Shoptail party? Bridalunch?

"I can't imagine—"

"It will only take a moment, but if we could speak privately, I'll get out of here, let you go back to enjoying your party."

"This is a setup, right?" one of the women asked. "It's like a practical joke. Dawn, did you hire a stripper? Because they sure screwed up if this is who they sent."

Elyse looked cross. "I told you guys that's not what I want. Not at the hen party, and certainly not here. Please."

"No, I'm the real deal. And this is about"—Tess thought for a second about what to say that would convey seriousness to Elyse without providing too much information to the others—"someone you used to care for, a long time ago. More than ten years ago. She's gone missing, I need to find her, for her own good."

"Alanna?" The emotion in Elyse's eyes was vivid, if unknowable. Tess nodded.

They went back to the dressing room. Tess would have preferred not to speak through a curtain, but Elyse could barely breathe, much less sit, in the dress she was wearing. The owner of the shop hovered jealously, refusing to leave until the dress had been removed and passed through the curtain. She shot Tess a look as if she were the bad witch at the christening, defiling this special day. What was that witch called? Elyse then put her own clothes back on and came into the tiny sitting room in the dressing area.

"What's happened to Alanna? Does it have something to do with Stephen's death?"

"We don't know," Tess said, which wasn't a lie. They didn't *know.* They would know when they found her.

"We?"

"I work for her mother."

"She killed Stephen, didn't she? She really did it this time."

"This time?"

"I mean—what happened before. She was out of her mind. I was there. I saw her. Saw the beginning. I was let go, before things got really bad, but when I looked back—I saw it, I really did."

Why was Elyse Mackie arguing the legitimacy of Melisandre's madness with Tess? It had the feel of an argument she had made before, with herself or someone else. Elyse was someone who had a vested interest in Melisandre being insane. Because otherwise, she was implicated, however indirectly, in Isadora's death.

"Have you seen Alanna recently? I know it's a long shot, but she's been gone for a day now and she had to go somewhere, seek out someone whom she trusted."

"I did see her. She came to my work, out of the blue. We went for coffee. I couldn't believe how beautiful she was—or how much she looked like her mother."

"Was there a reason she came to see you?"

Elyse sighed, averted her gaze. "You work for her mother, right? So you probably know. Fine. I had an affair with Stephen. Alanna saw us. Together."

Tess nodded as casually as possible, as if the information were new to her.

"After, the thing, with Isadora, after what happened, Stephen hired me back. I was happy to go. I was in love with him. He led me to believe that we would be a couple. Officially, eventually. When it was—what was the word he used?—appropriate. The girls had been through so much, and there was still the trial to get through. We were a lot more careful, the second time around, but we, um, started up again. Then, out of the blue, right before the trial, he terminated my employment and ended our relationship. Just like that. The thing was, I had signed a nondisclosure contract when I returned. I could be sued. For more money than I'd ever have."

So there was something Stephen and Melisandre had in common—their love of nondisclosure contracts.

"Didn't you think it odd that your lover made you sign something like that?"

"He said everyone in his employ had to sign the same contract or it wouldn't be legally binding on the others, or something like that. I was twenty-five. I was in love. And maybe he was, too, but looking back, I think he just didn't want to be troubled to find a new nanny. Anyway, I got mad. When I got fired the second time. So I called the state's attorney and asked if the clause was binding in a criminal trial. They said it wasn't. But the problem was, all I could testify to was the affair itself, the fact that Alanna had seen us. Only Alanna could testify as to whether her mother knew. I was told to be prepared to appear in case they needed to corroborate Alanna's testimony, but then—mistrial. It never happened. Melisandre sought a trial by judge the second time around and— Well, that was fair. She was insane when she killed Isadora. I never doubted that. Stephen and I—we talked about it once, only once. Obviously, we wanted to believe that it wasn't revenge, for what Alanna saw. What woman would do that?"

Elyse Mackie seemed to shrink as she spoke. Tess looked at their surroundings, noted again the overreach on Elyse's part. The chairs on which they sat looked like antiques, probably running to four figures each. It was as if, after all these years, Elyse was trying to have the wedding she'd thought she was going to have if she married Stephen Dawes. She was trying to be Melisandre, big and golden.

"Is that what Alanna wanted to know when she came to see you? If she had, indirectly, caused her sister's death?"

"Actually, what she wanted to know was if there was a deal."

"A deal?"

"She believed that her parents had an arrangement. They both benefited if Alanna didn't take the stand. It would hurt Stephen's reputation if the affair got out, but it would also hurt Melisandre's defense. She had decided that her parents worked it out together—what it would take to get a mistrial before Alanna was called to the stand."

"What did you tell her?"

"The truth. That I wasn't exactly close to her father around the time of the trial, that he had fired me and stopped taking my calls. I said she should ask him these things directly. The filming had started for the documentary, and I had decided on my own not to tell that part of the story, even if asked. But they didn't ask me, which I found interesting. After all, Melisandre knows, right? And she was acquitted, so she can't be tried again. Interesting, like I said. Like she was holding it back for some reason. Or, maybe, as Alanna suspected, there was a deal. Anyway, I called Stephen and gave him a heads-up. About Alanna, about how the filmmaker didn't ask about us."

250 / LAURA LIPPMAN

A heads-up. Tess lifted her gaze from Elyse, surveyed their surroundings. "Why would you do that? He had been pretty cruel to you."

"I was—I was thinking about Alanna. I didn't want him to be blindsided, or to say anything that would hurt her."

"So you called Stephen, out of the blue, and said, 'Hey, your oldest daughter is beginning to ask a lot of questions about what really went down twelve years ago. She knows you're a piece of shit, but now she thinks her estranged mother, back on the scene, is a piece of shit, too, that she was in on the perjury?'"

"I didn't say that exactly."

"I'm sure you didn't say a lot of things *exactly.*" Tess got up, walked over to a rack of dresses, looked at a price tag. That was a lot of Spanish olive oil. "You probably didn't say, Give me money or I will talk about the affair. But he gave you money, didn't he?"

"He offered me a gift when he heard I was getting married. I thought it was kind, under the circumstances."

"Did Alanna believe you? That you didn't know anything?"

"Why wouldn't she?"

"I don't know. Maybe because, once upon a time, when she was a little girl, her mother was sick and you slept with her father?"

Elyse was a feisty one. She blushed, but it was more in anger than in shame. "I was in love. And maybe I was silly and stupid—okay, I was—but I thought it was real. I thought I meant something. Stephen used *me.*"

"You must have been really angry with him."

"For a time. Yes. But clearly I got over it." She gestured at the dresses.

"Was fourteen thousand enough?"

"What?"

"Fourteen thousand. That's the federal limit on gifts last I heard. The amount that the donor doesn't have to declare on his taxes. Will that even pay for the dress you had on?" When Elyse didn't answer right away, Tess said, "Any money he paid you, it's going to come out. Even if he handed you a paper bag of cash. One penny over fourteen thousand and there will be a record."

"It wasn't— Look, leave me alone."

"Oh, I don't need to have anything more to do with you. But I'm going to tell the homicide detectives what I know, and they're going to come talk to you. Does your fiancé know how you're paying for your wedding?"

"Not the whole wedding. Just—some extras. Some things I couldn't have afforded, like a custom-made dress, better food. Steak instead of chicken."

"Steak instead of chicken." Tess's echo was meant to mock, demean, provoke. It worked.

"Look, do you know what it's like to be close, really close, to money, but not have it? The Daweses were good to me, but I was good to them, too, and I stood by Stephen during the worst time of his life. Then, just like that, it was over. *Oh, Ruby's starting prekindergarten, we'd be wasting your time. Here's a bonus, go back to school, finish your degree.* When I saw Alanna the other day, all I could think was how easy she was going to have it. She has a *Mercedes*. Seventeen years old and she pulls up in a bright red Mercedes. Okay, fine, a tragedy happened, but she was barely five. She has everything—money, family, those looks. I'm sorry, I just couldn't feel bad for her. And I wasn't going to give her an opportunity to feel any more sorry for herself. So I told her I didn't know anything about what her parents might have done, or not done."

"I'll ask you again—did she believe you?"

"What?"

"I mean, she knows you. Maybe she saw through your lies. I've known you less than fifteen minutes and I can tell you—you're not a very good liar."

"I don't know where Alanna is."

"Yeah, unfortunately, that's the one thing I do believe."

Tess left the shop. Elyse's friends had become more boisterous; a third bottle was upended now. Maybe a private-eye stripper could be hired on the spot. She helped herself to a puff pastry filled with some creamy mushroom thing. Steak instead of chicken indeed.

Noon

The view from Melisandre's apartment was greedy. That was the only word for it, she decided, as she stood at the glass windows and stared into the all-gray day—gray skies, gray water, gray buildings. Her view—Stephen's view, the one he had created for this apartment—took in the cityscape along the harbor, but it also had the depth and the breadth of the bay beyond. Her view was Baltimore, past and present and future.

But even in its sweep, there was something melancholy about the view, a sense of a place past its prime. To think that this had been one of the biggest cities in the United States when Melisandre was born, that this harbor had been a bustling beehive of activity. They had made things in this city once. Not her father's people. She was never quite sure from where their money derived, simply that they had lots and lots of it. Why had her mother, a London beauty, fallen in love with a Baltimorean, rich as he was? She could have had anyone. And he was older, too, already losing his looks. Yet her mother swore it had been love at first sight. He had arrived in London that very day and was persuaded to go to a party to counter his jet-lagged body's desire to sleep. On such small decisions, a life was made. Go to the party. Go to the regatta. Flirt with a man. Marry him. Have his children. Outlive him.

The charges against Melisandre were going to be dropped. She was sure of that. She had never doubted that. The trade-off would be that Alanna would be charged. As an adult, Tyner had explained. Even if the case were moved to juvenile court, which Tyner thought unlikely—this state's attorney would never miss a chance to prosecute a rich young white girl—Alanna's name would be out there. Right now, missing, not even officially a person of interest, she had privacy, of a sort. But she was going to be found and then she would know the pain that Melisandre knew. Which meant Melisandre was a failure as a mother. The job of a parent—even a parent who had been denied the right to be a parent—was to forestall, as long as possible, all sadness, general and specific. Boo-boos, disappointments, heartaches.

Being in the public eye as an accused killer.

But Alanna would be acquitted. Melisandre also had no doubt of that. The case against her was circumstantial at best. And even if Alanna were convicted, it would be of a lesser charge, with possibly no prison time. It would be understood that things had happened in anger, that there was no plan, no premeditation.

But she wouldn't be convicted. She wouldn't be convicted. She could not possibly be convicted.

Where are you, Alanna? She should have some insight. She had known her daughter so well once. She had known every inch of her body, every mark, down to the tiny birthmark on the left knee, the one that looked like Australia. But she also had known everything that went on inside her. Alanna had been transparent, as see-through as a jellyfish. Ruby was the complicated one, even at age three. Alanna was the one who wore her heart on her sleeve. Had that changed?

All Melisandre really wanted was a family, her family. Was that too much to ask? Like someone cheated out of her fortune, she had come back to stake her claim. At least she would have Ruby. She could be Ruby's mother. And maybe Alanna would come to love her when she saw how Melisandre stood by her during the trial. She was going to pay for the lawyer, too, this Bustamante woman who Tyner had recommended, although Melisandre found her coarse and unattractive. Gloria Bustamante claimed they had known each other, back at Howard, Howard & Barr when they were young associates, but Melisandre had no memory of her.

She felt bad about the film. She hadn't meant to disappoint Harmony, and she had been sincere about the project. It wasn't really her fault that all of this had happened. True, Harmony had seemed to hope that Melisandre would dissuade her from leaving, but if Harmony hadn't quit, Melisandre would have ended the film on her own. Besides, she didn't play those games. People should know their minds. Her lips crimped, imagining how others would mock those words in her mouth. But she did know her mind now. She had won her mind, at great cost and effort. *Out of one's mind* made no sense as a bit of imagery. To Melisandre, to be out of her mind was to stand back, have clarity. She was never more sane than when she was out of her mind.

A thought tantalized her, like a scent or a bar of music. It was urgent, important. What was it? *Harmony's film*. She needed to get *everything* back. She had checked the Dropbox today, and two videos were missing. Strangely, they were the ones she had shot. Where were they? She didn't mind Harmony having the interview with Stephen, but there was no need for anyone to see the one with Tyner. Had Harmony made copies behind her back? Why would she care about those interviews? Melisandre liked the girl, but these videos were hers, she had paid for them. A little face-to-face intimidation might be required. And it might have to trump the search for Alanna. What were the odds that Tyner's dim little niece could find her, anyway? Tyner had terrible taste in the women with whom he surrounded himself. That lawyer. His so-called niece. She wasn't his blood, and they bickered as if they hated each other. His wife, although she was attractive enough. For a bookstore owner.

Focus on Alanna. Alanna is the top priority. She would be okay in the long run. Tyner said everything would be okay. Tyner always said the right thing, unlike some people. But Alanna needed to surrender. The detectives' arrogance was in their favor. Reluctant to admit they might be wrong about Melisandre—more reluctant to see their error reported in the press—they would not issue a warrant for Alanna. Felicia, coached by Tyner, had been told to say that Alanna often disappeared. It helped that Alanna had no plausible way of knowing that Ruby was going to talk to the police, that Tyner could make the case she wasn't on the run out of fear. But they were looking for her. Where was she?

And just like that, Melisandre knew where her daughter would be found, at least once darkness had settled in. She had all but sent up a flare. Melisandre called Tyner—she made it a point never to speak to his not-really-niece directly—and shared her sad intuition with him.

7:00 P.M.

Alanna, the track star, had no talent for running when the destination was not fixed. Irony, much? But where could a homeless seventeen-year-old girl go? She had taken three hundred dollars out of an ATM, using an emergency card her father had given her. Her father— No, don't think about it. Don't think about him. Be strong. Besides, that was before anyone would have started looking for her. When had they figured out she wasn't coming home? The calls had started Thursday evening to her cell—Felicia, Ruby, some local numbers she hadn't recognized.

Fuck you, Ruby.

Of course Ruby had recognized the source of the notes. Those books were burned into their heads, line by line. Alanna hadn't even seen those books in years, didn't realize that Ruby had kept them, but she would never forget them. She had read them to Ruby. Did people remember that Alanna could read at age five, that she had been the smart one once? Not every word, not at age five, but those books had formed the core of their bedtime ritual. She hadn't known, at the time, that those were going to be the good old days. Did anyone recognize good times while they were happening?

Why had she written those notes? She couldn't have seen where things were leading, how awful everything was going to get. She had expected her mother to get it, to recognize the source, to see that Alanna was onto her. *And then what?* She no longer remembered what the point was. She no longer was sure of anything. All she knew was that she couldn't keep driving. The motels that took cash weren't places she wanted to stay. She had slept in the car last night, but it was terrifying. And she had parked somewhere so obvious that she couldn't believe she wasn't found. Was anyone even looking for her?

She got drive-through Wendy's for dinner. Fast food used to be a glorious indulgence. Felicia had kept a healthy kitchen, and her father— Alanna choked back another sob. If she had never confronted him, would this be happening? Had she once again set everything in motion? What was wrong with her? She was like some bizarre angel of death.

She was the Lonely Doll.

She pulled into the parking lot, the only car here at this hour. Could she really manage another night in this place? It had gotten so cold, about three this morning, that she had run the heater off and on, worrying it might kill her with fumes. Hoping it would kill her. Why not? This was her alpha and omega, the place where everything began and ended. She had finally found the courage to face it. X marks the spot. Here is where the world ended on August 8, 2002.

Her mother and father, beneath the tree. Her mother beneath the tree, her sister in the car. The air shimmering, as it does on a hot

August day in Baltimore. Like the witch in Hansel and Gretel, her mother had cooked Isadora. But had she known what she was doing? And if she was crazy, did that mean Alanna would be crazy, too, someday? Should she claim she was crazy now? Would that make everything better? Would anything ever be better?

A rap on her window. She screamed and jumped so hard she almost hit the car's roof. Then she looked up into a vaguely familiar face. Oh, *that* woman, the woman who had come to the house to speak to Felicia.

"Alanna," the woman said through the glass. "I'm here to get you to your lawyer, okay? I'm on your side."

"You work for my mom," she said, edging away from the window. She had longed to be found, but now she felt even less safe.

"I work for your mom's lawyer. But there's a criminal defense attorney, a good one, ready to meet with you. We'll come up with a good cover story for why you've been missing for twenty-four hours. But I'm afraid you will have to talk to the police. Not tonight, but by Monday. Sooner, if you want to go to the funeral, but we're going to try to work out a deal. They know, Alanna. About the notes, about the sugar bowl, about Tony, about Friday night."

"The Sugar Bowl? I don't even know who's playing."

The woman smiled as if Alanna were trying to be funny.

8:35 P.M.

It had taken a few minutes, but Alanna finally agreed to leave her car in the boathouse parking lot and get into Tess's minivan. She glanced in the backseat, taking in the mess.

"I have a kid," Tess said.

"A daughter?"

"Well, yes."

Gone was the poised, sarcastic girl that Tess had met—was it really only four days ago? She seemed almost catatonic, standing in the parking lot, indifferent to the chill in the air, staring into Tess's backseat.

"Is that *In the Night Kitchen?*" she asked, reaching between the front seats and picking up a book that Carla Scout had managed to wedge there. She settled in the passenger seat and flipped the pages slowly as Tess started to drive.

"Nothing is the matter," she said to herself.

"What?"

"Never mind."

She had stopped at the page that showed the boy, Mickey, falling naked through the sky. It had been covered with angry blue whorls of crayon.

"Oh, shit," Tess said. "I'm afraid my daughter did that. She's a little klepto and she grabbed that book from your mother's apartment the other day. She knows better than to draw in books—but, well, she's three."

"*I'm afraid my daughter did that.* Is that what my mom is telling everyone right now? Maybe it's not your daughter's fault. Did you ever think of that?"

"Um, sure. But who else would have done it?"

"I don't know. She's your daughter. You should defend her."

"Your mother has been defending you all along, Alanna. She was told Tuesday about your boyfriend, the fact that you came into town the night your father died. But your mother wouldn't let me go to the police. And when the information about the notes ended up in the paper, she fired me, thinking I was the source."

"Tuesday," Alanna said. "Tuesday."

She continued to turn the pages, reaching the end of the book, starting over, lingering on the defaced page, moving her fingers over the crayon marks. That was one part of toddler acting-out that Tess could never understand. Why was it so hard to learn not to write on books and walls and furniture and bed linens? Why did small children assume that the world was literally their canvas? Although Carla Scout was generally pretty good about it. Budding thief, yes, but not a vandal by nature.

They were two blocks from Tyner's office, where Gloria Bustamante waited—along with Melisandre, but Tess had thought it better not to mention that part—when Alanna said: "If I confess, I have leverage, right?"

"That's for Gloria to discuss with you, but—yes, the truth is best. If you want to have any hope of control over what happens, you'll have to tell the truth."

"That would be a first," Alanna said. In the streaking, in-and-out light of the streetlamps, she was the oldest seventeen-year-old girl that Tess had ever seen.

Saturday

10:00 A.M.

The 9:34 Acela had been sold out, except for first class. No problem, Melisandre had said. The Acela would save time and she paid for Tess's time. So Tess sat in first class, trying to pretend it was something she did all the time, an impression somewhat undercut by her refusing the breakfast—until it was explained that it was free. So *that* was the sixty-dollar difference between this and a regular business-class seat, which wasn't exactly cheap. She hadn't been to New York since Carla Scout was born, and she usually rode one of the discounted private buses.

But she wouldn't even see New York's skyline today. Once at Penn Station, she walked underground to the subway and got on the 1 train, trying to convey on some deep molecular level that she was not at all intimidated by the frenetic Brueghel painting around her. She bought a MetroCard and, after only a small bit of confusion, found the platform for the uptown train, then took a seat where she could unobtrusively keep an eye on the map, anxious not to miss her stop. Sure, she had her phone and could probably find her way to Harmony's apartment if she overshot the Inwood stop, but it had been a long time since she had to move through a city she didn't know intimately. Then again—she was alone! On a Saturday. *She had read a novel on the train.* And stared out the window, eaten her free, not-bad breakfast without interruption. The two hours and twelve minutes of solitude almost made up for being on a make-work errand that she was convinced was Melisandre's way of keeping Tess away from the main business at hand. Melisandre still seemed to blame Tess for the fact that her daughter had emerged as the primary suspect in Stephen Dawes's death.

As Tess understood the plan, Gloria would reach out to the state's attorney over the weekend and arrange for Alanna to sit down for an interview after her father's funeral. Depending on what kind of agreement was reached, they might be able to put her in juvie, but they'd never be able to keep it confidential. A seventeen-year-old charged with a felony no longer had automatic anonymity. And even if the judge granted her juvenile status, which Tess doubted, the genie of confidentiality could never be wrestled back into the bottle.

Yet, with all this going on, Melisandre suddenly had a bee in her butt about her "proprietary materials." She told Tyner—in front of Tess, although she made a point of never speaking to her directly— that she realized Harmony was still accessing the video even after she had tendered her resignation. Melisandre had changed the password to the Dropbox account, but two videos, the ones she had shot, were missing. She found that odd and wanted to make sure that Harmony was not going to release the one with Stephen.

"She could sell it, for big bucks. Stephen's last night alive and all. Some sleazy website would buy it," Melisandre said.

"I heard it was pretty dull," Tess offered. She might as well have been a mouse squeaking in the corner. "What's on the other video?"

"It's not important," Melisandre said. "The thing is, we have to make sure that Harmony knows she can't use these materials and we have to get anything she might have in her possession."

"But if you changed the passwords—"

"She could have downloaded the material before I did that. Perhaps before she quit."

"She quit? You didn't fire her?"

"Of course she quit."

"Because, you know, you're quick to fire people." It was all Tess could do not to point to her own face and say, "Ahem."

"Harmony and I parted on good terms. The project was dead. That wasn't my fault. Nor was it hers. And I agreed to pay her salary for the next two months. That said, she has a strict nondisclosure in her contract with me, and I will not have that violated."

"Did you learn that from your ex? The value of a nondisclosure policy?"

Melisandre could do a pretty good Medusa glare. "Perhaps I did. If only I had learned to lie as well as he did. The things he apparently told Alanna—claiming I colluded with him on the mistrial, that I signed away my rights for money. What horrible lies. He showed no empathy for Alanna, who's clearly more fragile than he realized."

Yet the fragile girl had refused to be in the same room as her mother. She was in Tyner's office with Gloria Bustamante, while Tyner, Melisandre, and Tess waited in the conference room. The brief moment of reunion had been something to behold—Melisandre reaching a hand out to her daughter's hair, the girl stepping back out of range and turning her face away, muttering: "I can't do anything if she's in the room." Melisandre had clearly been jolted by this.

Then again, if he had paid Melisandre for her children— No, Melisandre was especially convincing on that point. Why would she need Stephen's money? She had plenty of her own, even when it was controlled by a trust before her mother's death. They had halved various accounts because it was expedient, Melisandre explained. She had surrendered her rights because Stephen convinced her it was in the children's best interest. He had said they were scared of her, that she had become monstrous in their eyes. He had lied to her.

His best friend, his mistress—the guy did have a track record for misleading people, Tess had to admit.

"I did what I thought was right at the time," Melisandre said, looking Tess directly in the eyes. Person to person, mother to mother. "But what is right can change over a span of time. We see that every day, in arguments over language. What was right ten years ago isn't what's right today. My daughters need me. Now that I'm no longer going to be a suspect in Stephen's death, I should be their guardian."

Was it wrong for Tess to think: *And paying for Alanna's legal representation is a great way to show a court that your petition to have your rights reinstated is worth review.*

Their mother-to-mother moment didn't last long. When Tess balked at going to New York City on a Saturday, Melisandre didn't care that Tess needed to make child-care arrangements, much less that they had to be unorthodox ones, given that someone was keeping close tabs on Tess and her family.

So Tess and Crow started the day with Carla Scout in Tess's car, heading to Johnny's, a restaurant with a parking lot whose configurations made it a difficult place to lurk or follow a car as it left. Crow and Carla Scout promptly went out the delivery door and back to Crow's car, while Tess lingered over a cup of coffee and kept watch through the window. The plan was for Crow to take Carla Scout to Kitty's, where Tess would pick her up when her train returned.

At 125th Street, the subway emerged from the ground, something Tess had not expected, and she was treated to a view of Harlem. She knew nothing of the neighborhood she would be visiting, but she inferred that it hadn't been hipsterized, not yet. It looked—honest—not unlike some of Baltimore's working-class neighborhoods.

She called Harmony from right outside her apartment. Risky, taking a train—almost three hundred dollars, Tess marveled again, and that was one-way—without knowing for sure if the person was going to be there, but Melisandre had been firm. Harmony must have no advance warning of the visit. The young woman had no job, no boyfriend, Melisandre said. Where would she be on a Saturday afternoon in March?

Yes, Tess thought now. What could one possibly find to do in New York City on a Saturday? And—*fuck me*—no answer. But then her phone rang and it was Harmony, calling back.

"I'm walking home with some bagels," she said. "Can I call you when I get there?"

"Actually, I'm standing outside your apartment."

"Why?" Harmony's voice sounded cautious.

"Oh, you know Melisandre. Everything is urgent, urgent, urgent. She's got her panties in a bunch about some missing videos."

Harmony laughed. "Well, they're probably very nice, expensive panties, but—I'll see you in less than a minute." True to her word she rounded the corner forty-five seconds later.

The young woman who walked up to Tess seemed more relaxed, happier than the person she had met in Baltimore not even two weeks ago. Harmony offered Tess a bagel. Full from her train breakfast, Tess wanted to say no, but it seemed like a bad idea to say no to a New York bagel. Up in Harmony's small but charming apartment, Tess chose a sesame and slathered it with chive cream cheese.

"My neighborhood's not chic," Harmony said. It wasn't offered as an apology, just fact. "But it has a good bagel place. I missed good bagels in Baltimore. No offense."

"None taken," Tess said. It was by far the best bagel of her life.

This would be worth an extra sixty dollars on Amtrak. If it was served with a mimosa.

"So what's up? What's missing?"

"Melisandre is freaked out because she can't find the two videos she shot, including the one with Stephen."

Harmony laughed. "You know why she can't find them? *She* never uploaded them."

"What?"

"She did send me a copy of the Stephen interview, but as an e-mail attachment. I would have uploaded it myself, but by the time I realized what she did—well, the password had been changed. Which is fine, it is her material. I have no use for it. But I can't upload stuff if I don't have access to the Dropbox, right?"

"So you have copies of what she did because she sent it to you and she inferred some conspiracy? Sheesh. She thought you were going to sell Stephen's video to, I don't know, some sob sister on CNN."

"I wouldn't violate my contract with her."

"I don't think that was the issue."

"Sure it was," Harmony said. "But let me just tell you, there is nothing worthwhile in the interview with Stephen. Nothing. Then again, I don't think that's what Melisandre is worried about. She's probably worried that I saw the other one. I didn't watch it, but I read the transcript when it was forwarded to me."

"What was the other one?"

Harmony busied herself with her coffee mug, as if it were the most fascinating thing she had ever seen.

"Harmony—"

"She interviewed Tyner, made him go over what happened the day Isadora died. She went to see him. Did you know that? She went to see him. That day. Isadora was apparently left in the car there, too. She had retained Tyner a month before she killed Isadora, but wouldn't tell him why she needed a lawyer. I didn't know any of this."

"What did they talk about?"

"How she was still in love with him."

Goddamn *Missy*. She had engineered this mission so Tess would be out of the office all day Saturday. What was she up to?

"*Then*," Tess said firmly, using the tone Carla Scout adopted when she thought certainty was all she needed to achieve a desired result. "How she was still in love with him *then*."

Harmony gave her a half smile. "And now. But she didn't hear what she wanted to hear, at least not while the camera was on. When I read the transcript, that's when I knew the film was never the point. And that's why I quit."

"Wait, you said Melisandre was a fuckup, that you didn't see the Tyner video."

"Melisandre is an inconsistent fuckup. She didn't send me the video of Tyner or upload it, but she remembered to use our transcription app, which kicked an e-mail back to me five days later. That's how it was set up. If you use the transcription app, it's automatic. The tape goes to the service, the transcript comes back five business days later."

"Five days seems like a long time."

"It is, but it costs less. What's the old adage? You can have cheap, fast, good—choose two. I chose good and cheap. The app we used discounts sharply for every day you're willing to wait. I transcribe all the videos myself, so it's not urgent. I just like to have lots of backup. There was some, um, controversy about how my last film was edited. I wanted to have records of exactly what the raw footage contained. Not only video but these third-party transcriptions."

"She probably didn't send the Tyner video on purpose, because it was embarrassing to her." *Please tell me it was embarrassing to her.* "And forgot that the transcription app would kick in."

"Probably. Because when she went to see Stephen, she remembered to send me the video, but she forgot to use the app. She was pretty sheepish about it, not that it mattered. She was not the ideal partner in some ways. But it was my decision to end the project, not hers. I think she did want to make a film, but it was secondary to—other things. She came back to Baltimore for her children. And for Tyner. I see that now. She wanted to create a new family for herself, a second chance. I can't be angry at her. Not for *this*."

"I can— Wait, is there something else? Something that does make you angry?"

"When you called and said you were here, I thought you had figured it out. But I can't tell you anything. The contract, remember?"

"Can we play Charades? Twenty Questions?"

Harmony thought for a moment, then motioned to Tess to remain seated at her old-fashioned art deco table, then came back with an accordion file. "I kept all the receipts on the project. Melisandre's bills were charged to the film. She submitted her receipts to me, so I could keep track of the overall budget. She was on a per diem, too, a very high one. Still, she submitted all her bills to me because I kept the budget."

"So?"

"Have a look. Oh—and would you like some sugar with your tea?"

"I'm not having— Wait—are you saying—?"

Harmony pretended to lock her lips with a key.

Tess began digging through the receipts. There were several grocery bills, all from the Whole Foods near the Four Seasons. They were remarkably the same—and quite admirable. If you could judge a woman's character by her grocery bills, then Melisandre was a saint. She went—well, probably sent someone—about once a week, buying largely fresh produce, nuts, almond milk, maybe a little cheese.

There were four bills overall, one for each week Melisandre had been in Baltimore. The first one showed a purchase of brown and white sugar cubes. *Tyner bought those for the tea he prepared.* He said

Melisandre was used to doing things in a certain style. But it turned out she didn't even use sugar anymore.

Nothing on the second receipt, or the third. But the most recent receipt, the one from ten days ago—Melisandre also had bought organic sugar in bulk, eight ounces. There had been a sugar bowl. The sugar had been vacuumed up. But you didn't vacuum cubes, and if you had cubes, as Melisandre did, and you didn't bake and you no longer cared for sweets, then why—

"She roofied her own trainer?"

Harmony gazed at the ceiling. "I can't say anything. If anyone asks me, I went to the bathroom and you dug through these receipts while I was out of the room. Look, I can't *prove* anything. But Melisandre was worried about the lack of incident in the film. When she didn't get access to the girls— I don't know, I guess she decided to create some drama. But she'll never admit it."

"She might if I bluff hard enough." The sugar bowl. No wonder Alanna had drawn a blank. She didn't have a clue about what Tess was referring to. Everyone had assumed that the note sender was also the person who had tried to dope Melisandre's sugar. And Melisandre probably never expected a healthy young man to have such a dramatic reaction. "Harmony, may I— Could I see the transcript of the video with Tyner?"

"Technically, no. But I think I'll go back to the bathroom. Notice that I'll be walking past a wooden filing cabinet, where all the materials relevant to my last project are filed under *M*."

"For Melisandre?"

"For Medea. She wanted to call it *The Medea Project,* thinking it witty. She said that's who people thought she was, so why not embrace it? I was hoping to talk her out of that eventually."

"Medea killed her children out of vengeance."

"Melisandre doesn't see it that way. She says she killed them to save them, to spare them lives as slaves when their father remarried."

4:00 P.M.

"Funny, isn't it?" Gloria Bustamante took a sip of coffee, made a face. It was very old coffee, on the burner in Tyner's office since morning. "Meeting like this after all those years ago at Howard, Howard & Barr. Of course, it was just Howard & Howard then."

Melisandre nodded noncommittally. She had no memory of Gloria. Why would she have noticed this plain woman? Her hunch was that Gloria had left Howard & Howard before she was hired there, then grafted her memories onto Melisandre's life after she became *known,* for want of a better word. It happened. Lots of people thought they knew Melisandre.

But she also sensed something gleeful in the woman's demeanor. Gloria had been closeted with Alanna for hours today. And she had done good work. The state's attorney's office had not only agreed to wait to speak to her until Monday but had also given Alanna permission to attend her father's funeral, with assurances that she would not be picked up by the cops.

"Is Alanna going to confess?" Melisandre asked Gloria now.

"I can't speak to you about that," Gloria said. "Privilege."

"I'm paying."

"You know that's not relevant."

"Is she okay? I'm worried. She seems so fragile."

"She has some, ah, interesting ideas. I almost wish she were a little more fragile. Well, more malleable. She has definite opinions about what she wants to do. I wish I could tell you more, but, I'm sorry, I can't."

"I'm her mother."

"Not on paper."

Oh, that was cruel. Melisandre felt the rush of blood to her face, then remembered Gloria as she had been twenty years ago. The sly, ugly girl, hanging out with that gorgeous African-American lawyer, as if he would ever look twice at a woman like Gloria. There had been a third one, too. Gay, southern, given to seersucker. A tight little unit, smug and superior to the other associates for no reason Melisandre could discern.

"That seems to be a topic of particular interest to Alanna. Guardianship, I mean. She wants to petition to be emancipated. It is her hope that if she were granted status as an adult, she would come into her share of her father's estate and be able to pay me on her own. I said that the absence of a will would slow the process down. She says she'll pay you back."

"Don't be ridiculous. I won't take her money."

A shrug. "That's between the two of you, of course. The thing is—and this isn't related to her trial—she wants a say in where Ruby will end up. She thinks she should stay with Felicia."

"Only she doesn't have a say, does she?"

"No, she doesn't. I told her that. The court will probably defer to Ruby, given her age."

"Does this affect what Alanna will do on Monday? I think you should push for a trial, no matter what."

Gloria took another sip of scorched coffee, sighed as if it had suddenly become nectar. "I can't tell you that. She specifically told me not to tell you that. She just wants to know what it's going to take for you to stand aside and let Felicia have Ruby."

Melisandre decided to change her tactics, try charm instead of righteousness. "Why did she do it?" she asked in a low, wheedling tone. "I mean, I assume she was very angry with him, but—"

Another Cheshire cat smile. It did nothing for that plain, froggy face. "Any answer I give to that question would violate my client's privilege. Sorry."

"I don't think you're the least bit sorry. What has she been saying to you? Why do you dislike me so much? You know, everything that happened, to me, it was probably because I had an undiagnosed mental disorder and now Alanna may have it, too. You need to be aware of that. I feel horrible because that's my true legacy to my daughters. But if Alanna killed Stephen, then you have to consider that. She was probably not in her right mind at the time."

"I don't dislike you, Melisandre. I didn't *like* you, twenty years ago, when you swanned past me with your nose in the air. You were just one of those people who was always looking over the shoulder of the person in front of you so you could find the next person over whose shoulder you wanted to look. But I didn't dislike you. The two things are distinct, like and dislike. I never knew you well enough to dislike you."

"I think Tyner has chosen poorly," Melisandre said. "I am going to speak to him about this. I am paying, after all. Will you still be sitting here when my checkbook closes?"

"I might. It's a darn interesting case. Besides, Tyner left an hour ago, to be with his wife."

That hard crunch on that last word. What did this toad know?

"He'll be back here in fifteen minutes if I call him and tell him I need him. Besides, I want him here when his niece returns from New York."

He was there in ten minutes.

6:15 P.M.

When Tess saw Johns Hopkins Hospital on its hilltop perch in East Baltimore, she called Kitty to say she would be at her home in less than twenty minutes.

"Is Tyner there with you?" she asked.

"No, he went back to the office. Melisandre called."

"I need to talk to him. Face-to-face." Tess was dreading the conversation, but having it over the phone would be a big mistake. She wanted to show him the receipts, lay out Harmony's theory. He would know that Harmony was the source, but that was okay. As long as *Melisandre* didn't know what Harmony had indicated, she should be fine.

Tess had read Tyner's transcript on the train. It was disturbing. The fact that Melisandre had hired a lawyer before Isadora died— what was that about? Tess might as well get the conversation over now, go straight to his office, then pick up Carla Scout at Kitty's.

"Look, I hate to impose, Kitty, but can you keep Carla Scout another hour or so?"

"No imposition." But Kitty's voice sounded strained.

"Oh, shit, I'm so inconsiderate. She probably needs dinner. Look, she eats anything. Or doesn't eat anything, sometimes, but I don't worry about that. Feed her whatever you have on hand. I would say order a pizza, but only if you know a place that meets Crow's standards."

"When Crow dropped her off, he said she could have Papa John's."

"He did? Wow, interesting change of heart. I don't think she's ever had a pizza that wasn't made at home, or in some place that uses the word *artisanal* on the menu. Then again, everything is artisanal now. Okay, then Papa John's it is. Just cheese, though."

"And you'll be here when?"

"Soon, I hope. Maybe an hour or so."

"Crow told her she could have a Berger cookie, too."

"Sure. Train going into the tunnel. See you soon!"

Tess surrendered herself to these final seconds of solitude, unsure when she would be alone again. She could have made an earlier train, but she had availed herself of her free hour in Midtown—walking around, absorbing the city's energy, stopping at the Algonquin for a martini, which meant she had had to refuse the free wine in first class. She needed two hours and twelve minutes to burn off the effects of that martini. The trip home had not been quite as pleasant as the one to New York. She was dreading trying to persuade Tyner that Melisandre had tainted her own sugar bowl. And it didn't mean anything, in the big scheme of things. It was the least important allegation against Alanna. This fact also seemed to indicate that Tony Lopez was telling the truth. He hadn't used his hotel connections to get into Melisandre's suite.

Tess gathered her things, which included a bag of bagels for tomorrow's breakfast. Her car had fogged up in the humid chill of the parking garage and, as she waited for everything to defog, she told herself she didn't need another bagel right now. Oh, Berger cookies. She had to get Berger cookies.

Wait—Berger cookies had trans fats. It had been all over the paper at the end of last year. Berger cookies had trans fats, and the small Maryland-based company claimed it couldn't make them any other way if the substance was banned as proposed.

And Papa John's—whatever the quality of the pizza, Crow would never suggest buying pizza from a business owned by someone who had tried to circumvent the affordable health care act. Had Kitty lost her mind?

No, not Kitty. Never Kitty. Kitty was sending Tess a message: Things were not as they should be. She was in trouble.

Which meant Carla Scout was in trouble, too.

6:20 P.M.

"When will she be here?" the man with the gun asked.

"In an hour or so. She has to go see my husband at his office."

"Will he be with her when she comes back?"

"I don't know. Possibly." Would it be better to tell the man that Tyner was in a wheelchair? Would that make him calmer? Or simply more lethally confident?

"Does she have a key? Can she get into the apartment on her own?"

"No, I'll have to go to the door. I mean, we don't even have a buzzer. I'll have to go down in the elevator and let her in."

"An elevator for a three-story building. You must be pretty lazy." So he didn't know about Tyner. "Well, I'll be up here, with her. I'll hold her in my lap."

He tried to pick Carla Scout up. She wriggled away. "NO HUGS." She was playing with a toy from Kitty's girlhood, a large cloth painted to look like a town, with roadways and green spaces and railroad tracks.

"Do you really know how to use that? The gun?"

"Of course I do. Don't think you can get it away from me."

"I wouldn't dare try. I just worry—the way you gesture with it. That strikes me as dangerous."

"Don't worry about me. Worry about yourself."

"Why? What are you going to do?"

"My life was ruined. I'm going to ruin her life."

"How?"

The question flustered him. He was about forty, but an old-looking forty—pudgy, with a patchy red complexion. He had come to the bookstore ten minutes after closing, knocking frantically on the door, saying it was an emergency, he had to buy a gift for his young daughter. The employees had gone home and she was almost finished balancing her receipts for the week, but Kitty took pity on him and let him in, led him to the nook of children's books, where Carla Scout had spent much of the afternoon and was still playing.

It was then that he showed her the gun and told her to take him upstairs.

He did not offer his name, and he refused to say what he wanted with Tess, other than the chance to ruin her life. Kitty prayed that he did not have the imagination necessary to realize what would truly be the worst thing he could do to Tess.

"I used to date a cop," she told him now. This was true. "Your gun looks very new. Shiny."

"Bought it three days ago. All nice and legal. I didn't have any problem with the background check or the fingerprints. I'm entitled to own a gun. And yet— Well, never mind."

It was not a particularly powerful-looking gun. It wasn't the weapon that a crazy man would take into a schoolhouse or a mall. But it wouldn't take that powerful a gun to destroy Tess's life. One bullet would do it.

"How did Tess hurt you?"

"She knows."

"But she didn't do physical harm to you, or anyone you love. I'm pretty sure of that."

"As good as. And she's a hypocrite. She'll take anyone's money. She'll work for a baby killer if there's money in it. She was working for that Melisandre Dawes woman."

Lord knows, Kitty didn't want to argue Melisandre's side of anything right now. "She was acquitted. Not guilty by reason of criminal insanity."

"She had a good lawyer. I had a bad one. That's how this country works. If you can't afford a good lawyer, you're screwed."

"We have at least an hour. And I'm a really good listener. Maybe if you talk to someone, you'll feel better."

"I doubt it," he said. "It's been five years and I feel worse every day."

6:35 P.M.

Tess made it to Kitty's in under ten minutes. If a cop tried to pull her over, she would just lead him straight to the bookstore. She had considered calling 911, but what would she tell them—*My aunt wants to give my daughter Berger cookies, so clearly something is wrong?* No, she would get there, assess the situation, and then call 911.

Before Kitty had married Tyner, Tess had lived on the top floor of the building that housed the bookstore, in a small apartment with a large deck. She had locked herself out often enough to know how to break into what was now Kitty and Tyner's master suite. She climbed the fire escape along the back of the building, poking her head cautiously above the deck railing. The bedroom was dark. Unfortunately, the French doors to the deck were locked, as were all the windows. But Tess knew that the old windows could be opened from the outside if one had the patience to fiddle with them—to push and lean, push and lean. It was hard to have patience when all she wanted to do was smash the window and go crashing into the apartment. But, no, she had to be careful. She had no idea what awaited her. And she had no weapon. She couldn't have taken her gun on the train, and she hadn't wanted to keep it in her glove box while the car was in a public garage, so it was at home, locked away in the gun safe.

After an interminable five minutes of pushing and leaning, the screws lifted from the old, soft wood—thank God Kitty had never replaced the windows on the top floor. She had, however, blocked the window with a dressing table that was slightly higher than the sill, and Tess had to wiggle around it, trying not to disturb Kitty's myriad perfume bottles. One went over, but the floor had a fluffy rug that muted the sound. Alas, the perfume spilled from the old-fashioned cut-glass bottle that Kitty used, and some got on Tess as it toppled. Great, she was now the Joy-scented ninja. If they didn't hear her coming, they'd smell her.

The old staircase, used only by Kitty now, was creakier than Tess remembered. She took off her boots and crept down in stocking feet. There was a door at the foot of the stairs, a leftover from the days when the top floor was a separate unit. This led directly into Kitty's living room. Tess cracked the door, dropping to her knees. The living room was dark, but she could hear voices, Kitty and a man. The tone was strangely conversational. Had Tess overreacted? Continuing on hands and knees, she followed the sound of the voices into the large kitchen and dining room.

Unfortunately, this put her at eye level with Carla Scout, who looked up and cooed in the sweetest voice possible: "MAMA!" She then held out her arms to Tess and tried to run to her. A man stood up, a man with a gun in his hand. Tess had the shortest second in history to decide what to do next.

She punched him in the balls, which were conveniently at eye level. He went down, she grabbed his gun and started kicking him. And kept kicking him until the blood in her head and ears subsided and she realized that Carla Scout, safe in Kitty's arms, was screaming for her to stop. She stood over the man, who was curled in the fetal position, shielding his testicles from a second assault.

"Who are you?"

"You know me. You ruined my life. You took my daughter away from me. You know me."

She didn't.

7:30 P.M.

They did have pizza, after all, although not Papa John's. Tess called Crow, who left work and brought them Matthew's pizza, which they offered to the detectives. As they ate, they tried to explain to Carla Scout why Mama had beat the shit out of someone in front of her, but it was difficult.

"He was a bad man," Crow said.

"Like Captain Hook?" Carla Scout asked.

"Sure."

"But we don't hit!" Carla Scout pointed out. "We never, ever hit."

"No, we don't. But he was a very bad man. He was going to—to hurt someone. Mama had to hit him to make him stop."

"But, Dada, hitting is always wrong."

"It is. Mama's sorry."

And Mama was sorry. Truly. The man with the gun was Emmett Verlaine, and his surname jogged Tess's memory in a way his face never would. *Verlaine v. Verlaine,* an ugly divorce; not that there were any pretty ones in Tess's experience, but maybe only the ugly ones made it to the desk of a private detective. Tess had worked for his ex-wife. Verlaine had wanted joint custody but didn't get it. This had nothing to do with Tess's work, which had centered on Verlaine's financials, and everything to do with his track record for violence against his former wife. But someone had to be blamed, and Verlaine decided that it was Tess, that everything that had gone wrong with his life—quite a bit—had started with her accessing his credit score and doing a sweep of his financial life. His wife had moved to Texas in January, and there was nothing he could do to stop her. Then he had seen Tess with her daughter. He had started following her, meaning at first only to scare her, upset her. But when he realized she was in Melisandre's employ, some switch had flipped. He wanted to teach her a lesson.

"She's a hypocrite," he told the detectives. "Cares only who's paying her bills."

He claimed it had been his intention to kill himself, to make Tess and her daughter watch the horror of a man blowing his brains out. Maybe it had been. The police took him away, and Tess had to keep herself from calling after him: "Do you really think I'm a crappy mother?"

Instead she asked Kitty, who had poured healthy glasses of red wine for both of them. Crow had taken Carla Scout home. The girl was still worrying over Tess's bad behavior. "No hitting, Mama," she called out as she left. "Never, ever."

Great. She was probably worried that Tess was going to kick her in the crotch one day.

"No, Tess. I already told you once. I think you're doing a good job."

"It's just so hard. And it's forever. You can walk out on a marriage. You can't ever walk out on a kid."

"And yet people do. Every day. I did."

"No, you— *What?*"

"I got pregnant when I was in high school. I don't think I have to tell you that abortion was not an option for Kitty Monaghan. So I went to a home for wayward girls, as we were still called then, had a baby girl, and went back to school in the fall as if nothing had happened. And, in a way, it hadn't. You were born the same month. So, ever since then, I've had a sense of what my daughter would be doing, developmentally. When she would have talked, walked. Started pistol-whipping strange men."

"I didn't pistol-whip him. Jeez. But, Kitty—I'm a private investigator. If you wanted to find her—"

"No, no. That's her choice, not mine. There's a double-blind registry, called ISRR. I've known about it for a long time, but I've always been afraid to put my name in."

"Why?"

"Because once I do that, I'll know for sure that she hasn't put her name in."

"Aunt Kitty, that logic is flawed on about a half-dozen points. She might not know about the registry. She might be in there, waiting for you. What do you want?"

"I don't know. When I was a teenager, I knew I didn't want to be a mother. And I still know that about myself. I have no regrets. I just hope *she* has a nice life, that I did give her a better chance than she might have had with two teenage punks. God, I hope she got my brains."

"You mean, you hope she's shrewd enough to know that dropping the names of certain cookies and pizzas would trip the alarm bells in my head? I bet she is. And gorgeous, too."

Kitty turned her back, busied herself with rinsing dishes. Was she crying? Tess thought it better not to inquire. And then she decided it was better still to go put her arms around her aunt and just, for once, say nothing at all.

Sunday

3:00 A.M.

Tess had been asleep for only an hour when she jerked awake. Carla Scout was crying, probably reliving the fight in a nightmare. *Well done, Emmett Verlaine, well done. We'll be dealing with this for a while.*

By the time Tess got her daughter back to sleep, she was too wired to return to bed. She wandered through her slumbering household. Tomorrow—today—she still had to talk to Tyner. She didn't want to bring up his odd interview with Melisandre. It wasn't germane, although she had shared the transcript with Sandy. Then again, the transcript was probably the reason Melisandre was freaking about those "proprietary materials," why she had been so urgent about Tess's mission to New York.

Tess moved silently through the house, setting things to rights, picking up books and toys, washing her own wineglass. She had used wine to blunt the day's emotions, to no avail. Emmett Verlaine had meant nothing to her. If his name weren't unusual, she wouldn't have remembered him at all. Yet she had come to mean everything to him. She reached for her left knee, for the scar that reminded her she was lucky to be alive. A friend had died the night she tore open her knee. His name had been Carl. In the Jewish tradition, Tess had named Carla Scout for him, allowing Crow to choose the middle name.

"I guess someone with a daughter named for a character in *To Kill a Mockingbird* should expect to have a Boo Radley encounter," she had said to Crow in bed that night.

He had laughed. "Tess, you had a Bob Ewell encounter. *You're* Boo Radley, coming out of nowhere to save your family. The Tiger Mothers have nothing on you."

It was nice to laugh together. But it didn't mean the events of today would be readily banished. That note, the one in the grocery bag. How Tess had hated feeling judged as a parent. But she would continue to be judged. She knew that. She would judge others. Emmett Verlaine had felt judged, too. He was a horrible person. Yet horrible people can feel real pain.

Tess found Carla Scout's copy of *In the Night Kitchen* in the front hallway and carried it to the girl's room. But, no, her copy was already there. This must be the one she had taken from Melisandre's house, with blue crayon scribbles all over it and, toward the end, even some practice letters: A A A.

Only Carla Scout hadn't started making letters, not recognizable ones.

Maybe it's not your daughter's fault. Tess had thought Alanna was cautioning her to assume that was so in all cases. But, no, she meant it literally. This has been Alanna's book, as a child. She recognized these crayon marks. She knew the book was hers. She knew— Oh, man.

Okay, there was no way Tess could sleep now. She glanced at the clock: 4:00 A.M. How early could she call Detective Tull? Did the fact that he was a friend mean she had to be kinder or crueler to him on a Sunday morning?

She waited until 7:15, about ten minutes past sunrise, and he affirmed her hunch. But the call to Tull was the easy one to make. The call to Tyner was going to be much harder.

9:45 A.M.

Sandy was fifteen minutes early for the meeting with Tyner and Tess. That was intentional. He had the box of electronics seized the day after the murder, provided by Tyner's very obliging receptionist. He also had a thermos of his own coffee, which he knew was borderline rude, but he preferred his coffee to anyone else's.

"Thanks for agreeing to meet here," Tyner said. "I didn't want to leave Kitty alone, after the events of yesterday. She's still sleeping in, a sure sign of how upset she was. She'll stay in bed past nine on a weekend, but she never *sleeps* that late. Besides, I'm sure Tess is wrong about this. It won't be the first time she's gone off half-cocked."

"She is emotional," Sandy said agreeably, wanting to sound agreeable. He and Tyner had never been alone, without the buffer of Tess. On paper, they should get along. But it was hard to know. And any rapport they had was probably going to disappear once Sandy said what was on his mind.

"Have you—" Tyner asked.

"Not yet. I thought we should all do it together. You, me, and Tess. Her brainstorm, her show."

"She's running late," Tyner said. "She's not always punctual. It makes me crazy."

"No, I'm early. On purpose. I needed to talk to you. Man to man."

"Is it about Tess? I concede, she's impossible at times, but—"

"No, this is about you."

"Excuse me?"

He had started, he might as well plunge in. "Don't fuck up what you've got, okay?"

"Excuse me?" Sandy glimpsed the fearsome Tyner that he had thought was largely a figment of Tess's imagination. Maybe if you had known this guy since you were a young woman, maybe if he had been your rowing coach, he was fearsome. Sandy, unencumbered by this history, just saw a prickly guy who used anger as a bully might.

"I've seen the transcript. From your interview with Melisandre. Tess showed me."

"How—why— This is unconscionable. Harmony Burns had no right to share that."

"No one wanted to meddle, okay? Just so you know. You were, like, collateral damage. The transcript exists because— It's not important. The transcript exists. I read it. And I'm here to tell you, as a guy, that you are fucking things up. And I know why."

A man in a wheelchair can't storm away in a huff. But he can make little circles, backing and filling as if trying to get into a tough parking spot. "You've been in Tess's employ for only a year and you're picking up her worst habits. Nosy. Intrusive. Know-it-all."

"Which doesn't mean I'm not right. Look, I had the greatest wife in the world. My wife was strong, stronger than me, although she weighed maybe a buck and change. She was tiny. On our first date— That's not important. I'm trying to tell you, I know what it's like to be married to a woman who doesn't seem to need you, you know? And maybe I know what it's like to want a woman who leans on you, makes it seem like you're the only person who can help her. Maybe I had a time or two when I thought that's what I wanted. That's neither here nor there. What I'm trying to tell you is that these women, who seem so together, who act as if they don't even care if you show up every day? They need you, too. Don't lose sight of that."

Tyner crossed his arms over his chest like a sulky child. "I never did."

Sandy could stop there. But he wouldn't. "She could have used you last night. And where were you? With Melisandre."

"That's a rotten thing to say."

"I know. But you know what? I want you to figure out now, before we do what we're going to do, that you're not responsible for Melisandre. You couldn't save her then and you're not responsible for what's happening now."

"I wish I could believe that were true."

"It's nothing but ego to think otherwise. Yeah, she came back for you. Her daughters, but also you. Still not your fault."

A long, brooding silence. Sandy sat on the other thing he wanted to say, about how Tyner shouldn't worry about his inability to protect Kitty physically. That would be too much. Besides, it wasn't about having the use of one's legs. That was the point.

"We okay?" he asked Tyner.

"I suppose so. It's not like we're buddies."

"Easier to hear things sometimes from people not so close to you. One more thing? Don't tell your wife. About that interview. It's never going to see the light of day."

"I won't."

"Well, then, that's all good. Want some coffee?"

"I suppose I can brew it," Tyner said. "Kitty uses a French press—"

"However you make it, it won't be as good as mine." Sandy rummaged through the cupboards for some cups, came up with two mugs featuring an impressionistic drawing of a woman being chased by a devil. There was a look on the woman's face that made Sandy think the devil would be sorry if he ever caught her.

"We are the weaker sex, you know," he said, pouring the coffee.

"Let's keep that between us," Tyner said.

Noon

Tess surveyed the spread she had arrayed on the table in Tyner's conference room. It wasn't as lavish as what he had offered the first time Tess had met Melisandre here, not even two weeks ago. But the coffee was fresh, provided by Sandy before he headed out on his assignment, and the bagels were from New York. She had sliced a half dozen and bled on only one of them.

Melisandre declined everything but coffee.

"How's Alanna?" she asked. "Is she still staying at Gloria Bustamante's? It's sad that she doesn't want to see her sister, but I suppose that's to be expected. Is she still going to her father's funeral?"

"These are really good bagels," Tess said, a conscious nonresponse. "From New York. A day old, though, and I've learned that even good bagels don't age that well. I guess I'm kind of a bagel rookie in my way, despite being Jewish on my mother's side. I never had a New York bagel before. This is like a whole different species from what they serve at Suburban House."

Melisandre didn't even look at the food. She burrowed deeper in the chair, pulling her wrap closer as if the room were cold.

"I got the bagels when I went to see Harmony. I'm sorry that I couldn't report to you in full yesterday, but something came up." No reason to share her family drama with Melisandre. Although perhaps it would make for a nice bonding moment. "I had a stalker of sorts. Started sending me notes. Harmless at first, then it escalated. Pretty hairy stuff."

True to form, Melisandre asked no questions about what had happened to Tess, said only "My situation didn't escalate."

"Really?" Tess said. "What about the sugar? Don't you assume that was the second prong of Alanna's attack against you?"

She watched, interested to see how nimble Melisandre could be.

"She never meant to harm me. I'm sure of that."

"What about when she went to the house Friday night—do you think she intended to kill her father? Or was she looking for you?"

"*No.*" A shocked, offended no. Good. Melisandre seemed to sense her reaction was over the top, and modulated accordingly. "First of all, I don't think what Alanna did was premeditated. She and her father quarreled. Perhaps Stephen raised a hand to her and she reacted. Who knows?"

"So you *do* believe Alanna killed your ex-husband. I thought you told Tyner that you wanted her to go to trial because you expect her to be acquitted?"

"No, no— I mean, *if* she is responsible, that's the only explanation. That she went there to confront him and something went horribly wrong."

"Felicia told her you would be there, meeting with him. Perhaps Alanna meant to confront both of you. By last Friday night, she was furious with both of you, according to her father's old friend, Ethan Hinerman."

"Her father had lied to her. About the circumstances of our custody arrangement. He told her he essentially bought her and Ruby from me, a cruel distortion of the facts. I wish she had asked me about it. Because I would have told her what really happened."

"It must be so hard to know both your daughters hate you."

"Both?"

"Oh, I'm sorry. I just assumed that Alanna told Ruby everything she knew. They're close, right? Or were. Before Ruby decided that she had to go to the police and tell them about Alanna. About the notes, the car seat, which convinced her that Alanna had been out with Joey Friday night."

"I— Well, I don't know."

"Right. How could you know? It's not like you've seen either of them for ten years."

Tess busied herself with her backpack, bringing out the flavored cream cheeses she had picked up at Sam's Bagels that morning. "I have some good cream cheese. No lox, though. I didn't figure you for the lox type. Then again—turns out you're not the bagel type. There's orange juice, fresh. They have this totally cool machine at one of the local grocery stores that makes it for you while you watch. And Sandy made the coffee. It's from our earlier meeting, before he headed out for an errand."

"An errand?"

"More of a job, I guess, but it's for Alanna. You're paying for Alanna, so it's not a conflict for me to do stuff for Gloria. I checked that with Tyner and Gloria this morning. It's unorthodox, but there's no legal reason I can't do legwork for her as long as I remember to keep everything discrete."

"Where did you send Sandy?"

"That's a trick question, right? You're testing me, making sure that I respect the boundaries. As I said, I have to keep everything discrete. Keeping things separate—it has to be done sometimes. But you know the value of that, right? Divide and conquer."

"I don't have a clue what you're talking about."

Tess pulled the copy of *In the Night Kitchen* from her backpack. "So, straight-up confession. My daughter took this from your apartment last week when I went to get the personal electronics. Your phone, the iPad, the laptop, the camera you used when you interviewed Stephen. Harmony wants the camera back, by the way. It's expensive. I admit, I wasn't paying close attention, didn't realize my daughter had taken this book. I'm sorry. I want you to have it back."

Melisandre did not reach for the book.

"I hope," Tess said, sliding the book closer to her across the table, "that you weren't too worried when you couldn't find it."

"Why would I have been looking for it?"

"Because you gathered up all the books, the sources for the notes, and gave them to Ruby, right? Except, one was missing. I checked with Detective Tull this morning. Ruby brought four books—*The Lonely Doll, Curious George, The Cat in the Hat Comes Back,* and *Love You Forever*—to headquarters on Thursday. But she couldn't bring *In the Night Kitchen,* the source for one of the notes, because you couldn't find it, I'm guessing. Because my daughter had taken it. Alanna recognized it when she got into my car."

"Recognized the book, you mean. Wouldn't anyone?"

"No, this *copy.* A book defaced in blue crayon by a child who's learning to write. A very precocious child. And guess what letters she practices over and over, on the endpapers?" Tess flipped to the end of the story. "They're not very good, but you can make them out. A L A N N A."

Melisandre pulled on her gold chains, and Tess flashed back to their first meeting, the moment she had identified her tell.

"I had gathered up a lot of the girls' things from storage to make their rooms feel more homey. This book must have been among their possessions. But I didn't have the others. Ruby will tell you as much. They're hers, she brought them from the house. They have her name in them."

Tess sat on the edge of the table. She almost sat in the cream cheese but caught herself in time.

"She'll stick to that story. For a while. That errand, the one I sent Sandy on? It was to see Ruby. He's talking to her right now. And he'll be gentle as possible. But the detectives won't. When I tell them that they had the right person all along—and that you set Ruby up to lie to them—they'll be relentless. They don't like to be fucked with. They're funny that way."

Melisandre smoothed her hair. It was almost like watching someone play the theremin, the way her hair responded to her hands, settling, curling, coiling.

"I didn't ask Ruby to go to the police, much less tell her what to say to them. Quite the opposite. We never spoke of the notes at all. She did tell me that Alanna had quarreled with her father, gone into town—probably to see him, although Ruby couldn't be sure. I said I would support her in whatever she chose to do, but that I could not give the police any information about Alanna."

Tess willed herself to slow down.

"How did Ruby find you?"

"On Facebook." Melisandre smiled. "I'm there under the name Missy Harris. I was proud that she figured that out. But we aren't 'friends.' She used it to write me privately."

"And when did she first write you?"

"The day after filming was canceled. She was disappointed. She wanted to see me. And of course I was eager to see her. So we figured out a way to meet in places where people wouldn't notice us."

"Your apartment?"

"On the grounds of Fort McHenry." Then, quickly, with a hint of slyness. "Ruby's never even been in my apartment."

That wouldn't prevent you from getting the books to her, if she asked for them. But Melisandre was right. The notes didn't matter. Oh, she was so right about that.

"Ruby's never been in your apartment," Tess repeated. "But you've seen her—how many times? You said the first meeting was the day after filming was canceled. Was there another time?"

"This week. She needed me. You can imagine how upset she was. We saw each other Monday, spoke on Wednesday." Again, there was that look, the realization that she had a nugget of truth that accrued to her side. "That was before the notes were published. And *she* called me."

"At your suggestion?"

"What?"

"Facebook chats are archived," Tess said, having no idea if this were true, or if she could get access to them. But she had heard somewhere that the British Library was archiving everything on the Internet, so maybe it was true. "If she called you because you told her to, because you wanted to keep the conversation offline, we'll know that eventually."

"I prefer to speak by telephone," Melisandre said. "I'm sorry if you find it suspect that I asked my emotionally overwrought daughter to talk to me instead of typing into a little box."

"And that was Wednesday? The day you spoke?"

"I think so. Yes, I'm sure of it. We spoke Wednesday afternoon and I told her only that she must do what she thought was right, that I would support whatever decision she made. I think seeing the little boy's car seat in Alanna's car disturbed her more than anything. The realization that Alanna either took him inside—or left him in the car, outside."

"The little boy? You mean their brother."

"I don't think of him that way. Especially now that Stephen's gone. It's like a setup to a fairy tale. His widow will never do right by the girls."

Tess decided to create a long, luxurious silence by eating a bagel. They really didn't taste as good on the second day, but she wasn't eating it for flavor or even sustenance. She wanted to create an unbearably empty space that Melisandre might rush to fill. But Melisandre knew better. She sipped her coffee, glanced at her watch.

Tess swallowed her last bite and just went for it, hoping the result would be more Hail Mary pass than Pickett's Charge.

"And when did you decide to frame Alanna?"

"Excuse me?"

"Good mock outrage," Tess said. "Not too over the top."

"You are ridiculous. Does Tyner—" Melisandre stood as if to leave.

"Know everything? Yes, he does, Missy. Yes, he does. *Everything*. He even knows what it sounds like when a man is dying from massive blood loss."

Melisandre sat back down.

"Here's the sequence as I see it," Tess said, checking her fingers for any leftover cream cheese before she used them to tick off the events. "On Friday night, you killed your ex-husband. You did a flurry of busywork to make the case that you couldn't possibly have just come from the scene of a homicide—typing up your notes, sending the video to Harmony via e-mail attachment. That's why the video wasn't in the Dropbox file, by the way. You never got Harmony's protocols exactly right. The same was true when you filmed Tyner. Both times, you failed to upload the video to Dropbox. You didn't send the Tyner one at all, but that was probably calculated. You sent the short one with Stephen as an e-mail attachment. So it wasn't Harmony's fault that they weren't there, and she didn't do anything untoward with them. Except maybe make it possible for me to find the transcripts of both."

"She's not allowed to speak of the work she did for me," Melisandre said. "I hope she can afford to pay the fine for breaching confidentiality."

"You'll find that nondisclosure statements don't apply in criminal cases. You should remember that from Elyse Mackie. She tipped off the state's attorney about her affair with Stephen, told them Alanna had walked in on them. If Alanna had testified at your trial, she would have been called to verify that. But Alanna didn't testify, thanks to the arrangement you had with Stephen."

"*Arrangement.*" It was the first sense of any real emotion on Melisandre's part. "I made a deal with the devil. He told me he could get me a mistrial, that I would fare better with a judge than a jury, that he would then write a victim impact letter that beseeched the judge to understand how mentally ill I was. He would admit at last what he had never admitted—that he sat back, ignored my distress, left me untreated because he had no empathy for me. All I had to do was give up my children. He manipulated a fragile, guilt-ridden woman into walking away from her own daughters, but disguised it as a favor to me."

"And now he's dead."

"Yes, and I'm the best guardian for the girls. Ask Ruby what she wants. She prefers for me to take care of her. Not that woman Stephen married, not his mother. Me."

"What about Alanna?"

"She's seventeen. It doesn't matter as much. As I understand it, she's going to petition the court to be an emancipated minor."

"Yes, and as you understood things, she was going to be charged as a juvenile and probably do no time at all, or be sent to a relatively low-key juvenile facility. To be fair, you can't be faulted for not keeping up with the changes in the juvenile system since you've been abroad." At Melisandre's surprised look, Tess added: "Tyner told me that you expected Alanna to be under the jurisdiction of a juvenile court. You *counted* on it. Even as you told us that you would never do anything to hurt Alanna, you were busy framing her. Sharing with Ruby the text of the notes, giving her the books so she could play show-and-tell at police headquarters. Clueing her in on Tony Lopez, too; all the while insisting that you would never tell the police about Alanna's trip to see him Friday night. Sending a reporter an anonymous note, then corroborating every detail when he called you, pretending to Tyner that you were naïve about how the press worked. You framed one kid so you could care for the other? That's a hell of a Sophie's choice, Melisandre."

"Ruby needs me. Ruby wants to be with me. I didn't kill Stephen. I can't help what Alanna thinks. I have to do what's best for Ruby."

Tess stared at the book in front of her. Yesterday, under the baleful gaze of Emmett Verlaine, she had promised herself not to judge other parents again, lest she be judged and found wanting. But this wasn't about being a mother. It was about being human.

"My daughter has this hideous stuffed animal, a kangaroo in a clown suit. Clownie. I never expected it to last—it's an ugly, generic thing—but I think it's going to be with her until she goes to college.

Anyway, whenever she's arguing for something—she's three, she argues a lot—she says, 'But Clownie wants me to have it.' 'Clownie wants me to have a second dessert.' 'Clownie wants me to have another show.' Listening to you talk about Ruby, it's like 'But Clownie wants me to frame his older sister so I can take care of him.' Only Ruby is clueless, isn't she? You made Ruby believe that her sister had killed their father. You confided in her, leaked information to the press that she would recognize, alerted her to read the story when it was online. Then you sat back, clutching your pearls—well, your signature gold chains—too overwhelmed to know what to do."

Melisandre reached a hand toward her chains, jerked it back.

"Ruby may verify that I gave her those books," she said. "But only after she asked for them. Besides, you work for Tyner and, by extension, me. Anything you know belongs to me."

"Tyner's listened to the audio, Melisandre. You may never have remembered to upload your videos, but you did engage the transcription app both times. I guess if Harmony hadn't quit, you were planning to fire her—leaking to the newspaper was a nice twofer that way. You would blame her for the article, then fire her according to the impetuous pattern you had already established. That way, you wouldn't have to worry about her receiving that transcript when the app automatically kicked it back. She'd be off the project and you'd have removed her e-mail from the notification list, so it couldn't be forwarded to her. You probably even managed to cancel the transcription. But you forgot that the audio lived on, still on your old phone. Tyner and I listened to it this morning."

"How is that possible?"

"Get your head *in* the cloud, Melisandre. You ran the transcription app while you were interviewing Stephen. The recording's on your old phone, the one I collected so police wouldn't seize it. Sure, you got a new phone and the old one is dead, would require a new account to be used *as a phone*. But all we had to do was charge it,

Melisandre. You don't need a phone number to listen to the recording."

"I don't believe you," Melisandre said. "There is no audio because none of this happened. Stephen and I talked. He gave me a short statement for the film, said he would reconsider the issue of the girls later. I left. I don't know who killed him and I hope to God it wasn't Alanna."

Tess reached into her purse, pulled out a notebook, and began to read. "'You're a fool, Missy. You're still in love with Tyner. This isn't about the girls. Even when you were in your right mind, you never cared about them. You were—'" Tess had to swallow hard to read the next part. "'You were always a rotten mother. Not because you killed Isadora, but because you never put your daughters' needs ahead of yours.'"

"You—you made that up," Melisandre said, but she was bright red.

"I think you know I didn't. I think you know it's word for word what was said. It was there, on your old phone. You could change the password for the Dropbox account, kill out the new transcript when it arrived by e-mail. But this recording couldn't be undone until you got access to your old phone."

"And Tyner heard it?"

"Tyner heard it. And you know what, Melisandre? I think he felt—we both feel—that we might have pushed someone, too, if he had said those things to us. It wasn't premeditated, clearly. Leaving him to die—that's a different matter."

It had been hard, listening to the recording. Tess's victory buzz over her brainstorm to check the phone for the recording had faded quickly. God, the things that spouses, even former spouses, knew about each other. Then the crash, after he said that killing Isadora was the least of Melisandre's sins. Tess had shut it off, not wanting to listen to the sounds Stephen made as he lay dying, but she hadn't been fast enough to cut off the sound of breaking glass, his first scream of agony. How had the transcription service let it go? But they thought they were transcribing scenes from a film, probably assumed it was fiction.

"Go with Tyner to the state's attorney tomorrow. Enter a plea. You don't have to tell anyone how you tried to frame your own kid. Heck, it will look like you're trying to save her now. If you do that, I don't have to release the tape. Tell them it was like the time with Silas, that you froze and Stephen was dead before you could do anything. That's not implausible."

"That's *true*," Melisandre said. "I did freeze. I never—I thought—I really thought we could reach a place where we could agree, where he would let me start over with Alanna and Ruby. But all he cared about was thwarting me. He filled Alanna's head with lies until she didn't know what to think anymore. He would have done the same with Ruby eventually."

Tess had boosted herself onto the table during their conversation in order to loom over Melisandre, have a superior posture. Now she dropped to the chair beside her so they were on the same level. Face-to-face. Mom-to-mom.

"You were sick the day you killed Isadora. You were sick and so many people didn't believe you. And now, if this gets out, even more people will doubt you. But I do believe you. About Isadora. It must have hurt, to have Stephen throw that back in your face, when he claimed to have forgiven you. When you deserved to be forgiven. For that."

"I could never hurt one of my children if I were in my right mind."

"Yet you were prepared to sacrifice Alanna to save yourself."

"I really thought she would be acquitted. After all, she didn't do it. And Tyner says Bustamante is such a good attorney. When Alanna started talking about entering a plea, I didn't know what to do."

"She knew. The second she saw that book in my car and heard

where it came from, she assumed that you and Ruby had colluded against her, that she was outnumbered. The greatest kindness you could do would be to persuade her that Ruby was your dupe in this."

"She'll never believe me."

A voice came over the intercom. "I might."

Melisandre's head shot up, her expression a mix of emotions that frightened Tess a little. She knew what the woman in front of her was capable of. Sudden acts of violence, followed by a bizarre paralysis. "Is she—?"

Tess nodded. "After you came in, they set up at the receptionist's desk, Alanna and Gloria. They've been listening all the time through the office intercom."

And then Alanna was standing in the door, her lawyer behind her.

"I never knew," Alanna said, "that you didn't want to leave us. I always assumed you did. That you didn't want us, or love us. That you let us go because it was what *you* needed. And when you came back, Daddy told me I was right. He said you didn't care about us, that you didn't want us."

"Alanna." Melisandre's voice was pleading and, yes, loving to Tess's ear.

"He shouldn't have done that," Alanna continued. "But that doesn't excuse what you've done. I understand now that neither of you ever put us first. I have worried, for so long, that I would turn into you. That I would be crazy, that I would hurt people I love. But I'll never be like you."

"Alanna—" Melisandre held out her arms to the girl who so resembled her. But the girl took a step backward.

"I need to go now. I want to be with my sister. They're burying our father today. We're all we have. Me, Ruby, and Joey. That's my family. And I have to take care of them."

May 11

"It's actually supposed to be a sixpence," Kitty said.

"What?"

"It's supposed to be a sixpence, but if 'you haven't got a sixpence a dime will do.' And I brought a sixpence, the one I used."

"Of course you have a sixpence. So if I use yours, does it count as a twofer? I mean, it's borrowed, right?"

And with that, Tess slid the offered coin into her shoe, which happened to be a lovely shade of blue. So there it was—something borrowed, something blue. The shoes were new, too, which meant that most of the age-old bridal ritual had been achieved below her ankles.

The something old was an antique ring, a square-cut diamond that had belonged to Crow's grandmother, much too precious for daily wear and not at all her style. This ring deserved a movie star or a reality-TV housewife. "Can I have it?" Carla Scout had asked greedily. "When you're forty," Tess had said. "Until then, it's going to live in a safe-deposit box."

The day was hot for early May. "As if hell is filing an objection," Tess kept saying. They had chosen to marry at home on a Sunday because it still was their only mutual day off. And they had initially agreed that only family would attend. But *family* was hard to define. Just their parents and Carla Scout? If they included aunts and uncles, the number of attendees swelled to almost thirty, thanks to Tess's prolific grandparents. Yet it was unthinkable not to have Kitty or Uncle Donald, Tess's mother's brother. Plus, Tess considered Whitney family. And Lloyd Jupiter, the homeless teenager mentored by Crow, who was about to begin work as a PA on another season of *House of Games*. In the end, Tess had thrown up her hands and said: "If it's my fucking day, then I'm going to invite whomever I choose to the ceremony and have a blowout of a party that everyone is invited to attend."

It was the last time she said "my day," at least unironically. Carla Scout, however, was convinced that the day was all about her and was very disappointed that the cake was not as she had dictated (rainbow) and that her dress was not purple, her current favorite color. She also wanted to walk all three dogs down the aisle on ribbon leashes. But there was no aisle. Just a very crowded living room, where Whitney, who had applied to be a Universal Life minister in order to preside, led them through the most basic vows possible. The only personal touch was the moment when, instead of asking the parents to give their "children" away, Carla Scout was asked to approve of her parents' marriage.

"Of course," she said and burst into tears when people laughed, thinking they were laughing at her. But they were charmed by her airy lilt, the way she pronounced it, "Of cawse." She still had difficulty with *r*'s.

Despite the heat, the wedding party had then proceeded to a tent set up in the park at the foot of their hill, where they ate barbecue, drank beer and wine, and danced late into the night. It was really more family picnic than wedding, and that was fine with Tess. She didn't need to be celebrated for marrying her daughter's father.

Besides, Carla Scout was inevitably the true center of attention.

Tess watched her daughter dance and twirl, eat all the frosting off her cake, have a meltdown over being denied the right to keep the bride and groom figures, fall asleep under a table, then rise again when the music started. Her father's daughter.

"She packs more into a day than anyone I've ever known," Tess said to her mother.

"So did you, at that age," Judith said. "God, you drove me nuts, sometimes."

Tess found her mother's candor cheering. "Really? You didn't spend every minute of the day just wrapped in a gauzy haze of love for your only child?"

"No, I was too busy living in complete fear all the time. That's the unfair part about being a parent. The bad stuff—the fears, the anxieties—that never takes a break. There's always something to worry about."

"What did you worry about with me?"

"Primarily, your hair." That was a joke, an old one, between mother and daughter. "And the fact that you were an only. Everyone should have a sibling. Your father and I came from such big families and liked it. I always felt as if you deserved a sister."

I have a cousin, Tess thought, remembering Kitty's confidence, then realizing her father and mother must already know. She was the one from whom the secret had been kept. Tess and Tyner, although Kitty said she had confided in him a few weeks ago. Somewhere, there was a girl born the same summer as Tess, another Monaghan. Kitty was adamant that she didn't want to look for her—yet.

"I would have liked to have had a sister," Tess said. "I think. I don't know. I don't really mind being the center of attention. Neither does Carla Scout, in case you haven't noticed."

The girl had already rebounded from her nap and was dominating the dance floor with her father, who had used his connections to hire the Klezmer All-Stars for their wedding day.

"Speaking of sisters," her mother said, "how are the Dawes girls?" Like a lot of Baltimoreans, Judith Monaghan had taken a lively interest in the saga. Tess herself had no appetite for the stories that had unfolded in the wake of Melisandre's plea, her agreement to serve time for manslaughter. Tess's heart ached a little to see Melisandre vilified again as a baby killer. Yet she had almost sacrificed another daughter, and she had done *that* in complete sanity. Tess knew she shouldn't judge her. Yet she couldn't stop judging her.

"Sort of okay. Ethan Hinerman is going to be the trustee of their estate. Alanna acknowledged that she has no clue how to handle the money, once it's all figured out. She also realizes she has to have a civil relationship with Felicia in order to stay close to Joey. I doubt they'll ever have any real relationship with Melisandre. But, in a weird way, I hope they do."

"Parents have to forgive their children anything," her mother said. "I'm not sure it works the other way around."

"I'm not even sure it works that way. Some things can't be forgiven. And yet—she loves them. Melisandre really loves her daughters. I'm sure of that. She loves them, yet all she has ever done is create a legacy of pain for them. She shouldn't have gone away. She was right to come back, to try to reconnect with them."

"She killed a man. She killed their father."

"I know. And then tried to blame Alanna for it. She's a horrible person. But I can't help thinking what a thin line separates good parents from bad parents. I have days when I get so angry, when Carla Scout gets on my last nerve and I scream at her and I have to stifle the desire to shake her or even paddle her. I hate it when I scream. I worry that I'm screwing up, every day."

"Welcome to the club," her mother said.

"Does it ever end?"

"No," she said, smoothing back a strand of hair that had slipped from Tess's unaccustomed topknot. And, for once, Tess let her mother fix her hair without comment.

It was almost midnight when the party broke up and Carla Scout was eased from her flower girl's dress and into her bed.

"Can I get ma'ied?" she asked Tess. "Can I kiss someone?"

"Sure," Tess said. "Who do you want to marry?"

"You, Mama."

Tess's heart felt like the great glass elevator in *Charlie and the Chocolate Factory*—lurching sideways, then up, up, up. She knew she should explain why this could never be, that Carla Scout could marry a girl, but not her mother. Or her father, to whom she would probably propose tomorrow.

But all she said was "Why not?"

Still in her dress—a vivid print, now decorated with grass stains and Carla Scout's chocolate fingerprints, which was one reason Tess had chosen a vivid print—she watched her daughter's eyes flutter and close, fighting sleep with every fiber of her being. The girl didn't want to miss a thing. Once her eyelids were finally shut, Tess noticed they had a purplish cast, as if her beautiful blue eyes were shining through. The girl was gorgeous. She was impossible. She was everything. Why had Tess done this to herself? Why had she handed all her happiness to this small, impetuous creature? Was there any rational case for parenthood, or did the universe trick you into it? What if she failed her? What if she did something that Carla Scout could not forgive? If she lost her daughter, what would she do to get her back? How far would she go? Would she kill someone who stood between her and her child?

Tess remembered Emmett Verlaine, curled up like a potato bug on Kitty's floor. *Yes.*

Crow had fallen asleep, but he awakened when Tess climbed into bed and spooned him.

"That was fun," he said. "Why did we wait so long?"

"It never seemed to matter. Being married. And then it did. Because of Carla Scout. But then there was never time. Because of Carla Scout."

"Yet we found time. We pulled this together in two weeks. When you wanted to find time, you found it."

"Are you saying we didn't get married because I wasn't really committed to you?"

"No. I'm saying there's always time for what you really want. For what we want. We may never have as much money as we'd like. And our days may seem overfull, but if we want something, anything, really desire it, I have to believe that we can figure out a way to get it. A trip to Europe. A bigger house."

He flipped over so he and Tess were face-to-face.

"A bigger family?" she asked.

"Is that what you think I want? Or is it what you want, Tess?"

"I think it's what I want."

"You should be sure."

"I'm never sure about anything. I wasn't sure about you, remember?"

"It will be harder."

"I know."

"Exponentially harder."

"I know."

"It—"

"Oh, shut up and let's make another one."

Author's Note

Blame mom-brain. I can't remember everyone who helped me with this book. Probably because everyone helped me with this book. Husband, family, friends, neighbors, people on social media, former colleagues. My agent, my editor, everyone at William Morrow. The team at Faber & Faber. The FLs. The moms on William Street and the moms on Eighth Street. Some dads, too, particularly the one who helped me fact-check a detail about Inwood.

The stay-at-home writer and the stay-at-home parent have a lot of interesting overlaps. This book is dedicated to my nanny, who has no overlaps with the nanny in this book. When my daughter was born, a lot of people happily predicted that I would no longer write at the same pace. They were wrong. Sara Kiehne deserves most of the credit.

Laura Lippman
Baltimore, 2014

About the Author

Since Laura Lippman's debut in 1997, she has been heralded for thoughtful, timely crime novels set in her beloved hometown of Baltimore. Now a perennial *New York Times* bestseller, she lives in Baltimore and New Orleans with her family.